When SHADOWS FALL

RILEY SKOV

WHEN SHADOWS FALL

Edited by Clio Editing Services.

Proofread by Red Adept Editing.

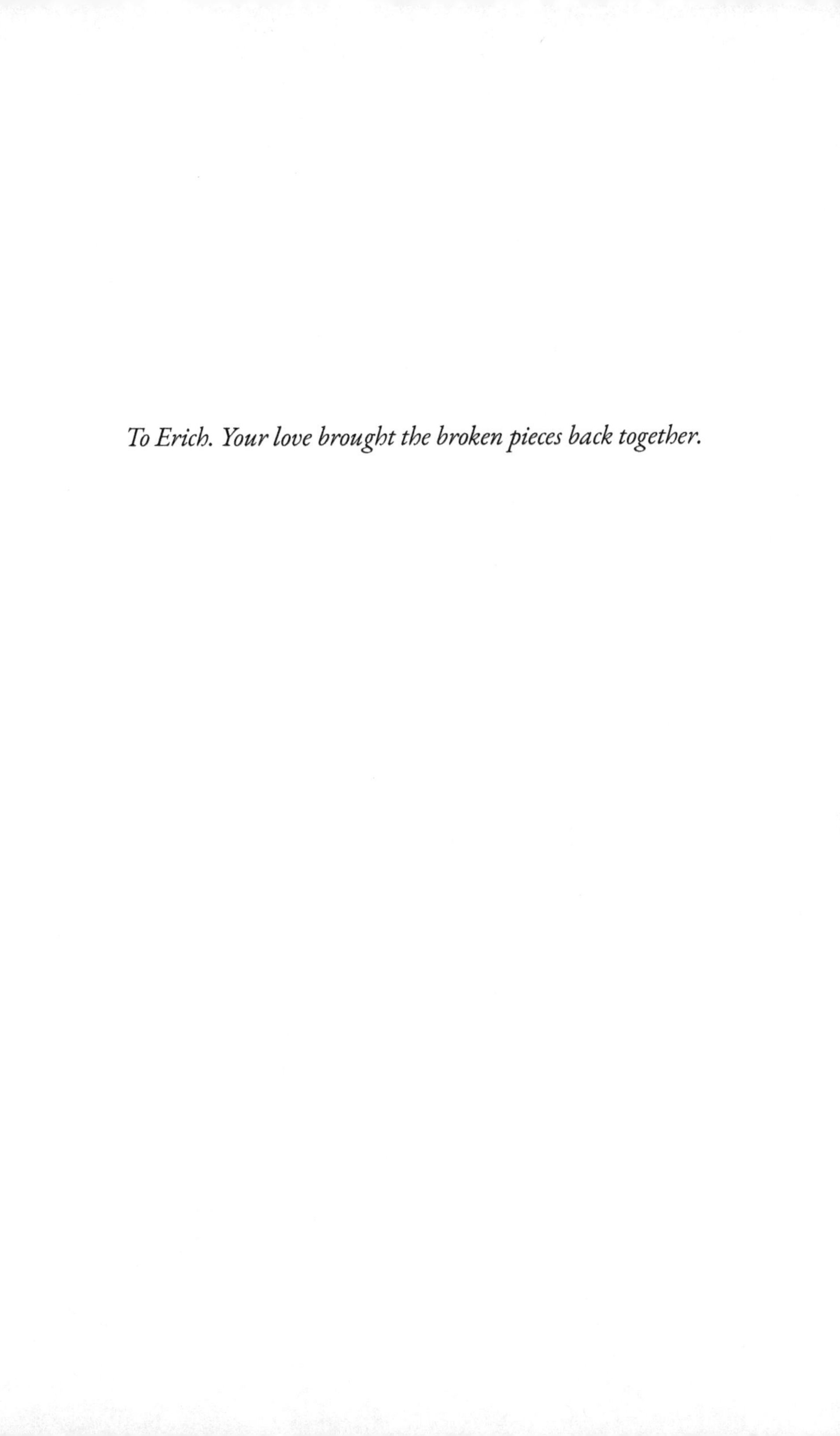

To Erich. Your love brought the broken pieces back together.

Prologue

Terror gripped my body as I stumbled over unfamiliar terrain. My breath was ragged, threatening to burst my lungs, the darkness so consuming, I navigated by shades of black. It wasn't the fact that I was in the woods in the dead of night. It was that these weren't *my* woods, and I had no idea if I was running toward help or right into the devil's outstretched arms.

The pine needles beneath my feet, squishy with rain, muted the sound of my footfalls. Unfortunately, that meant my pursuer had the same advantage.

A twig snapping to my right whipped my head around. Was it the storm shearing smaller branches from the trees? Or was my lead shorter than I thought?

I clenched my jaw, willing my feet to keep going, to push through the heaviness that had settled in my legs, making every step harder than the last.

He's counting on you. You have to get out.

The rain fell in blinding sheets, even through the thick canopy of overlapping pine branches, and the wind howled as it ripped through the trees, twisting the drenched fabric of my sweater around me. The sting of the water and cold on my face taunted me with the reality that this was not a nightmare from which I would wake.

Passing the thick black silhouette of a tree standing sentinel, I threw my back against the rough bark and consciously fought to slow my breathing, the ragged bursts of air making it difficult to hear and threatening to reveal my location.

I closed my eyes and strained my ears.

Nothing.

Nothing but the sound of rain falling and small creatures scurrying amongst the fallen foliage that blanketed the woods.

I swiveled my head, scanning my surroundings, but it was pointless. The darkness was too profound. Getting out of these woods alive would be a damn miracle. I was tempted to crawl under some brush and hide until morning. But I couldn't do that. I wasn't the only one running out of time.

He's probably dead by now.

I gritted my teeth and forced the thought aside, refusing to entertain that possibility. Sending up a silent prayer that I was headed in the right direction, I stepped away from the tree and started forward again, quickly glancing over my shoulder. When I turned back, my stomach lurched and my steps faltered. A shadow unfurled from the dark mass of trees dead ahead and stalked toward me.

CHAPTER 1

Alex

THREE WEEKS EARLIER . . .

I GLANCED at the clock on the corner of my desk, my agitation growing by the second. Each tick of the second hand echoed like a death knell, loud and mocking in the surrounding silence. I placed my hands on the stack of notebooks in front of me, each one carefully labeled and aligned precisely with the one beneath it. The colorful tabs sticking out from between the pages matched the collection of pens sitting beside them. The tidy order of it all lent a sense of comfort and control that steadied the emotions trying to overwhelm me.

Standing behind the large oak desk, my eyes trained but unfocused on the bare surface, I ran through my mental checklist of everything I needed. The ticking of the clock grew louder, as though the infernal gadget was trying to shove me out the door.

"All right, all right. I'm going. I don't need *you* to weigh in on the matter too."

A year ago, I might have questioned my sanity had I found myself having a full-on emotional confrontation with a clock. Now? I considered it a perfectly healthy form of displacement for all of the anger and anxiety.

I kicked my chair further behind me, the wheels rolling easily across the hardwood floor, and started to round the desk. The sound of rapid clicking, soft at first and growing louder, halted my steps. A slow smile bloomed on my face as I waited for my visitor to enter the room. As usual, she didn't keep me waiting long.

Skidding to a halt at my feet, my husky dropped to her belly, her tail sweeping the ground in rapid strokes, her crystal-blue eyes trained on me with expectation. When I didn't bend down to pet her quickly enough, she let out one demanding bark and swished her tail faster.

Laughing, I placed my fists on my hips. "No sassing me, little lady."

Aderes responded by rolling onto her back, waiting for me to pet her white belly. She knew I couldn't resist the belly. Kneeling beside her, I stroked the short fur with the tips of my fingers. As she closed her eyes and rewarded me with a goofy grin, I could feel my own tension slowly settling from a roar to a low hum. However bad things got, my girl always managed to bring me back to center.

The respite, however, was short-lived. The sound of my phone vibrating like a jackhammer across my desk intruded on the moment and set my heart to a gallop. I growled and snatched the wretched device, pausing to check the caller ID.

My stomach clenched when my eyes settled on the display, the phone continuing to buzz in my hand while I stood frozen, wishing I could return to the quiet of five minutes ago. My thumb hovered above the screen, my teeth chewing the soft skin of my lips raw. As much as I wanted to decline the call and pretend it had never come through in the first place, I knew avoidance wasn't going to make this problem go away. I'd tried that already.

With a deep inhale, I let my thumb fall to the screen and swiped to answer. Before I could speak, a voice laced with displeasure snaked through the line. "You better not be avoiding me."

I closed my eyes and tried to make my voice sound normal. "No, of course not."

"Good. Because believe it or not, everything I do is because I care about you."

I believed it to a certain extent, but I wasn't a young girl without experience. I knew how the game worked. "I know," I said, trying to head off the conflict brewing like a dark storm on the horizon.

"Good. So, what have you got for me?"

My tongue darted out to wet my lips. "Um, nothing I'm ready to share."

Silence. The knot in my stomach doubled in size.

"Alex, this is unacceptable."

"I'm working on it. It's just . . . rough."

"That's fine. I just need *something* to show the publisher. They need to see progress, and they're being particularly demanding about it given the past twelve months."

My dread turned to guilt in a flash. I knew Cass meant well and she was just doing her job. She was paid to be in my corner after all, and I hated that, as my agent and publicist wrapped into one, she was having to take blows that were meant for *me*. I released a deep sigh, and as usual, she read it like it was in black and white.

"You don't have any pages to send me, do you?"

"No," I admitted. "I'm trying, Cass. I really am. I just keep drawing a blank. It's like I've completely lost my ability to weave a story."

She must have heard the defeat in my voice, because her typical hard-ass tone softened. "Alex, I know this has been a hell of a year, but you've still got a life to live. Unless you want to lose your career, too, you're going to have to figure out a way to stop punishing yourself and move forward."

"I'm not punishing myself, Cass. I just can't concentrate."

"Wasn't that the point of moving to Podunk, USA? So you

could get away from the noise and all the distractions and just write?"

The question was rhetorical and hung thick in the air with its intended effect. As always, I yielded first in our standoff. "I don't know what you want me to say. I'm trying. That's the best I can do."

I placed the phone between my ear and shoulder and bent to pick up the black messenger bag leaning against the front of my desk. Long locks of mahogany hair fell forward in large spirals, creating a curtain around my face. I tucked them back behind my ears as I straightened, smoothing the tresses until they lay perfectly flat.

I could practically hear the gears turning in Cass's head as she clicked her pen repeatedly, no doubt trying to decide which tactic would have the greatest likelihood of success. "Alex, if you miss another deadline, they're going to drop you, and there's not a damn thing I'm going to be able to do about it. If that happens, you're going to have to pay back that hefty advance."

Ah, the threats tactic. I fought to keep my tone even as I shoved my laptop, notebooks, and pens into my bag with way more force than necessary, once again choosing to displace my anger onto inanimate objects. "I'm aware of that, Cass."

She pressed on as though I hadn't responded. "Not to mention, given your reputation lately, and the way your fans are growing restless, I'm not even sure I'll be able to convince another publisher to take a chance on you."

I zipped up my bag and left it on my desk as I walked to the picture window adjacent to my workspace. The deep golden rays of afternoon sunlight streamed through the window, giving the floor around me and the bookshelf on the opposite wall a gilded cast. I wrapped my free arm around my middle and stared out at the grass and maple trees in my side yard. The leaves would be falling soon, but I would relish every moment of the bright red and orange hues of fall while it lasted. Growing up in Southern California, I never got to enjoy much of a change in seasons.

Nature's display of the passing of time was one of the reasons I had settled in this small mountain town.

As though sensing that it was futile to press the matter further, Cass sighed in resignation and said, "Just get something, *anything*, to me this week. Okay?"

Though I had serious doubts as to whether I could back it up, I said, "Okay."

Shifting into friend mode, Cass adopted a tone of concern. "What about the *other* situation?"

I thought for a moment about how to respond, playing the scenario for each option out in my mind before committing. Turning from the window, I scooped up my bag and slung it over my shoulder before switching off the light and leaving the room.

"Oh, that? Nothing new to report, really. It's been pretty quiet." I bit my lip, hoping she'd leave it at that, but I should have known better. Cass was a bulldog, and she didn't let anything go.

"So you haven't had any more incidents since the last time we spoke?"

Not wanting to lie, I tried for a middle-of-the-road response. "Nothing worth mentioning." I scrunched up my face and walked delicately toward the kitchen as though it would bring this conversation to a close more quickly.

"Alex."

How did she do that? Even my mother, with her severe tone and mannerisms, couldn't force me into submission as quickly as Cass could with just my name. I released the breath I'd been holding and finally gave her what she was after. It was the only way this dreaded phone call would end. "Yes, there have been more incidents. Another letter emphasizing my physical assets and what he'd like to do with them."

"Anything else?"

I walked through my kitchen to the door that led out to the garage. Aderes was right on my heels, seeing me off as she always did. I twisted and leaned down, pushing my bag farther across my back so it wouldn't swing and hit her in the head as I scratched between her eyes where she liked it best. "Some more phone calls. But I don't even know if it's the same person. Chances are it isn't."

"The caller still isn't saying anything?"

"No, just silence, and occasionally, I can hear breathing."

"This asshole really needs to invest in a blow-up doll and get on with life."

I straightened and smiled ruefully at Cass's sarcastic sense of humor. She had no time for idiots who interfered with her results. And because she felt this creeper was interfering with my work, he was affecting her bottom line.

I entered the garage and climbed into my green Range Rover, throwing my bag into the passenger seat. Knowing this conversation wasn't over, I laid my head against the seat and closed my eyes, willing myself to channel whatever patience and common decency I had left.

The familiar squeak of Cass's filing cabinet competed with her words as she continued her interrogation. "What did the cops say when you reported it?"

"They didn't say anything because I haven't reported it."

"Excuse me?"

And round two begins. "I haven't reported it. There's no point." I pressed on without even the slightest pause to keep Cass from interrupting. "I don't want the cops or the media in my business. I had enough of that last year. This is just another creeper responding to some news footage he saw of me. I get obnoxious letters every week from men who think a woman actually *likes* having strangers explicitly detail all of the sexually graphic things they'd like to do to her."

I pulled my sunglasses from the visor and slid them up the bridge of my nose. "This will die down, Cass. The longer I'm out of the public eye, the sooner people will forget about me. And whoever is sending me these letters and doing the heavy breathing on the line will move on to the hottest new celebrity to hit the scene."

Cass's voice took on a hard edge. "If this turns into anything like last time, you're going to need that paper trail."

"Last time was different."

"Alex—"

"End of conversation, Cass." I punched the button on the garage door opener clipped to my visor and started the engine. "I've got to go. I'm headed into town to get some work done at the coffee shop."

My declaration had the desired effect. Cass was once again focused on my work and clearly delighted to hear I had no other plans for the evening than working on producing pages she could use to get my publisher off her ass.

"Excellent! A change of venue will do you good!" she said.

I could envisage her sparkling-white smile standing in contrast to her tan skin and brick-red lipstick. She would, of course, be wearing her typical fitted skirt with a suit jacket, her long blond hair tumbling loosely around her shoulders. Cass had that classic Hollywood beauty of days gone by with a flare of modern badassery.

As I ended the call, she slipped in one last reminder about pages by the end of the week. Backing slowly out of my garage, I kept going until I hit the end of the drive and met the rural highway that ran along the front of my property. Fortunately, we didn't get a lot of traffic around here, or leaving my house would have been more danger than I had the ability to stomach.

Once I was on the road, I yielded to the hypnotic whir of tires on asphalt and the thoughts competing in my head. Cass hadn't reminded me of anything that wasn't a constant in my train of thoughts these days, but the phone call still managed to send my anxiety and frustration right back into overdrive. How was I supposed to be creative when all I could focus on was my career circling the drain?

I received letters daily from a multitude of fans who started with expressions of sympathy and ended with demands and scolding regarding the MIA status of my next book. It had gotten to the point where I avoided most of my fan mail and had considered hiring a virtual assistant to handle it for me.

Giving myself a mental shake, I turned the volume knob on my stereo and smiled when the driving beat of classic rock poured through the system.

Just get to the coffee shop, I thought, bobbing my head to the drums. *Everything is better with caffeine and a change of scenery.*

CHAPTER 2

Gabe

STATIC CRACKLED in my ear and was promptly followed by a sultry voice raising my call sign. "Twenty-Five Adam Two."

I keyed the mic at my shoulder. "Go ahead."

"Mrs. Walker is requesting an additional response to her residence."

I shook my head, a smile tugging at my lips. "Ten-four. I'll be en route shortly."

The double doors separating the front of the police station from the back opened, and my partner sailed through, throwing his head back and laughing. "Sounds like you've been formally requested to attend another tea party."

I raised my eyes without lifting my head from the paperwork in front of me. "She's lonely since her husband passed. If calling me out for tea under the guise of having me investigate strange noises helps her to cope, I can handle that."

Trevor shook his head and came to a stop next to my desk. The fluorescent lights of the station reflected off his blond hair, giving him an angelic glow that was most definitely misplaced. "And that, my friend, is why all the women in this town, young and old, are obsessed with you."

I didn't bother to answer and instead chose to refocus on the paperwork. I didn't need to get into another conversation about my dating life. Or lack thereof.

Picking up on my not-so-subtle hint, Trevor dropped the subject as decidedly as the file he slapped down in front of my face. "Another body showed up in the coroner's office with the tongue cut out." His tone was grim, far from the teasing cadence he'd had just moments ago. A look passed between us, conveying an understanding that didn't require words.

"Fuck." I breathed the curse as I picked up the manila folder and leaned back in my chair. Having read far too many autopsy reports lately, I deftly thumbed the pages, knowing exactly where to find the details I wanted first. "Charles Bailey. I don't recognize the name, do you?" I didn't bother looking up. I was too engrossed in the grisly images of the eviscerated victim, studying every detail to confirm what I already knew.

"No." Trevor adjusted his duty belt as he took a seat on the corner of my desk. "It's gonna be a pain in the ass trying to figure out who he was a CI for."

I grunted my agreement as I shut the file and threw it back on my desk. "They're taking them out faster than you can sweet-talk a woman out of her clothes."

Trevor smirked and looked at me sideways. "Only if I'm not trying that hard."

I tipped back in my chair and ran my hands over my face. The station was quiet today. The other officers on duty were out enjoying the sunshine while the brass sat quietly behind closed doors, praying no one was going to bring a shitstorm to their doorstep. Most days, those prayers were answered.

While Eden Falls had its own police department, we were small. With only fifteen patrol officers and one K9 unit, our resources were nearly depleted whenever we *did* actually get something exciting.

Sliding back into my desk, I started straightening papers and closing files. My reports would have to wait. "We should head over and check on the kid," I said. "Make sure everything is still copacetic on his end."

Trevor nodded slowly and stood. When he turned to face me, thumbs looped over his duty belt, I could see that the question haunting me was also written in the creases of his brow.

With a solemn gaze, I asked Trevor, "What's your gut telling you, partner?"

His sky-blue eyes dulled under a heavy burden. "Hell if I know." He studied the floor for a moment. "If we really want to bring these assholes down once and for all, he's our best shot. Still . . ." He shook his head.

"Still," I continued for him, "are we really willing to allow him to continue paying the price?"

Trevor nodded.

The question was one that weighed on my conscience daily. I wondered if I had become so hungry for the goal that I was blind to whether the end really justified the means.

I pulled my sunglasses and keys from the top drawer of my desk, hooking the sunglasses on the front of my shirt and slipping the keys into my pocket. "Let's go touch base. We'll fill him in on the latest development and share our reservations about continuing. At the end of the day, he's earned the right to be treated like a man, and he needs to have a say in how we move forward."

"You just gonna leave Mrs. Walker hanging?" Trevor asked, his taunting smile back in place.

"Shit. I almost forgot." I pulled my cell phone from my breast pocket. "I'll call Dispatch and have them let her know it'll be a bit."

Halfway through the first ring, the voice of my favorite dispatcher came on the line.

"Dispatch, this is Quinn."

"Hey, Quinn. How's it going?"

I could hear clicking as Quinn's fingers flew over her keyboard. "Hi, Gabe. Good, thanks. How's everything with you?"

Temporarily distracted by Trevor pantomiming something impossible to decipher, I scowled and shook my head at him, looking away. "Good, good, thanks. I have a favor to ask, though."

"Shoot."

"Something's come up, and I need to go make contact with someone. Can you call Mrs. Walker and let her know that it'll be a bit, but I'll head over as soon as I can?"

Trevor was now two-stepping in front of me. Every time I swung away, he stepped in front of me again.

"Of course," Quinn replied. "I'll give her a ring right now and put your call back in the queue."

"Thanks, Quinn. You're the best."

Hearing that I was getting ready to disconnect, Trevor signaled for me to wait. Exasperated, I said, "Hang on a sec, Quinn. Trevor has something to add."

I pulled the phone away from my ear and leveled him with another scowl. "What?" I barked.

He looked as giddy as a schoolboy who'd just convinced a girl in a skirt to climb the flagpole. "Tell her I'm going to arrest her if she doesn't give it back."

Even with the phone inches from my ear, I could hear Quinn's feral growl on the other end of the line. Judging by her response and the smug grin on Trevor's face, I had just been an accomplice in Trevor's never-ending pursuit of getting a rise out of Quinn.

I put the phone back to my ear and said, "Quinn, I'm gonna let you get back to work. Thanks for taking care of Mrs. Walker."

I returned the phone to my breast pocket and lifted my chin toward the door, signaling to Trevor I was ready to take off. "Do I even want to know what that was about?" I asked.

Trevor scrubbed a hand against his jaw, still very amused with himself. "Ah, nothing much. I stopped by Dispatch the other day and accused Quinn of being a thief."

My eyes popped out of my head. That wasn't exactly the kind

of joke you threw around lightly with anyone who worked in law enforcement. "Why the hell would you do that?"

Trevor chuckled. "Relax. Once I had her good and worked up, I told her she could protest all she wanted, but I knew without a doubt she was a thief because she had stolen my heart."

We pushed through the double doors leading to the front of the station as I said, "Considering she's all business, I'm sure that went over well in front of all her partners."

"Oh man, for a minute I thought her head was going to come off and start spinning." Trevor was laughing so hard, he had tears running out of the corners of his eyes.

"Just keep me out of it," I said, pulling my sunglasses from the front of my shirt and putting them on. "I'm not dumb enough to make an enemy out of Dispatch. She's going to start giving you so much paper you'll be wiping your ass with it."

"Nah, she's all show. Deep down, she can't stop thinking about me." Trevor flashed his pretty boy smile. The one that made most of the women in town give him whatever he wanted. Quinn was a different story, though, and I suspected that was part of her allure where he was concerned.

After a short walk, we reached the only real coffee shop in town. The sign above the door had the words *Rise & Grind* in a rainbow shape over sunbeams rising like steam out of a coffee cup. The red brick building stood in sharp contrast to the black trim, the modern yet quaint style a favorite of mine. Grind was part of a strip of businesses that flanked the busiest section of Main Street. You could find just about anything you'd need within a three-block radius.

Inhaling deeply, I allowed the cool air to suffuse my lungs as I admired the bright colors of fall, which were out in full display in the trees that lined the street. Cars moved slowly from one end of town to the other, stopping to allow citizens to cross in front of them. One of the best features of this place was that no matter how determinedly time marched on, the pace remained slow and easy.

Down the street, one of Cindy's yoga classes must have just been dismissed because a gaggle of women in bright-colored spandex and cotton flooded from the building and collected in chatty little circles despite the crisp autumn air.

"Mmm," Trevor hummed, gazing in the same direction. "I swear God's gift to man was yoga pants."

A laugh rumbled in my chest. Yanking open the door to Grind, as the locals called it, I ushered him inside. "Let's go, Casanova. I'm not in the mood to head off one of your crazy conquests today."

As soon as we entered the café, the intoxicating smell of coffee and pastries beckoned like a seductress. All of the regulars were present and accounted for. The old men who sat closest to the door, their tables pushed together, looked up and saluted as Trevor and I walked past. The young moms with their toddlers and infants sat opposite the old men, bouncing the little ones and smiling as they passed phones back and forth, sharing their photos and videos.

Before I even made it halfway to the register, a squeal pierced the veil of idle chatter and a rosy-cheeked angel with bobbing blond curls launched herself at me. I scooped her up and was rewarded with a temporary air supply issue as her chubby little arms wound tightly around my neck.

"Me and Momma were coming to see you," she informed me when she pulled back to look at me.

"You were?"

She nodded.

"Well, I couldn't wait that long." I tickled her belly and shifted her weight to my side as I proceeded to the pickup counter, where her mother was waiting for their order.

Lily giggled over my shoulder. I suspected my partner was back there making all kinds of stupid faces. With the love-filled look of a proud momma, my sister watched us approach and leaned in for a hug with Lily pressed between us.

"Hi," she said. "How's your day going so far?"

"Not bad, but just got a whole lot better." I blew a raspberry on Lily's neck and laughed at the indignant face she made. "What are you girls up to?"

Liz looked stylish and full of energy, as always, but I could see beneath the exterior as only a brother could. Her short brown hair was cut and styled in what she called a pixie cut. I guessed that's because it made her look like a brunette Tinkerbell. Especially with her petite frame. And though her violet-blue eyes were still the star of the show, the sparkle had been dulled by the shadow of private pain.

Liz ran her hand along her bare neck, tilting her head from side to side, trying to loosen knots. "We were going to stop by to visit you and then head to the store to get the fixings for dinner."

Lily had been busy tracing the outline of my badge with her finger, her tongue sticking out as she concentrated. But at the mention of dinner, she piped up. "We're making s'ghetti!"

"You are?" I made my eyes big. "With lots of sauce and meatballs?"

"Uh-huh." She nodded, her expression grave.

In my years as an uncle, I had learned that food is a very serious subject for a child.

Seeing that their drinks were up, I gave Lily a kiss on the cheek and handed her to Liz. "I'd better let you go, then. The sooner you two get to the store, the sooner I get to eat!"

After seeing Lily and Liz off, Trevor and I moseyed up to the register to order. I rubbed my eyes, squinting against the sensation of little bits of sand scratching across my retinas. We'd both been pulling too many hours lately, our thirst for justice a brutal mistress.

"Hi, guys! What can I get you?" Bree's fingers hovered over the buttons on the register. She was a constant fixture at Grind. As the only manager, I figured she probably felt the need to ensure the ship always had a captain on deck.

"Hi, Bree. The usual, please."

"You got it. Two house coffees. One with cream and two sugars, the other black. Anything else?"

"Nope, that'll do." I opened my wallet and pulled out two fives.

Bree shook her head. "Don't even think about it, Gabe."

I smiled and shoved the money into the tip jar.

As I returned to the pickup counter, I caught the eye of the kid who was getting to work on our drinks. I lifted my chin and shifted my eyes toward the back of the store. He nodded once, almost imperceptibly, and went back to his business.

Trevor was busy fiddling on his phone, so I propped my arm on the counter and scanned the shop, confirming our sleepy little town was still sleepy. The second my eyes landed on the small table in the corner, cast in shadow as the only area in the café the light from the floor-to-ceiling windows couldn't touch, thoughts of everything else took a back seat.

I had come to think of that table as *her* table. It was the one she seemed to like best, as it was where I most often found her. Long mahogany hair fell softly down her shoulders. And though her back was to me, I knew bright-green eyes, the color of Irish hills, were focused like a laser on the laptop in front of her. She was as still as a statue, and from the look of it, her cursor sat blinking on a blank page. Everything about her screamed high class, from her designer purse right down to the red sole of her shoe peeking out from under the table, where she had one foot crossed behind the other.

A hard shove to my shoulder snapped everything else back into focus. Especially Trevor's face, which was begging for me to pound it like meat.

"What?" I glanced around, pretending I had been scoping things out.

"If you don't go ask that very fine lady out, *I'm* going to. And you know that once she's been with me, you're not going to have a chance after that."

I snorted but otherwise ignored him.

Trevor's tone softened. "Look, man. All kidding aside, she's the first woman I've seen you really look at since—"

My head snapped around, and his words died on a breath.

He cleared his throat and clapped me on the shoulder. "I just want you to be happy. She's a gorgeous woman and fresh blood. I think you should make a move."

I craned my neck to check the status of our drinks and realized Bree was standing close by, cleaning the espresso machines. Her eyes shifted from the woman I'd been staring at to me. When she realized I was looking at her, she smiled and pretended to be very intrigued by the steam wand.

Great. By sundown, the whole town will have new fodder for the ongoing gossip regarding my relationship status.

Jace placed our drinks on the counter. I snatched them up in a hurry and made a beeline for the exit, intentionally keeping my eyes focused on the street beyond the windows. I was *not* interested in the gorgeous, leggy woman at the shadowy table, and I'd be damned if I gave anyone else reason to question the truth of that statement.

As I approached her table, which was situated to my right, I turned my head even farther to the left so Trevor would have a clear view of how uninterested I was as he brought up the rear. Just as I was inches from a clean exit, my traitorous partner, and now former best friend, body checked me. I watched in slow motion as the piping-hot coffee in my hands jumped out of the cups and landed on the woman I'd been avoiding. As if that wasn't bad enough, I had also managed to bump the table as I tried to regain my balance, and *her* coffee sailed all over the papers she had laid out in front of her.

She gasped, lifting her arms away from the spattered pages. Her white blouse, made of a delicate fabric that floated around her each time she moved, now had brown splotches all over it. She was looking down at her clothes like someone who had just been shot but couldn't believe it. I looked around for Trevor and saw the bastard outside, angling from view.

I cleared my throat, trying to figure out what the hell I was supposed to say after assaulting a woman. In the end, I decided to keep it simple. "I'm very sorry, ma'am. Hang on a second. I'll grab some napkins."

I hustled over to the small counter near the entrance that held napkins, creamers, and sweeteners. I could feel every eye in the place boring into my back. *I'm going to kick the shit out of that asshole.*

Napkins in hand, I went back to the table and started dabbing her paperwork, praying I hadn't ruined anything that would take hours to replace. The woman was pulling her wet blouse away from her body to keep the thin fabric from sticking to her. As she tugged, the neckline dipped low enough to provide a very decent view of her cleavage. I forced my eyes back to the mess on the table and handed her some clean napkins without looking at her.

"I really am sorry." I cleared my throat again. "I'll pay for the dry cleaning on your blouse and replace your coffee." I chanced a glance at her but couldn't decipher what she was thinking.

She dabbed gently at the coffee stains on her top. "Thank you, but that won't be necessary."

Red splotches appeared on her neck and cheeks, making me feel even more like an asshole. She was either pissed or embarrassed. Either one was unacceptable.

"Miss—"

She flicked those pretty green eyes up to me, her thick black eyelashes making the impact of her gaze even more potent. The moment our eyes locked, I momentarily forgot about the mess and everyone else in the vicinity. Her lips, soft and full, parted ever so slightly. An almost overwhelming urge to taste her caught me off guard. Something flared in her gaze but was gone so fast I wondered if I'd imagined it, because in the next moment, her entire demeanor shifted, and the atmosphere between us took on a frigid chill.

"I can manage this, Officer. Thank you just the same." She

dipped her chin and began to shuffle together all of the papers on the table.

Her words were polite enough, but her tone held an edge that said this conversation was over. Taking the hint, I wadded up the used napkins and mumbled something to the effect of "Have a nice day."

Before heading out, I went back to the counter and caught Bree's attention. When she reached me, I leaned forward and spoke quietly. "Can you do me a favor and get that woman another of whatever she was drinking?" I didn't even bother to clarify which woman I was referring to because the entire coffee shop was still captivated by the unfolding drama.

"Alex? Sure thing."

Alex. The name suited her. It was definitely better than referring to her as the leggy woman.

I handed Bree a ten-dollar bill and told her to keep the change. On my way out, I glanced in Alex's direction. She was still seated but bent over, shoving the sullied papers into her black bag. Just before I reached the door, the sound of teeth clicking drew my attention to the group of geezers. They were all smiling and wagging their eyebrows at me.

I was going to kill Trevor.

CHAPTER 3

Gabe

WHEN I STEPPED OUTSIDE, the sun shone on me like a spotlight. I circled around to the right of the building and found Trevor leaning against the wall with his arms crossed and a giant smirk on his face. I brushed past him with nothing more than a scathing glare.

"Ah, come on!" he hollered after me, jogging to catch up. "I just thought you needed a little push. Literally." He belted out a laugh, finding his own joke hilarious.

"You're a dick." The heat from my anger felt thick beneath the heavy fabric of my uniform and bulletproof vest.

As we neared the backside of the building, Trevor sobered and put his hand on my shoulder, forcing me to stop and face him. With both of us standing just over six feet tall, we were pretty much eye level with each other.

"I'm sorry," he said. And he actually looked like he meant it, but knowing Trevor, he could burst out laughing at any moment, delighted by the fact that I had fallen for his fake apology.

I eyed him skeptically.

"I mean it," he said. "It wasn't my goal to embarrass you, and I *really* didn't intend to cause you to spill coffee all over the poor woman."

I ducked my head and ran my hand through my buzz cut, agitated by the horrific memory.

Trevor's baby blues shone with sincerity. I took a deep breath and slowly blew it out, giving my brain the signal to reset.

The sound of a dumpster lid being thrown open and glass-filled trash bags landing inside the metal bin came from the alley behind the row of businesses we stood beside.

As the tension left my body, the creases in Trevor's forehead dissipated as well.

"It's a good sign, man," he said softly, testing the waters. "The fact that a woman has your attention again is a good sign." He nodded as though his conviction were contagious and, by *him* believing it, I would automatically believe it too.

A small smile tugged at the corner of my mouth, and I shook my head. I turned to continue our walk to the alley and said half in jest, "She doesn't have my attention. That's a brand of trouble I don't need. Her shoes alone would set me back three paychecks."

We rounded the building and came to a stop outside of the rear entrance to the coffee shop. When I reached to open the door, Trevor caught my wrist. My brow furrowed, the look I gave him asking what the hell he was doing practically holding my hand.

Trevor's tone was as grave as his expression. "You can't move forward as long as you're holding on to the past, partner." He waited a moment for his words to sink in before releasing his hold on me.

It wasn't like Trevor to be so serious. And it definitely wasn't like him to spout shit that sounded like it had come from some philosophy handbook.

I had no idea why he was so hung up on the idea of me and this Alex woman. It wasn't like I never gave a woman the time of day. I just didn't do serious. Besides, the fact that I *did* find her captivating for some reason I couldn't figure out was all the more reason I was determined to keep as much distance between us as possible.

She'd come into town a few weeks back. Word on the street was that she was some famous author from Los Angeles and had just bought a house here.

I knew her type. Her fancy clothes, perfect makeup and hair, and designer purse all screamed money and a love of material things. She'd get tired of this small town real quick. She'd miss the glitz and glamour of big-city life and hightail it out of here just as fast as she'd ridden in. There was no way in hell I was getting involved with a shallow woman with a distaste for simple living and a habit of judging men by the size of their paycheck.

Shoving the last ten minutes and a pair of mesmerizing green eyes from my mind, I opened the door to the café and followed Trevor inside.

Jace was already waiting for us, shifting his weight back and forth, from one foot to the other.

"Hey," he said, raising his chin as we approached.

The lighting in the back of the shop was dim. A small bathroom the size of a coat closet stood at one end of the narrow hall for employee use only, while the wall opposite held several hooks decorated by jackets and aprons. I knew from having checked the premises during routine patrol that an office and small kitchen made up the middle portion of the business, with everything else situated up front and within sight of the customers. All of the pastries were made in-house in that cramped little kitchen, which was probably why they were some of the best I'd ever had.

"Any changes?" I asked, keeping my voice just above a whisper.

Jace's black eyes held a tinge of anxiety and a whole lot of determination. His shaggy brown hair was ruffled, as though he'd been running his fingers through it. At least when he was in need of a haircut, most of his earrings were concealed from view. I was aware of Bree having gotten more than one complaint from little old ladies about hiring someone with a bunch of piercings and tattoos. But God bless her, she had promised to give Jace a chance, and that was more than I could get any of the other business owners to agree to.

Jace shook his head. "It's been pretty quiet. Same old shit."

"Has anyone been acting any different toward you?" I asked.

He shook his head again and shoved his hands in his pockets. The kid was wound tighter than a spool of twine.

"Things are heating up, Jace." I cast a glance at Trevor. "We're not sure you should continue."

Jace removed his hands from his pockets and pounded his index finger into his open palm. "Look, I said I was going to help you bring them down. And that's what I'm going to do."

I started to reply, but he cut me off.

"I knew the danger when I agreed to this," he continued. "But this is just something I have to do."

"Jace, I get where you're coming from, but we just had another body show up on a slab with the tongue cut out. That easily could have been you."

He exhaled sharply and scraped his thumb over the inch-long white scar that sat above his right eyebrow. "I appreciate that you guys care about what happens to me. I really do. There's only one other person I can honestly say has ever given a damn. But I'll never be able to consider myself anything more than a pile of shit and waste of space if I don't see this through."

Trevor and I exchanged glances. We both knew this was a fork in the road for this kid, and we weren't about to rob him of the chance to change his reality.

I canted my head. A silent expression of both support and respect. "All right, Jace. We'll be keeping a close watch. If I get a whiff of anything that smells off, we're calling this thing and getting you the hell out of Dodge. You hear me?"

His face was placid as he nodded, but gratitude gleamed from his eyes. Eyes that held way too much experience for his eighteen years.

Knowing that we needed to end this meeting before anyone

got suspicious about Jace being gone too long, Trevor turned and exited the way we had come.

I gave Jace a stern look. "Watch your back."

"Don't worry," he said, sliding his pant leg up. "I don't go anywhere unprepared."

I glanced down and saw the metal gleam of a switchblade sticking out from the top of his ankle-high boots.

Had it been anyone else, I would have confiscated the weapon. But, considering Jace was putting his life on the line to serve a community that had turned its back on him long ago, I decided to pretend I hadn't seen a thing. If this op went sideways, that blade could mean the difference between life and death.

CHAPTER 4

Alex

I USED the last of the napkins the officer had brought over to wipe down my purse, which had been sitting on a spare chair and was assaulted nearly as badly as my notes. Glancing down at the coffee stains on my white chiffon top, I had the sudden urge to strip it off and drive home in my bra. I was an absolute mess, and it made me feel like I had ants crawling underneath my skin.

A white paper cup dropped to the table in front of me. I looked at the cup and then up at the deliverer. Bree stood with her hands on her hips, a pitying gaze traveling down my ruined top.

I offered a polite smile and said, "I believe you have delivered this to the wrong table. I didn't order another drink."

"I know," she said, swiping a strand of dishwater-blond hair behind her ear to join all the others that had escaped her messy bun. "Gabe bought it for you."

"Gabe?" I looked behind her at the counter, expecting to see a man waiting and watching for the signal that it was okay to approach.

Bree hooked her thumb toward the door. "The officer. The one that spilled coffee all over you."

"Oh!" I shook my head. "I told him not to worry about it."

"Yeah, well. He's all chivalry, that one." Bree crossed her arms, the bones from her shoulders bringing her blue T-shirt to a peak on either side of her head. She was a pretty girl, in an understated way, though she could easily stand to put at least another twenty pounds on her wispy frame. And though she appeared to be in her mid-twenties, her eyes held a sharpness and her demeanor a presence that made me wonder if her lanky frame simply gave the illusion of youth.

"Seemed like you two really hit it off," Bree continued, a sly smile forming.

I chuckled and looked toward the door the officer had disappeared through a moment earlier. I could still feel the weight of his gaze, those deep brown eyes and inky-black lashes threatening to pull me to depths to which I didn't wish to go. His humble apology had caught me off guard. Given his stern appearance with that dark buzz cut and pressed uniform, I had fully expected him to be another one of those cops that considered it beneath him to ever apologize, even if it *was* warranted.

Realizing I'd been ignoring Bree, who was still standing beside me while I was off in my thoughts, I smiled up at her and raised my cup. "Well, thank you for bringing this over. It was very thoughtful of him." I slid my purse up to my shoulder and scooted to the edge of my chair to indicate I was ready to leave. "I'd better head home and change into something a little less conspicuous."

Bree laughed and started to walk back to the counter. "See you soon," she called over her shoulder.

By the time I arrived home, my shirt was dry and my motivation low. The coffee shop had proven a bust. Just like every other time I'd been in there since I had moved to this town. Which was often. I had dealt with writer's block before, but this was different. Even with writer's block, I at least had a story idea and characters chattering away in my head. This block, though—this was absolute. No ideas. No characters. Nothing but a gaping black hole.

When I entered the house from the garage, Aderes came

running to greet me, her little paws slipping on the hardwood floor in her excited scramble. She walked her front feet up my leg so I couldn't go a step farther without giving her some affection. She was about the only thing that could distract me from getting out of my disastrous clothes.

Once she was satisfied, I deposited my bags in the office and continued down the carpeted hall to the master bedroom. Peeling off the soiled garments, I padded to the walk-in closet. Though it was nearing evening, the darkening sky outside had more to do with a rapidly approaching storm than the hour, so I moved to where all of my long-sleeved garments hung.

Wearing nothing but a white lace bra and panties, I pursed my lips and studied my options. Somewhere between eyeing a blue knitted sweater and a rose cashmere wrap, my attention drifted to the memory of a pair of dark eyes with thick lashes. I could still see him looking down at me, the heat from his body chasing the goose bumps on my skin as though he were actually standing right in front of me. Electricity erupted across my flesh as my imagination conjured strong arms wrapping around my waist, holding me firmly from breast to toe against his muscled frame.

I had noticed him before.

I tried not to. But he was difficult to ignore.

He was the kind of man who dripped with sexual prowess and commanded attention. I liked it best when he wore a T-shirt and jeans. Though the uniform was sexy as hell, too. The T-shirts, though—they put the strength of his arms on full display with the way the sleeves strained against the contours of his muscles.

My senses seemed attuned to him. Whenever he entered Grind, no matter what I was doing or how engrossed I was, a tingle skipped across my skin, and I knew if I looked up, I would find him there. Today was no different. The only surprise was the disappointment I'd felt when I'd seen him with that beautiful woman and the little girl in his arms. Undoubtedly his wife and child.

Thinking of the way that little one had squealed and jumped

into his arms caused a smile to spread across my face. He was so good with her. The way he doted on and cajoled her, she would never have to question how much she was loved.

The smile slipped from my face, replaced by grief for another little girl who had never known the security of feeling truly loved.

Shaking my head against the weight of heavy emotion pulling at my chest, I brought myself back from distant memories and forbidden desires.

I reminded myself that I wasn't open to a relationship anyway. That ship had sailed, and I had no intention of ever stepping aboard again.

Closing the door firmly on my wandering mind, I grabbed a soft green sweater and black leggings. Once dressed, I collected my soiled garments from the floor and left them soaking in the washing machine, hoping I could salvage my top. With a glass of red wine in hand, I pulled my notes and laptop from my bag and settled on the couch in front of a fire, Aderes curled up next to me.

The first drops of rain snapped against the windows and the patio doors to my left. The remnants of day backlit the shadowy trees and shrubs surrounding my house, highlighting the force of the growing wind as their limbs danced maniacally.

"Okay," I took a deep breath and let it out slowly. "I can do this. I've done this dozens of times before. No pressure."

Sure. No pressure. Your publisher is only threatening to drop you. Your fans are growing more impatient by the day, and if you blow this contract, you'll have to figure out how to pay back the advance you used to run away.

I swallowed another big gulp of wine and stared down at the wrinkled, coffee-stained notes in my lap. Honestly, I thought that cop had done me a favor. There was nothing here worth salvaging.

I tossed the stack of papers onto the coffee table in front of me and scooped up my laptop. After staring at the screen for several minutes, I set the laptop down beside me and rose from the couch, circling to the back of the room where the kitchen opened off the living room. Yanking open the refrigerator door, I gazed at the items on the shelves without really seeing them.

How the hell can I ever write another romance?

Would I be having this much trouble if I was trying to write a mystery, or maybe horror? Horror would be good. Then I could just write down the details of my life and be done with it.

Okay, I was devolving into a pity party for one. Not good. I slammed the door shut on the fridge and returned to the sofa, knowing full well I wasn't hungry, just procrastinating.

Aderes was deep in slumber, her lips flapping with each exhale. *Oh, to be that carefree.*

I slid the computer back onto my lap and wiggled my fingers. "I am not leaving this spot until I have something on this page."

A particularly strong gust of wind slammed into the living room windows, the darkness outside so complete I could no longer distinguish anything else. Rain fell in sheets, the drip from the overflowing gutters distinct from the rest of the downpour. Just as the lights began to flicker, my cell phone released a piercing cry, sending my heart into my throat. I picked up the device and hesitated when I saw *Unknown* on the caller ID.

Before the call could go to voice mail, I swiped to answer.

"Hello?" I waited for a reply that I didn't truly expect.

The silence on the other end of the call had that white noise quality to it that indicated the line remained open. The crank calls had started last week, and I'd tired of them quickly. At first, I thought a member of the media must have gotten ahold of my private number. But with each call that resulted in silence, I had quickly discarded that theory. If it was a member of the media, they wouldn't be shy about trying to bait me into a conversation.

Then the letters started. Whoever was sending them was clearly harboring an obsession with me, detailing all of the things he'd like to do to me sexually, most of which involved some form of sadism. The letters were nothing I hadn't experienced before, and they were sent to my author PO box in Los Angeles and forwarded to my home address, so I wasn't especially worried.

Still, the timing of the mysterious calls and the distasteful letters was a bit suspect.

I continued to listen to the silent phone call for a minute, hoping to pick up a clue in the background as to who might be calling, but as usual, it was a pointless endeavor.

Throwing the phone down on the couch, I refocused on the laptop screen. Not even ten seconds later, another call shattered the silence.

Growling, I snatched up the phone and answered. "If you don't have the guts to say anything, quit wasting my time!" I hung up and threw the phone down again.

Through the living room windows, a bolt of lightning illuminated the entire sky before the world outside descended back into darkness. The lights flickered more vehemently this time but remained on for the moment.

"This is just great. My clothes get ruined. I haven't written a single word. The electricity is about to go out, and I'm being harassed by a middle-aged man in his parents' basement with his hands down his pants. What a great freaking day!"

My phone blared again, and a bloodcurdling screech erupted from someplace inside of me that I didn't know existed.

I grabbed the phone and switched it to silent before placing it face down on the coffee table. Pushing off the couch, I walked into the kitchen again and pulled a flashlight, two candles, and a lighter from the catchall drawer.

A boom of thunder blasted overhead as another streak of lightning cast its spiderweb of electricity across the sky. The lights flickered once more and died.

"Shit."

I turned the flashlight on and stood it on end so I could see what I was doing to light the candles. Aderes's high-pitched whines drifted over the back of the couch and grew more distressed with each additional blast of thunder.

"It's okay, sweet girl. I'm coming."

I left the candles on the long counter that separated the

kitchen from the living room and walked back to the couch with the flashlight. The fire provided all the light I needed at the moment, so I saved the flashlight for bathroom trips.

Just as I was about to sit back down to snuggle Aderes, her whines morphed into a warning growl, her eyes locked on the patio doors, hackles rising. I stared at the doors, straining to see outside, but rain splatters and darkness were all that was visible. I told myself it was just some animal she heard scurrying around in the brush, yet the goose bumps on my arms and the hair on the back of my neck refused to listen.

A scrape against glass came from somewhere near the front door. Aderes jumped to her feet and ran to the door, barking ferociously. I swallowed against the lump in my throat. If it had come from one of the windows, I would have chalked it up to the bushes that sat close to the house. But there was nothing anywhere near the front door that could have caused that noise.

Aderes suddenly went still, her ears twitching as she changed their angle, trying to locate something. In a flash, she pivoted and ran straight for the patio doors and launched another barrage of warnings at an unseen foe.

My hands began to shake. I stood completely still, as though the slightest movement would bring my nightmares crashing into my reality.

Another flash of lightning sliced through the obsidian night, with it a flash of movement that traveled too far, and stood too high, to be an animal or a tree. My fear screamed at me to move. With trembling fingers, I snatched my cell from the coffee table, all the while debating whether I had really seen anything or my eyes and the storm were playing tricks on me.

I didn't want to be one of those pansies that called 911 freaking out about an intruder, only to have the cops arrive and discover it was something completely innocuous. Deciding I'd compromise by calling the nonemergency line and calmly requesting a check of the premises, I flipped the phone over to locate the number, and my stomach dropped.

Twenty-seven missed calls, all from *Unknown*.

My breath lodged in my chest. I couldn't pull my eyes from the screen.

What if?

What if I had been dismissing something that wasn't as benign as I had thought?

But surely if the creeper had my address, he wouldn't be sending letters to my PO box. Unless . . .

Unless the person sending the letters wasn't the one making the calls.

I protected my privacy fiercely. If someone had managed to get ahold of my cell number, could they have located my address as well?

Aderes went still, drawing my attention back to her and my patio doors. Her hackles were raised from her neck to her tail, every bone in her body rigid.

I went back to my phone and started to dial 911. Before I could finish, light flooded the house as the electricity came back on. The whir of electronics filled the silence, and Aderes dropped her tail.

Slowly, I moved to the patio doors, standing off to the side so I wasn't framed by the glass. When I flicked the switch on the wall, the backyard lit up. Nothing appeared out of place except for a large bag ensnared in one of my trees, the plastic flapping wildly in the wind.

Was that the movement I'd seen?

Aderes sniffed around the edges of the double doors. The backyard butted up to a large wooded area, with no fence dividing the two. All kinds of wildlife liked to venture into our yard. It drove Aderes crazy. Perhaps she really had sensed an animal.

Deciding I had likely been overreacting, I walked around the house, flipping on all of the outdoor lights, and then returned to the couch.

Having had enough excitement for one day, I shut my laptop and turned the TV on. As I flipped through channels, looking for a good movie, I glanced outside every now and then. Each time I failed to find something out of the ordinary, my nerves settled a little more. Aderes walked back to the sofa, hopped up, circled twice, and plopped down.

After finding a good black-and-white to watch, I pulled the afghan from the back of the couch and covered my legs. The storm was easing up a bit, the rain turning to a soft pattering. The thunder, a memory. All seemed normal. And yet, I couldn't shake the feeling that Aderes and I hadn't been alone during that storm.

CHAPTER 5

Gabe

THE CRACK of billiard balls slamming into one another smoothed out some of the tension I'd been carrying around the past few days. Ever since that latest CI had shown up so hollowed out his own mother wouldn't recognize him, I couldn't stop fearing that at any moment, I was going to get a call informing me that Jace had just been recovered in a similar condition.

Lost in thought, I spun my cue between my fingers, keeping the thick end of the stick planted on the floor. Sitting with one hip situated on the wooden railing that separated the raised platform where the billiard tables stood from the rest of the room, I was able to keep one eye on the game and the other roaming the dim bar, searching for anything that seemed out of place.

Like most nights, Rustlers boasted a pretty decent-size crowd. My sister and Bree were sitting at a table in a distant corner, nursing a red drink in a martini glass. It was Liz's weekly Girls' Night Out ritual, where she invited one of her girlfriends to join her for cocktails on the one night of the week her husband, Mark, would agree to a babysitter.

When Liz suddenly swung her gaze my way and caught me checking up on her, she stuck her tongue out. Noticing the peculiar behavior, Bree followed Liz's line of sight, smiling and waving when she saw me. I waved back and shot Liz a cocky smirk before continuing my assessment of the place.

Rustlers wasn't a high-class bar by any means, but it was the preferred watering hole among all the locals. The walls and the floors were built of the same light-colored pine. The bar top itself was rustic, crafted out of a dark, rough wood and given further character by the many brawls that had left a fair number of gouges and scars over the years. Neon signs in various shades of pink, orange, and green decorated the walls amid decades-old photographs of various locals who had left their imprint.

The stage, which sat adjacent to the billiard tables, was empty tonight. It was situated at the front of the room, whereas the pool tables sat in a more central location. So, though they were both elevated to the same height, the platform I was standing on provided a better bird's-eye view of all the happenings going on. The stage wasn't used nearly as often as the old jukebox sitting along the wall near the bathrooms, but some of the local bands were pretty damn good. The energy on those nights was through the roof, and some of the best times I'd ever had in this town had been spent listening to live music in this place.

"You always were shit at this game!" Trevor's voice cut through my distraction. I swiveled my head back to the table, where we were having a friendly game between coworkers. As usual, Trevor was trying to throw Garrett off his game by talking trash. Garrett lowered his chest to the table and slid the pool stick back and forth between his fingers. The single bulb hanging in a cheap green shade above the table cast harsh shadows across his features and turned his sandy-blond hair to ash. I bit back a laugh at the look of intense concentration on his face. Trevor was good at getting under Garrett's skin. Garrett knew it, and he was doing his damnedest to show Trevor up.

After several more seconds of lining up his shot, he finally thrust the pool stick into the cue ball and turned bright red when the stick glanced off the side of the ball, sending it only a few inches farther than where it had started. Garrett stood up with a string of curses that would have made a sailor blush.

With a victorious smile, Trevor moved in for the kill as Garrett moseyed over to his partner, Nash, with a whipped expression. Despite the fact Garrett had most likely just lost the game for the two of them, nice guy that he was, Nash simply smiled and patted Garrett on the back.

Ten seconds later, Trevor sank the eight ball and waggled his brows at Garrett. I shook my head, thinking that one of these days, when Garrett was a little less wet behind the ears, he was going to figure out the sweet game of getting even. When that day came, I hoped to hell I wasn't standing next to Trevor.

"It's okay, Pee Wee," Trevor said, ruffling Garrett's hair. "One of these days you'll be able to keep up with the big boys."

"Fuck off," Garrett said, going for the triangle to rack a new game. "Ten bucks says I kick your ass this time."

I couldn't be a part of watching Garrett lose both his dignity and his money all in one night. Apparently, Nash felt the same because he returned his pool stick to the rack and said, "Afraid you boys will have to play the next one without me."

"What?" Trevor looked offended and glanced at his watch. "It's only eight-thirty, you old lady!"

Nash laughed, completely unperturbed. Unlike Garrett, he had some years on him, and he wasn't so easily baited. I liked that the chief had paired those two together. Garrett was a smart kid and ambitious as hell. Nash was wise and patient. I had already seen a lot of growth in Garrett just in the few months he'd been under Nash's tutelage. Another year and he was going to be one of the best officers we had.

Nash started pulling on his brown bomber jacket. He wasn't a huge guy, standing at five eleven, but power radiated in every inch. It must have been the Puerto Rican in him. He was often all smiles, but the second someone crossed the line, his entire demeanor changed, and men twice his size cowered like pups.

"Come on," Trevor pleaded. "Just one more game." When

Nash didn't respond, Trevor added, "Are you really going to leave Junior hanging?"

Garrett's expression became mercurial, shifting from indignant to doubting and landing on false bravado with his chin raised and his chest puffed out.

Nash lifted his left hand and wiggled his ring finger. "Why would I stay here with you dickheads when I've got a smoking-hot woman waiting for me at home?" Instead of waiting for an answer, he flashed his white smile, saluted, and walked away.

I nodded at him as he sailed past, then took my own pool stick back to the rack.

"You're not leaving too, are you?" Trevor's eyes were practically begging me to stay.

I crossed my arms and squared off with him. "No. But I'm done playing tonight." Scrubbing a finger beneath my bottom lip, I pretended to scan the room again, afraid that if I looked Trevor in the eye, he'd see through me like toilet paper at the bottom of the bowl.

He twisted to look over his shoulder and then turned back with a knowing grin. "Which one is it gonna be?"

My eyebrows came together. "What the hell are you talking about?"

"The blonde or the redhead?"

I looked past him again, and this time I actually focused on the people. A blonde with her man-made assets on display in a low-cut tank top and her redheaded friend, in an equally revealing mini skirt, were giving me the green light. When they realized I was looking at them, the blonde ran her tongue slowly around her over-glossed lips and stuck her breasts out even farther. The redhead, who was standing at their high-top table, acted like she needed to adjust her strappy high heel and bent low enough for me to see that she wasn't wearing so much as a thong.

It was like any other night. There were plenty of women signaling to me that I didn't have to go home alone and unsatisfied if I didn't want to. Every once in a while, I took advantage of the buffet of sex options being offered up to me. Not that I took any of those hookups to *my* house. Sharing a piece of property with Liz and our parents, I was very careful about who I brought around. I definitely didn't want Lily and Connor's future relationship choices being influenced by what they saw their uncle doing. I had higher hopes for them.

Hopes that were more in line with Nash's life choices—the lucky bastard. Every time we played pool, he was the first one out the door, anxious to get home to a beautiful woman who was waiting for him with a smile, a warm body, and open arms meant just for him.

Sensing that I obviously wasn't in the mood for jokes tonight, Trevor let his grin slip from his face as his eyes turned stony. "Dude, when are you going to stop acting like you're the kind of guy who could ever get any satisfaction from a one-night stand and go back to being the guy that dotes on just one woman?"

I rolled my eyes and started to shove past him. Trevor brought a hand up to my chest and stopped me hard. "It's been two years, brother. You need to move past it. Otherwise, she wins over and over again."

I could practically see the waves of heat coming off my body, fists clenched as tight as my jaw. Trevor was walking a *very* fine line, and he knew it. His body became rigid, muscles ready to react if it came to that. The air between us crackled from the tension, and I wasn't sure if it was the blood rushing in my ears, but the conversations around us seemed to quiet suddenly.

I reminded myself this was my best friend. We'd been inseparable since grade school. We'd gone through the academy together and been partners ever since we'd gotten off field training. He was more than a friend. He was a second brother.

Slowly, I released the breath I was holding. The volume in the bar gradually grew louder, and my fingers uncurled to hang limply at my side. "That's not something we're going to talk about again," I said.

Trevor stared at me for a moment, seeming to contemplate

whether he was ready to agree to that. Finally, he gave a brief nod and returned to the pool table where Garrett was patiently waiting, his eyes darting between us with a question he didn't dare ask.

Taking up my position against the railing again as Trevor broke the balls, I looked back at Liz and Bree one more time to make sure they were still good. Hearing the familiar creak of the bar's heavy door as it swung open, I glanced over to note who was walking in. I was always vigilant about knowing who and what was around me, a skill I had honed while serving overseas, but lately, my vigilance had kicked into overdrive. Trying to bring down one of the most feared motorcycle gangs in the continental US would do that to a cop.

I stilled when the low light of the bar gleamed on a head of rich mahogany. Every step she took—the sway of her hips, the swing of her arms—was full of grace and captured my attention like the hypnotic lull of a snake charmer's melody. Creamy skin with a flush of pink contrasted with darkly lined eyes that shone with green fire. Her body had a language all its own, and it was a language *my* body craved to study.

Alex's eyes took in the room before settling on the bar. As she walked to the short end of the bar nearest her, she seemed completely unaware of the dozens of men mentally undressing her with every step and all the women throwing daggers with their eyes. Sliding between two patrons, careful not to touch them, she watched Scott behind the bar, trying to catch his attention.

She didn't have to wait long. As soon as he looked her way, he did a double take and hurried over to her. Placing his hands on the bar, he leaned in close so she could speak in his ear. When he pulled back, he offered Alex his hand and shook it while he flashed that charismatic pretty boy smile that kept the ladies tipping and sipping all night long.

Scott took off toward the kitchen, so I assumed the pretty author was picking up an order to go. She looked incredibly uncomfortable sitting by herself at the bar—like she didn't know what to do with herself in a place like this. She was dressed in a long sleeve dark-blue shirt that really set off the red in her hair. And the V-cut of her neckline was tasteful but also showed enough skin to make a man wonder about the parts he *couldn't* see.

One of the regulars who was always drunk by five-thirty was trying to strike up a conversation with her, but her tight-lipped smile clearly indicated she wished he would pass out and leave her alone.

The urge to go to her and kick the shit out of anyone who bothered her rose up like a tidal wave, the force of it catching me off guard. I didn't like to see women hassled. I always stepped in when I witnessed a situation where it looked like a woman needed assistance in getting her point across to some asshole with a hearing problem. But this was different. The drunk might have been annoying her, and she might have felt a bit self-conscious with all of the attention she was getting, which had now become obvious even to a blind man, but it wasn't like she was in any danger. Yet I had to tell myself—firmly, and many times—to stay the fuck where I was.

Don't do it, you schmuck. That is a woman that has trouble written all *over her.*

I knew her type. Big city with lots of money and a distaste for blue collars. The kind that spent Saturday nights at galas and red-carpet events, dripping with jewels and dressed in an expensive label. No doubt she had watched one Hallmark movie too many, gotten the idea that a small town in the middle of nowhere was a charming notion, and decided to "invest" in a second home. Hell, this was probably a third home for her.

I hadn't Googled her as I knew others in the town had, but the gossip mill in Eden Falls was strong. And that was the only thing I hated about this place. Well—that and the murderous drug-running bastards who were trying to turn it into their own private playground.

I knew enough to know this woman had the level of fame and fortune that would ensure she wasn't going to stick around long.

The big-city types always moved in and out quickly once they realized a small town was just too boring compared to the lifestyle they were accustomed to.

To me, though, that was a big part of the charm. Simple living meant a man could live a hell of a life without having to go out and kill himself at a desk job that he hated while he racked up wealth and simultaneously destroyed his marriage and any respect his kids might have once held for him.

Seeing that the drunk now had his hand on Alex's shoulder, I stood from the railing. The guy's hand continued to inch lower and lower as Alex kept leaning back, trying to put distance between them. Any second, his hand was going to flop down onto her boob. *Over my dead body.*

Without even realizing I'd made the decision, I descended the stairs and stepped onto the main floor, carving a straight line to Alex and the drunk who was about to lose a limb and anything else that touched her before I got there.

When I rounded the bar, those green eyes shifted from the drunk to me, a flash of relief crossing her face so fast, I wasn't sure I'd read her expression correctly.

The drunk sat between us, completely unaware of my presence at his back, even with Alex staring at me. I slapped my hand on his shoulder and shouted above the country song blaring from the jukebox. "Hey, buddy, you need to go sleep it off outside."

The drunk turned at a glacial pace. His glassy eyes looked up at me, and at first, the belligerent look warping his features made me think this was going to turn into a thing. But then recognition dawned, and we were suddenly best friends.

"Hey—I know you," he slurred, a bit of drool running out the side of his mouth. "You're that cop." He wagged a beefy finger at me and squinted like he was trying to remember something very far out of reach.

"Yeah," I said. "I'm that cop. And I'm cutting you a break by telling you to go sleep it off."

I caught the attention of another regular standing nearby who

I often played pool with when my partners had already left with female company. "Joe, can you do me a favor and take this guy out to his car so he can get some rest?"

Joe nodded and came right over.

I reached into the drunk's pocket and pulled out his keys, handing them over to Joe. "Once you've got him settled, give these to Scott. He'll make sure the guy walks home if he's still drunk when he wakes up."

When I was convinced Joe had everything under control, I turned to Alex.

She offered a polite smile. "Thank you for doing that."

"No problem. It was the least I could do after what happened the other day."

Lines formed across her forehead, and she hesitated for a moment before responding. "I'm sorry if I was a bit short with you. It had been a challenging afternoon."

I leaned against the bar so I was facing her profile. "And then I go and make it better by spilling coffee all over you." I offered a wry grin and was rewarded with a thousand-watt smile on her end. And . . . wow. If I thought she was a stunner before, that smile about brought me to my knees.

As if catching herself, her smile wilted, and she ducked her head, tucking an imaginary lock of hair behind her ear. She had her sternum pressed against the bar, arms folded on top. The action pushed her breasts up and provided another very nice view of her more-than-adequate cleavage. I gave myself a mental facepalm, reminding the stupid half of my brain that this wasn't the kind of woman we needed to get involved with.

What the hell was the matter with me? It wasn't like she was the only beautiful woman in town. And it definitely wasn't as if I was hard up and overdue a sexual release. Okay—maybe I was overdue, but it was by my own choosing. She wasn't even the kind of woman I went for. I liked my women like I liked everything else —simple. And this woman might have been a lot of things, but simple sure as hell wasn't one of them.

I waited for her to say something else, but she remained silent, her gaze locked on her hands stacked neatly in front of her.

Maybe it was the fact she didn't flirt with me the way other women did that made her so compelling. Yeah, that must have been it. It was just my primal instinct to chase and capture challenging prey.

A glass shattered at the other end of the bar, and Alex's head whipped up, a look of fear and panic in her eyes.

I watched her for a moment, trying to piece together what had just happened. Before I got my answer, Scott returned with her food.

Alex hopped off her barstool, bag in hand, and flung her purse over her shoulder. She smiled up at me and said, "It was nice speaking with you. Thank you again for your assistance with that gentleman."

Her prim and proper facade was firmly affixed once again. But I hungered for another glimpse of the woman with the dazzling smile that could put the stars to shame.

"I'm going to walk you out," I said. I placed my hand on her lower back and started to usher her to the door, hoping my assertive tone would keep her from arguing.

I should have known I wasn't that lucky.

Her eyes widened, and she looked up at me over her shoulder. "You really don't have to do that. I'm parked right out front."

"It's not a problem. And frankly, I'm not about to let you walk to your car alone with the way half the men in this bar are looking at you."

As if noticing them for the first time, her eyes darted to the various faces following us out the door. Snapping her mouth shut, she didn't say another word until she climbed into her SUV and thanked me again.

Standing in that parking lot under the glow of the Rustlers sign, I watched her taillights disappear into the night, and somehow, I knew if I wasn't careful, history was going to repeat itself.

CHAPTER 6

Alex

THE MORNING LIGHT filtered through branches thick with pine needles and reflected off dewdrops that sparkled like millions of tiny diamonds. The dirt and fallen foliage that carpeted the woods was still damp, creating a soft landing for each footfall. I pushed my body forward, letting the steady thump of my steps and rhythm of my breathing pull me deeper into the zone and away from the myriad thoughts and worries that plagued me every moment I wasn't running.

This was *my* time. My escape. Running through these woods was the only relief I got these days. I always left my phone at home, and the trail through the woods behind my house was my favorite place to run because I had never seen another soul out there. No phone calls. No one talking to me, scolding me, or demanding answers from me. No text messages. No emails. No crazy letters. No lawyers. Only quiet and air so fresh it burned.

Each breath escaped in a puff of white condensation that washed over me as I pushed harder. The muscles in my legs strained to match the pace I demanded. The pain felt good, like I was actually achieving something. Despite the exertion and the fact that I was dressed in thermal leggings, a long-sleeve top, and a vest, the bitter cold still managed to cut through my defenses—just like that police officer.

Gabe. I rolled his name around, matching the image of the man to the meaning of the name and wondered how aptly it suited him.

No matter how many times I tried to evict him from my mind, no matter how many miles I put behind me, the memory of him kept stealing into my thoughts.

I didn't think I'd smiled even once this past year. Then he comes along and makes me do it twice in one week.

Despite my trying to focus on the trail, the forest melted from view, and Rustlers appeared before me like a mirage. Recollections of last night, the hazy bar and the way my stomach had somersaulted when I'd seen Gabe walking toward me all dark and lethal-looking held me captive. I'd been so busy trying to keep a low profile, just wanting to get in and out with my food, that I hadn't even noticed he was there at first.

A gentle slope in the running trail had me pumping my arms harder, both to keep my pace from slowing and to push the man out of my head. I did *not* want to think about last night. I did *not* want to think about Gabe with his chocolate eyes and a physique so hot it could melt the Arctic. And I certainly did not want to think about the nonstop fantasies my traitorous libido kept sneaking into my imagination.

Focus on the pain, Alex.

My muscles were screaming, trying to convince me to slow to a walk. My lungs burned as they grappled for breath after breath. And I loved every minute of it. The pain from the exertion was my only reliable form of distraction.

Birds chirped in the endless expanse of trees lined up like a cheering squad. Branches creaked. Twigs snapped. It was nature's serenade, and out here, it felt meant for only me.

I crested another rise in the land, trying to determine if I was going to do my usual loop or push for extra mileage as part of that age-old tradition of procrastination. It was nearing the end of the week, and I still didn't have any worthwhile pages to send to Cass. She was going to stuff an apple in my mouth and roast me on a spit.

Before I could make up my mind, something caught my attention along the trail about fifty yards ahead. Keeping my eyes trained on it, I squinted, trying to make out what it was. I knew for sure it hadn't been there during my run yesterday.

Drawing nearer, I broke into a walk until I was close enough to decipher the enigma. Then my eyes widened, and adrenaline flooded my body as I stopped dead in my tracks.

The solitude I always found so peaceful had turned to terrifying in an instant. Dragging my eyes away from the tree, I turned in a circle, searching for any sign that I wasn't alone. The birds were still chirping, oblivious to the terror creeping in like a poisonous fog, threatening to choke me.

Ragged breathing filled my ears. It took a moment to realize it was coming from me. I fought to slow the rise and fall of my chest, recognizing that I was on the verge of hyperventilating.

Stay calm and think.

I had to get out of these woods. If whoever had put this thing on this tree was still here somewhere, waiting for me, there was no one for miles to hear my screams. No one to play witness to a nightmare made manifest.

Scanning my surroundings once more, I backed away and began retracing my steps. This was clearly a message meant for me. Planted by someone who knew my routine. Which meant that person would also expect me to complete the loop back to my house since that was the fastest way back. And that was exactly why I would do the opposite and return the way I had come.

Sprinting through the woods, I was no longer aware of the frigid air penetrating my clothes. I could no longer hear the birds or even feel the burning in my muscles. The only thing I was aware of was the icy-cold fingers of fear tickling my neck and tracing a path down my spine.

A horrifying thought sprang to mind as I calculated the

distance still remaining between me and my house. The black-and-white photo that had been nailed to the tree could have only been taken from one place—

My bedroom closet.

Someone had been standing mere feet from me, taking photos while I lay in bed reading, completely unaware. How long had they been hiding there? How had they gotten past Aderes? What had they done after I'd gone to sleep?

The thought of being unconscious while someone lurked in my home was too much to handle, especially as I contemplated my next move.

My phone, my keys, my car—they were all inside my house. A house that had already been penetrated by someone trying to . . . what? Scare me? Rape me? Kill me?

What if they were waiting for me inside? Expecting that I would see that photo and run back and lock myself in with them?

When I finally rounded the last bend in the trail, my house visible through a thick stand of trees, I slowed.

What the hell do I do?

I didn't know any of my neighbors. The closest one was a mile away, and this bastard could be anywhere.

But one thing was for sure. My dog was inside, and I wasn't going anywhere without her. Especially since this psycho had already found a way around her.

I squared my shoulders and sharpened my senses, watching and listening for anything out of place as I approached the house at an angle that would ensure I couldn't be seen through any of the windows. I always left the back door to the garage open when I ran so that I didn't have to carry my keys.

When I reached the door, I slipped inside and locked it behind me to lessen the chance that someone could follow me in and catch me by surprise.

I paused and stilled my breathing, listening. After a minute of hearing nothing out of the ordinary, I eased toward the door leading to the kitchen. Cracking it open, I peered through the slit.

I could see most of my kitchen and the living room from my vantage point. All seemed quiet. Too quiet. Silence had never been so suffocating.

My heart pounded against my chest. My fingers trembled. For the first time in forever, I wished I wasn't alone.

Pushing the door open farther, I stepped inside, grimacing when the rubber on my shoes squeaked on the hardwood floor. I paused again.

Nothing.

Sunlight streamed in through the patio doors. Dust particles floated in lazy, meandering patterns. The refrigerator hummed in monotone.

Everything was so normal and yet completely changed. Someone had been in my *home*. They had violated my space. My privacy. This no longer felt like a sanctuary. Instead, it felt like an illusion. Like the walls and doors didn't really exist, and anyone could traipse through my fragile psyche and the barriers I had built around me anytime they pleased.

I eyed my purse sitting on the counter at the far end of the kitchen. Slowly, I moved toward it, stepping with careful precision to mute my footsteps, my eyes scanning for movement that didn't belong.

I didn't dare call out for Aderes, but my heart rate galloped even faster as I considered all the reasons she hadn't come running at the squeak of my shoe.

Reaching my purse, I grasped it firmly and slid it toward me. The zipper might as well have been blaring through a bullhorn for all the noise it made in the deathly quiet space.

Once I had unzipped it enough to get my hand inside, I reached in and ran my fingers around like I was choosing a raffle ticket from a fishbowl. The purse lining scraped against my fingertips, each item in the bag easily identified and quickly dismissed.

Then, my hand stilled, and my stomach dropped.

Alex

WHERE THE HELL are my keys?

I unzipped the purse the rest of the way, still keeping my eyes up and scanning. If someone was in this house, I would *not* be caught off guard.

It didn't matter how many times I ran my hand through the items in my purse. My keys were not there. I shoved my fingers into my hair, trying to think.

Why the hell hadn't I listened to Cass? I should have just reported the damn letters and phone calls when they'd started. What if the person behind those incidents really had tracked me down and put that photo on the tree to taunt me? Was he watching right now? Getting pleasure from seeing me terrified out of my mind?

Focus, Alex. Just focus.

Maybe I should start walking toward town. This time of day, there would be a few cars on the road, so I'd at least feel like I wasn't completely alone, waiting for someone to come murder me. Then I could call the police and ask someone to come meet me.

A thump from the back of the house stopped me cold. I took

slow steps around the counter, angling myself so I could see all the way down the hall toward the bedrooms. My breath turned to iron in my chest, my heart beating so loudly I was afraid it would give me away.

I waited, unable to tear my eyes from the hall. Expecting someone to pop out any moment. A shadow fell across the wall opposite my office. I wanted to scream, but I was paralyzed. Unable to move. Unable to breathe. Unable to swallow against the lump lodged in my throat. My hands trembled even harder, rattling the metal clasp connecting the strap of my purse to the D ring.

The shadow grew darker. In my peripheral, I saw the pair of scissors I kept in the pencil holder on the counter. Just as I reached for them, movement flashed from my office as the source of the shadow barreled toward me.

My lungs deflated like a balloon that had been popped, my hand flying to my chest in relief at the sight of Aderes, safe, and the realization that a psychopathic killer wasn't sprinting toward me.

Aderes circled my knees, waiting for me to greet her. I was done messing around inside this house. I'd prefer my car so I could put as much distance between me and this place as possible, but I was going to have to settle for walking. With purse and phone in hand, I spun and went straight for the garage again. Aderes stayed close to my leg. I was mentally preparing to grab her leash from beside the door when I suddenly remembered something.

When I'd arrived home from Rustlers last night, I had been distracted by the memory of Gabe and the way he'd handled that drunk who'd been fondling me. I had set the keys down so I could pull a doggie biscuit out of the box I kept beside the door.

When I opened the garage door, I craned my head around the corner and spotted my keys right there on the shelf above the dog treats.

Thank you, God.

I snatched Aderes's leash from the wall and ushered her into the garage. Once we were both settled in the car, I punched the button on the garage door opener and hit the gas the second my car could clear the rising door. Only once I was on the main road, my driveway disappearing in my rearview mirror, was I able to take a deep breath. My hands continued to tremble, so I gripped the steering wheel hard, trying to bring myself under control.

My purse started to vibrate. I looked at the name flashing across my car's Bluetooth display and was relieved to see that it was Cass. When I answered, her voice boomed through the speakers.

"Alex, great news, Love. I got you a spotlight feature in *Happening Now*. They're going to run a six-page spread on you." Cass was talking a mile a minute, her chipper voice a half octave higher than usual.

"They agreed to focus primarily on your career. You know, all about you growing up privileged and everything but determined to succeed on your own. Of course, I couldn't get them to agree to completely ignore all recent events, but that's only going to be a very small part buried somewhere in the middle."

"Cass—" My voice broke. I tried to swallow the thick emotion building in my throat, the tears gathering in my eyes making it difficult to see the road clearly.

"Alex? What's wrong?" Cass's tone had lost all excitement. Hearing the genuine concern in her voice caused the tears to gather faster until they were streaming down my face.

"I—somebody . . ."

A million thoughts swam in my head, jockeying for position.

"Alex, take a deep breath."

I tried to comply, but violent sobs had me gasping for air, a fuzzy feeling settling in my brain. My sweet husky, sensing that I wasn't okay, leaned across the center console and licked the tears from my cheek. Feeling her warmth against my shoulder and her rough tongue on my skin grounded me.

I tried again to catch my breath. This time I was able to fill my lungs and release the air slowly.

"That's good, Alex. Just keep taking those deep breaths." Cass was trying to take control of the situation, and I loved her for it. Despite her hard-ass tactics when it came to business, as a friend, there was no one better to have in your corner.

"Now," she continued. "Are you safe, yes or no?"

"Y-yes." I took another deep breath. My vision began to clear, the dizziness subsiding.

"Okay. That's good. Why don't you pull over until we can get you feeling a little better?"

I shook my head, forgetting she couldn't see me. "No, I can't." I gripped the wheel harder, determined to make it to the police station without stopping.

"It's happening again, Cass."

"What's happening?"

"I'm being followed." Another sob tried to escape. I pushed it down, determined to regain control.

Cass was silent for so long I glanced down at the display on my dash, thinking the call must have dropped.

"Where are you now?" she asked.

"I'm headed into town. I'm going to the police station. I should have listened to you." I shook my head again, this time at my own stupidity. I had been so determined to protect my solitude and privacy that I had created the perfect environment for a predator to walk right through the front door—literally.

Cass let out a slow breath, the only sign of stress she ever showed. "It doesn't matter, Alex. You're going there now, and we're going to do whatever it takes to keep you safe."

Though she was thousands of miles away, her words soothed me, helping me to find peace within the storm. Cass never said anything she couldn't back up with action.

"I'm going to stay on the phone with you until you're inside the police station."

Five minutes later, I pulled along the curb that fronted the

Eden Falls Police Department. When I walked inside, Aderes trotting next to me, I saw an older woman sitting at a long counter. She looked up and smiled when the door closed behind me.

"Okay, Cass." I spoke quietly, trying my best to appear calm. "I'm inside."

"Call me as soon as you're done making the report."

"I will." I disconnected and slipped my phone into the pocket of my vest as I approached the counter, suddenly self-conscious by the way the woman's hazel eyes looked me over. At least I knew I didn't have mascara running down my face since I hadn't yet put makeup on today. But I was sure the tear stains on my cheeks were still visible.

"Hello, dear. How may I assist you?" The woman looked to be in her sixties and reminded me a lot of Betty White, her kind smile inviting me to spill all my secrets.

I cleared my throat and smoothed my hair. "I need to speak with a police officer, please."

"Certainly. May I ask what it's regarding?"

"Someone has been stalking me."

Betty's penciled-on eyebrows nearly reached her hairline. I had a feeling they didn't often deal with very serious matters in this town.

She pointed an arthritic finger at a bench sitting along the wall next to the counter. "If you'll have a seat, I'll ask one of the officers to respond immediately."

Betty White didn't mess around. I had barely gotten myself settled on the bench, Aderes lying on top of my feet, when an officer stormed through a set of double doors opposite the ones I had entered through.

He smiled and nodded as he came to a stop in front of me, but his eyes remained stoic and untrusting. "Ma'am, I'm Officer Garrett Carlson. I understand someone's been bothering you. Would you like to tell me about it?"

Not wanting to be in a subservient position, I stood, my eyes searching the floor as I thought about where to start.

"A few weeks ago, I began receiving anonymous letters of a sexually graphic nature."

Officer Carlson nodded slowly but didn't say anything, so I continued.

"Then I started receiving phone calls. Also from an anonymous source."

"And these phone calls were also of a graphic nature?" he asked.

I shook my head. "No. The caller never actually said anything. He just kept calling and leaving the line open."

"If he never said anything, how do you know it was a he?"

"I don't know for sure," I admitted. "I just assumed. Especially when I started to suspect it might be the same person sending the letters."

He nodded again but remained silent. I was keenly aware of Betty cocking her ear in our direction, pretending to focus on something in front of her.

I cleared my throat again, suddenly feeling self-conscious for reasons other than the state of my appearance. "Then, today, I was out for a run and I . . . I saw something nailed to a tree. When I was close enough to see it clearly, I realized it was a picture. A picture of me, taken from inside my house."

The only reaction from Officer Carlson was a slight lift of his eyebrows. "Have you ever seen that photo before?" he asked.

"No!"

Betty jerked her head up, eyes wide.

Heat flooded my cheeks. "I'm sorry, Officer Carlson. This has just been a very distressing experience. I'm sure you can imagine how alarming it would be for a woman, in the middle of the woods, alone, to find a picture of herself nailed to a tree. Especially when that picture was taken from inside her home without her knowledge."

Carlson squinted his eyes and studied me for a moment. I held his gaze.

"All right, ma'am." Carlson pulled a notepad and pen from his breast pocket and flipped to a clean page. "Can you tell me exactly where you found this photo?"

After I'd given detailed instructions on where to locate the evidence, Carlson told me to take a seat and to wait for his return.

An hour later, and on the brink of another breakdown, I was seriously regretting the choice I had made.

CHAPTER 8

Alex

"I don't know what you want me to say!" I thrust my fingers into my hair and tried very hard not to pull it out by the roots.

"Ma'am, calm down," Officer Carlson held his hand out like he was trying to stop traffic.

"Do. Not. Tell. Me. To. Calm. Down!" Heat crawled up my chest and climbed all the way to my cheeks. "I came to you for help, and you're practically accusing me of lying!"

"I didn't say that, ma'am."

Oh, but his eyes and tone said plenty. Ever since he'd returned from his little field trip, all he had done was insinuate that I was either crazy or making the whole thing up.

"Perhaps you simply went to the wrong location," I said.

"I followed the directions *you* provided. There was nothing out of place."

"Then whoever nailed that photo to the tree must have removed it after I saw it."

"And what would be the point in that, ma'am?"

My skin was beginning to feel too tight, and every time he called me ma'am, another surge of heat washed over me.

"Gee, I don't know, Officer. If I thought like a homicidal maniac, perhaps I'd be better able to do your job *for* you."

We squared off, both of us falling into silence and neither one of us breaking eye contact.

As most men did under the hostile glare of a vexed woman, he finally made the first move. "Wait here. I'll be back."

I bit my tongue to keep from saying something that was going to get me slapped with a citation for assaulting a peace officer. Too angry to sit, I paced the short distance between the counter and the exit.

Occasionally, Betty glanced up at me, but she seemed intent to remain a spectator rather than a participant in the sparring match Carlson and I had going.

My phone buzzed in my pocket. It was a text from Cass. *How did it go at the police station?*

I shook my head as I typed my reply. *Still here. They think I made it all up.*

What?!?! What do you mean?

One of the officers went out to the trail to collect the photo as evidence. It was gone. Or more likely, he couldn't follow the simple directions I gave him. Either way, he thinks I made the whole thing up.

I watched the dots dancing on my screen as Cass typed her response. *Did you tell him about the letters and phone calls?*

I closed my eyes, once again regretting that I hadn't taken Cass's advice sooner. *Yes. He questioned why, if someone has been harassing me, I haven't made any reports.*

Don't let them off the hook, Alex. They need to take this seriously.

I know, I typed back. *I'll call you when I leave.*

It was nearly twenty minutes before Carlson returned, likely trying to show me who had the power here. I crossed my arms and wiped my face of emotion as he approached.

He handed me a business card with a number written on the back. "Here's your case number. I'll write a report, but without any evidence to verify what you're telling me, there's nothing else I can do."

My jaw dropped, and I struggled to find the words to adequately describe how unimpressed I was with his effort. "What about the phone calls? I showed you my call log. And the letters? I told you I would bring them in."

He swung his arms open in a gesture that indicated we'd already been over this. "The call log just shows that someone, or multiple someones, have called from a blocked number. A lot of people block their phone numbers to protect their privacy. I'll still include it in the report, but there's just not much to go on. As far as the letters go, bring them in and I'll attach them to the file."

Realizing there was nothing more I could say to convince this guy to do his job, I slammed my mouth shut and bent to pick up Aderes's leash. She jumped to her feet, and we started toward the exit. Before I got to the doors, the phone at the counter rang. Two seconds later, Betty called after me.

"Ms. Reilly, would you come back here, please?"

I turned and hesitated, looking between her and Carlson, who no longer appeared arrogant but utterly confused.

As if sensing I'd had enough and was about to tell them where they could stick their case numbers on my way out the door, Betty gave me that disarming smile and said, "Chief Kelly is requesting to see you in his office."

Carlson's head snapped around to Betty, his eyebrows rising like towers. "What for?" he asked, sounding like an indignant schoolboy who had just had his hand slapped.

I tried not to smile, but his reaction was worth the price of admission alone, so I figured I'd see this thing through a little longer.

I canted my head. "Very well."

Betty walked me through the double doors behind the counter and toward the back of a large room that had desks scattered throughout and officers sitting at several of them. Figuring that Carlson had probably spent those twenty minutes back here telling the other officers I was crazy and making jokes at my expense, I kept my chin high and my eyes straight ahead.

When we reached an office situated in the middle of the back wall, Betty ushered me in and closed the door behind me.

An older gentleman with a short, round frame rose from his desk. "Ah, Ms. Reilly. Thank you for coming in. I'm Chief of Police Jim Kelly." The chief smiled and extended his hand.

With blue eyes that twinkled in a round, happy face and a white mustache that matched the horseshoe swath of hair covering the lower half of his balding head, the chief had a pleasant way about him. Still, after my experience with Carlson, not to mention my recent experience with law enforcement in general, I would remain skeptical until I was given a reason to feel otherwise.

Closing the distance between us, I shook his hand and waited for him to explain what I was doing there.

Chief Kelly waved a hand toward the visitor's chair in front of his desk. "Please, have a seat, Ms. Reilly."

A sheen of sweat broke across my face. I was still wearing my thermals from my run, and heat blasted from a small unit affixed to the wall beneath the large picture windows sitting opposite me. The picturesque view of snowcapped mountains rising in the distance did little to calm the anxiety running beneath my skin like a live wire.

Chief Kelly glanced at his phone and cleared his throat before giving me his attention once more. "Ms. Reilly, it's been brought to my attention that you believe someone has intentionally been trying to intimidate you—"

A sharp voice cut through the chief's explanation. "Noooo, Chief Kelly. As I've already told you, Ms. Reilly does not *believe* that to be the case, but rather that *is* the situation."

My eyes widened and fixed on the phone. *Cass.*

Oh, dear Lord.

Chief Kelly closed his eyes briefly and rubbed his forehead. I recognized that look. It was the look of someone who had just gone round for round with Cass and had come up wanting.

I sat up straighter and folded my hands in my lap, refocusing on the chief.

With a grim smile, Chief Kelly continued. "Your publicist is insisting that I provide you with a protection detail. However, as I have explained to her"—Chief Kelly scowled at the phone—"that is not something we do—"

Cass cut him off again. "And as *I* have explained to Chief Kelly, it is in their best interest to comply. You see, Chief, what I haven't yet had the opportunity to expound upon is what will happen to your department if anything should happen to Ms. Reilly as a result of this unstable stalker and your lack of due diligence."

The chief opened his mouth to reply, but the freight train that was Cass was just getting started. Without taking a breath, she continued in a chipper tone with an undercurrent of threat. "As a publicist, I'm sure you can imagine how many media sources I am in contact with on a daily basis, and I would not hesitate for a moment to ensure that each and every one of my connections is informed of the fact that you were made well aware of the threat to Ms. Reilly and yet failed to take the matter seriously. Considering the size of her fan base and the amount of media attention she receives, I'm sure you can quite easily visualize the shitstorm that will rain down upon you and your entire department should you fail to heed my warning."

Cass fell silent, allowing the chief to contemplate whether she was bluffing.

Chief Kelly's face was transitioning through various shades of red, his expression pinched.

I was so very grateful to Cass for getting the police department to take this matter more seriously, but I was equally horrified by her suggestion to put a protection detail on me. I did *not*, under any circumstances, want a bunch of strangers milling around my private space and following me all hours of the day and night. If I was finding it impossible to work in complete solitude, the way I preferred it, then how could I possibly expect to accomplish anything with someone standing over my shoulder?

The tension in the room became unbearable. I was not someone who tolerated confrontation and displeasure well. I reached down to Aderes and gently stroked her ears, drawing comfort from the baby-soft fur before breaking the silence. "Cass, I really appreciate how hard you're willing to fight to protect me, but I don't think securing bodyguards is the answer."

I had Chief Kelly's attention, but he remained quiet, chewing on the inside of his cheek, waiting for me to elaborate.

"I would, however, appreciate it if you would open an investigation, Chief, to determine who is behind these incidents. Additionally, I would like an officer to accompany me home and stand by while I pack a few things."

Cass hollered into the phone. "Pack a few things?"

Wiggling in my seat, I slid closer to the edge, my spine unable to get any straighter. It wasn't even ten o'clock in the morning, and I was thoroughly exhausted from this day. "Yes. I think it would be best for me to leave for a while until the police figure out who is behind this."

Chief Kelly eyed me as though he were putting together a puzzle and trying to visualize the full image from a few scant pieces.

"Alex." Cass had the tone of someone trying to explain something to a five-year-old. "Let's consider this for a moment. You take off for a while to get some distance and allow the police to investigate. First, there is a very high likelihood this person followed you to Eden Falls. So it stands to reason he would continue to follow you wherever you decided to go. You would remain as vulnerable as you are now."

I drew my lip between my teeth, Aderes's leash becoming frayed where my fingers worked the stitches.

"Second," Cass continued, "the police will be much more likely to catch this guy if you remain in one jurisdiction. If you keep moving, even if you report every incident, you'll be dealing with several different police departments who have no prior knowledge of this situation. You will be far better off staying in one place with *one* law enforcement agency handling your case."

I hated to admit it, but Cass made some very valid points.

When I didn't respond right away, Cass said, "Chief, kindly take me off speakerphone and give Ms. Reilly the handset."

Chief Kelly rolled his eyes, looking less than enthused about taking orders from a civilian, but he complied.

I stood and moved closer to the desk to keep from pulling the base of the phone to the floor.

"Alex, I get your reservation. But the truth is, you need to get back to writing, and the last thing you need to be worrying about is someone coming after you. Take the protection detail. Let the cops worry about this stalker. And *you* worry about your pages."

"Cass, the idea was to get away from everyone. How am I supposed to get any work done if I have a bunch of babysitters milling around all day?"

"How are you supposed to get any work done if you're constantly looking over your shoulder?" she fired back. "Besides, this situation could play to your advantage."

I frowned. "What do you mean?"

"Well . . ." Cass dragged out the word like she was trying to build suspense. "Your fans have a history of supporting you through challenges. If they catch wind of this, it could buy you some time. Get everyone off your back for a bit as the focus shifts from frustration over your lack of production to sympathy for everything you've endured these past couple of years."

I looked down at my feet, sliding one toe back and forth across a seam in the dingy carpet. I really hated this part of the business. Treating people's lives, *my* life, like a game. But the truth was, I couldn't argue with anything Cass had said.

As if sensing I needed just one more little push, she added, "Alex, this is what you pay me for. Let me handle everything else so you can just focus on writing your next best seller."

Sighing, I agreed and handed the phone back to Chief Kelly.

After a few more terse exchanges between Cass and the chief, the chief, looking wilted, hung up the phone, went to his door, and leaned out. "McNeil! Ryan! Get in here!"

My eyes went wide and about popped right out of my head and onto Chief Kelly's desk when Officer Sexypants and his partner walked in.

CHAPTER 9
Alex

JUDGING from the look on Gabe's face, he wasn't at all surprised to see me, but he *was* perplexed as to why he and his partner were joining us. Chief Kelly closed the door and situated himself behind his desk, while Gabe stood at a distance with his hands crossed in front of him, eyes focused on the chief. His partner, on the other hand, came toward me with a big grin and an outstretched hand. "It's a pleasure to meet you, ma'am. I'm Trevor Ryan," he said as we shook.

Trevor struck me as the kind of guy who liked to have a good time, didn't take anything too seriously, and was used to getting whatever he wanted by flashing that Hollywood smile.

I inclined my head and withdrew from his grasp, butterflies fanning their wings against my stomach lining as I waited for the chief to proceed with whatever this was.

"Officer McNeil, Officer Ryan," Chief Kelly began, "meet Ms. Reilly. Your new assignment."

My stomach dropped. Both men's heads whipped toward me and then back to the chief. Gabe was the only one to speak. "I'm sorry, sir. I'm not clear on what you mean."

"Ms. Reilly and her publicist have decided that it is the responsibility of this department to offer a private protection detail to Ms. Reilly, as she holds the belief that someone wishes to cause her harm."

Kill. Me. Now.

It was way too hot in this room. Sweat trickled down my back and soaked the wisps of hair at my neck. The heat washing over me from hairline to toes kept coming, wave after wave, and intensified under Gabe's harsh glare.

Chief Kelly looked like a happy little Irishman, but looks were deceiving. He did not like having his hand forced, and he was clearly determined to make this as miserable as possible for me.

Mission accomplished.

Gabe resettled his gaze on the chief. "Sir, all due respect, but I'm still unclear on the situation." If the creases in Gabe's brow got any deeper, he was going to give the Grand Canyon a run for its money. "We don't have the resources to provide private security to *anybody*." He swung his eyes back to me as he emphasized the last word.

I stared back at him, turning my features to granite and clenching my fists at my side to disperse the rage building inside.

As much as I hated confrontation, I hated being bullied even more. And that was exactly what was going on here. None of these people wanted to take this situation seriously, and I was going to end up in a ditch somewhere while they were busy slacking off around the watercooler.

Chief Kelly leaned back in his chair, a squelch coming from the hinge under protest. "I understand your frustration, McNeil. But unfortunately, Ms. Reilly is a very important person with very important friends. It has been made clear to me that it is in this department's best interest to comply."

What an asshole.

Gabe dismissed me in every sense of the word, turning his back to me and speaking to the chief as if I wasn't there. "Sir, we can't afford to be taken off our current case. You know the risks involved. Are we really going to risk innocent lives to play babysitter to some pampered city girl who can't take no for an answer?"

I stepped forward and opened my mouth to challenge his assumptions of the situation but was brought up short when he stuck his hand out to stop me without even turning to look.

"Ms. Reilly—" The chief's stern tone swung my head around. "You may go. Wait in the lobby. I'll have an officer follow you home."

I hesitated, partially as an act of defiance. I would go, but I'd be damned if I'd snap to attention. But the other reason for my hesitation was because I was still trying to find the words to shred Gabe as he had shredded me.

Finally, I folded like the doormat I was and, unlike Aderes, left with my tail between my legs.

* * *

GABE

As soon as Alex pulled the door shut behind her, the chief leaned forward and put his arms on the desk. "Look, men. I'm aware this is fucking bullshit. I'm going to spend the next month trying to rub out the teeth marks her pit bull publicist left in my ass."

"Who the fuck cares what they want, Chief? We've got bigger issues." I punched my finger into his desk to drive my point home. "If you take us off the Serpents case, you might as well sign Jace's death warrant."

Trevor shifted behind me but remained as silent as he had been since schmoozing Alex when we'd first walked in.

The chief rubbed his bald head before responding. "You have your orders, Officer. I want this situation resolved quickly, so I'm putting you two in charge of the detail."

I threw my arms up and looked to the stained ceiling. I was pushing my luck, but I didn't care. I could *not* be taken off my current case. The Satan's Serpents Motorcycle Club had been growing in power and violence at an alarming rate. Confidential informants were dropping like flies. There was no way in hell I was going to let that happen to Jace. Not after he had put his ass on the line by trusting me. Everyone in that kid's miserable life had failed him. I was not going to be another tally mark on the wrong side of that scoresheet.

"According to Garrett, she's either crazy or looking for attention," I said. "So why not put one of the rookies on this? It'll give them a chance to get some experience working an op while keeping Alex Reilly and her indulgent publicist happy."

The chief raised himself to his full height and stared daggers at me. "Officer McNeil, I've allowed you to disrespect my authority this *one* time because I know how devoted you are to the Serpents case. But this discussion is over."

He rounded his desk and stood directly in front of Trevor and me, eyes looking back and forth between us. "This may seem like a candy-ass assignment to you, but you had better understand this: I expect you to resolve Reilly's case promptly and satisfactorily. Like it or not, right or wrong, she has the power to bring a major clusterfuck to our doorstep." Spit flew onto my face. I kept my eyes straight ahead, standing at attention and staring out the windows behind the chief's desk.

"And if that clusterfuck hits our doorstep, it hits me. And if it hits me, you sure as hell better believe it's going to land all over you, too. Have I made myself clear?" He looked at Trevor and waited for confirmation.

Trevor nodded once. "Crystal clear, sir."

The chief swung his gaze to me, silently daring me to argue.

Every bone in my body screamed at me to keep fighting this. But if I wanted to keep my badge, I had no choice. And if I was going to keep Jace safe and bring down the Serpents, I had to keep my badge.

"Clear, sir."

CHAPTER 10

Gabe

As soon as we were back at our desks and well out of earshot of the chief, I gave full vent to my anger.

"What the hell kind of precedent are we setting by allowing civilians to dictate what we will and will not do?" I snatched a file folder from the cluttered surface of my desk, flicked it open, and then promptly slammed it back down. "This is just the beginning, you know." I pointed at Trevor, who sat perched on the edge of his desk, adjacent to mine. "Every time something ruffles this woman's Prada feathers, she's going to be back in here telling us what to do about it and threatening a lawsuit if we don't comply."

Hooking my thumbs on my duty belt, I paced the length of my desk, spun, and paced back before coming to a stop in front of Trevor again. "Considering she's already got the chief's balls in a vise, and the fact he seems to think we're his best option for dealing with her drama, we're going to be drowning in this bullshit on an ongoing basis."

Trevor's eyes crinkled at the corners. He didn't look half as annoyed as he should have, and that pissed me off even more.

"How can you be so fucking chill about this?" I demanded.

The asshole actually cracked a smile. "Think of it this way," he said. "Now you get to spend time cozying up to the hot author lady without having to spill coffee on her first. Considering the sparks that were flying between you two, I think I'll just grab a chair and some popcorn and enjoy the show."

I glared at him for a long moment before deciding I wasn't going to give him the satisfaction of taking the bait. I marched back to my desk, yanked the chair out, and kicked it aside. My fingers grabbed for every loose sheet of paper and file folder they could find and began randomly shuffling and stacking. I could feel Trevor staring at me like a hawk, eyes missing nothing.

We both knew what I was doing. He had hit a nerve, and I was trying to prove that he hadn't.

The last thing I wanted was to have to spend long hours in isolation with the sexy snob from LA. She was far too tempting. And I didn't *want* to be tempted by her. I wanted to keep my distance. Lots and lots of distance. At least until my body remembered that I wasn't some horny teenage kid who only cared about a gorgeous body and a pretty face.

Between turning Liz down when she'd asked Alex to participate in a charity event to support the schools and walking through the police station with her nose in the air—marching straight to the chief's office when she hadn't liked Garrett's response to her case—she had made it clear that this town was beneath her. And anybody who was too good for this town had no place in my personal life. And that included my fantasies and wet dreams.

Fuck. This was a nightmare.

Sensing that Trevor was still watching me, I spun and faced him. "What?"

"Easy, amigo." Trevor raised both hands defensively. "We're on the same team, remember?"

I blew out a breath and closed my eyes, letting my head fall back. When I refocused on Trevor, my blood had cooled from a boil to a simmer. "Sorry. This just couldn't have come at a worse time. The longer the Serpents walk free, the more vulnerable Jace becomes. His ass is already dangling in the wind. With us off the case, even just temporarily, he's a sitting duck."

Trevor's expression turned stony, and he nodded.

"I'm just not convinced this whole protection detail isn't a bunch of drama," I said. "Or worse—some stupid publicity stunt." I pulled my chair back in and took a seat, sliding down and letting my knees fall open. "This woman claims someone's been harassing her for weeks, but she doesn't report it until now? That doesn't seem off to you?"

Trevor raised his eyebrows and looked down at the cheap linoleum tiles. "It seems off to me, yeah. But the truth is, there's a lot we still don't know about this case." He met my gaze. "Everything we know about her situation, we've either heard from Garrett or the chief. Two men who aren't particularly happy with her. Whether they've got it right or we're missing facts doesn't really matter at this point, though. We're stuck with this assignment, so there's only one thing I can see to do."

"And what's that?"

He shrugged. "We work both cases."

I chewed on the idea, thinking through the logistics that would involve. We'd been best friends and partners for so long, our thoughts often ran parallel. This was no exception as Trevor began to lay out a plan.

"Once we get the detail on Alex established, it's primarily a matter of setting up shift rotations and tracking down the person behind the letters and the calls."

"Assuming there *is* a person behind the letters and the calls, and she and her publicist aren't just making it up."

Trevor inclined his head. "Either way, this should be a quick solve. Open and shut."

I nodded, tracking with his line of thought. "So, while one of us is babysitting and following the clues, the other is keeping an eye on Jace."

"Exactly."

"Chief's going to eat our balls for breakfast if he finds out we're still working the Serpents case while this protection detail is going on."

Trevor grinned. "Kinda makes life exciting, doesn't it?" He stood and rounded his desk, winking at me as he sat down.

I couldn't suppress the laugh that broke through the last of my irritation. Trevor was right. We could work both cases. And so long as we were diligent about working the supposed stalking situation, I doubted the chief would throw a fit about us putting in some overtime to stay on top of any developments with the Serpents. He knew as well as we did how big of a threat those worthless pieces of shit were to this town.

I sat up straighter and rolled into my desk. "Okay. I'm in." I pulled a pen and pad of paper from the center drawer of my desk so I could start drawing up a rotation schedule for the protection detail. "We get in. Get set up. Solve the case. And get back to life as usual."

Trevor gave a curt nod. "In and out like a teenage boy."

I laughed again and pulled up the department roster on my computer. The sooner we got to work, the sooner I could put this ridiculous assignment and the compelling author in my rearview mirror. For good.

CHAPTER 11

Alex

MY FINGERS HOVERED above the keyboard, the flashing cursor on my screen taunting me. Something was forming. A hazy image. *Come on, little guy. Come out and show yourself.* I concentrated on the whisper of an idea, feeling it start to slip away the more I tried to call it forth. Closing my eyes, I took a deep breath and let it out slowly, trying to force myself to relax so the image could sharpen. And then . . . *bzzzzzzz.*

The sound of a drill driving a resistant screw into ornery wood scattered the picture like smoke in a heavy wind. I ground my teeth together and shoved my fingers into the long strands of my hair. With the deftness of someone who has completed the same task hundreds of times, I wound my hair into a tight twist and secured it with the bobby pins I kept in the top right drawer of my desk.

Taking another deep breath, I rotated my neck left and right, trying to expel the tension.

"Okay," I said, wiggling my fingers over the keyboard. "Let's try this again."

Bzzzzzzz.

"Oh, for the love of God!"

I slammed my laptop shut and flopped back in my chair. This was pointless. Ever since Gabe—or as I was now calling him, Officer Arrogant Ass—and his partner had arrived early this morning, my house had turned into both a zoo and a war zone.

There were people crawling all over my sacred, private space. Stomping boots, slamming doors, drills, people shouting, and endless interruptions by Officer Ass himself had all conspired to keep me from getting a single word written. That was the zoo.

The first shot in the war had rung out when Gabe had invited himself into my office without so much as a knock to tell me in no uncertain terms how this whole protection detail was going to play out. I had still been fuming from the experience in the chief's office the day before, and I'd had all night to replay the scenario in my head over and over again, thinking of all the things I wished I had said. But before I could say even half of what I wanted to, he had turned around and walked out.

I should have gone after him, but the house was full of officers who had made it clear that they were no happier than Gabe about this assignment and that they had collectively decided I was a liar. Why they would think I was lying about something like being stalked, I wasn't sure, but the sentiment was apparent.

So, I had remained in my office all morning, Gabe and I locked in an endless power struggle every time he came in to interrupt me. Which was often.

I swiveled my chair toward the picture window and stared out at the trees in the distance, craving a run. Before long, I was transported back to the chief's office, my cheeks flaming from the memory. If Cass had still been on the phone when Chief Kelly had called Gabe and Trevor in to join us, maybe I wouldn't have felt so mangled.

The experience of standing alone in that room, so vulnerable I felt naked, while the chief and Gabe impugned my integrity and character had left me feeling helpless and humiliated. And it *definitely* made me further regret going to the police in the first place.

I hadn't wanted this protection detail either, but Gabe made his response to it personal.

I sighed deeply, trying to suppress the restless, squirmy feeling I always got when I was experiencing powerful emotions I didn't want to deal with. At least one positive had come from the whole thing. I now saw Gabe in a completely different light, so the fear of slipping and wanting something I shouldn't had evaporated.

As if I had conjured him from my thoughts, the devil himself came walking in.

Without knocking.

I swiveled around to face him and raised my eyebrows.

Gabe hooked his thumbs over his belt and planted his feet wide. "I need you to put together a list of possible suspects. Include any ex-boyfriends, anyone with a grudge against you, fans who seem a little too obsessed, and anyone who you've refused romantically."

Whom, my internal editor corrected automatically.

"I need it immediately." He didn't even wait for a response before he turned to leave.

"Get in line," I muttered.

Gabe halted and turned back to me, crossing his arms over his chest. "For a woman who *demanded* that police officers be personally assigned to her because she was so afraid that someone was following her, you're not exactly acting like I would expect."

I leveled him with my harshest scowl. "Meaning what?"

"Meaning, I would think that you would be much more cooperative. Happy to provide whatever we need to resolve this situation quickly."

I nearly ground my molars to dust and bit back a response.

Apparently, Gabe took that as a silent invitation to push me further. "Not to mention, I would think a single woman living alone and getting strange phone calls and obscene letters would file a report with the police." His tone was saccharin with a dash of accusation.

I mentally rolled my eyes, irritated that I needed to explain this for what seemed like the fourteenth time. "As I informed Officer Carlson, in my line of work, and especially with how much I have been in the media these past couple of years, it is not at all out of the ordinary to receive unwanted attention in various forms. That includes letters, and occasionally, someone manages to get ahold of my private phone number." I lifted my hands and let them fall back to my lap in a gesture of concession. "I just didn't think it was a big deal."

Gabe eyed me, his jaw flexing.

A blind man could have seen the skepticism written all over his face.

"Just get me that list. I want it within the hour." He turned to leave again.

I was quick to reply so I wouldn't have to chase him through a house of accusers. "I'll get it to you when I can."

My cool tone had him turning toward me slowly. He cocked an eyebrow as though to confirm he'd heard correctly.

I scooted back into my desk and opened my laptop.

Coming closer, he bared his teeth and said very quietly, "Let me be clear. Half of the police department is in *your* home providing you with white glove service because you were supposedly too afraid to be here alone." His tone was ice water running down my spine. "Every minute we're here, that's a minute we're not out protecting our town."

I turned my head to meet his hostile glare. There was nothing but frigid disdain in his dark eyes and the harsh planes of his face.

When I didn't respond, he turned and stalked out of the room.

I released a shaky breath, biting back the tears that burned in my throat. If he was trying to make me feel guilty enough to request the protection detail be rescinded, he was doing splendidly.

With trembling fingers, I moved my mouse around and

opened a new document. I succeeded in typing one name when an instant message chimed.

It was Cass, wanting to know how my pages and the protection detail were coming along. I scrunched my mouth to the side, trying to decide whether I should fudge the truth.

Considering Cass seemed to have the power of clairvoyance, I decided to just shoot straight.

No pages for you yet, I typed back. *Too much noise and everyone here hates me, so things are going about how one would expect.*

Don't let them get away with being assholes. You haven't done anything wrong, Alex.

I should have just left town.

NO. You are exactly where you need to be. Focus on work and forget the rest of the bullshit.

I shook my head as I typed my reply. *Easier said than done.*

That's because you care too much. Please at least tell me there is a uniform or two in that hillbilly town worthy of a steamy fantasy that will thaw your self-imposed celibacy.

I was appalled when my subconscious immediately threw up an image of Gabe and every mouthwatering cut in that fitted uniform on the projection screen of my mind. I shoved it away and gave my primal instincts a slap before responding. *You know that no mere mortal will ever compete with those spun by my imagination.*

Yeah, but your imagination won't leave you sweaty, wet, and begging for more.

I scrunched my nose at the vulgar image. *Gross.*

I had barely hit Send before Cass's next message chimed. *Lol. On the upside, that soundbite we sent out on all of your social media sites this morning is having the desired effect. Thousands of fans have responded saying how much they love you and are supporting you through this stalker thing. I think it will buy some time with the publisher.*

A wave of nausea swept over me. I really despised having to play all the games that permeated the entertainment world. I just prayed that this town was too small and everyone too uninterested in me and my life for anyone to have seen the media snippets Cass had sent out that morning.

I typed a quick response saying I needed to get back to work and returned to the list of possible suspects. At least that was one piece of writing that came easy.

CHAPTER 12

Gabe

Radio traffic crackled in my ear, keeping me informed of all the activity I was missing. Not that there was a lot happening around town at the moment. Mr. Finnigan had gone for a stroll on Main Street and had forgotten his pants again. The toilet paper terrorists had struck several houses during the night. And Mrs. Walker was reporting more strange noises inside her house.

Still, I knew the officers responding to those calls were dealing with people a lot more cooperative than the one I had been tangling with all morning. I stood in Alex's driveway—the sun like a spotlight on this theater production—and monitored the installation of motion-activated lights and new door locks.

This woman seriously had no clue about personal security. My twelve-year-old nephew could have picked the lock on the back door leading into her garage, which also happened to lead into the house through a door she never secured. And while the house had a porch light near the patio doors and the front door, the rest of the house was shrouded in darkness once the sun set. I knew this because I had done a drive-by late last night to assess some of the vulnerabilities of the property.

Satisfied with the progress being made on the lights and locks, I decided now was a good time to canvass the rest of the perimeter. It was a cool thirty-six degrees, but the crisp fall air did little to temper the heat simmering beneath my skin.

Trevor and I had spent most of the morning making all the necessary arrangements to ensure this assignment was as short-lived as possible. Fortifying the house. Collecting and poring over evidence in the form of call logs and the letters Alex had claimed to receive in the mail.

Though the envelopes didn't contain a return address, I verified that the postmarks indicated those letters had been posted in Eden Falls. That combined with the story her publicist had released this morning to a prominent online entertainment publication did little to convince me this whole stalker story hadn't been contrived to keep Alex's name in the press.

She certainly hadn't earned herself any friends at the department when word spread about the article. Trevor and I had spent most of the briefing that morning listening to those assigned to the detail bitch and complain about how this was all a farce and a waste of our very limited resources.

As I walked around the house, I tested each window to ensure it was secure and not easily manipulated from the outside. When I reached the back of the house, I stopped and swung my gaze around the yard, paying particular attention to where it butted up against the woods.

I didn't like the fact that anyone who desired could enter the property just by taking a long stroll through the trees. Not much I could do about that right now unless Alex suddenly decided to get with the program and hire a contractor to erect a privacy fence. Doubtful.

I grabbed the back of my neck, trying to coerce the knots that had formed in the chief's office yesterday to take a hike.

They, along with my numerous encounters with Miss Prissy Pants this morning, had landed me a tension headache the size of Texas.

I swear that woman was secretly enjoying having the Eden Falls Police Department at her beck and call. She sure as hell took pleasure in making *my* life difficult. Every time I issued her an order, she found some way to resist. Whether she argued with me directly or took the passive-aggressive route by dragging her heels, she never made anything easy.

I had decided two could play that game. The more difficult she made my life, I returned the favor tenfold by interrupting her as often as possible and bombarding her with tasks that I followed up on every five minutes. If she wanted a personal police presence, she was going to find out it wasn't nearly as fun as she'd thought it would be.

Continuing my perimeter sweep, I started toward another window. This one required pushing through thick rhododendrons that stood like sentinels in the flower bed lining the rear of the premises.

The ground was still soft from the rain we'd had yesterday afternoon, and I could feel the mud squishing into the tread of my tactical boots. When I looked down to assess how long it was going to take me to clean and polish them tonight, I noticed a set of footprints just under the window.

I squatted down to get a better look. The toes were pointed toward the window as though someone had been standing right in front of it. At first, I considered whether it could have been the officer assigned to stand guard last night. It would have been standard procedure to walk the outside perimeter every so often, checking for unsecured doors and windows. I already knew the answer, though.

The tread on those impressions looked more like a work boot than the tactical boots sworn personnel wore. Judging by the size and depth of the print, I would guess they were made by an average-sized male.

I pushed some of the lower branches on the shrubs away, searching for anything else out of place, but came up empty. As I stood, Trevor came around the corner. He was whistling the theme song to *Bad Boys* and started laughing when he saw me coming out of the bushes, wiping my hands against each other.

"When you gotta go, you gotta go, huh?" The corners of his eyes crinkled in his customary expression.

I ignored the comment and pointed to the footprints. "Take a look."

Trevor sobered and pushed his sunglasses on top of his head, squatting down as I had.

"What do you think?" I asked.

He shook his head. "Unless one of the workers did it, I'd say we have ourselves a situation." Trevor stood and walked backward to stand next to me, keeping his eyes fixed on the footprints.

"I've been monitoring those guys since they got here. They've only been around the front of the house so far," I said.

Trevor pulled his sunglasses back down onto his nose. "I'll get the crime scene guys out here to take photos and measurements. Hopefully they'll be able to give us an idea of this guy's height and weight."

I nodded, my mind going places I didn't like. Whether or not there was more going on here than some publicity stunt, I realized in that moment that I had allowed my emotions to completely overshadow my objectivity and good judgment.

I prided myself on being an officer who focused on facts. Too many cops drew conclusions without enough evidence to back them up. Confident they knew the answer from the get-go, they were blinded to pertinent information. And I had just done the same.

The sound of soft footfalls crunching on dry leaves and grass drew my attention to the corner of the house. I didn't have to wait for our guest to appear to know it was Alex. She was the only one around here who walked like the ground was covered in eggshells.

When she came into view, my breath caught at the sight of her mahogany hair catching fire in the sunlight. Her green eyes sparkled like the dew that still glistened in the shadows of the trees. And the angry flush in her cheeks that deepened every time she laid eyes on me conjured visions of a different kind of flush spreading over her naked body as she lay beneath me.

I stepped farther away from the side of the house as she approached, Trevor following suit. If I had indeed pegged this situation wrong, I didn't want Alex to see the footprints and have more to worry about until I had a better idea of what we were dealing with.

Casting a glance at Trevor, Alex settled her fiery gaze on me and thrust a piece of paper toward me.

"What's this?" I asked, taking it from her.

She pursed her lips. "The list you requested. Delivered within the hour." She folded her arms and cocked a hip to the side.

I fought the smile trying to hijack my face. Despite my best efforts, I couldn't help but notice how damn cute she looked when she was angry with me. Not to mention, I kinda liked being able to bring out the sass in her. I got the impression she didn't show that side enough.

I scanned the list, slightly amused and slightly appreciative of the fact she had ordered it by category and likelihood of guilt.

Trevor touched the brim of an invisible hat and bowed his head to Alex. "Ms. Reilly. How are you getting along today?"

Alex's weary eyes studied Trevor's face for a moment. Probably trying to decide if he was being sincere or sarcastic.

"I'm fine, thank you." Her demure response triggered a pang of guilt in my gut. It was obvious she was well aware of the fact that no one trusted her or wanted to be here. And I knew my attitude toward her and this assignment had fueled that fire.

Now that my instincts were starting to nag me about those footprints, I was beginning to feel like a complete jackass for possibly making her situation more difficult than it already was.

But I wasn't yet conceding that there *was* something sinister going on. I would, however, check my emotions and get back to focusing on facts, and I would lead the officers under us to do the same.

Alex started to walk away. I called her back, pointing to the paper when she halted in front of me. "The last boyfriend you have listed here was from eight years ago."

Her expression remained stoic. "Yes."

I scrutinized her face, waiting for her to elaborate. She didn't.

"So . . . you're saying you haven't dated anyone recently? Even casually?"

"That's right."

I continued to study her. She continued to stand like a marble statue. And Trevor continued to swing his gaze back and forth between us.

How was it possible this beautiful, sexy, smart, successful woman had not been in a romantic relationship for eight years?

I dropped my eyes back to the list and zeroed in on the name with a star beside it. Again, I pointed to the list. "This Maxwell Hargrove." I looked at Alex. "Who is he?"

Alex cleared her throat and focused on her shoes. Despite her tall frame, her oversized green sweater and black leggings made her look small and fragile. "He was arrested nearly two years ago for stalking me."

My eyebrows shot up. "And you didn't think to mention this before now?"

She looked up at me and scowled, every bit of demureness erased from that porcelain skin. "He's in prison, so, no, I didn't think it warranted a panicked reaction."

"Do you know for sure he's still in prison?" Trevor asked.

She shrugged. "He was sentenced to five years, and the police said I would be informed when he was released, so I assume so."

Trevor and I exchanged a knowing glance. Prisoners rarely served their full sentences, and victim notifications could be unreliable. At least now we had a solid lead.

I nodded and held up the paper. "Thank you for getting this to me so quickly."

Alex's eyes widened, her lips parting slightly. Instead of replying, she wrapped her arms around herself, nodded, and walked back toward the front of the house.

I faced Trevor. "You thinking what I'm thinking?"

A huge smile stretched across his face, his white teeth sparkling like he was in a gum commercial. "Oh yeah."

I laughed and pulled my phone out of my breast pocket. "Mind your Ps and Qs. We can't afford for you to piss her off."

Trevor put a hand to his chest and feigned shock.

When Dispatch answered my call, I asked for Quinn. She came on the line with her characteristic professionalism.

"Dispatch, this is Quinn."

"Hey, Quinn. Gabe here."

"Hi, Gabe. What can I do for you?"

The radio traffic coming through my earpiece echoed in the background of the call.

"I need to enlist your supersleuth skills. Can you handle it, or are you slammed?"

Her laugh was as rich as a mug of honey. "In Eden Falls? No, please, give me something more to do." The smile in her voice was contagious.

"You really are the best. As I'm sure you've heard, Trevor and I have been assigned to head up a case that involves an alleged stalking victim."

"Oh, yes. Garrett has informed the entire department."

I rolled my eyes. I was going to have to tell Nash to put a muzzle on his pup.

"I don't doubt it," I said. "I've got a list of names I need you to start researching. If you're able to eliminate any as suspects, Trevor and I will follow up on the ones that are more involved."

"Sure thing. I'm happy to help any way I can."

Before I could thank her profusely for her genuine awesomeness, Trevor opened his big fat mouth.

He leaned in so close, bringing his mouth near the phone, that it would have looked very questionable to anyone who happened upon us. "Quinn! Lady of my heart! How 'bout I pick you up tonight and we can do a little research together?"

I shoved Trevor away from the phone and mouthed, "Shut the fuck up!"

His grin grew even bigger, and he waggled his eyebrows. Even with my phone pulled away from my ear, we could both hear Quinn's response. "Keep that troglodyte away from me and I'll bury myself in research for as long as it takes to free you from this case."

Trevor clutched his chest, acting like he had just taken an arrow to the heart.

I laughed. "You've got a deal, Quinn. I'll drop the list off shortly."

After we hung up, Trevor and I finished canvassing the outside of the house and found several more sets of footprints matching the first.

Anxious to get the list of suspects to Quinn, I opened the door to my patrol car and propped my arm on top of it, taking one more look at the house.

We still had a lot of unanswered questions, but my gut was starting to tell me Alex might not have been fibbing about someone being inside her house. And if that was the case, whoever was behind this was just getting started.

CHAPTER 13

Gabe

THE SUN GLINTED off the hood of my dark-blue Silverado as I drove through town with the windows down. We had been locked in an uncharacteristic heat spell the past few days, and the townsfolk were out en masse enjoying the gift, knowing the harsh Montana winter would soon set in.

Keeping a steady cruise, I followed a lazy succession of cars, my eyes constantly scanning out of habit. A group of kids skipped down the sidewalk on my right, ice cream melting down their arms from the cones they held. Several old folk were sitting on the benches that lined Main Street, no doubt chatting about days gone by and the status of each child and grandchild.

The trees were still boasting their colors of crimson, orange, and gold, and the sky was cornflower blue. It was the kind of day that made you smile and wonder if God was giving you a glimpse of Heaven.

With one arm out the window and turning a slight shade of pink, my thumb drummed against the steering wheel, matching the fast beat of the hard rock song pouring through my speakers. Though it was *technically* my day off, I was on my way to Rise & Grind to check in on Jace while I took care of a few other errands. It had been several days since Trevor or I had been able to touch base with the kid, given all the hours we'd had to devote to establishing Alex's protection detail.

Fortunately, the legwork on the front end had paid off. The shift rotations for guard duty were going off without a hitch, and Quinn had made some good progress on the list of suspects I'd given her to start tracking down. She'd easily cut the list by half in just the past few days. Not that I was surprised. That woman could track down a white rabbit in a blizzard.

I was, however, starting to reconsider if maybe I had let Alex and her publicist off the hook too soon. Five days had gone by since the leggy author had come into the police station ranting about a picture on a tree and demanding a private security detail, and in those five days, absolutely *nothing* out of the ordinary had occurred. Still, I supposed it was possible that our presence could have scared the guy off. Made him reconsider if the effort was worth getting tased and going to jail.

If this radio silence kept up much longer, the chief was going to have a hard time justifying the continued draw on our scant resources. Maybe then Trevor and I could finally get back to focusing the bulk of our time and energy on Satan's Serpents.

As I neared the coffee shop, the glint of sun on chrome caught my eye. "Speak of the devil," I murmured as I squinted at the row of bikes parked a block up the street. "What the hell are they doing here?"

Having the advantage of being in my private vehicle, I eased farther up the road. When I had a clear view of the motorcycles parked in the empty lot of the flower shop, I pulled to the side of the road so I could observe their riders.

The patch on the back of those black leather vests was unmistakable. A red devil with a pitchfork was situated right in the middle, two blue serpents with green bellies slithering up either side until his head was wedged between theirs. A third serpent was wound around the pitchfork and had its mouth open in an evil hiss, the words *Satan's Serpents* written across the top of the image in white block letters, while Montana was written below.

The Serpents rarely came into this part of town, preferring to stick to the outskirts, where the good citizens of Eden Falls wouldn't try to run them out with pitchforks and rolling pins. With their clubhouse situated on the opposite side of town, they had no reason to be hanging around these streets. But what bothered me most was that these weren't just any Serpents.

There were five bikes lined up and facing the street. I narrowed my gaze on the rider in the middle. Tall with a solid build and salt-and-pepper hair kept short to match his perfectly trimmed goatee. Though he wore a pair of wraparound sunglasses, I could practically see those icy blue eyes glowing through the tinted lenses.

Drake Dawson. President of Satan's Serpents. The man was as intelligent as he was violent. Always managing to keep his dirty deeds from ever touching him in a way that could be traced back and proven in a court of law.

I plucked my phone out of the cupholder and tapped Trevor's name on the screen.

If he didn't have it on silent, his "Danger Zone" ringtone would inform him I was calling.

He answered before the second ring. "What's up, brother?"

"Hey, I've got a snake pit on Main."

"Please tell me you mean an actual snake pit."

"Dawson and his right-hand men are camped out at the flower shop. They can see Grind from where they're parked."

Trevor's breath came out in a hiss as the air passed through his clenched teeth. "Fuck. You don't think they made him, do you?"

I heard Trevor's engine turn over. He was on duty today and had probably been parked somewhere monitoring traffic.

"I don't know," I said. "I doubt they'd be watching him if they already had their answers, but it might mean they suspect something's up."

Grind was to my left. I could see Jace through one of the large windows that stood on either side of the front door. He was behind the counter making drinks, likely completely oblivious to the fact that his president was a hundred yards away.

Fuck. Why did I have to get pulled from this case right now?

Had we missed something because we'd been so distracted with Alex's situation? I'd promised Jace I would have his back. That I would do everything in my power to keep him safe and help him find a better future.

Trevor read my silence like only he could. "We're not going to let anything happen to him, man."

I released the air from my lungs, returning my gaze to the Serpents, noting every movement. "It pisses me off that this town doesn't even know what he's doing for them. All he's ever gotten from anyone around here is accusations and a reminder that he's trash from the wrong side of the tracks. If they only knew he was putting his life on the line to bring these guys down, maybe he could at least walk down the street without people glaring at him."

Trevor's radio squawked in the background. He turned it down before replying. "I know, bro. When this is all said and done, they *will* know. He's got a long way to go to overcome the sins of his past, but the important thing is he's getting that chance and he's taking it."

Done watching and waiting, I decided it was time to have a little get-together with Drake Dawson and his band of Merry Men. I killed my engine and exited the truck. "I'm gonna go rattle the cage. See if I can get them to tip their hand."

"All right. I'm three minutes out."

"Copy."

By the time we disconnected, Drake had spotted me walking toward them. Even without being able to see his eyes, the smirk on his face said plenty. Like his men, he sat astride his bike, booted feet on the ground, arms crossed. Beside him, the club's VP adjusted his vest, his hand caressing the left lapel to ensure the firearm in his shoulder holster was hidden from view.

Every nerve in my body was on high alert. I saw every twitch, every shift of weight. Though my black T-shirt was fitted around my chest and arms, it was loose enough in the waist to hide the Glock at my hip. These guys weren't dumb enough to do anything in broad daylight with dozens of witnesses when they knew I didn't have anything on them. At least, not enough to put them away for good. Yet.

Still, a cop who let his guard down was a cop whose days were marked. A smile tugged at one side of my mouth. My casual stride belied the tension in my muscles. I was ready for a fight if they decided to throw down.

"McNeil." Drake dipped his chin to acknowledge me.

I nodded back. "Drake." I gave his crew the once-over. People continued to pass by, casting fearful looks at the biker gang.

The air sizzled between us. A centuries-old battle line drawn in the sand between good and evil.

"What are you doing here, Drake?"

Drake spread his arms wide and looked to the sky before settling back on me. "Enjoying this beautiful day. What else?"

A couple of his men chuckled.

"And you decided to spend it sitting in front of a flower shop?" I flashed a doubtful smile. "Considering a move from drug running to horticulture?"

A muscle in Drake's jaw twitched. We stared at each other for a long moment before he said, "We both know you haven't got jack shit on the Serpents." A sneer slowly spread across his face. "So why don't you scamper on back to your playpen, Boy Scout."

I stepped closer, causing two of his men to jump to their feet. Keeping my eyes locked on Drake, I lowered my voice. "You're not half as smart as you like to think, Dawson. Get your fill of fresh air now, because your days of freedom are numbered."

Tires crunched to a stop directly behind me, signaling that Trevor had arrived. He was getting out of his black-and-white, but before he reached us, Drake leaned forward on his handlebars and spoke just above a whisper. "It's a small town, McNeil. Everyone knows everyone . . . and their relations."

Drake straightened again when Trevor came to a stop beside me. It took every ounce of willpower to keep from giving Drake the reaction he had hoped for, but my body was vibrating with crimson rage. If he so much as breathed on my family, I'd be the one doing hard time for the things I would do to him.

"Flower shop is closed, gentlemen." Trevor's tone was pleasant, drawing a sharp contrast to the tension hanging in the air. "And this is private property, so I'm going to have to ask you to leave."

Drake turned his gaze to Trevor and gave an artificial smile. "Sure thing, Officer. We've accomplished what we came here for." Nodding to his companions, Drake fired up his Harley. The others followed suit, their engines roaring to life, shattering the serenity of the quiet street.

Before they drove off, Drake looked at me and smiled. "Give my best to the family."

Once the sound of their engines had become a distant hum, Trevor turned to me and put his hands on his waist. "What the fuck was that about?"

I shook my head. "Nothing I didn't expect."

CHAPTER 14

Gabe

TREVOR and I walked back to his patrol car and propped ourselves on the hood. "Have you had any luck tracking down information about who that CI on our slab was working for?" I asked.

Trevor shook his head and kicked his foot back to plant it on the car's bumper. "No, but I've got feelers out to my contacts in the surrounding departments, and I reached out to the feds in the nearest field offices."

I ran my hand across my head. I'd left home without a hat that morning, and the sun was burning my scalp through my buzz cut. "I hope to hell that whoever used that CI to infiltrate the Serpents has got more on them than we do."

Trevor snorted. "No shit."

I pushed off the car and clasped Trevor on the shoulder. "I'm going to head over to Grind and touch base with Jace."

"Copy that. I'll hang in the area to make sure those assholes don't double back while you're in there."

As I turned to cross the street, two women in bright spandex approached, yoga mats rolled up under their arms. They were all smiles and fluttering eyelashes as Trevor joined them on the side-walk. "Well, hello, ladies." He shoved his sunglasses on his head and flashed his signature grin. "How are you two lovelies this morning?"

The women giggled, and I recognized them as regulars at Rustlers. Trevor had gone home with each of them, and sometimes both of them, on more than one occasion.

Leaving Casanova to his guilty pleasures, I jogged across the street and ducked inside Grind.

Bree was working the register and offered a big smile when I approached. "Hi, Gabe. Day off?" Bree's hair was swept up in her usual messy bun, with dark-blond tendrils falling down around her face. From her flushed cheeks and messy hair, I surmised it had been a busy morning.

"Hey, Bree. Yeah, it's going to be the only one for a while. Figured I'd take care of some errands while I can."

I flicked my eyes to Jace, who was off to my left, busy making drinks. "How's he doing?" I asked in hushed tones.

Bree glanced at Jace, a wry grin forming. "Good. He's still fighting the apron policy, but he's punctual, and he works hard."

I laughed. I had tried to get Jace a job at the auto shop. He loved having his hands in grease, and he was good with machines, but I couldn't convince anyone other than Bree to give him a chance. When I'd told him about the position at Grind, he'd screwed up his face and said he wasn't working anywhere that forced him to wear a dress.

After I ordered a drink and tried once again to pay but was refused, I strolled over to the pickup counter and caught Jace's eye.

"How are things?" I asked.

Jace looked out at the patrons, taking note of who was around. "Weather's turning. It's getting hot." His gaze bored into mine. "Not sure why."

I turned that information over in my head. He was telling me something was up with the Serpents and things were getting more dangerous, but he wasn't sure what or why. That coupled with the fact that Drake Dawson and Satan's Serpents' leadership had slithered out of their usual terrain to park themselves in the heart of Eden Falls had my warning bells going off like fireworks on the Fourth of July.

"Sounds like you might want to get out of town for a bit," I said. "Go someplace cooler."

He nodded thoughtfully and shrugged. "We'll see."

The sounds from the street grew louder when the door to the coffee shop swung open. Jace glanced up and lifted his chin to say hi to the person walking in. He wasn't warm with very many people, so I turned my head to see who had just entered.

Emmy, a cute girl of about seventeen, walked toward us with an energetic gait. Her soft brown hair with natural blond high-lights glowed like a halo above her round face and rosy cheeks.

"Hi, Officer McNeil." Her self-conscious wave and beaming smile were so characteristic of Emmy that she was the unofficial sweetheart of Eden Falls.

I ruffled Emmy's hair when she came to a stop beside me. "Hi, Emmy. What are you up to?"

She giggled in response to my teasing. "I'm putting up flyers. My band got our first real gig."

My eyebrows lifted. "Wow, that's great! Where are you guys playing?"

Emmy combed her hair back and handed me a flyer. "Rustlers. Friday night. Scott said as long as we enter through the back and stay away from the main floor and the bar, we can play there, but we have to leave as soon as we're done."

I nodded, reading the details from the paper in my hand. Emmy's toes turned toward each other, and her fingers gripped the remaining flyers until they developed deep crinkles. I looked up, wondering why her body language had changed so abruptly.

When I saw her looking at Jace, her bottom lip between her teeth, it all made sense.

She pushed her hair back again and cleared her throat. "Do you think you'll come, Jace?"

Jace was busy steaming milk and offered only a glance in

Emmy's direction before shrugging and saying, "Dunno. I'll have to wait and see what's up that night."

Emmy's hopeful smile slipped from her face. And with a cruel sense of timing, fate stepped in to land a crushing blow.

A young woman with bleach-blond hair and breasts falling out of her push-up bra and slinky camisole strolled up and shouldered Emmy out of the way. I reached out to steady Emmy as she sidestepped toward me and tried to regain her balance.

The young succubus leaned forward on the counter to give Jace more than an eyeful. After only two minutes of shallow conversation, the blonde walked away with triumph in her step, and Jace was grinning like an idiot about his hot date for Friday night.

So much for Emmy's concert.

Sensing the hole burning into the side of his head, Jace turned to look at Emmy. "What?"

The idiot somehow seemed genuinely confused.

Emmy's normally angelic face looked like ten degrees of Hades with her lips mashed together and her eyebrows drawn into one line. "Nothing, Jace Maloy. Absolutely nothing."

Emmy spun on her heel to face me, her lower lip fighting a tremble. "Goodbye, Officer McNeil. It was really lovely to see you."

Damn, this girl was breaking my heart. "Bye, Emmy. I'll try to make it Friday night if work doesn't interfere."

After giving me a brave nod, she turned and left in a hurry, pushing through the door to Grind so hard she nearly bowled a man off his feet.

I leveled Jace with the best fatherly expression I could manage for someone who didn't have kids.

He gave me the same response he'd given Emmy. "What? Why does everyone keep looking at me like that?"

"I wouldn't look at you like this if you bothered to pull your head out of your ass."

Seeing that Jace had no idea what I was talking about, I

decided to spell it out for him. "Jace, Emmy, a very sweet girl who has been your friend for a long time despite all the shit she's taken for it, and who has a crush on you, just asked you to come support her at her first gig on Friday night. And instead of saying yes, you gave her a half-hearted maybe and two seconds later said yes to an easy fuck instead, and you did it right in front of her."

Jace placed my coffee on the to-go counter and planted both hands on the surface behind it. He looked at the door where Emmy had disappeared and then grinned and shook his head. "Nah, it's not like that with us. We're just friends."

My eyebrows shot up. "Let me give you a piece of unsolicited advice." To his credit, all humor left his face, and he gave me his full attention. "Girls like that blonde you just jumped at the chance to be with are a dime a dozen, and they've got all the depth of a soap dish. They're easy to get, which means they're easy for *anyone* to get, and they'll leave you looking like an asshole the second something better comes along." I picked up my coffee and snatched my shades off my head. "Girls like Emmy, on the other hand, are the ones you wait for. And unfortunately, they're often the ones we didn't know we wanted and needed until we've fucked things up so badly, we don't have a snowball's chance in hell of getting them back."

Jace twisted the bar rag sitting on the counter.

"And here's one more piece of advice," I said. "A snake can get close enough to bite before you even know he's there." I held Jace's gaze to drive my point home. When he looked out at the street through the huge front window, I knew he'd gotten my warning about the Serpents hanging around.

When I climbed back into my truck, I dropped my coffee in the cupholder to hurry and answer my phone. It was Trevor.

"What's up? Did the Serpents come back?" I asked.

"No. The coast is clear."

Trevor's tone left me with a sense that I still wasn't going to like what he had to say.

"Garrett just called me to advise that he's sick and can't make his shift tonight."

I placed my middle finger and thumb over my temples and squeezed. A headache was coming on fast. "Okay. Who else is available, then?"

"Everyone who's assigned to the detail, other than you and Garrett, is working either today or tomorrow. So, unless you want someone who's dead on their feet standing watch or working patrol tomorrow, we don't have anyone else."

I chewed the inside of my cheek, thinking through our options.

Trevor told me to hold while he responded to radio traffic, then came back on the line. "I know you've got that family dinner tonight and you promised Lily you'd be there to celebrate, so why don't we just pull someone who's not assigned to the detail. Just temporarily."

I thought about it for a second, extremely tempted. But I already knew my answer. I expelled an irritated sigh. "No. I'll take the shift."

"You sure?" Trevor sounded like he was worried I was about to blow a spark plug. This fucking detail was turning out to be an even bigger pain in the ass than I'd first thought.

"Yes. I'm not going to further deplete department resources for this thing."

"What about your dinner?"

I turned my engine over and threw my truck in gear. After making sure no one was coming, I punched the gas. "I'll figure it out."

Trevor whistled through his teeth. "Okay, amigo. But Lily's going to have your balls for badminton if you miss that dinner."

I'd hand them over before I ever broke a promise to my niece. I knew what I had to do, and one thing was for sure—this headache was going to get a whole lot worse before the day was over.

CHAPTER 15

Gabe

WHEN I PULLED up to Alex's place that night, it was in my own vehicle rather than a black-and-white. The sun was setting behind the mountains, the dark peaks cast in shadow and rising beneath a sky of indigo blue with only a few remaining streaks of pink and orange. I pulled my jacket from the truck before slamming the door and marching toward the house with all the enthusiasm of a man walking to the guillotine.

When I reached the front door, I knocked brusquely and walked in without waiting for an answer. The officer on duty stood from the couch and stretched. Clearly, he'd been sitting there a while.

"This whole protecting life and limb business a little too boring for you, Emmett?"

"Ah, come on, Gabe. Don't bust my balls." Emmett plucked his department-issued down jacket from the back of the couch and yanked it on. "You know this is all a bunch of bullshit anyway."

My molars slid against each other, tension creeping into my jaw. I was pissed that my officers were slacking off, but I also knew I had contributed to this rampant attitude among them. It was time to tighten things up.

"Emmett, we have no idea *what* the situation is yet. So, until we learn otherwise, you will remain vigilant and conduct yourself with the utmost professionalism. Understood?"

Emmett looked like he was trying to decide if I was serious or attempting to pull a fast one. He clearly decided wrong because he broke into a grin and chuckled.

With two steps, I was on him like maggots on shit, my chest bumping his as I looked down the bridge of my nose at him. "I obviously wasn't clear. If I ever catch you napping on the job again, you're going to be wishing for a meter maid position by the time the week is out."

All humor was gone from his face. He stood at attention and said, "Yes, sir," waiting for me to dismiss him.

I made him squirm under my gaze for a few more heartbeats. "You're dismissed," I finally said.

Emmett ducked around me, heading for the door like the place was on fire.

"Emmett," I barked.

Turning slowly, he waited for another ass chewing.

"Pass that message along to the rest of the detail."

"Yes, sir."

The door had barely closed behind him when I heard soft footsteps padding down the hallway. Alex was barefoot and wearing a pair of skinny jeans with a flowing maroon top. Her dark hair fell around her shoulders, looking as though she'd been anxiously running her fingers through it. The effect gave the appearance that she'd just taken a tumble in bed, and damn if that thought didn't make my dick jump to life.

I tried to say something, but my mouth went dry, and a bobbing Adam's apple was the best I could manage.

What the hell was wrong with me? There was a constant stream of half-naked women throwing themselves at me on a regular basis at Rustlers, and none of them could so much as hold my attention for more than a few seconds. But fucking Alex Reilly comes walking toward me with disinterest at best and disdain at worst, practically dressed in a nun's habit, and I'm rendered dumb, horny, and completely useless.

She stopped several feet in front of me, the soft yellow glow from the dim lamps scattered around the foyer and the living room behind me giving her skin an incandescence that made it impossible to look away.

She wrapped her arms around her waist and spoke as though she expected me to bite her head off. "I thought Officer Carlson was on duty tonight."

Praying that my voice would come out as more than a squeak, I swallowed hard. "He was. He's sick, so I'm covering."

Her eyes traveled down my body and my groin tightened again.

"You're not in uniform," she said, her forehead furrowed.

Feeling self-conscious under her gaze, then irritated that I was feeling self-conscious, I shoved my hands into my pockets, then promptly withdrew them so I could cross my arms and regain the upper hand. "No, I'm not. I have somewhere to be tonight, and since I can't leave you here alone and there's no one else to stand by, you're coming with me."

Alex's expression morphed from apprehensive to alarmed in the flap of a hummingbird's wings. Once again, I was rendered speechless. I had expected some resistance. Maybe even a flat-out refusal. But scared? That had never been a consideration.

She started shaking her head and taking steps backward. "N-no. I'm not going anywhere with you."

Still unclear as to what the fuck was happening, I defaulted to what I knew and had used with great success on countless criminals. Command presence and intimidation. I stalked toward her slowly, sensing she might just turn and run into her bedroom at the end of the hall and lock herself in if I spooked her. The chief would never sign off on damages if I kicked her door down because she refused to join my family for dinner.

"Let me be very clear," I said, my tone indicating this was not up for discussion. "I promised my niece and the rest of my family

I would be at dinner tonight. And because you simply *had* to have a babysitter, my only options are to leave you here or take you with me."

"Then leave me here," she said, continuing to take small steps toward her room.

"I can't," I said from between clenched teeth.

"Then call someone else."

My voice boomed, and I threw my arms out at my sides. "Do you really think I would be here trying to coax you into dinner with my family if there was someone else I could call? This is no picnic for me either, lady, but I'll be damned if you're going to be the reason I break a promise to my niece."

Alex stopped moving backward, but she was far from agreeing. Everything from the way her shoulders caved inward to the look of panic in her eyes told me she was trying to figure out an escape.

Losing all patience, which was something that had happened to me maybe five times in my life, I growled and turned my back to her. Planting my hands on my hips and counting carpet fibers, I focused on taking a slow, deep breath. When I felt confident I wasn't going to either spank her or throw her against the wall and kiss the stubborn out of her, I turned back around and tried very hard not to focus on the pouty lips parting in surprise.

"Ms. Reilly . . ." My voice was low, my tone calm.

"Yes?" she whispered.

I took two more cautious steps. "If you don't put your shoes on and park your ass in my truck, I'm going to throw you over my shoulder and take you to dinner barefoot."

If she'd looked alarmed before, a five-alarm fire was now ringing in her head. She backed toward the bedroom again, an arm stretched behind her, feeling for the door.

"You wouldn't do that!"

Without a word, I swallowed the distance between us before she knew what was happening. When I reached her, she let out a yelp as I bent and pulled her over my shoulder, wrapping an arm around the back of her legs to hold her steady.

She squirmed and kicked her legs. All fear gone, the fury of fight taking over.

"Put me down!" she yelled, beating the small of my back.

"Nope. I gave you a choice, and you chose wrong."

I spun around, careful not to slam her head into the narrow walls, and marched for the door. She was going to freeze her ass off on the way to the truck, but the engine would still be warm enough to get the heater blasting as soon as she was inside.

Her dog, hearing her mistress hollering, came running from somewhere on the opposite side of the house. Hackles raised and teeth gleaming, her growl left no need for interpretation.

"She'll bite you!" Alex squeaked from somewhere near my ass.

"Yeah, well, she won't be the first female to try it."

"Somehow I am not at *all* surprised."

When I opened the front door, an arctic blast rushed inside and practically turned my bones to ice. We didn't have snow on the ground yet, but damn, the temperatures could sure plummet at night this time of year.

The frigid air must have cooled Alex's temper and convinced her I wasn't messing around, because where she'd sounded like a she-devil a moment before, she now had all the charm of a Southern lady.

"Officer McNeil, if you would kindly set me down, I'll go put myself together and be ready to leave shortly."

Considering I had just given Emmett an ass chewing on professionalism, and the fact I *never* lost my cool on the job, I decided to take a chance on believing this wasn't some kind of trick.

When I set her down, she flipped those long locks back over her head like she was in some kind of sexy shampoo commercial. When she started to stumble, I slid my hand around her waist, realizing she was probably dizzy from all of the blood rushing from her head.

Those gorgeous green eyes looked up at me, her rapid breaths washing over me like angel kisses. Mesmerized didn't begin to describe the spell I was under.

My gaze fell to that luscious mouth again. I could *not* stop thinking about that mouth. The tips of my fingers pressed into her low back, that fucking shirt the only thing keeping my skin from melting with hers.

Someone up above either loved me or hated me, because as our bodies moved closer one centimeter at a time, just as my mind fully shut down and my dick took over, that damn dog of hers let out a bark shrill enough to give me permanent hearing damage.

From the looks of it, Alex had been in her own trance. She jumped at the dog's intrusion, her eyes rounding like she'd just realized what was about to happen. Her hand came up between us and pushed against my chest as she backed away. Without a word, she tucked a lock of hair behind her ear, dipped her chin, and retreated down the hall.

CHAPTER 16

Gabe

THE DRIVE to Liz's house couldn't have been more awkward. Alex remained silent and sat perfectly still, looking out the window the entire time. And without anything else to focus on, my brain kept coming up with increasingly vivid fantasies of what I'd rather be doing with her right now. I seriously needed to get a grip before I ended up doing something that earned me the chump award—again. The challenging part was that I was in uncharted territory, having never in my life been *this* fixated on a woman.

Relief washed over me when we finally turned onto the ranch, taking the second driveway, which led to Liz's house, as well as my own, farther up the hill. A thick layer of frost covered the grassy fields. Beneath the moonlight, it gave the earth a soft blue luminescence that was both ethereal and eerie. There were so few houses out this way that, aside from the occasional porch light, the moon and stars were the only thing keeping the night from swallowing all signs of life.

"We're here," I said to Alex as I parked alongside the wraparound porch. I unfastened my seat belt and hopped out to open Alex's door for her. When she stepped onto the running board, she paused, her gaze taking in the spacious farmhouse. Like me, Liz had designed their home herself. She had a real eye for colors and architecture. The house was one story, painted white with dark wood beams and black fixtures. She had lined the front porch with black lamps every four feet, so at night, the entire space was enshrouded in a soft glow, as though it were defying the dark.

Alex, remembering I was waiting on her, stepped down from the truck and followed me to the house. The crickets and bullfrogs serenaded the night, masking the sound of the crisp grass crunching beneath our feet. The sound of country living had ruined me for ever living in the city.

As soon as I opened the door to the house, the scent of baked chicken and bread, and the sound of laughter and children's giggles, beckoned me inside. I stood back, allowing Alex to enter first. The house was warm, but she kept her arms wrapped tightly around her.

I cleared my throat and stepped closer. "Here, let me take your jacket."

Silently, she pulled the garment from her shoulders and allowed me to slide it down her arms. As I was hanging it on the coatrack by the door, the sound of little feet running down the wooden planks of the hallway had me grinning like a fool.

"Uncle Gabe!"

Lily bounded toward me, her blond curls bouncing like springs and blue eyes blazing. When she launched herself at me, I bent to catch her, swinging her high and earning lots of giggles. Then I brought her down to my hip and angled her toward Alex.

"Alex, this is my niece, Lily. Lily, this is Miss Alex."

Lily extended her hand the way I had taught her. "Hi, Miss Alex."

Alex smiled with such joy and sincerity that, for the first time, I realized I had never seen her with her guard down until this moment. Lily had that effect on people.

Grasping Lily's hand and giving it a shake, Alex said, "Hi, Lily. It is so nice to meet you."

"You too. You're really pretty." Then, looking at me, "Hah, Uncle Gabe?"

Heat crawled up my neck. I glanced at Alex and then back at Lily. "Yes, she's pretty. Where's your momma?"

Lily wriggled free and slid down my leg. "She's in the kitchen. Come on!"

Unable to avoid Alex's gaze any longer, I offered a small smile and ushered her farther into the house. "I'll introduce you to everyone. But I should warn you, they're an excitable bunch, and they have no concept of boundaries."

Alex followed me toward the dining room, wringing her hands and biting her lip. Her shyness was yet another surprise. I would have thought with all of the parties and events she undoubtedly attended in her line of work that she would walk into any room and own it.

We passed through the living room, sparsely decorated with a large flat-screen TV, brown leather couch, and matching recliner. The pictures on the walls and end table were the highlight of the room. When we passed through the large opening leading to the dining room, all chatter ceased.

Alex was hiding behind me, so I reached around and, placing a hand on her low back, pulled her forward.

"Everyone, this is Alex. Alex, this is my family." Pointing to the old cowboy on my left and moving in a clockwise manner, I said, "This is my father, Tuck. That beautiful woman next to him is my mother, Alice. Then we have Connor, my nephew. Mark, Liz's husband. And I believe you've already met my sister, Liz."

Alex was quiet, her gaze traveling between Liz and me. Probably wondering how I knew she and Liz had already been acquainted. The blush on her cheeks told me she was slowly putting it together.

Liz, in true form, marched over to Alex and wrapped her arms around her. "We are *so* happy to have you join us. Just make yourself at home, sweetie. Can I get you something to drink?"

Alex, looking a little petrified, shook her head. "No, I'm fine, thank you. It's so kind of you to allow me to join all of you."

I locked eyes with my mother, silently begging her to make the situation less awkward. The same violet eyes she had given to Liz held a trace of humor and understanding. "Alex," she said, tapping the table beside her, "why don't you have a seat next to me? I'd love a chance to chat and get to know you better." Then, turning to my nephew, "Connor, go get Miss Alex a glass of water, please."

Connor dashed out of the room as Alex sidled over to the empty chair beside mom. The knot in my chest eased. Now that I was surrounded by my family, I knew the rest of the evening would be easier.

Catching Liz's wink and not-so-subtle nod toward the kitchen, I followed her. Once we were in the kitchen, Liz started dashing around, putting the finishing touches on dinner. Lifting the lid on the gravy, she dipped a spoon in to taste it. "It's sure been a long time since you brought a woman home for dinner."

I leaned against the kitchen sink and folded my arms. "I didn't bring a woman home for dinner. It's work. That's all."

Her eyebrows lifted. "Mm-hmm. It'd be okay to bring someone home, you know."

When I didn't answer, she pressed further.

"I like her. She's beautiful, and she has a nice energy about her."

I snorted. "What, you're reading people's auras now?"

"No," she said, dragging the word out. "But you don't have to be psychic to get a vibe off people." She lifted a shoulder. "I'm just saying, she's got a good vibe."

"That's funny, because it seems to me, not too long ago, you were ranting about how unneighborly and standoffish she was."

Liz planted her hands on her hips and pinned me with a glare that only a sister could manage. "Okay, fair enough. But I judged her prematurely, and I think you have too."

"I haven't done anything with her. I'm just her bodyguard."

"Say what you want, Gabe McNeil, but I've been your big sister for as long as you've been alive, and I *know* you have already made up your mind about that woman. It's written all over your scowl."

I ran a hand down my face, caught between my survival senses telling me to just let Liz rant and my pride telling me to shut this down right now.

Something Liz had said piqued my interest, and curiosity won out over both survival and pride. "What makes you so sure you misjudged her?"

Liz snatched a pot holder from the counter and bent to take the chicken out of the oven. "Some of the girls in town googled her shortly after she arrived. Turns out she had a good reason for turning me down on that charity auction."

"Oh yeah? And what reason could possibly make you take no for an answer?"

Liz sighed and turned to face me, lowering her voice. "Her husband died suddenly. About a year ago."

My stomach plummeted and took all my fight with it.

"She was married?"

"Yes. He died in a car accident about nine months before she moved here." Liz waved her hand around. "So, it makes sense that she would say no to an event that would require her to be auctioned off for a date."

Liz was on the city council, and her role involved spearheading all of the community events, which included the annual fall dance, preceded by an auction where the men got to bid on dates for the dance. She had been so excited when an actual celebrity had landed in town and hadn't wasted any time trying to get Alex on the auction block. Alex had turned her down flat without any explanation, and we had all dubbed her a big-city snob who couldn't be bothered to contribute to raising money for the schools and their extracurricular programs.

Damn. Pieces of the puzzle that was Alex were starting to fall into place. I thought back to that list of suspects she had given me. No wonder there weren't any recent boyfriends on it. I was starting to feel like a complete asshole. For someone who took pride in remaining objective and collecting all the facts before passing judgment, I sure was making a lot of assumptions where Alex Reilly was concerned.

The dining room opened off the kitchen, and from my vantage point, I could see Alex sitting beside my mother, appearing deep in conversation. Somehow, she no longer seemed to have such a hard edge. Where I had once observed superiority, I now saw vulnerability.

I forced myself to look away and scrubbed my face, trying to erase the confusing feelings bubbling to the surface.

A hand gently squeezed my arm. When I looked at Liz, her sad smile said all the things I didn't want to hear. "Brother, it's okay to like her. And it's definitely okay to admit it. You can't keep letting your past hold you back from what you really want."

"And what is it you think I want?"

"What you've always wanted." Though the kitchen and dining room were connected, the area was spacious enough that with everyone involved in conversation, the likelihood of us being overheard was slim. Still, Liz kept her voice low. "You can still have what Mom and Dad have. You can still find a good woman and settle down in this small town to raise your kids the same way you, me, and Mason were raised."

I went to the fridge to get the milk, but really, I was just trying to escape Liz. And she knew it. When I turned around, she was standing right in front of me with her arms crossed. My sister was tiny. Her five feet four inches was no match for my six three, but she had a way of carrying herself that made even the toughest of guys think twice about steamrolling her.

"Gabe, Olivia was a bitch."

I tried to walk around her, but she sidestepped and blocked my path.

"You're loyal to a fault," she continued. "And that's why she was able to do so much damage before she left. I know you think this town considered you a damn fool, but that's not true. We all knew you were too good for her, and though it broke everyone's heart to watch you live through that drama, we were happy to see you free of her once and for all."

I ground my teeth together. "Liz, this is not up for discussion."

Putting both hands on my chest, she softened her gaze. "You like Alex, Gabe. It's obvious to anyone with eyes to see. Don't let the memory of Olivia keep you from being happy."

I took a deep breath, trying to shove away all the things from my past I didn't want to think about and the anger rising against my sister for forcing me to revisit them.

"Liz, I know you mean well." I kept my tone soft, reminding myself she was coming from a good place. "But I am *not* interested in Alex, or any other woman. I'm happy with my life the way it is, and you all need to accept that and stop trying to push me into something I don't want."

"But I *know* it's what you want, Gabe. When we were all growing up, Mason was always talking about getting out of here and seeing the world, but you and I always knew we wanted to settle and raise families here. It's the whole reason you decided to get out of the Marines rather than making the military a career, like Mason has."

I walked to the cabinet where the glasses were kept and pulled the pink plastic princess cup down, filling it for Lily. Over my shoulder, I said to Liz, "You need to get your own marriage right before you start trying to give me relationship advice."

When she didn't snap at me as I had expected, I looked back at her and immediately regretted my words. She was pale, and all of the fight and sparkle had left her eyes. Without a word, she went to the stove and started scooping the gravy into a dish.

"Liz, I'm—"

"Don't worry about it. You're right. I'm not the one who should be telling you how to live your life."

Before I could finish apologizing, she filled her hands with dishes and left the kitchen.

When had I become such a fuckup with women? It seemed like I could never say or do anything right anymore unless it involved a no-strings-attached one-night stand.

Gathering the remaining dishes, I followed Liz to the dining room, hoping the second half of the evening would be easier than the first.

* * *

ALEX

MY HEART SWELLED at the sight of Lily, her cherub face awash in the glow of the sparkler candles on her cake. She clapped along with us as we all cheered to celebrate the reason for this dinner. Throughout the meal she had regaled me with the details of how she had landed the lead role in her class play, *The Princess and the Frog*, making sure I knew she was the princess, not the frog.

Never had there been such a celebration in my home growing up, even for events that would traditionally warrant some fanfare. To see that Lily's entire family had come together to celebrate a five-year-old's elation at landing a part in a play left me feeling both overjoyed and mystified.

Once the lights were back on and the candles removed, Liz began cutting the cake.

She handed a piece to Lily, who promptly jumped down from her chair and, with her tongue sticking out of her mouth, carefully picked up her plate and brought it over to me. "We can eat our cake together," she said as she scrambled into my lap.

Liz caught my eye and mouthed, "Is that okay?"

I smiled and nodded, accepting the cake she passed to me.

Gabe was seated to my left at the end of the table, and the look of both surprise and disappointment at his niece's choice of laps was nearly enough to send me into a laughing fit.

Thinking back on how this evening had started, I could hardly believe how relaxed I felt. When Gabe had thrown me over his shoulder with every intention of loading me in his truck like a sack of feed, I had been on the verge of shattering. The last thing I wanted was to be around a bunch of people, especially strangers. But surprisingly, Gabe's family was a lot warmer than the man himself. Well, most everyone.

I eyed Mark at the other end of the table. The man hadn't said more than a few words all evening. Was he always like this, or had he read the tabloids and formed an ill opinion of me? Somehow, he didn't strike me as a man who would spend his time getting wrapped up in celebrity news.

Not wanting to be rude by speaking to everyone but him, I made an effort to include him in the conversation.

"So, Mark, what is it that you do?"

He flicked his eyes toward me but never actually looked at me, choosing to stay hyperfocused on his cake. "I'm an accountant."

He had the appearance of a jock with his athletic build and sandy-brown hair, so I was expecting something more physical, like construction. "So you're good with numbers, then. I've always been envious of people with that talent."

He didn't reply, and the chill that descended had nothing to do with the plummeting temperature outside.

Liz glanced at her husband and then plastered a bright smile on her face. "I'm with you, Alex. Numbers have never been my thing, but I *love* to plan and organize parties and events."

"Yes." Alice nodded enthusiastically. "And she is quite good at it."

The warmth and love between Liz and her mother was truly enviable. Alice, with her white pixie cut and vibrant eyes, looked like an older version of Liz, and the two seemed inseparable. I found myself constantly watching them, wondering what it would be like to have that kind of relationship with my own mother.

Lily's giggle drew me back to my end of the table. "He got you again, Uncle Gabe! You're not doing very good."

Gabe and Connor were engaged in a battle of thumb war, and Gabe had just allowed Connor to pin his thumb again. Feigning frustration, Gabe reached over to Lily and tickled her belly, earning a shriek of laughter.

I had been trying all evening, but I could not for the life of me reconcile the man sitting beside me, his expression full of adoration for these two children, and the grouch who had brought a black cloud down around my house.

How many personalities did this man have?

Lily leaned her head against my chest and looked up at me, curling her finger so I would come closer. When I brought my ear down next to her mouth, she whispered, "Uncle Gabe doesn't have a princess. *You* should be his princess."

Heat flooded my chest and traveled up to my cheeks. Why I should be embarrassed by Lily's suggestion, I had no idea, but the thought of me and Gabe together unleashed a hurricane of butterflies in my stomach, which caught me off guard even more than the comment.

I watched as he and Connor began another round of thumb war. The muscles in his forearm flexed with each strike and counterstrike, the sleeves of his black T-shirt straining against his powerful arms.

With a lightning-fast swoop, he caught Connor's thumb and claimed victory on this round. When he reached across the table to muss Connor's hair, the boyish grin that lit up his face made my breath catch. But that was nothing compared to the tingles that exploded across my body when he turned that dark gaze on me, nothing but smoldering heat crackling the air between us.

I swallowed hard, trying to tear my eyes away from him. But it was no use. He had me pinned with just one look.

"Come on, Uncle Gabe. Another round," Connor pleaded.

He looked to be around twelve or thirteen, just beginning to show hints of the man he would become. He'd inherited his uncle's chocolate eyes and his father's sandy-brown hair, and I had no doubt they were going to have a heartbreaker on their hands.

Gabe fixed me with an impish grin before turning back to Connor. "Afraid not, kid." He hooked a thumb toward me. "I've got to get this one home."

Gabe stood, signaling it was time to go, the rest of us following suit. A few minutes later, Gabe and I were backing down the drive. His family, minus Mark, stood on the porch, wrapped in warm coats and huddled close together, waving as we disappeared into the night.

Once we were on the road, I stole a glance at Gabe. I could barely make out his features in the dark cab, but the moonlight slicing through his window cast a ghostly glow across half his face, while the other half was hidden in shadow. The effect made him appear even more fierce than usual.

I took note of his eyes as they scanned the road and the fields that surrounded us, occasionally glancing in the rearview mirror. Regardless of where he was or what he was doing, his eyes were always moving, taking in details around him. I briefly wondered if it was a cop thing, but I hadn't noticed the other officers being half as observant.

I cleared my throat, feeling the need to break the silence. "Thank you for allowing me to intrude on your family's celebration tonight."

Gabe turned his head and cocked an eyebrow. He didn't reply right away. Instead, he kept that hawklike gaze on me as though he were studying every detail of my face. Finally, he turned back to the road and said, "Thank you for coming. My niece would have been very upset had I not been there."

I tried to bite back a laugh as I thought of how his polite response belied the truth of how I'd wound up at Liz's tonight. The harder I tried to suppress my amusement at the mental images of him throwing me over his shoulder earlier, the more determined my giggles grew to escape. To my mortification, a snort escaped instead.

Gabe's head whipped around, a look of utter shock on his face.

"I'm sorry," I said, trying to speak through the fit of giggles. "I was just thinking about how I really didn't have much choice in the matter." Tears leaked out of my eyes and streamed down my cheeks.

A rumble emanated from Gabe's chest, his shoulders shaking. Before long, he was caught in his own fit of laughter. It was all downhill from there. The harder he laughed, the harder I laughed, and vice versa.

I wrapped my arms around my belly, trying to ease the soreness setting in. When we finally got control of ourselves several minutes later, I used my palm to wipe away the tear streaks and tried to catch my breath.

I couldn't remember the last time I had laughed that hard. Truth be told, I'd thought I had lost the ability and was dismayed to realize Gabe, of all people, was the one who'd brought it out of me.

The rest of the drive home was filled with easy conversation and comfortable silences as we wound down from dinner, the atmosphere between us entirely different than it had been since this protection detail started.

When we pulled into my driveway, an uneasy feeling washed over me, but I couldn't discern why. Gabe adjusted himself in his seat, sitting taller and leaning forward. The movement caught my attention, and when I glanced at him, I saw that the relaxed facade he'd had only a moment ago had been replaced by a fierce scowl. His eyebrows were drawn together, eyes rapidly scanning the house and driveway.

"Gabe?" My voice was barely more than a whisper. His form was so rigid, part of me feared he might snap if I made any sudden movements or loud noises.

"The light's off," he said, eyes trained on the large window to our right that provided a view of the open space between the foyer and the hallway leading to the bedrooms.

I swiveled my head to look, and my stomach plummeted when I realized what he meant. We had left the hall light on so we wouldn't walk into darkness when we returned. But now, the whole house was pitch-black.

Alex

Transfixed by the ominous aura enshrouding my house, I realized now that that was what my subconscious had been trying to tell me when we'd arrived. My eyes darted to the motion-activated lights Gabe had installed, noting that they should have been triggered when we'd pulled into the drive.

I unfastened my seat belt. Gabe reached over and placed a gentle hand on my wrist, his eyes still fixed on my home.

"I'm going to clear the house," he said. "But I don't want to leave you out here alone."

I swallowed the lump in my throat. "What do you want me to do?"

"I want you to stay right behind me. When we reach the house, stay by the front door until I tell you otherwise."

I nodded and waited for him to make the first move.

With one more scan of our surroundings, Gabe pulled a small flashlight from his glove box and exited the truck, drawing a gun from the holster on his hip. He walked around to the passenger side and opened the door for me. As I stepped down and took up a position behind him, I felt the air around us vibrating with the energy that radiated from his body.

Slowly, he stalked toward the front door. I copied his movements, keeping my back to the house, stepping one foot over the other. He tried the doorknob and found that it was still locked. Snatching the key from my purse, I passed it to him and waited with bated breath for the moment that door swung open.

Condensation rose from my lips, and my body shivered, but whether it was from the cold or adrenaline, I wasn't sure. Gabe, however, looked solid as a rock. His movements were smooth and soundless.

As Gabe worked the lock, my mind started conjuring images of a figure dressed all in black rushing him the second we stepped inside. I saw the glint of a knife one moment and the muzzle flash from a black handgun the next.

Once Gabe had the door unlocked, he silently passed the keys back to me and began turning the knob. I gripped the keys so hard, the metal teeth bit into my fingers, but I was too afraid to put them back in my purse for fear I would drop or rattle them. Besides, they were the only weapon I had.

Inch by inch, the door swung open, an abyss waiting on the other side. Gabe took two steps over the threshold and paused, his gun raised and sweeping in a slow arc from left to right. When he stepped in farther, I followed close behind until I was just inside the door. Pressing my back into the wall, I waited for my eyes to adjust. Gabe was already moving toward the living room, nothing visible but the faint outline of his broad shoulders.

He cleared the kitchen next, moving so quickly that my eyes were only just acclimating to the dark when he circled back and started toward the hallway. When he crossed in front of a window, moonlight arced across his face. Then he came to a sudden stop and looked down. My eyes followed his and locked on a small white bundle on the ground.

A scream erupted from my throat, eyes filling with tears until the horrible image shimmered and danced. I flew to where Gabe stood, forgetting the danger we still faced. Dropping to my knees, I heard a sob tear from my throat as I lifted Aderes's head onto my lap.

Gabe moved past me like a ghost and disappeared from view. I stroked Aderes's silky fur as my tears fell faster and landed on her cheek. Unable to stop the heart-wrenching sobs pouring from my soul, I crumbled into my girl, my forehead pressed to hers.

Not long after he'd left, Gabe jogged back into the room, flipping on light switches. As the house roared to life, he wasted no time in returning to where Aderes and I were tangled on the floor. Gabe placed a hand under Aderes's nose and raked his eyes along her body. It was only then that I noticed a very slight rise and fall to her abdomen.

"She's still alive, Alex."

The tears fell even harder at the sight of her pink tongue hanging from her mouth. She might not have been gone yet, but death was at the doorstep, and I could feel its cold breath on my heart.

Without another word, Gabe scooped Aderes into his arms, his long strides carrying him swiftly toward the door. I stared after him, still in shock and confused by his actions.

"Alex! Let's go!" He barked the command, and somehow my body was obeying without conscious thought.

Gabe was already at the truck and ripping the back door open when I stepped onto the front porch. My senses returning, I jogged after him. He turned with Aderes still in his arms and jerked his head toward the back seat.

"Get in and I'll hand her to you."

I dove into the truck and helped to pull Aderes onto my lap. Gabe was in the truck and flying down the driveway in reverse in a matter of seconds. I leaned down to Aderes, kissing her soft cheek and murmuring words of comfort. If these were her final moments, I needed her to know how much she was loved. I needed her to know she wasn't alone. That she didn't have to be afraid. But most of all, I needed her to stay.

Gabe accelerated down the ebony highway. The light from his phone ignited the truck's interior. He punched a button and a moment later had someone on the line.

"Doc, it's Gabe. I have a dog in critical condition."

I strained my ears trying to hear the other end of the conversation, but the sound of the truck's tires eating up the road drowned out everything else.

"Yeah, I can be there in five," Gabe said.

I didn't even bother asking where we were going or who he'd been talking to when he hung up the phone. I was too busy praying this evening wouldn't end in even greater tragedy.

By the time we entered the heart of Eden Falls and parked in front of a veterinary clinic, it felt like hours had passed.

Gabe jumped out of the cab and circled around, gently pulling Aderes from my lap and cradling her against his chest as he headed for the door. An older man with white hair and balding on top pushed the door open and waited for us to enter. From his scrubs and white coat, I presumed he was the veterinarian. He directed Gabe to a room in the back and immediately began inspecting Aderes when Gabe set her on the steel table.

After pressing a stethoscope to Aderes's chest and abdomen, he checked her eyes with a light and ran his fingers across her stomach.

"When did her symptoms start?" he asked, looking at me over his small, round spectacles.

I tried to answer, but the words caught in my throat and were obliterated by another onset of sobs.

Gabe placed an arm around my waist and pulled me into his side. "She was fine when we left earlier this evening around six," he said. "When we returned around nine, we found her on the floor, barely breathing and unresponsive."

The doctor nodded and continued his examination. "Her breathing is depressed and her heart rate lethargic. Is there any chance she could have gotten into any poisonous chemicals?"

I shook my head. "N-no. I keep everything l-like that in a cabinet in the g-garage, too high for her to get into." I tried to take a deep breath so I could pull it together and be of some use, but the tightness in my chest kept my lungs from fully expanding.

"Is she on any kind of sedative? Something like Trazodone, to help with anxiety, or anything like that?"

I shook my head again.

"Any medications of yours she could have gotten into?"

"N-no." A new wave of sobs racked my body, the lack of oxygen making me lightheaded.

Gabe gently squeezed my waist. His touch grounded me, and I drew strength from his steel frame and the calmness of his presence.

"She could have been poisoned, Doc."

My head snapped back so I could look up at Gabe. His face was grim, and his eyes held an edge.

The doctor raised his eyebrows, causing the wrinkles on his forehead to deepen. He waited for Gabe to expound.

"Ms. Reilly has been receiving threats and harassing phone calls and letters. When we arrived back at her residence tonight, there was evidence that someone had infiltrated her home." Gabe nodded toward Aderes. "I believe her dog was intentionally harmed."

My eyes swung back to Aderes, her breaths growing more shallow and infrequent. She was suffering because of me. If I had just gone to the police sooner . . .

I should have left town when I'd found that picture on the tree. I would bleed for the rest of my days if Aderes didn't make it through this night.

CHAPTER 18

Alex

AN HOUR LATER, Gabe and I were sitting in the lobby of the veterinary clinic waiting for Dr. Jacobs, as I now knew him, to finish up with Aderes. While he was confident she would recover, he wanted her to stay overnight for observation. Unable to leave until I could see for myself that she was awake, Gabe had graciously agreed to wait around until she regained consciousness.

With nothing to do but replay in my mind the horrific events of the evening, I glanced around the lobby, trying to focus on details. The room was spacious, consuming the front third of the building. White floor tiles matched the white walls, creating a cold atmosphere when combined with the fluorescent lighting. Pictures of dogs and cats with happy faces and in cute poses hung in frames around the room, softening the sterile feel of the place. Wooden chairs with blue cushions that had seen better days lined the L-shaped room. A handful of the chairs were situated on the short wall while the majority lined the exterior wall, which was composed of floor-to-ceiling windows that showcased the street.

Gabe and I sat in the corner, adjacent to each other. He had his back to the short wall so he could face the front door, and my back was to the long wall so I would know the second Dr. Jacobs emerged from the examination room.

My legs were crossed, the top one swinging rapidly as I chewed on my lip. My shoulders sagged under the weight of the evening. I used every ounce of remaining energy to keep myself upright. Gabe sat perfectly still beside me, his head reclined against the wall, eyes closed. His breathing was so deep and steady, I questioned whether he was still awake.

I took the opportunity to study him more fully. Whenever he was around, whether it was because he was the officer standing watch over me or because he was checking in on things, I avoided eye contact. His disdain for this assignment had been obvious from the start, and I felt more guilty every time I looked in his eyes and saw his frustration reflected back.

But that wasn't the only reason I avoided looking at him for more than a glance. Despite our rocky encounters as of late, my body reacted to him in a way to which I wasn't accustomed. It rattled me enough as it was, but it would be worse if he were to take one look at me and *know* the effect he had.

Before tonight, anytime my body took on an agenda of its own, I'd firmly reminded it that he was married and had a child. Learning that Liz was his sister and Lily his niece had shredded that protective barrier. It left me searching for and reciting countless reasons why I still should not and would not allow my libido to run the show. Especially where *he* was concerned.

I uncrossed my legs and bounced my heel, glancing toward the examination room again. The office was so silent and still, one could imagine the world had moved on and forgotten to carry this place with it.

Stealing another glance at Gabe, I looked down to the gun fastened on his hip, his gleaming silver badge beside it. A hand rested on each of his legs, strong fingers spread and relaxed. He had scooted down in the chair so his upper body could recline a bit. His knees had fallen open, one of them brushing my left leg and sending spirals of heat pulsating from the point of contact.

Though he looked like he was down for the count, apparently his senses were still sharp, because he opened his eyes and looked right at me. Horrified that he had caught me studying him, I felt heat sweep across my face.

"I wasn't sure you were still awake," I said with a nervous chuckle.

One corner of his mouth lifted in a wry grin. "I don't sleep on the job. Just listening for anything out of place."

He sat up and stretched his arms overhead, his muscles flexing in the process. "How are you holding up?"

I released a deep breath and nodded thoughtfully. "I'm okay."

I allowed my eyes to canvass his face despite the fact he was still doing the same to me. This night had been revealing in many ways, not the least of which was the fact that I had grossly misjudged the man sitting beside me. Had it not been for his quick action and cool head, I knew without doubt that tonight would have ended very differently.

Most men would have probably chastised me for becoming hysterical over a dog and putting us in greater danger by announcing our presence when someone could have still been in the house. And most would have probably called Aderes a lost cause given the condition in which she was found. But Gabe hadn't even thought twice about doing everything in his power to save her.

My purse sat on my lap. I hugged it closer to my chest, trying to find the right words. Apparently, writer's block extended beyond the page.

"Gabe—"

His dark-brown eyes locked with mine, and my heart opened, releasing the words my brain could not find.

"I'm so grateful to you for what you did for us tonight." I dipped my chin, my hair falling forward to shield some of the vulnerability I felt. "I know it probably sounds silly, but Aderes and I—all we really have is each other." The sting of tears burned the back of my throat. I swallowed against the pain that was trying to break through the door I kept it locked behind. "I honestly don't know what I would have done if I had lost her."

I lifted my head, allowing Gabe to see the raw emotion on my face. The emotion I tried so hard to hide from the world. Something had shifted tonight, and somehow, I felt safe letting him see the truth. Or part of it, at least.

Gabe offered a sympathetic smile. "I'm glad you don't have to find out."

We fell into silence again, Gabe staring at his boots. A crease formed across his brow, the wheels in his head nearly audible.

"What is it?" I asked.

He pressed his lips together and waited a moment to answer. "Doc asked if you had Aderes on any type of sedative." Gabe's eyes were still focused on his boots, but they moved back and forth rapidly as he processed whatever was going through his head. "I'm assuming he was trying to determine if you had given her too much."

I nodded. "Yes, but it definitely couldn't have been anything like that. The only thing I have ever given her is flea and heartworm medication."

Gabe's eyes found mine. "Something's been bothering me since you first said you believed someone had been in your home."

My lips turned down. "What's that?"

"Aderes is very protective of you." He inclined his head and looked up at me through those thick black lashes with a slight grin. "I got a taste of that firsthand this evening."

I chuckled and then immediately felt sad again thinking of my sweet girl and the way she always had my back. Even to her detriment.

Gabe continued. "Every time I've seen you in town, it's always been at the coffee shop, and then that one time at Rustlers, and you've never had Aderes with you."

I nodded slowly, trying to track where he was headed. "That's right. I don't get out much, but when I do, it's almost always to go to Grind to write. I don't bring Aderes because people can't resist her, so I get interrupted too often when I'm trying to work."

"Which means," Gabe said slowly, his eyes squinting at the

floor, "that someone was able to enter your home and take that picture of you without Aderes interfering."

I leaned forward, my hands wrapping around my knees. "Yes, I had wondered about that briefly that day I found the picture and went home to get her. But with everything that's happened since, it slipped my mind."

Gabe's eyes snapped to mine. "I think whoever has been stalking you has been drugging Aderes to gain access to your home. And to you."

Like a key in a lock, Gabe's words opened a part of my subconscious. Memories and images started to coalesce, forming a hazy picture.

"What is it?" Gabe asked, scrutinizing my face.

Tingles skipped across my skin as realization dawned. "There were several nights over the past few weeks when I returned home from a session at Grind and Aderes wasn't there to greet me like she usually does. I'd go looking for her and find her conked out either on the couch or my bed." My leg started to bob up and down again, my hands gripped the seat beneath me. "Each time, she woke up when I started to pet her, but she remained lethargic for the rest of the evening. Since she was always back to her normal self the next day, I didn't think much of it."

Gabe grew very still as his eyes narrowed and his voice dropped to a lethal whisper. "This guy comes and goes from your home whenever he wants. There's no way of knowing how many times you've been locked inside with him. Or how many times he's stood right beside you, close enough to touch. But one thing's for sure." Gabe leaned forward, capturing my gaze. "He doesn't fear the police. And in his mind, nothing is going to keep him from you."

CHAPTER 19

Gabe

IT WAS a crisp Saturday morning with baby-blue skies when Alex and I pulled up to the baseball field. The parking lot was already almost full as all the locals greeted each other and descended upon the field. The parking lot sat higher than the park itself, so from our vantage point, I could see the baseball diamond and the bleachers beyond.

Liz stood near the chain-link fence that protected the spectators from stray balls, talking to a few of her girlfriends. As I rounded the hood of my truck, Alex was already pushing her door open and hopping down. Her long hair swung from the opening in the back of her baseball cap, and with the way her ass looked in those faded blue jeans, I wondered why in the hell she didn't dress down more often. Not that she didn't look just as good in everything she wore, but I definitely preferred this low-key country girl thing she had going on today.

Aderes jumped down from the truck, her leash jangling as she gave a good shake. She looked up at Alex with those crystal eyes, tail wagging and tongue hanging out of her mouth, and earned herself that thousand-watt smile and a scratch behind the ears. Alex had been a completely different person since we'd brought Aderes home yesterday. It was as if all of her other troubles had become lighter in the wake of nearly losing her closest companion.

"Ready?" I asked as Alex straightened and turned to gaze at the field.

She nodded and followed me down the grassy knoll to where Liz waited.

"Hi!" Liz practically pounced on Alex, throwing her arms around her and rocking their entwined bodies back and forth. "I'm so glad you came! Now we can sit together, and I won't have to listen to the Gaggle Geese over there gossiping about everyone the whole time."

Alex followed Liz's eyes to the group of old ladies perched on the front row of the far bleacher. Their heads were already bent together as they whispered and cast furtive glances at their targets.

Alex laughed, her green eyes sparkling. She reached a hand behind her head to pull down on the back of her baseball cap, and when she did, the threadbare fabric of her T-shirt pulled tight across her breasts, outlining her delicious curves. My hands twitched at my sides, itching to reach out and trace every contour until it was committed to memory.

The woman was the fucking devil's candy. I blew out a slow breath and reminded myself to get a grip before I tossed aside all of the really good reasons I had for keeping her at arm's length.

Tearing my eyes away before I ended up with a situation that would get me arrested at a family event, I scanned the crowd for the officer who was supposed to stand guard over Alex while I played in the annual Cops vs. Firefighters Baseball Game.

"The kids over on the jungle gym?" I asked Liz.

She shaded her eyes and twisted to look back at the playground. "Yep. They're all pretending they're either cops or firefighters. Except Lily." Liz turned back to me with an ironic grin. "She is a police officer princess and threatened to stomp on anyone's toes who tried to tell her there is no such thing."

I laughed. "That's my girl."

Trevor appeared out of nowhere and rested his forearm on my

shoulder. "Oh? Finally decide to break up with Blow-Up Annie and get yourself a real date?" He looked at Alex standing on my other side and winked. *Asshole.*

I wouldn't have believed it if I hadn't seen it with my own eyes, but Alex actually snickered and looked away, trying to hide it.

Trevor had that wild look in his eyes that usually resulted in me nursing a whole lot of regret. I needed to get him away from Alex before he said something that would force me to kill my best friend.

"Have you seen Shoemaker?" I asked. "He's supposed to stay with Alex during the game."

Trevor shook his head, then looked around. "He probably just got stuck on a call. If he's not here by the time the game starts, she can sit on the bench with us until he arrives." Giving Alex a shit-eating grin, he added, "She'll bring up our hot quotient and distract the hose draggers."

As if on cue, Bryan stopped at our circle on his way to the fire-fighters' dugout. "Morning, all." He grinned and raked his eyes over the group, pausing when he landed on Alex. I wondered if his red hair and light eyes that had landed him the prized December page in last year's charity calendar would capture her attention.

When I shifted my eyes to her, it felt like someone elbowed me in the gut. She was smiling at Bryan with such warmth, I had my answer. She had never looked at me like that.

I ground my molars and looked away. What the fuck did I even care? I. Was. Not. Interested. In. Alex. Reilly.

Okay. That was a stretch. She was sexy. And smart. And classy. And stronger than she thought. All things that I admired in a woman. But that didn't change the fact that she was a big-city girl who would get bored with this town sooner rather than later. And I, for one, wasn't going to be the schmuck left in her wake when she drove south past the city limit sign without looking back.

Bryan stretched his hand out to Alex. "Hi, I haven't had the pleasure. I'm Bryan Jameson."

Alex accepted his grasp and introduced herself, allowing him to hold her hand a little too long.

I tried to focus elsewhere to distract myself from the love connection taking place right in front of me, but I couldn't get my damn eyes to obey orders. After a few seconds of those two exchanging small talk, I was ready to blow a gasket.

While Bryan was in the middle of answering a question posed by Alex, I interrupted. "Shouldn't you be warming up, Jameson? Wouldn't want you blaming your loss today on a pulled groin muscle."

Bryan's smile grew even bigger as he locked eyes with me. "I would if I expected a challenge, but I don't anticipate it'll be a terribly taxing game."

I crossed my arms and deepened my scowl. Bryan laughed and turned his attention back to Alex, who was now looking between us with uncertainty. "Alex, I hope you enjoy the game." Reaching out to shake her hand once more, he added, "I'm certainly glad to know you'll be in the stands. I look forward to seeing more of you."

Alex blushed the color of an overripe tomato. "Thank you. It was very nice meeting you."

Hearing a snort, I snapped my gaze to Trevor, who was trying —*not very convincingly*—to hide his laughter.

Just then Shoemaker jogged up to the group. "Hey, guys. Sorry I'm late. I—"

"What the hell took you so long?" I snapped.

Shoemaker's eyes went wide. He looked back and forth between me and Trevor like he couldn't figure out why one of us looked ready to murder him while the other was practically bent over in hysteria.

Before Shoemaker could offer any excuses, I motioned to Liz and Alex. "Take these two to the bleachers and *don't* let Alex out of your sight."

Alex and Shoemaker walked toward the stands, Alex glancing back after a few steps, her brow furrowed. An uneasy feeling settled in my bones as I watched her move farther away, Aderes trotting at her side. I'd fucked that up big-time. I plucked the cap off my head and raked my hand over my hair.

Liz was still standing in front of me, her arms folded and a knowing look in her eyes. "Don't worry," she said. "If women were easily dissuaded every time a man said or did something stupid, the human population would have died out long ago." Shaking her head, she turned to join Alex and Shoemaker.

Trevor straightened and used his palm to wipe the tears from his eyes. I glared at him, trying to decide if I could get away with punching him in front of all of these people.

"Oh, come on," he said. "*That* was some funny shit." He started cracking up again and put his hand on my shoulder to steady himself. "I know you and Bryan have always had a friendly rivalry, but for a minute there, I really thought I was going to have to pull you off the poor bastard."

I shoved Trevor's hand from my shoulder and started to walk toward our dugout.

"Hold up!" Trevor called after me. "We need to talk about something real quick."

Hearing the gravity in his voice, I stopped to hear him out.

"I didn't want to say anything until we got the girls situated, but I got some information on the dead CI."

My eyebrows lifted. "How long have you been sitting on this? You didn't think I'd want to know right away?"

Trevor raised his palms to me. "Chill, amigo. The call just came in about an hour ago."

"So? What did you find out?"

"He was undercover for the feds. DEA to be exact."

I stilled. "Are you shitting me?"

Trevor shook his head. "He was serving time in a federal pen for some pretty serious drug charges. The feds cut him a deal. If he agreed to work undercover, infiltrating Satan's Serpents and feeding information back to them, they would drop the rest of his sentence."

"How long was he under?"

"Three years."

I ran my hand across my mouth, digesting the turn of events.

"Did they tell you anything else?" I asked.

"Not really. The fed I talked to was pretty tight-lipped about it. Honestly, I'm surprised he reached out at all." Trevor shifted his weight back and forth, his shoes scratching against the pebbles in the dirt. "He caught wind that we were searching for information on someone matching the CI's undercover identity. Wanted to know where we found him and in what condition. Apparently, the guy had failed to check in with his handler, and they'd lost track of him."

"If the feds are sharing notes with us about their investigation, scant as they may be, it doesn't give me a lot of hope that they're having better luck than we are in getting anything significant on the Serpents."

Trevor nodded and looked out at the field, squinting against the sun.

"Did you check on Jace this morning?" I asked.

"Yeah. He's doing all right. Nothing new to report."

"Have you seen the Serpents hanging around in town at all?"

"No."

A breeze kicked up and whipped inside my shirt, cooling the sweat that had begun to gather between my shoulder blades. "I don't know, man. Maybe it's best to just pull him and get him the hell out of town. We'll find some other way to get what we need on those bastards. If the feds are running a sting, I don't want Jace getting caught in the net."

Trevor grunted his agreement. We were quiet for a moment, both mulling over the situation, when he asked, "Where are we at with that list of Alex's?"

"Between me and Quinn, we've been able to clear everyone

except for one." I canted my head and gave Trevor a *guess who* look.

"Maxwell Hargrove."

I nodded. "No one else on the list has had any major run-ins with law enforcement. A few with DUIs or minor drug charges, and every single one can be accounted for either when Alex reported that picture nailed to the tree or when Aderes was drugged."

"So then what's the deal with Hargrove?"

I crossed my arms and shrugged. "He was sent to prison following the stalking incident with Alex and was released on parole three months ago. They failed to notify Alex when he was released."

Trevor snorted. "The justice system at its finest."

"No shit." We started to walk toward the dugout where our partners were congregating. "I put a couple of calls in to his parole officer to find out if there's any way Hargrove could have been in Eden Falls in the past few weeks. I haven't heard anything back yet."

When we reached the dugout, I searched the stands for Alex. She and Liz were absorbed in conversation, the wind whipping her ponytail around. Fresh-faced and totally casual, she looked like a small-town girl enjoying a day in the sunshine with friends.

Sometime between dinner with my family and seeing her with Bryan this morning, my feelings for her had shifted. I had begun to accept that I'd misjudged and underestimated her more than once, and now—I questioned if *this* Alex, the Alex in blue jeans and a baseball cap sitting in the bleachers with my sister, could be the real Alex.

I dared to stare for a moment longer, my heart sinking when I realized it wasn't a question but a hope.

* * *

ALEX

THE COLD HARD metal of the bleacher bit into my thighs, but I hardly noticed as I closed my eyes and lifted my face to the cool breeze and warm sun. Excited murmurs rose from the crowd like waves about to crash upon the shore. It seemed as though the whole town had turned out, dressed in either blue or red, to show their support. I looked down at my T-shirt, wondering if I stuck out like a sore thumb in my violet top. Gabe hadn't mentioned anything about team colors, or I would have worn blue to show my support for the men and women who had been protecting me through this whole ordeal.

I considered how I must look now, compared to how I had been dressing for the past several years. When I'd lived in Los Angeles and had been required to make a number of appearances for the sake of my career, I had been informed in no uncertain terms that I was never to be caught portraying an image other than a chic, successful, confident woman.

The first time the paparazzi caught me in a pair of sweats and without any makeup, it was enough to ensure I would never so much as open the blinds in my house again without being dressed to the nines and looking red carpet ready. They had, of course, ensured I looked even more hideous than reality by doctoring the photos until even *I* could hardly recognize myself.

It felt good, though. Watching a baseball game in a pair of jeans and white Keds while a town full of people who all knew each other cheered for their team and snuck in a few teasing jabs at the other side.

I scanned the field looking for Gabe and found him off to the side, warming up with Trevor. He bent to stretch his hamstrings, and I surprised myself when I realized I was practically drooling while staring at his backside. I was *not* a woman who leered at men.

Maybe the draw was just the fact that this guy kept me spinning. It was unusual for me not to have someone figured out within the first five minutes of meeting them. Gabe McNeil, however, remained a mystery.

I leaned toward Liz. "Is everything okay with Gabe? Some-times I feel like I can't keep up with his changing moods."

Liz chuckled. She had her feet propped up on the bleacher in front of us, her arms resting on her knees. "Well, he actually keeps a pretty cool head by nature, but he's had a few things stealing his focus and testing his control lately. Of course"—she shrugged—"it didn't help that Bryan chose to arrive at that particular moment." Liz smiled as though she harbored a secret.

"Do they not like each other?" I asked.

"Nah, it's all in fun. They've been rivals since high school. They were both fantastic athletes, always performing neck and neck and trying to outdo the other." Liz brushed a gnat from her shoulder and squinted toward Gabe. "They were also in the top of their class academically, and of course, girls were obsessed with them. I think they secretly appreciated that they had each other as competition, though. It gave them an edge. Kept 'em sharp."

I contemplated the interaction I had witnessed between the two men as Bryan walked to the pitcher's mound and the crowd released a cacophony of cheers. For such a good-looking man, he had struck me as humble and sincere. It was nice talking to someone who seemed genuinely happy to meet me rather than branding me a liar or mentally unhinged.

Yet my attention once again drifted to the taciturn man in blue, eyes roaming over his surroundings and never missing a thing. Gabe stood in the dugout with one arm extended, fingers clutching the trim on the low roof. The muscles in his arm rippled each time he adjusted his position, shirt riding up just enough to display part of the V at his hips.

When it was his turn to bat, it didn't escape my attention that several women in the stands, dressed in cutoffs so short that Victoria no longer had a secret, stood and cheered for him by name. My fingers curled into my palms, nails biting as they pene-trated the top layer of skin.

Get a grip, Alex. With everything going on in my life, the last thing I needed was to start feeling possessive about a man who wasn't even mine. Besides, that part of my life was over. From the moment I had put Robby's body in the ground, I had decided the only thing that would get my attention from then on was my work.

My stomach clenched, the feel of sunshine dulling as if a bank of clouds had swept in and stolen the golden warmth. Just thinking about work was enough to make me ill these days. Though I had managed to get some words on paper since this whole protection detail had started, none of it was good. And after the incident with Aderes, I had completely lost focus again.

Liz waved in my peripheral. I turned my head to her and followed her gaze until I saw Bree, smiling and heading our way. It was the first time I'd seen her with her hair down. It fell in waves down her back, standing out against the blue of her T-shirt. Though she also wore red capris, so I figured she was here to cheer on both teams.

"Hi. Trouble making up your mind?" I asked, flicking my finger down her form as she sat beside me.

She looked down at her ensemble and laughed. "I didn't want to hurt business by picking a team, but between you and me, I'm pulling for the blue today."

"Your secret is safe with me."

Liz leaned across me so she could address Bree. "Are you just getting here?"

Bree shook her head and pulled a stray hair from her lip gloss. "No, Mrs. Walker caught me over there." She hooked a thumb toward the far left of the field. "Spent the first half of the game talking my ear off. I finally told her I needed to go find some water and took off."

Liz laughed. "That poor woman. She's so lonely now that Mr. Walker is gone."

Gabe had just crossed home plate, and his cheering squad went crazy. Bree looked over at a gaggle of them in the bleachers to our right. "Jeez, does Gabe really get around that much?"

Liz glanced at the women and rolled her eyes. "I think it's the fact that he refuses to get involved with anyone that makes him more desirable. Makes the chase more exciting, I guess."

Bree nodded in a way that made me think there was subtext I was missing. "It's been *two* years," she said.

Knowing it wasn't any of my business, but unable to stop myself, I asked, "What's been two years?"

Bree and Liz exchanged glances.

Finally, Liz said, "It's been two years since Gabe's fiancée walked out." Her voice was low, and she looked around to ensure no one was paying attention.

I didn't know what I had expected, but *that* certainly wasn't it.

For whatever reason, Liz decided to expound. "Gabe was engaged for a while to a woman we went to high school with. They didn't date in school or anything, though Lord knows she tried a number of tactics to get his attention." Liz ran her fingers through the back of her short hair. I admired her delicate features and the way she could pull off that sassy hairdo.

"They got together a couple of years after he'd left for the Marines," she continued. "He was home on leave, and for reasons I *still* don't understand, he finally gave her a chance. Nobody around here liked the match, but"—she shrugged—"what can you do when a grown man has made up his mind about something? Anyway"—she wiped her hands down her pant legs—"he came home for good. She didn't like his choice to leave the Marines, so she left for something better."

I lifted my eyebrows. "Something better?"

Bree cut in. "It happened just before I got to town, but everyone was talking about it so much, I felt like I had witnessed the whole thing." She leaned in closer and whispered. "She left him for another man. Someone she had been seeing for a while."

My eyes shot to Gabe. He was standing near the dugout, laughing at something one of his teammates had said. I turned Bree's words over and over in my head. *She hadn't wanted him.*

She left him. A sharp pang of guilt lanced through me. Suddenly, I didn't want to hear anymore.

"She was such a bitch," Liz said, shaking her head, her violet eyes blazing. "She didn't just leave town. She *humiliated* him first."

"How?" What was wrong with me? I did *not* want to hear this.

Liz's stony expression said it all. "For men, money is a score-card. Olivia made sure everyone saw Gabe as the loser. She not only boasted about the fact that she'd had this wealthy, powerful man dangling on a string while she was engaged to *my* brother, she also returned to town twice after she left to flaunt that she'd struck it rich. Fancy clothes, fancy car, expensive jewelry. Talking about how happy she was and how she finally had everything she deserved."

Liz sat there simmering and shaking her head for several moments before adding, "Trevor and I begged Gabe to leave her when he returned home. We told him we'd seen her at Rustlers on more than one occasion acting single while he was away."

"What did he say?" I asked.

She turned to me with a sad smile before returning her gaze to her brother. "He stood by his woman. Loyal to a fault, that brother of mine."

"And he hasn't been in a relationship since," Bree added.

Cheers from the crowd dulled until they were almost nonexistent. My heart ached for Gabe. Though there was a lot I still didn't know about him, I knew he was a proud man. To think that someone he had loved and committed his life to had treated him so cruelly hurt as though I had lived it myself. Another slice of guilt cut across my core, squeezing my insides until I almost couldn't breathe.

The rest of the game was a blur. Too distracted to pay atten-tion, I was startled when everyone around me rose and began plodding down the bleachers. I followed Liz and Bree to the stairs that ran along the railing, Officer Shoemaker at my elbow the entire time.

When we made it to the grass, Liz and Bree left to congratulate Gabe and his team on the victory before heading to their cars, while Shoemaker and I hung back. Since Gabe stayed to help with the equipment, there were only a few people still milling around by the time we made it to his truck.

He opened the rear door on the passenger side so I could load Aderes. She jumped lithely onto the floorboard and then again onto the seat, twirled once, and settled on Gabe's flannel shirt. She'd been obsessed with that shirt when we'd brought her home from the vet, so he'd left it there for her, anticipating more truck rides.

"You okay?" Gabe asked as he held my hand while I climbed into his tall truck. The warmth of his fingers was far more comforting than it should have been, his calloused hands a testament to the fact that he was a man who earned everything he had.

I tried to form a convincing smile. "Yes. Just a little tired from the sun, I think."

Judging by the way he scrutinized me, I suspected I hadn't quite pulled it off, but he didn't press further.

The drive home was quiet. I could see his reflection in my window as I gazed out at buildings that eventually gave way to an ocean of evergreens butting up against the mountains in the distance.

He'd turn to look at me every now and then, but he never spoke, and I was grateful. I didn't want to have to explain what I was feeling or the thoughts that darkened my soul. I could lie, I supposed. But oddly, I didn't want to lie to *him*.

When we finally pulled into my driveway, I was relieved at the opportunity to close myself in my office and let the facade I had been so accustomed to putting on each morning slip for a bit. As soon as we were through the front door, Aderes went in search of her food and water, and I went in search of sweats.

"I'm going to change and then try to get some work done," I said to Gabe.

He nodded. "Okay. I'm here if you need anything."

I could feel his eyes on my back as I made my way down the hallway, thoughts swirling and tumbling. I tried in vain to push them down. When I reached the door to my bedroom, I gently pushed against the smooth wood, the whooshing sound of it gliding over the carpet oddly soothing.

As I looked down at the floor, the hair on the back of my neck rose. When my gaze lifted, my breath caught before a bloodcurdling scream shattered the silence.

CHAPTER 20

Gabe

ALEX'S terrified scream ripped through the house. In one motion, I ran toward the back of the house, drawing my gun and preparing for the worst. When I hit the entrance to the hallway, the first thing I saw was Alex sprawled backward on the floor, scrambling away from her bedroom.

Reaching her in a matter of seconds, I paused at her side. "Alex! What is it?"

She raised a shaking finger, pointing at the half-open door to her bedroom, and though her lips formed words, no sound came out of her mouth.

Inching forward, gun leading the way, I nudged the door open farther. Clothes were strewn about the room, pulled from the open dresser drawers and the walk-in closet adjacent to her bed. The perfume bottles atop her dresser were bowled over, one of them smashed and dripping liquid into the top drawer.

I eased into the room, the barrel of my gun drawing an arc from one corner to the next as I listened for signs of another presence. It was eerily quiet, as though the room mourned its desecration.

When my eyes took in the crumpled lavender comforter on Alex's bed, my jaw tightened along with the grip on my Glock. A white envelope was perched on one of her pillows, her name scrawled hastily in red ink.

I stepped one foot over the other as I made my way to the bathroom on the left side of the room. It took me only a second to clear it before moving to the walk-in closet, which also held no intruder.

Though I was confident Aderes would have alerted us if someone was still in the house, I returned to Alex and, placing a hand on her shoulder, told her to stay put while I checked the rest of the house.

I found her office in a similar state, papers scattered over the floor and every surface. Books pulled from the shelves, their battered skeletons boasting crumpled pages and a few torn covers. And the fact that her laptop was smashed beyond repair told me this was definitely not someone looking for an easy payday. This was the work of someone who wanted Alex locked in a psychological prison of pain and fear.

When I returned to her, I found her still sprawled on the floor, staring in disbelief at her bedroom. Kneeling down, I grasped her arm and gently pulled her up. With the way she was trembling, I was hesitant to let go, so I placed a hand on her lower back and guided her into the room.

At first, her body went rigid, but with a few coaxing words, she relaxed enough to follow my lead. As much as I hated to sit her on the bed, where someone had clearly been lying, and doing God knows what else, it was the only place, other than the floor, for her to take a seat.

I took her face in my hands and tilted her head up so I could get a good look at her. She was as pale as the white bedsheets, her pupils dilated and eyes unfocused. Running my hands up and down her arms in an effort to warm her cold skin and rouse her from the shock, I had a sudden urge to pull her into me and hold her close. I wanted to chase away the nightmares and promise her that nothing bad was going to happen.

But plenty of bad things had already happened to her, and so far, I hadn't managed to do much to remedy the situation. Alex blinked up at me, her gorgeous green eyes starting to register reality.

"Nothing is going to keep him away," she whispered, her lower lip trembling.

I ran my thumb across her cheek, her soft skin a contrast to my calloused hands. "*I* am going to keep him away, Alex. He may have gotten into your home, but he's not going to get anywhere near *you*." I held her gaze, urging her to hear the promise in my words.

She took a deep breath and released it slowly. Convinced she wasn't going to crumple to the floor, I took a cautious step toward the head of her bed.

Snatching the envelope off her pillow and holding it by the corner, I examined the handwriting on its front.

"Do you have tweezers?" I asked.

She nodded and rose from the bed, heading for the bathroom. A moment later, she returned and handed them to me. I used the hem of my T-shirt and the tweezers to separate the document from the envelope. A piece of tri-folded paper emerged, gaping from the contents wrapped inside.

When I lifted the document, several thin sheets of paper floated onto the bed. Alex gasped and covered her mouth as she stared down at them.

Using the tweezers, I began flipping all of the newspaper clippings right side up and spread them out so each one was visible, all the while keeping one eye trained on Alex.

Every clipping held an image. Several of them showed a crumpled vehicle wrapped around a telephone pole and taken from different vantage points. The others were of Alex, either alone or with a man.

Combined, the images depicted a tale of glam and glitter descended into tragedy. In some of the photos, Alex was smiling and every bit the successful author who lived a glamorous life. In others, she and a blond-haired man in expensive suits and polo shirts had their arms wrapped around each other. And finally, images of Alex, dressed in black and wearing oversized sunglasses, frown lines creasing her porcelain skin.

I raised my eyes to Alex, finding her still transfixed by the photos.

Next, I moved to the note. Unlike the envelope, it was typed, precluding any type of handwriting analysis. I kept the page turned away from Alex and scanned the contents.

When I was through, I ran my eyes over her face and read her body language. She was teetering on the edge, but I had a feeling she'd be able to shed light on the subtext of the letter.

"Alex."

Slowly, for the first time since those newspaper clippings had fallen like the ashes of her past, she raised her eyes to me.

"Alex, I want to read this letter to you. It's not going to be easy to hear, but I need to know what it means to you. Can you do that?"

She swallowed hard, her body swaying ever so slightly. One nod was all she managed.

Still holding the paper with the tweezers she'd given me, I began. "My beautiful Alexandra, though you've hidden yourself away, you will always be revealed to me. You are mine, put here on this earth for my pleasure and reward. Fate has proven nothing will stand between us, as your departed husband has learned. His life was taken for taking something that did not belong to him. Soon, Alexandra. Soon."

Tears slid silently down Alex's cheeks. When she dropped her head, they splattered like raindrops on her T-shirt. No sobs. No ragged breaths. Just unspoken pain.

I went to the bathroom and returned with a box of Kleenex and a small trash can. After the incident with Aderes, all suspicion of Alex and her involvement in this stalking situation had vanished. But if it hadn't, seeing the raw and bleeding wounds that had just come to the surface would have convinced me of her innocence.

She pulled a couple of tissues free and dabbed at her cheeks. I waited, content to give her hours if that was what she needed. A minute later, she raised her tear-stained face to mine. The pain in her eyes was expected; the resignation was not.

Fear. Pain. Anger. Those were emotions I expected and could deal with. Resignation coming from this woman who had been so fierce in her own way scared the hell out of me.

She cleared her throat and swallowed. "Not many people call me Alexandra." Her voice was monotone, devoid of emotion, as though she were reciting the periodic table. "My parents call me Alexandra. The only other person to call me Alexandra in my adult life was Maxwell Hargrove. He loved saying my full name. It was as if he couldn't say it enough."

Alex's fingers toyed with the tissue, pulling it back and forth between her hands.

"What else can you tell me?" I kept my voice soft.

She glanced at the pictures on the bed and then looked away again. "Those are the newspaper clippings from when Robby died."

"Your husband," I clarified.

"Yes."

"Were any other vehicles involved? Any signs of foul play?"

Alex shook her head. "No. It was ruled accidental. His toxicology report showed a BAC of point-two-four. He lost control of the car and hit a telephone pole." She rubbed her palms back and forth on her legs. "It happened at three in the morning, so there weren't many cars on the road."

My forehead scrunched as I studied the black-and-white images and the print beneath. Just because no other cars were thought to be involved didn't mean someone couldn't have been waiting for the right opportunity to stage an *accident*. If Alex's husband had a tendency to get rip-roaring drunk, it wouldn't take long for someone to learn his pattern and take advantage of his altered state while he was behind the wheel. Not something Alex needed to know.

I moved in front of her, my thighs resting against her knees. Without thinking, I reached for her cheek and gently wiped away a stray tear with my thumb. She didn't seem to think anything of it, but it surprised the hell out of me and set off warning bells. I needed to get some distance. I was getting too wrapped up in this case.

No. More accurately, I was getting too wrapped up in Alex. I took a step back and shoved my hands in my pockets to keep them from acting on their own. "Tell me more about Maxwell Hargrove."

Alex dabbed at her cheeks again and tossed the Kleenex in the trash can. Her tears had subsided, but I preferred them to the vacant stare that had replaced them.

"He was a deranged fan," she began. "I attended this charity event to promote a shelter that cared for abused animals. He saw me in the media coverage, and that's where his obsession started." Alex pulled the baseball cap from her head, her ponytail snaking through the opening in the back. Tossing the cap aside, she reached up and slid the hair tie down her long strands, the soft curls falling free and fanning over her back and shoulders. Raking a hand through the hair at the crown of her head, she closed her eyes, like she'd been waiting all day to let her hair down.

"It started with a bunch of phone calls and creepy notes," she continued. "Some of the notes came in the mail, always to my personal address, rather than the PO box I use for business. Others were left on my car when I was out and about."

"The letters and phone calls you said you were getting prior to finding your picture on that tree—were they the same as before?"

She tilted her head, her lips pursing as she searched her memory. "The letters were similar. He always wrote about all of the sexually degrading things he wanted to do to me—about how he wanted to *possess* me. But the phone calls were different."

"How so?"

"Before, he always spoke. He'd tell me that I was his, and he'd often repeat what was in the letters. His calls were initially disgusting, and he was clearly infatuated, but it wasn't until after law enforcement really started going after him that his calls became hateful. Full of anger."

"But with the more recent calls, no one ever spoke to you?"

She shook her head.

I folded my arms, sifting through everything I knew about this case, comparing it to Alex's experience with Hargrove. "Is there anything else that's similar between what you've been experiencing and your prior situation with Hargrove?"

Alex's gaze landed on the newspaper clippings again, and she slowly nodded. "The incident that led to his arrest was when he broke into our house. We were out at lunch and returned home to find my clothes strewn all over the place. Pictures had been broken, some of them removed from their frames. Robby's clothes were all shredded and lying like piles of confetti on the floor. And—"

Alex's long eyelashes fluttered as she glanced at me, hesitating.

"And what?" I asked.

A crimson blush rose in her cheeks. "He had masturbated on my side of the bed," she said, her eyes falling to her lap.

Even if Maxwell Hargrove wasn't the one currently harassing Alex, I had the sudden urge to track him down and feed him his own genitals. Consciously relaxing my jaw before I ground my teeth to dust, I said, "You mentioned this was the event that led to his arrest."

She nodded. "Given the totality of everything that had happened with him, and the DNA he left behind, law enforcement was able to obtain a search warrant for his residence. They found the photos that were taken the day of the break-in, as well as several pieces of my lingerie. They found a lot of other things, too, but those items were pretty damaging." Alex shifted on the bed and crossed her arms. "He didn't even try to deny it. He boasted about how many times he had been in my house without me even knowing." The bitterness punctuating each word gave me hope that she wasn't giving in to this asshole yet.

She fell silent, and I got the sense she needed a moment to process everything. I pulled my phone from my jeans pocket. "I need to get our people out here to collect evidence and take photos. Are you going to be all right here for a minute?"

Alex nodded without looking up.

"Try not to touch anything until we've collected what we need."

I left the room to make my calls, starting with Dispatch to get our version of a crime scene unit out to Alex's as quickly as possible. While I was at it, I had them give me the law enforcement inside line to the parole office handling Hargrove's case. I'd given Maxwell Hargrove's PO plenty of opportunities to follow up with me. I was done playing nice and was going straight to the guy's supervisor.

An hour later, our two crime scene techs were combing through Alex's house, destroying the last shred of privacy she'd been clinging to. Given the go-ahead, Alex was in her bedroom trying to erase all evidence that a faceless intruder had had his hands all over her personal belongings.

My phone vibrated in my pocket. When I glanced at the screen, the Los Angeles area code kicked my pulse up a notch.

"Officer McNeil," I answered.

"Officer McNeil, this is Supervising Parole Agent Henry Griggs returning your call. I apologize for the delay in my response, but I wanted to obtain the information you're seeking prior to speaking with you."

"I appreciate that," I said, moving away from Alex's office, where the techs were currently working. "What can you tell me about Maxwell Hargrove's case?"

The pause on the other end of the line told me I wasn't going to like what I was about to hear. "I spoke with Hargrove's parole officer. Apparently, Hargrove has been MIA for the past few weeks."

My grip tightened on my cell phone. First the prison fails to inform Alex that Hargrove was released on parole, and then the parole officer on his case doesn't deem it necessary to inform the stalking victim that her attacker has absconded?

Griggs continued. "He failed to show up to his job one day and just never returned. When he also failed to check in with his parole officer, the officer responded to Hargrove's home and found it empty, with food rotting in the sink and fridge. Hard to tell with some of these guys and the way they live, but it looked like he had already been gone for a bit."

"What are you doing to track him down?" I asked, trying to diffuse the heat that was working its way up my chest. Considering I needed this guy's cooperation, I couldn't afford to lose my temper.

Griggs sighed into the phone. "A warrant has been issued for Hargrove's arrest, but unless he gets in trouble with the law, we're not likely to find him. These guys jump ship and go underground all the time."

I let my silence do the talking. After a long, awkward moment, Griggs cleared his throat and said, "May I ask why you're inquiring about all of this, Officer McNeil?"

"Yeah." My voice held an edge sharp enough to cut steel. "Hargrove's victim is being terrorized. I'm working her case, and it bears a lot of similarities to Hargrove's MO. The fact that no one thought to notify the victim of his release or that he absconded may have just given him the edge he needed to infiltrate her life before anyone caught on."

To his credit, Griggs didn't try to defend himself or his officer. "There is no denying we dropped the ball on this. I will personally see to it that this case is given top priority, and if there is anything else we can do to assist, I'd like you to call my cell phone directly."

After he provided me with all of his direct contact information, we disconnected. I glanced down the hall to where Alex was loading her arms with a pile of clothes from her floor, undoubtedly preparing to throw them in the washing machine on the hottest setting.

As I watched her move about, grace in every step, her face set with determination and focus, I realized that this was no longer strictly business for me. Try as I might to deny that I had any feelings for Alex, the primal urge inside of me demanding that I defend and protect what was mine told me I was in trouble where she was concerned.

The only thing that terrified me more than that realization was the thought that had been hacking at my brain like an ice pick. Though it was entirely possible Maxwell Hargrove was the perpetrator we'd been looking for, I didn't yet have enough evidence to determine that conclusively. And if, by some slim chance, it wasn't him, we were back at square one, dealing with a diabolical mastermind wearing a face that could belong to anybody.

CHAPTER 21

Alex

THE MORNING after my house was ransacked, I crawled out of bed feeling like I had been used as someone's punching bag. The knots in my neck and shoulders sent sharp pains down my arms and back, and a headache pounded behind my eyes. Still groggy and fighting the temptation to crawl back into bed and hide from the world, I checked the clock on my bedside table.

Nine o'clock. Way later than I was accustomed to rising.

The scent of coffee wafted under my bedroom door and beckoned me to the kitchen. Trevor was on watch today. He was always good about putting a fresh pot on when he arrived.

Pushing myself up off the soft mattress, I shuffled to my bathroom, hoping to ease some of my knots with a hot shower.

Ten minutes later, clean and feeling a bit looser, I went to my dresser and took my phone off the charger. As soon as I unplugged it, the screen lit up. My eyes rounded, and my stomach dropped when I saw a long list of text messages, missed calls, and voice mails from what seemed like my entire contact list and a lot of unknown numbers.

One name jumped out and sent waves of nausea rolling through me.

Cass.

I had a dozen missed calls, four voice mails, and countless texts from her alone. I felt my world crashing down around me without even knowing what the issue was.

A whisper in my head told me to put the phone back and pretend I hadn't seen anything. But I'd tried that tactic before, and I always ended up a breath away from a nervous breakdown and still having to deal with the monster I didn't want to face.

After an attempt at a calming breath, I listened to one of Cass's voice mails first. "Alex, we have a *big* problem. Call me back immediately and do *not* talk to anyone until you do."

My fingers started to shake. I glanced down at the voice mail below Cass's. It was from Robby's mother. We hadn't spoken since the day of his funeral.

Heeding Cass's warning, I touched her name on the screen and put the phone to my ear, bracing for her answer.

"Alex? Where the hell have you been?"

I cringed. I knew Cass well enough to know this curt tone was coming from a place of concern, but I was too fragile to brush it off right now. The events of yesterday were still too fresh. And now—I felt like something was burrowing a hole in my stomach as I waited to hear what awful event had taken place.

"I was sleeping." I cleared my throat to get rid of the raspiness from not having used it for hours.

Cass's voice took on the quality of someone who is trying to break bad news and they're afraid of how the other person is going to respond. "Alex, there is no easy way to tell you this, so I'm just going to give it to you straight."

Cass was nothing if not direct.

"Your divorce papers were leaked online early this morning."

The ground fell away, and suddenly, I was falling through space. I tried to clutch at the dresser, but my fingers slid across the smooth surface and lost contact. As I fell, the bottles of perfume I had put right after finding them scattered the day before toppled over again, a huge clatter resulting.

"Alex? Alex, are you okay?"

I tried to suck in air, but my lungs refused to take it.

The door behind me flew open, banging into the wall. Trevor was on the floor next to me before I'd even realized he had entered the room. His hand gripped my arm, which still held my cell phone to my ear.

"Alex!" He shook me. "Alex! Look at me!"

I turned my face to his, barely registering the concern etched deeply into his features.

Trevor gently slapped my cheek, the subtle sting pulling me from my stupor and somehow encouraging my lungs to suck in a deluge of air.

I scrambled to my feet and ran for my office, leaving Trevor in my wake. By the time he caught up to me, I was already at my desk, opening my iPad.

I set the phone down and put Cass on speaker. She was still screaming into the phone, trying to get me to answer.

"I'm here," I said, barely audible even to myself. Trevor stood in front of me, his hands braced on his hips, waiting for someone to explain.

As I navigated to the online media sites, Cass began to fill me in on the situation. "The press is all over this, Alex, and the fans are not responding well." Cass's high heels clicking in the background told me she was headed somewhere fast.

"Whoever did this leaked *everything*," she continued. "Even your personal correspondence with your attorney, including what happened when you told Robby you wanted a divorce."

My hand flew to my mouth to cover the scream trying to force its way through my vocal cords. My eyes scanned the numerous headlines and articles that seemed to be populating by the minute. I clicked on a few of them and let my eyes wander down to the comments section.

"Alex! Did you hear me?" Cass was shouting into the phone again.

"Yes," I whispered. "Cass . . . no one knew about the divorce except for my attorney, Robby, and you."

My soft accusation hung between us. After a moment of silence, my friend Cass was back on the line, having set Cass the agent and publicist aside for a minute. "Alex, I would never betray you like that." Her words were quiet and laced with hurt. "I have never told a soul about the problems you and Robby were having or what happened afterward, and I never will."

I had only told Cass about the divorce because I'd known when it went public there would be a media storm. I had been branded, early in my career, as America's sweetheart. A good girl from a privileged upbringing who'd built everything she had by the sweat of her own brow. An author who always made time for her fans and tried to connect with them as authentically as possible.

But then Robby had died before the papers were filed. There had been no public record of our failed marriage, and I wanted it to stay that way. Not because of my celebrity status or what it might do to my career, but because I didn't want that ugliness to be how people remembered Robby and me as a couple. I wanted to let him rest in peace.

Finally, I said, "I believe you, Cass."

The sound of her heels clicking had ceased. Her voice no longer held slight tremors from her frantic pace. "Look, just don't go online, and put your phone out of sight while I deal with this."

"Too late," I said.

Trevor eased around the desk and looked over my shoulder at the string of vile comments running up the page like a ticker tape.

Looking down at my phone, I went into my text messages, wanting to bear the weight of their content while I had Cass on the line. Maybe I could draw on some of her unwavering strength.

I opened one text after the other. After reading the third one, I choked on a sob. Trevor placed a hand on my shoulder and squeezed.

Hearing the tears, Cass was once again concerned. "Talk to me, Alex."

I tried to take a breath to steady my voice, but the gasps and tears just kept coming. "They hate me, C-Cass."

"Who?"

"Everyone. Robby's family. Our f-friends. My parents." I wiped my face with the sleeve of my sweater. "They're all blaming me for what happened."

My shoulders continued to heave. My worst fears and everything I hated about myself were being validated by everyone who knew me and many who did not.

Cass sighed again. "Fuck them, Alex. They don't know shit, and you shouldn't care about what people like that think."

Rage slowly started to build beneath the pain and humiliation. She didn't get it. She didn't know what this was like. To have your face and your private business plastered all over the internet and television for the world to judge and condemn. This wasn't the first time this had happened to me, but it was the most brutal so far.

A new comment populated on the site I was monitoring: *What a disgusting human being. She pretends to be so broken up about her husband dying, but it was all for attention. She clearly didn't give a shit about him.*

Cass pressed further. "Just do as I said and stay off your phone and the internet. I'm about to head into a meeting with your publisher." Her heels were clicking again. "Between all of this negative media, the missed deadlines, the fact you *still* haven't submitted pages, and the way your fans are roasting you, I'm hanging on by my nails trying to convince them not to drop you once and for all."

Something inside me snapped, a dam of fury and fire breaking free, bent on total destruction. I picked up the phone and held it close to my mouth. In careful words delivered with medical precision, I spelled out how I felt about her predicament. "I don't give a *fuck* about the publisher *or* the fans."

Before she could respond, I punched the end button and threw the phone down on the desk.

I scrolled up to the images of the scanned documents that chronicled my private failures and deepest shame. As my own words jumped off the screen, taunting and tormenting, the rage that had fueled me to finally speak my mind a moment ago vanished. In its place, a chasm formed—cold and silent. To it, I willingly relinquished my life.

CHAPTER 22

Gabe

THE MOMENT I walked through Alex's front door, I could sense a heavy presence. The house was eerily still, the only movement coming from the particles of dust riding the sunbeams that lanced through the windows and patio doors. Movement in my peripheral had me turning toward the kitchen. One look at Trevor, his lips pressed into a thin line and his eyes weary, confirmed that something was off.

"Hey, partner," he said as he scraped a hand down his tired face.

I met him where the kitchen entrance and foyer met. "Why do you look like you just went ten rounds with a crazy ex?"

He huffed, the corner of his mouth curving up. "It's been a hell of a day. Have you been online at all?"

My eyebrows drew together. "Not except for trying to track down any trace of Hargrove. Why?"

Trevor looked over my shoulder toward Alex's bedroom. I twisted and saw that her door was shut.

"Whoever broke in here yesterday stole documents from her filing cabinet." His expression turned to stone. "Private documents that were never meant to be seen by anyone but Alex and her lawyer. They included divorce papers she'd given to her husband but never had the chance to file."

The air left my lungs. "Divorce papers? She was leaving him?"

Trevor nodded. "Since she never filed, the documents were never made public. He died shortly thereafter, and she kept their marital problems to herself, with the exception of her attorney and that piece-of-work publicist of hers. Now"—Trevor gripped the back of his neck and rotated his head like he was trying to work out some serious tension—"the media, her fans, and even her own family and friends are all roasting her."

I glanced at Alex's closed door once more. "How is she holding up?"

"Well, she's been locked in her room for the past six hours, and that was after she unleashed a can of whoop-ass on her publicist, who was busy scolding Alex on all of the ways she's fucking up her career."

I closed my eyes and dropped my head. Alex had already looked on the verge of breaking yesterday after finding her house invaded and that creepy-ass note on her bed. Before I could ask Trevor anything else, a click from down the hall told me Alex was emerging from her room.

Trevor straightened, and I turned so I was shoulder to shoulder with him, watching Alex shuffle down the hall. Her hair, usually gleaming and perfectly styled, looked as though she hadn't brushed it since yesterday. It was piled on top of her head, several tendrils falling from her bun, giving her the windswept appearance of someone who'd just completed a long run. Her face was free of makeup, her eyes puffy and red. And instead of tailored slacks and expensive high heels, she wore a pair of gray sweats that were easily two sizes too big, an oversized gray sweatshirt, and a pair of thick socks that scrunched at the top.

Despite her disheveled appearance, her beauty was still undeniable, but she didn't look like the Alex I had come to know. The most noticeable difference was her eyes. They no longer sparkled.

Alex trudged into the foyer and moved past us like a ghost,

seeming to not even register our presence. We followed her with our eyes as she proceeded through the living room and out the patio doors. Aderes ambled beside her, her lethargic movements matching the energy of her mistress.

When Alex reached the patio table, she pulled out a chair and turned it toward the woods before sitting down and drawing her knees to her chest, her arms wrapped around her shins. Aderes licked Alex's hand once and lay down on the deck beside the chair.

Trevor blew out a long breath. "I didn't know what to do. I don't know how to handle women when they're emotional." His voice rose until he sounded like he was on the verge of hysterics. Trevor was good with the ladies but only when he and they were looking for a little action. Anything deeper was completely out of his comfort zone.

I watched Alex for several moments, trying to figure out what she needed and how I could give it to her. Trevor cut into my thoughts before I came up with anything.

"You said you were working on tracking down Hargrove. How's that going?"

I snorted. "Let's just say I'd have better luck picking the winning lottery numbers."

Trevor chuckled. "That good, huh?"

"I'm working every angle I can think of, but with the resources at our disposal, it's slow going." I walked into the living room and stared out at Alex. "I put out a BOL yesterday before I went off duty. Hopefully we'll get a bite. One thing's for sure, this guy knows how to go to ground."

Trevor stretched, his voice rising as he arched his back and raised his arms overhead. "I'll keep working on it while you're on watch. Things are at a standstill with the Serpents right now anyway." He walked into the kitchen and began rinsing cups and placing them in the dishwasher. The low counter separating the kitchen and living room allowed us to continue our conversation.

"What do you mean?" I asked.

He shrugged. "Everything's been quiet. Jace hasn't had anything new to report, and the feds have resumed their tight-lip policy. For now, I'm just continuing to keep an eye on the kid."

That news made me nervous. Nothing was ever quiet where the Serpents were concerned. If anything, it was just the calm before the storm.

I hooked my thumbs on my duty belt and breathed in deeply, my cheeks puffing out as I exhaled my frustration. We had enough on our hands as it was. No sense wasting time coming up with the countless possibilities of what Dawson and his gang could be up to. The best we could do was continue to monitor the situation and stay close to Jace. Until then, there was a mahogany-haired beauty in need of some serious intervention.

I considered what I would do if I were in Alex's position and my whole life had turned into a firestorm in a matter of weeks. I'd be hitting the iron and punching bag until there wasn't an ounce of sweat or rage left in me. The idea of breaking a sweat reminded me that Alex had first made a report after she'd found that photo while she was out running.

"Hey, Trevor." I walked to the counter, placing my palms on the surface. "Alex likes to run, doesn't she?"

After loading the last of the dishes, he shut off the water and began drying his hands. "Yeah. She and I actually talked about that once. I asked her what she liked to do for fun, and she said reading and running." He smirked. "I teased her about being both a jock and a nerd. Just like a woman. They can never make up their minds."

I glanced over my shoulder at Alex, contemplating how she'd respond to a challenge right now. Deciding it was what she needed even if it wasn't what she *wanted*, I recruited Trevor for a special mission. "Can you run to the department and grab my gym bag from my locker?"

He looked like I had just taken a hard right when he thought we were going left. "Sure. Why? Are you gonna use your stinky socks as some kind of scent therapy to shock her back to life?"

I picked up a pad of paper from the counter and threw it at his head. He ducked to the side and straightened with a cocky grin.

"And I'm going to need you to hang around for a bit to keep Aderes company," I said. "You up for that?"

"You want me to babysit a dog?"

When I didn't answer and instead stared blankly at him, he shrugged. "All right. I'm always up for a good time." As he walked toward the door, under his breath, he added, "It'll probably be the best date I've had in months."

* * *

ALEX

THE AFTERNOON SUN glowed with the burnt orange of autumn leaves. I stared across my lawn to the Douglas firs that guarded the trails that had once been my solace and escape. The biting chill in the air barely registered against the numbness that had settled into every crevice of my soul. Soft snores rose from the slumbering husky beside me, her hind foot jerking every few seconds as though she was caught in a nightmare—or perhaps, just an extension of my own.

Hateful words in various accents and pitches rose and fell in my mind, one yielding to another in a never-ending carousel of vitriol. I now knew with absolute clarity what the world and those whom I had loved and trusted thought of me.

Interestingly, I discovered at some point in the past few hours that one really could shed all of their tears, leaving nothing behind save an empty well and only memories of emotion.

I was used up. Empty. Done.

A form moved into my periphery. I didn't bother to look up. Whomever it was, whatever they wanted, it didn't matter anymore.

Gabe moved in front of me. After pausing for the briefest of moments, he knelt down and placed his hands on either side of my chair, capturing me in the expanse of his arms.

I continued to study the tree line without truly noticing it.

"Alex." My name on his lips was soft and sweet like buttercream. More a whisper into the void than a statement of fact.

I didn't respond. I didn't have the energy to lower my eyes to his.

A rough hand settled on one of mine. His thumb caressed the ridges in the back of my hand, formed by the death grip I had on my knees as I pulled them closer to my chest. Maybe if I could make myself smaller, the world would forget about me, and I could just slip away into oblivion.

"Alex, look at me."

Gentle though it was, his words were a command nonetheless. One that my subconscious seemed content to obey. My eyes fell until I was swimming in irises so dark, I could see myself reflected in them. His gaze drew me in. Like a moth to a flame, I floated toward him, outside of my body where I was distanced from the pain.

"Alex, I want you to come with me." Gabe continued to stroke my hand, coaxing me back from the black hole. I wasn't sure if I wanted to let him, though. Moving toward Gabe meant feeling things. It meant letting the world in again. Opening myself up to everything that could hurt me.

The hole didn't feel good, but it also didn't hurt. It just was.

Gabe's other hand came down on my arm, his thumb working in the same gentle strokes. Warmth fluttered across my skin, currents of electricity close behind. The velvet of his voice, the tenderness in his eyes—it was hypnotic. I was caught in his spell, gliding toward him and powerless to stop it.

He slid his hands farther up my arms, gently tugging, enticing me to stand with him. I was on my feet without knowing how I'd gotten there, my forearms leaning into his chest. His hands held me steady.

"We're going for a run," he said, never ceasing with the gentle strokes, building friction between us that threatened to spark into wild flames.

He started maneuvering me toward the house, my feet his willing accomplice. "Go get dressed," he said. "I'll meet you back here in five minutes."

I glanced at Aderes, who was now sitting and watching us, her sweet head tilting from side to side as she looked between us, hanging on Gabe's soft timbre.

He shook his head. "Don't worry about your girl. Trevor's going to take good care of her while we're gone."

My eyes traveled back to his, searching his soul for answers to my questions. Did he think I was awful too? Why was he doing this? Why was he being so gentle with me? Was he really this kind, or was he fooling me too?

With one more nudge from Gabe toward the patio doors, my feet carried me to my room, my body following his orders without conscious thought.

When I reemerged on the deck, Gabe had his back to me, hands on his waist. The sunlight glinted off the spandex in his blue running shirt, the material clinging to every rise and fall of muscle in his strong arms and defined back. The garment moved with him like a second skin.

Gabe turned when he heard me approach. His eyes ran down my body, probably assessing if he was going to have to carry me back. I was dressed in black running pants, made to weather the cold, a long-sleeve fuchsia top and a puffy white vest.

"Do you have music to run with?" he asked.

I pulled my phone and earbuds from the pocket of my vest and held them up in answer.

He nodded and extended an arm toward the woods. "Let's go." When we stepped onto the trail that bordered my property and fed deeper into the mountainside, Gabe stopped and faced me. "Here's the deal. You put your music on and run as far and as fast as you want. Don't worry about anything else. I've got your back, and I'll be with you every step of the way. Okay?"

I almost couldn't comprehend what he was saying. No one had let me run since this whole protection detail had started. Was he really going to just let me take off into the woods like I didn't have a care in the world?

The look in his eyes told me that was exactly what he was saying. Gabe was giving me my trails. My freedom. And he was going to keep me safe while I tried to silence the storm.

I nodded once, then turned to face the path unfolding before me. The rise and fall and turns in the terrain kept me from seeing everything that was ahead. But with Gabe beside me, somehow knowing everything that was to come wasn't so necessary.

I took a step forward and leaned into it, my heel digging into the soft earth as my other foot glided forward and fell with even greater purpose. Soon, I was sprinting through the dim woods, trees flying past me like images I refused to gaze upon. The beat of drums coming from my earbuds crescendoed as I crested another hill, and with every surge forward, my heart thumped harder, and my worries became lighter.

Scared, at first, to run through the precious woods my stalker had turned into a living, breathing night terror, I glanced over my shoulder every so often to ensure Gabe was still there. He was. Every time.

His eyes were always scanning, his posture tall and his form formidable. He kept pace with me easily, and when I looked back once more, he captured my gaze and gifted me with the warmest smile I'd received in a very long time. After that, I no longer needed to look back. I knew he was there, and I knew he was doing this for no other reason than to give me support where I otherwise had none.

We ran for about an hour before I finally turned back. Like mine, Gabe's shirt was soaked through, but his breathing was still steady. When we were about a half mile from the house, I slowed to a walk so we'd have enough time to cool down properly.

Gabe drew up alongside me, and I tugged the earbuds free, placing them back in my pocket. Panting, I placed my hands on my hips and took a couple of deep breaths.

Gabe was still surveying our surroundings, his hawklike gaze zeroing in on every creature that scurried and every branch that creaked.

I stopped for a minute and turned to him. His brow furrowed as he mirrored my body.

"Gabe . . ." I looked deeply into the eyes of the man I had once considered an enemy. "I—" Why was this so hard?

He waited patiently for me to find the words.

"Thank you," I finally managed, nodding my head to emphasize the overwhelming gratitude I felt toward him.

An easy smile broke across his face. "You're welcome, Alex."

We resumed our walk. I closed my eyes and lifted my nose in the air, drawing in the rich scent of damp earth. We were covered in shadows, the large branches of giant evergreens reaching overhead to cocoon us in a magical space while cool air caressed my face.

This moment, alone with Gabe, was serene—even blissful. Though I couldn't fully explain it, I felt safer with him than anyone else. Not just physically, but emotionally. And that feeling beckoned to something inside of me, compelling me to lay my vulnerabilities bare before him.

"I didn't want anybody to know about the divorce," I said. I kept my eyes straight ahead, but I could sense Gabe hanging on my words. "I'm a very private person," I continued. "And I *love* what I do. I'm so grateful for every publisher and every fan who has made my dream possible."

I fisted my hands in my pockets and watched my feet, focusing on each step. "But I hate how much it forced me into the public eye. All of the parties and elbow rubbing. Never being able to go anywhere without wearing designer clothes and a full face of makeup." I shook my head, unable to find exactly the right words to express how much I hated that part of my career. "In a lot of ways, once I became truly successful, it felt like my life was no longer my own."

Gabe listened silently. When I went quiet, he looked over at me, his open expression and silence encouraging me to continue.

I took a deep breath and released it slowly. "I just didn't want anyone knowing about the divorce yet. I knew they would find out eventually, but I wanted me and Robby to have time to process it and figure out how we were going to move forward without all of the complications that come with getting other people involved. Then"—I ran my hand over the top of my head, smoothing my hair down—"after he died, it just didn't seem right to taint his memory with something that negative. Especially when it didn't even matter anymore."

We fell into silence, our footfalls on the damp pine needles and shifting dirt the only thing penetrating the muted woods.

Finally, Gabe spoke. "I can appreciate what it's like having a bunch of people in your business who don't belong there." His eyes were fixed in the distance, his jaw flexing.

"Liz told me about Olivia," I quietly confessed.

The corners of Gabe's eyes crinkled, and a grin slid up his face. "See?" he said, turning his face to mine.

I laughed. A full-on, heartfelt belly laugh. I couldn't believe I had actually *laughed.*

Gabe ran a hand along his day-old scruff. It was the first time I'd seen him not clean-shaven. Honestly, he could have glued cotton balls to his face, and he'd still be the most handsome man in Eden Falls—and beyond.

"The truth is, Olivia and I should have never been together. We had different values." Gabe raked his eyes across the landscape. "Trevor and Liz, even my own parents, tried to warn me against her. But I was too ignorant to listen."

"Loyal, is the way Liz tells it."

He laughed. "Yeah, one of my biggest supporters, that sister of mine."

My heart ached for the love Gabe's family shared. Anyone need only glance at them to see it.

"I wasn't upset because Olivia left," he continued. "I was furious because of the *way* she left. She ensured the whole town would be talking about it for a long time. Every time I walked into a store, or patrolled my beat on foot, I had people stopping me to tell me what they thought of the situation. Conversation stopped when I entered a room. Whispers followed me when I left."

Gabe stopped walking and squared his body to mine. Face-to-face in the naked woods, our regrets and shame given shape and voice, I saw a fractured soul and shredded heart that mirrored my own.

"It sucks, Alex. There's no way around it. People are nosy and much more interested in pointing out what's wrong with everyone else's life than fixing what's wrong with their own. But just because someone else holds an opinion doesn't make it true. Only *you* know what lies in your heart. Only *you* know all of the facts of what went on between you and your husband. Your reality is no one else's right to judge."

The conviction in his declaration captured the air from my lungs. My eyes searched the face of my most unexpected supporter. Who would have thought this tough, handsome, complicated man would have turned out to be the *one* person who actually understood?

Gabe jerked his head toward the house, which was now visible through the tree line. "Let's get you back before the sun sets and we freeze out here."

I smiled and picked my way over some fallen limbs. A chime coming from Gabe's pocket had me glancing over my shoulder at him. His steps faltered for a moment as he looked down at his phone, his easy-going energy of a moment ago replaced by something coiled and dangerous.

My smile fell. "Is everything okay?"

He looked up and returned his phone to his pocket, nodding, though his lips were pressed into a firm line.

Gabe continued walking, placing a hand on my lower back as he drew even with me, gently urging me forward. The tension emanating from him was so palpable, I dared not press the issue. But one thing was certain. There was menace swimming in his dark eyes, and someone was going to pay for it.

CHAPTER 23

Gabe

THE GRAY CLOUDS hanging low and dark in the sky matched my mood as I drove toward town. It had been two weeks since we'd placed the protection detail on Alex, and we were no closer to catching the asshole who was terrorizing her than we had been on day one. The crime scene techs hadn't even been able to pull so much as one clean print after all of the hours they'd spent combing through Alex's house after that damned letter had been left on her bed.

Add to that the text I'd received from Jace yesterday when Alex and I were headed back from our run, and I was pretty much feeling like a complete waste of space. Alex's case was supposed to be open and shut, an easy whodunnit. Now, here we were with zero leads on one case and a kid hanging with his ass in the wind on another. Working both cases had proven a lot more challenging than Trevor and I had first imagined. We were burning the candle at both ends and still managing to come up short.

Between me, Trevor, and Quinn, someone was always on the hunt for Hargrove. From everything Alex had told me about him, he didn't seem the subtle type. Whether or not he was capable of pulling off the perfect crime and leaving not a trace of evidence, it didn't jibe with his MO. He was arrogant and boastful, not patient and calculating. He hadn't bothered trying to clean up after himself before because he'd *wanted* Alex to know every move he made.

Still, I couldn't write the guy off. His prior fixation on Alex and the timing of his metaphorical jailbreak was just too coincidental. Maybe he was changing things up this time. His strategy the first time around clearly hadn't worked, and this time he was a fugitive who didn't have the luxury of moving around quite so freely.

Coming to a stop at one of the few traffic lights in Eden Falls, my turn signal clicking like the second hand on an old-fashioned stopwatch, I turned the situation over in my mind. The memory of Alex curled up in her deck chair, her eyes and face puffy, came rushing to the surface, and my stomach tightened. We needed to close this case, and fast. I was doing everything in my power to help her hold it together, but this stalker was dismantling her life one attack at a time, and so far, I had proven completely inadequate in stopping him.

It was looking more and more like the only way we were going to end this assault on Alex and refocus our attention on the Serpents was to catch this guy in the act. Until then, Hargrove was our only real lead. The only way to move forward at this point was to find a way to either prove or disprove that he was behind the whole thing.

The traffic light turned green, and I made a left onto Main, heading for Grind. I did my best to shake thoughts of Alex and Hargrove from my mind so I could focus on my immediate goal. The last thing I wanted was to compromise Jace's undercover status because I had my head up my ass.

I surveyed the streets as I drove through the business center of town, glancing at every face that passed. Cars lined both sides of the thoroughfare, forcing me to drive slowly in case a pedestrian popped out in front of me.

So far, the clouds had resisted dropping the deluge hanging in their bellies, but their low coverage kept Eden Falls much warmer than I'd expected. I'd chosen to wear a black long-sleeve Henley, believing the weatherman when he'd said it would be breezy and wet. I shoved my sleeves up, baring my forearms, as I canvassed the street for a place to park.

Just as I was about to pull into an empty space in front of the coffee shop, two men on bikes caught my eye, their Satan's Serpents cuts hard to miss. I hit the gas and continued down the street past both the coffee shop and the Serpents. Pulling out my phone, I punched Trevor's contact and waited for him to pick up as I drove around the block.

Trevor's voice came on the line, bright and lilting. "You've reached Stephanie at one-eight-hundred-spank-you. How may I direct your call?"

"We've got a situation." My tone brought Trevor to attention.

"I'm almost to Grind," he said, all humor gone from his voice. "You need lights and sirens?"

"No, but there are two Serpents parked on Main, a half block west of Grind."

Trevor breathed a curse. "Did they see you?"

"No. I drove past as soon as I spotted them. They were busy shooting the shit and trying to look tough."

"I think it's time for the welcoming committee to pay them a little visit."

Having circled the block, I parked on a side road where I could just barely see the two bikers across the street and to my left. I was on the same side of Main as Grind but far enough down that I'd have to travel behind a separate strip of shops to reach the coffee shop.

"I'm parked on First. When you get here, keep them busy long enough for me to slip into the alley."

"Copy that."

A minute later, Trevor's black-and-white pulled behind the two bikes. I waited as he unfolded his long body from the low car, his hair glowing like gold in the overcast light. Trevor walked around the rear of his car and approached the men from the side-walk, drawing their attention away from me.

Slipping out of the truck, I darted to the back of the long building housing several small shops. Jogging past a series of dumpsters and dodging a door that was thrown open in front of me with barely enough time to swerve, I reached the end of the building and glanced around the corner. Another side street and a quaint square decorated with a fountain and small tables stood between me and Grind.

There were very few people on foot today. Apparently, they had all believed the weatherman too. Having so few people out and about made it easier to assess if there was anyone around who I wouldn't want to see me slipping in the back door of Grind, but it also meant it was harder for me to go unnoticed.

After scanning the parked cars for occupants and finding none, I jogged across the street and through the square. Once I was inside Grind, I shot Jace a text, simply writing *Here*. Not two minutes later, he was standing in front of me, anxiously wiping his hands down his apron. His sable eyes and matching hair were stark against the pallor of his skin.

I ran my gaze over him, my eyebrows drawing together as I read his body language. "What's going on, Jace? Do we need to pull you out?"

Jace shook his head, his eyes darting to the front of the shop.

"There are two Serpents parked half a block away," I said. "We need to keep this brief so I can slip out of here without them seeing me."

He brought his attention back to me. He looked so riled up, if I didn't know him, I would have suspected he'd taken narcotics.

"They've got something *big* in the works," Jace said. "Somehow they found out the Reapers are running protection on an arms shipment." Jace raked a shaky hand through his hair, the tattoo on his bicep peeking out from beneath the sleeve of his white T-shirt.

"Why would they care about something like that?" I asked.

"Dawson's obsessed with gaining more power. He's planning an ambush on the Reapers. He's convinced that if he takes them down by proving they can't handle their shit, the Serpents can steal all of their business."

The Reapers were a motorcycle club that dominated most of the territory along the northern Montana border. If Dawson managed to take them out of the game, he'd have control over the entire northern half of the state. As far as I knew, Dawson and the Serpents had only been involved in drug running and minor prostitution so far. If he was planning an ambush on a gang running munitions, clearly he was looking to level up.

Jace turned his head to glance toward the front of the shop again.

"Is there something else going on?" I asked. "You look like you're about to shed your skin."

He combed his hair back again. "I found out how they keep making all these CIs."

My eyebrows shot up.

"Dawson is paying spies. People who have no ties to the club." Jace leaned in closer, his voice barely audible. "It could be anyone. So just because you don't see a Serpent around doesn't mean Dawson doesn't have a set of eyes on you."

I ran my hand across my mouth, mentally flipping through all of the possible implications of the ticking bomb that had just been dropped in my lap. Dawson was more clever than I'd given him credit for. No wonder he had always been able to weed out the informants so fast.

I placed a hand on Jace's shoulder and squeezed. "We're going to have to figure out some other way to meet up. Until then, only contact Trevor or me if you absolutely have to."

Jace nodded.

"When and where is this ambush on the Reapers supposed to take place?"

"I'm not sure." He scraped his thumbnail across the white

scar above his eyebrow, the way he always did when he was stressed. "Soon, though, from the sounds of it."

I pressed my lips together and gave a curt nod. "You did good, Jace. This could be the break we've been waiting for."

Jace's tight smile conveyed how much this situation was wearing on him. I hated that because of Alex's stalker, we hadn't been able to monitor the Serpents more closely and rattle their cage a bit. Though we'd managed to keep a pretty close eye on Jace, we hadn't made any movement in the case. The longer we waited to act, the more danger he was in.

"You'd better get back up front. Remember"—I squeezed his shoulder again—"don't contact us unless it's critical. Lie low while we figure out what to do with this information."

I watched Jace as he hurried away and then pulled my sunglasses from the top of my head. I stepped into the alley before I had my shades in place, and I rounded the corner of the building just as the two Serpents Trevor had been detaining drove by—one of them looking right at me.

CHAPTER 24

Gabe

I QUICKLY RETREATED to the shadows, my back pressed against the cool brick wall.

Fuck! What the hell had I been thinking stepping out into the open like that without checking my surroundings first?

I *wasn't* thinking. That was the problem. I'd become distracted lately, and I was losing my edge. Still pissed at myself, I pulled my cell out and called Trevor. Glancing around the corner of the building and seeing that the street was once again clear, I crossed the square and headed back to my truck the same way I'd come.

Trevor answered without preamble. "Where are you?"

"Almost back to my truck." Stepping around a small puddle that might well have been piss, judging from the smell of the alley, I added, "I might have been made."

Trevor expelled an exasperated breath but didn't say anything.

"I fucked up leaving Grind. I stepped into the square without clearing it first. Our two buddies were riding by and one of them looked in my direction."

"Shit. I held them as long as I could, but they got antsy, and I didn't have PC to detain them." There was a muffled sound as Trevor shifted his phone. "Did he recognize you?"

"I don't know. I'm not even sure if he saw me. His shades were on, and I was barely out of the shadows. He didn't show any reaction, but still—"

"Yeah. If they were there because they suspect Jace of turning, they wouldn't have risked giving anything away."

Reaching my truck, I climbed inside and started the engine, allowing the cool air from the vents to wash over me. Trevor was still parked dead ahead, perpendicular to the street where I was parked. He was leaning against the trunk of his cruiser, one arm crossed over his chest and his legs crossed at the ankle, looking like he was carrying on some boring conversation.

"There's more."

"Of course there is." Trevor looked directly at me, though to anyone watching, it would appear he was simply taking in his surroundings. "What? You decided we needed to add a little fucked-up to an already fucked-up situation?"

After I filled Trevor in on the details of my conversation with Jace, we both agreed that it was time to start making arrangements to get Jace out.

I checked my watch, noting that it was time to get going if I was going to relieve Carlson on time. "Since you're taking over Alex's detail from me in the morning, why don't we spend some time before she wakes up working out how we're going to run the sting on that ambush."

"Sounds like a plan." Trevor drew his aviators down his nose and looked over the top of them at me. "Enjoy your night," he sang.

I tried to fight the grin spreading across my face, but it was no use. Trevor's laugh was the last thing I heard as I hung up and turned my truck toward Alex's house. Maybe I wasn't ready to admit it to anyone else, and I was barely admitting it to myself, but I had been waiting all day to make this drive. Once I was on the open road, I hit the gas, accelerating toward a pair of emerald-green eyes and lips that could make a preacher sin.

* * *

ALEX

BUTTERFLIES SWIRLED in my stomach with such force I thought I might actually vomit. Any moment now, the rumble of Gabe's truck would fill the quiet void of my driveway, signaling that it was time. I sat at my desk, staring at the blank screen of my brand-new laptop, my hands on my thighs, gripped tightly together. I couldn't stop questioning what I was about to do, and yet, there wasn't a doubt in my mind that it was what *needed* to happen.

A forceful breath traveled from my lips, causing the hair that framed my face to flutter. Rising from my desk, I walked to the picture window. I shoved my hands in the pockets of my jeans and stared out at the low fog that had rolled in during the past hour. The opaque mist clung to the dull grass and danced exotically around the trunks of naked trees.

Winter was bearing down, the cold, gray days matching my internal reality. A solitary ray of golden sunshine from the sinking flame broke through the cloud coverage, painting everything it touched in a gilded glow. A smile touched my lips as I likened Gabe to that ray of warmth. Just like the sunbeam on a blustery day, he had broken through the depression and despair enshrouding my soul. He had been the one touch of warmth that beckoned me from the edge.

The weight and stress of these past two weeks, on top of the many layers that had piled over the past two years, had become too much. I couldn't continue like this if I had any desire to salvage what was left of my life and my career. That realization had come shortly after Gabe and I had returned from our run yesterday, and I'd spent the better part of the night staring up at my ceiling, trying to decide what to do about it.

Thinking back to what Gabe had said about my reality not being anyone's right to judge had forced me to look at how I had spent my entire life hiding my true self for fear of what people would think. And it had forced me to admit that I was afraid to tell the truth because of what happened when I'd last tried.

But it was time to unbury my secrets, to bring the shadows into light. And Gabe was the one I wanted to confess to. He was the only person who had supported me through two of the worst weeks of my life without anything to gain in return.

I pulled the edges of my cream sweater together, wrapping them tightly around me. The darkness was descending with haste, my anxiety growing with each deepening shade of twilight. The penetrating silence was part of what I had loved about this house when I'd first seen it. But now, it brought into sharp focus how very alone and alienated I was. Part of that had been my own doing. When I'd moved to Eden Falls, I had done so with the sole purpose of cutting off contact with everyone in my life except Cass.

At the time, it was the only way I felt I could escape and reclaim the part of me that was true. The part that I had tucked away and pretended didn't exist. Every relationship Robby and I had shared—all of our friends and family—had been superficial and destructive. Each one of them obsessed with status, money, and prestige. I was just so damn tired of playing a part in it all. And I'd been doing the same thing with Robby. Playing a part.

I had finally woken up one day, tired and depressed, taken a look around at the big house, the expensive clothes, all of the status symbols, and admitted the fact that my husband and I didn't love each other.

I would never forget the feel of the plush white carpet against my bare feet, the silk of my nightdress against my skin, as I stood in our massive bedroom, alone, realizing that the only truth in my life was my writing, and it was slipping away like water through my fingers.

The growl of Gabe's engine drifted through the open door of my office, my hands turned cold, and my breath grew shallow as I steeled myself for what I was about to do.

It's time to stop hiding from this.

I turned from the window and headed for the entryway of my house. Officer Carlson plucked his jacket from the back of a kitchen chair and draped it over his arm. He offered a tight-lipped smile as he saw me approach and nodded once before heading for the door. He hadn't exactly warmed to me, but he was no longer hostile either. At this point, I'd consider that a win.

From my front window, I saw Gabe come around the hood of his truck, and my stomach lurched again. His long strides were relaxed, but there was something in the way he carried himself that conveyed a lethal edge. It was hard not to admire his physique, especially when he was dressed down like he was today. His dark-wash blue jeans hugged his butt and the thick muscles of his thighs. He had the buttons undone on his Henley shirt and the sleeves pushed up his forearms. It was just enough skin to make my imagination want to fill in the rest.

But what really halted my breath was the complicated story written in the depths of those chocolate eyes. They told the tale of a man who loved deeply and bled for the people and things he believed in. A man who had given his heart and loyalty to a woman who didn't deserve it. And they told of a man who yearned for something he dared never to hope for again.

I knew that story well.

And with one look at the man who had seen me breaking and refused to let the pieces fall, I knew I was putting my faith in the only person I could. Gabe might think me a monster after he heard what I was about to tell him. Perhaps he would withdraw the only support I had left.

Nausea rolled through me like waves on a violent sea at the thought. But I had been carrying too many secrets, too many shadows, for far too long. That was going to change tonight.

CHAPTER 25

Alex

GABE WALKED through my front door, his eyes sweeping the house and halting when they landed on me. His gaze locked on mine, and I smiled, suddenly self-conscious. The corners of his eyes crinkled with only a whisper of a smile on his own lips, and that was enough to turn the hurricane in my stomach into a summer breeze.

"Hi," I said, hands in my pockets, walking toward him.

"Hi." Gabe closed the door and met me where the foyer, the hall, and the living room met. He glanced at the patio doors. "There's a storm coming in. How do you feel about a fire?"

I inhaled deeply through my nose, allowing fresh air to fill my lungs until it felt like they might burst. "That would be nice. I'll put some coffee on."

Grateful for something to keep me busy while I tried to figure out a way to start this conversation, I moved into the kitchen. Every once in a while, I glanced at Gabe. He was seated on the rock hearth, getting the kindling to catch. The amber glow from the flames illuminated his features, emphasizing the sharp contours of his square jaw and straight nose.

"How was your day?" he asked, turning his body so he could look at me over the long counter separating our two spaces.

I scooped heaping tablespoons of dark grounds into a filter, relishing the rich scent of the bold roast. "It was fine, thanks. How was yours?"

Gabe nodded, then looked over his shoulder to check the flames. "Uneventful." He grabbed a few logs from the metal box beside the hearth and threw them on the burgeoning fire. "Did you get any writing done today?" He brushed his hands against each other and came to stand at the counter.

After pouring the water into the coffee maker, I hit the brew button and moved to stand in front of Gabe, with only the counter between us. "No." I wrapped my arms around my middle and cast my eyes to the sparks shooting up from the crackling wood. "I've never had this much trouble putting words on paper."

Gabe stared at me for a long moment. I grew uneasy, wondering what he was able to see with that penetrating gaze of his. Finally, in a gentle timbre, he said, "It'll come, Alex. When it's meant to . . . it'll come."

I drew my focus back to him, trying to commit to memory every line, every scar. All the little nuances that made up the whole.

Gabe was so different from anyone I'd ever known. He was *real*. Even though his directness had injured my fragile ego in the beginning, there was comfort in knowing that he was always truthful. Even if the truth wasn't pleasant.

He stood there, allowing me to study him, his body language showing he was comfortable. Relaxed. Like he was an open book and had no fear of anything I might see or judgment I might pass. Lord, what would it be like to have that kind of self-assurance?

Taking another calming breath, I said the words I'd been putting off since he'd first walked through the door tonight. "Gabe, there's something I'd like to tell you." I chewed my lip and dropped my eyes to the counter. Then, deciding I was done being a coward, I squared my shoulders and looked him in the eye. "It's not something that's easy to talk about, but I feel the need to explain some things. Would that be all right?"

One nod and an open expression was my answer.

We moved to the couch. It wasn't a long couch. Big enough for two adults to sit comfortably. Gabe took one end, draping an arm over the back of the couch, his knees falling open in that relaxed way of his. I took the other end, pulling one knee into my chest and tucking my other leg beneath me.

I cleared my throat. "I'm not really sure where to start."

"The beginning is usually best."

I managed a nervous chuckle. "Right." Tucking a lock of hair behind my ear, I stared off into the red-and-orange flames, trying to figure out where the beginning was. "Well, I guess I should start by telling you a little about my family and upbringing."

The sound of rain tapping the glass on the patio doors and windows accompanied me as I unfolded the ugly details of my past, laying them out, one by one, for Gabe to witness.

"I was raised in a very wealthy, prominent family," I said. "As a result, I had a lot of opportunities growing up, but it was also a severe environment. A lot was expected of me, and there was no affection. Cold praise when I did well. Harsh criticism when I fell short."

I glanced at Gabe to gauge his reaction. His expression was as stoic as ever, so I pressed on.

"I grew up with Robby. Our families traveled in the same social circles, and we had become good friends. When I was fifteen, we started dating. Our parents were elated." Noticing I was wringing my hands to the point of turning my fingers white, I wrapped my arms around my knee and forced them to stay put.

"Robby and I dated all through high school and most of college. We enjoyed each other's company, but I often found myself asking if that was enough." I shrugged. "I just always thought there should be something more, but at the same time, my parents had never regarded each other with anything more than indifference. They acted more like business partners. So, I questioned if maybe I held an unrealistic notion of what love should look and feel like because of all the books and love stories I had devoured growing up."

Unable to hold still, my fingers dropped to the hem of my pant leg and fiddled with a loose thread. I took a deep breath and forced myself to keep going, knowing that if I stopped, I might lose the strength to finish. "I figured the only way to find out was to broaden my horizons, so I told Robby I wanted to see other people. And for a little while, I did. But he and my parents never accepted the breakup, and I felt horrible for hurting him. So"—my shoulders caved in, and my voice began to tremble—"in the end, I was weak. I caved under their constant pressure to reconcile, and I went back to what was comfortable and familiar."

I raised my eyes to Gabe and forced more air from my lungs in an effort to remove the tremor from my voice. "After we graduated, the next logical step was to get married. Robby wanted it. I wasn't so sure. But our parents pushed hard for the union. So that's what we did."

Gabe's expression hadn't changed in the slightest. He was listening with the same intensity that he approached everything else. I had his undivided attention, which made me feel both nervous and cared for.

My voice dropped to a whisper as I struggled to say aloud the truth that had been written on my heart for so many years but that I had been unable to bring into the light of day. "The truth is, Robby and I were never in love. We were together because we made each other look good, and by extension, we made our parents look good. We both graduated top of our class from every educational institution we'd ever attended. We had successful careers, and all of our friends were the 'right' sort of people. From the moment we were thrust together at the various country club functions and ever-revolving elitist parties, we had become Robby and Alex, the power couple. By the time we married, we had played the part for so long, we just continued to fill our respective roles."

I cringed inwardly. I hadn't even gotten to the worst part yet, and already, I felt a thousand fissures erupt across my resolve. Gabe must have sensed it, because he removed his hand from the back of the couch and put his arm around my shoulders. The tenderness of the act surprised me. And maybe that was what knocked me off-balance enough to keep going.

Drawing strength from his touch, the graze of his fingers brushing back and forth across the top of my shoulder, I pushed through the discomfort clawing at the walls of my stomach. "The night that Robby died, I told him I wanted a divorce. I was miserable, and I couldn't pretend any longer." I looked deep into Gabe's eyes, praying he could see my honesty—that he would believe me. "I *did* love Robby. We had been friends before we were anything more. I didn't want to hurt him, but I truly believed we would each be happier if we could just be honest with ourselves and with each other and stop living that *lie*."

A tear leaked out of the corner of my eye and rolled gently down my cheek. I swiped it away and kept going, determined to purge my sins. "Robby was furious. He accused me of wanting another man. He told me our families would be crushed and that I was destroying everything we had worked for. He said I was being selfish. Then, when that didn't get me to change my mind, he started begging me. He got down on his knees and wrapped his arms around my waist. He was crying, and he just kept asking me not to do it."

My own tears were escaping one right after the other, matching the relentless drops of rain streaking down the windows. Gabe leaned away and grabbed the box of Kleenex sitting on the end table. He passed it to me and then put his arm around my shoulders again. I took a moment to breathe and regain my composure. This was it. The moment I had been dreading most. The mark I'd been carrying on my soul for the past year.

My eyes found Gabe's, and I refused to look away as I made my confession. "For the first time in my life, I was being honest about how I felt and what I wanted. I told myself I couldn't give in to Robby's demands, or anyone else's, if I was ever going to be free of the cage that had been built around me. The cage I had voluntarily remained within. So, I knelt down in front of him and told him I wasn't going to change my mind and that one day he would see that it was for the best."

My voice climbed in pitch as my words tumbled out, keeping pace with the tears that had turned into a steady stream. "He stopped crying and looked at me like he didn't recognize me. Then his features contorted into this mask of rage. He stood and went for the door, and I ran after him. I grabbed his arm and begged him to stay and talk to me. But he threw me off, grabbed his keys off the table by the door, and left. That was the last time I saw him alive."

I hiccupped and dabbed at the tears clinging to my eyelashes. "The police arrived on our doorstep at four the next morning and informed me Robby had been drinking, lost control of his car, and hit a telephone pole. They said his death was instant."

My breaths were coming in ragged sobs, and I fought to bring them under control. Uncurling my legs, I placed my feet on the floor and propped my elbows on my knees, burying my face in my hands. "Robby never got that drunk. And when he did drink, he didn't drive. He died because I pushed him over the edge. Because I wanted something deeper than what we had, I broke his heart and sent him to his grave." My body shook with the force of my pain, my words thick with emotion.

Gabe was quiet for a long while, and I was sure he was thinking all of the horrible things I was thinking about myself. But when a warm hand landed on my back and began drawing soothing circles, I dared to glance at him. Gabe's eyebrows were drawn down, matching his frown.

"Alex, come here." Gabe gently gripped my shoulders and eased me back until I sunk into the couch. He turned his body so he was facing me. "You are not responsible for other people's decisions, Alex. You showed Robby respect by being honest with him, rather than stringing him along or running around on him behind his back, making him out to be the fool."

Gabe gathered my hair from around my face and pushed it over my shoulders so that it fell down my back. "*He* chose to go out and get drunk and then drive that night. *You* did not force that on him. Shut out all of the other voices, Alex. They don't matter. You were trying to give Robby and yourself a chance to actually be happy. You never set out to hurt him, and that's the difference."

Relief that Gabe didn't think I was a monster battled against the guilt I'd been holding on to since Robby's death. But I could feel a small and vulnerable ray of light starting to peek through the gray clouds.

"You've got to stand up for yourself, Alex." Gabe scooted closer and placed his hand on my thigh. "Quit letting people silence your voice. The reason you feel so beat up right now is because you're taking punches without throwing any of your own. So get in that arena and start swinging."

Thunder roared overhead; the rain was falling in sheets of violent symphony. And from somewhere deep inside, I felt the rise of a battle cry. Gabe's words suffused my blood with a warrior's call, and I could feel the courage to fight growing like a timid bud through the last of winter's snow. I wanted to fight it all. The guilt. The shame. The stalker who had terrorized my mind and violated the only space that felt safe. I wanted to fight my family. The public. And the media. I was *done* trying to please people who wouldn't even care if I fell off the face of the earth except to enjoy the salacious gossip it would provide.

Something in Gabe's eyes flared, and I found myself falling into their depths. He lifted his hand from my leg and placed it on my cheek. With his thumb, he wiped away a tear I didn't even realize had lingered. Leaning into him, I laced my arms around his neck and held him tight, inhaling deeply. I relished the warmth of his cheek against mine. The strength of his arms banded around me. The woodsy scent of his aftershave. The beat of his strong heart against my own.

I pulled back just enough to be able to look into his eyes, our noses almost touching. His hands slid down my back until they reached my waist, his fingertips pressing into my skin ever so slightly. Our breathing became shallow pants that mingled and intertwined until they became one.

As the weight of the pain that had been my constant companion for so long began to lessen, one thought echoed through my mind as a whisper.

I want this man.

I need this man.

I needed him to wrap me in his embrace and hold me close. I needed him to make the world disappear, if only for a little while.

Another thought bubbled up from the hell I'd been living, threatening to ruin the first breath of air I had breathed in a long time. *It's a betrayal to Robby. He's lying in a grave. I don't deserve something this good.*

But what if Gabe was right? It was true that I hadn't forced Robby to go out and drink and drive that night. The opposite. I had wanted so badly for things to remain amicable between us, but he hadn't been willing to stay and work through it with me.

As my warring thoughts pulled me further and further out of the bubble I was in with Gabe, he slid his body closer to mine, wrapped an arm around my lower back and pulled me into him as though he could tell I was slipping, and he wasn't going to let me fall.

Gabe lowered his face to mine. Slowly, at first, giving me every opportunity to pull away. When I didn't, he covered my mouth with his own, his lips firm in the taking but gentle in the delivery. I pressed into him, trying to erase every bit of space between us. My lips matched his push and pull, and as our mouths melted together, Gabe deepened the kiss. When his tongue slid against mine, he drew a moan from me, almost without my awareness. I wanted more. I wanted to stay locked in this moment forever. The building ecstasy. The safety of Gabe's arms. The rain falling, and the fire crackling.

For the first time in my life, I turned my mind off and yielded to what *felt* right.

CHAPTER 26

Alex

GABE BROKE THE KISS, and as he pulled back, the sense of emptiness began to return. I opened my eyes to search his. He answered my unspoken question with a small smile as he gripped my hand and pulled me from the couch. Without a word, he drew me behind him and led the way to my bedroom.

My eyes roamed over his broad shoulders, relishing the way his shirt clung to the contours of his back, and down to his narrow waist. He carried himself with so much confidence and ease, as though he had nothing in the world to prove and every reason to believe he could handle whatever came his way.

When we reached the bedroom, Gabe left the door open just enough that the light from the living room allowed us to see each other in soft shadow. Drawing me into his arms, he pulled me firmly against his chest. My arms wound around his waist, and I kept my eyes locked on his as he traced his hand up my body and slid it beneath my hair to gently grip my neck.

The feel of his calloused hands on my skin sent a ripple through every inch of my body. When he eased toward me and lowered his lips to mine once more, I rose up on my toes to meet him, anxious for another taste. The stroke of his tongue was slow and indulgent. His lips moved against mine with a strength and rhythm that made my core pulse in want of more.

Gabe used his body to nudge me backward, slowly walking us to the bed. When the mattress hit the back of my thighs, he broke the kiss but held my gaze with such intensity that the butterflies returned to my stomach with the force of a gale wind. His fingers moved to my shoulders and slipped beneath the edges of my sweater, slowly sliding the garment over my skin until it fluttered to the floor.

A boldness I had never experienced before swept through me, driven by the growing need to feel Gabe inside of me, to bring him close and savor the tenderness and affection he offered. My fingers fumbled with the hem of his shirt and grazed his smooth skin as I pushed it up his body and over his head.

Dark ink along the edge of his bicep drew my gaze to his arm as my fingers traced the outline of a breathtaking piece of art. Various shades of black and gray swirled together to form a globe with an anchor behind it and a bald eagle sitting on top with his wings spread. On a banner that wrapped around the entire image were the words *Semper Fidelis*.

My fingers continued to graze the tattoo, and when I lifted my eyes to Gabe, he was watching me, patiently allowing me to canvass his body. My frame melted into him, my chest rising and falling with increasing frequency as my breaths grew shallow with desire. I was nowhere near as controlled as he was. His body was still, his breaths even, but the heat burning in his eyes left no doubt that he wanted this as much as I did.

Gabe's hands slipped beneath my tank top and molded to my body, skimming every curve from my hips to my shoulders, dragging my shirt higher and higher until I was free of it. Then he gripped me by the waist and lifted me onto the bed as if I weighed no more than a bird. He nudged my legs open and stepped between them, capturing my mouth as his hands cradled my jaw. Every move he made was an intoxicating contradiction. His actions smooth and unhurried but with an underlying hunger, as though he was holding himself back from something he wanted to devour.

Another moan traveled past my lips, and he drank it in as his hands roamed my back. He found the clasp of my bra, and with one flick, the elastic gave way, and the straps fell down my shoulders a bit. Gabe pulled back just enough to slide the garment down the length of my arms, his eyes locking on my breasts as the fabric snagged on the peaks of my nipples and then pulled free. Tossing the bra behind him, he returned one hand to the back of my neck while his free arm banded around my waist, drawing me closer until my core pressed against him.

The feel of his bare chest against mine, his dark smattering of hair brushing across my nipples, was nearly enough to push me over the edge. My body rubbed against him, begging him to take me. But Gabe was nothing if not controlled. His thick erection pressing against my core told me how much he was fighting temptation. And it was driving me crazy.

Gabe's fingers moved to the button on my jeans. A moment later the denim fabric was sliding down my legs, along with my silk panties, in an excruciatingly slow manner. I leaned back on the bed, holding Gabe's eyes as he unfastened his own jeans and shoved them to the floor. Slipping an arm around my waist, he positioned me farther up the bed as he lowered himself over me.

The feel of him pressing against my entrance made my hips rise to meet him, urging him inside. Gabe's eyes silently swept my face. "Are you sure you're ready for this?" he asked, his voice husky, concern etching lines in his brow.

I smiled and nodded, quietly reassuring him that I was okay. I was better than okay. And though thoughts of Robby and the fact that I didn't deserve something this good fought to take control of my mind, I pushed them away each time, determined that nothing was going to ruin this moment between Gabe and me. Those ghosts would still be there tomorrow, but this moment was one of those experiences in life where you know it's a fleeting gift to be cherished.

Gabe brushed my hair from my face and drew a trail of kisses along my jaw and down my neck. He nibbled at my collarbone, his fingers sliding down my side and along my leg. When he slid down my body, the friction of his skin against mine drew a gasp from my lips. But it was nothing compared to the explosion of sensation when his warm mouth drew my nipple between his teeth.

I threw my head back, my hips bucking against him, fingers clawing his back. His grip was like a vise, holding me steady, forcing me to be patient. But I didn't want to be patient. I had had enough darkness. I'd experienced how cruel and frightening this world could truly be. I wanted just a moment, a breath in time, to feel only bliss. To feel the way that Gabe was making me feel right then. Cherished. Protected. Accepted for who I really was.

My fingers climbed his back and slid into his hair, my nails scraping against his scalp, pulling him closer. As Gabe shifted his attention to my other nipple, dragging his tongue in slow circles around the peak, he slid his hand down to my sex. The moment his fingers began to rub against the sensitive nerves, I came unraveled. I pressed my head deeper into the mattress, my hips rising and falling like thrashing waves in a monsoon. I bit my lip, trying to endure the painful ecstasy that continued to climb until it was almost unbearable.

Gabe slowed his strokes, bringing me back from the edge ever so slightly. I was panting hard, my knees gripping his hips. When he rose from the bed, cool air washed over me, raising goose bumps on my skin. I lifted my head to see what he was doing. He picked up his jeans and then dropped them back on the floor a moment later. As he returned to me, he pulled a condom from its wrapper and slid it into place.

When he settled between my legs once more, I held him close. His mouth went to my neck, sucking and kissing, sending currents of electricity skipping across my skin. And when his lips found mine, his tongue slipped inside, delivering strokes so slow and sensual that my body rocked against him, demanding to be stroked elsewhere.

This time, Gabe answered the demand. Pressing his erection to my opening, he kissed me deeply and pushed inside. His strokes were shallow at first, the sensation shooting off fireworks along every nerve, making me lightheaded with euphoria. I felt my body stretching in a way it hadn't in a very long time.

"You're so tight," Gabe breathed as he pushed in a little deeper, careful not to go too far too fast.

Realizing I was tensing, I forced my mind to shut down again and my body to give in to the pleasure Gabe was giving me. The moment I yielded, Gabe slid in all the way with one smooth thrust of his hips. I savored the feel of being wrapped around him as he pulled out and drove into me again. With the same excruciating control as before, he built the tension, wave upon wave, as he fell into a steady rhythm.

I closed my eyes and reveled in every touch. Every kiss. Every stroke.

Gabe planted a trail of kisses down my throat as his hand moved down my body to grip the back of my thigh. He moved his hips faster, thrusting a little harder, pulling me into him. My hands traveled down his back, his muscles tensing and relaxing beneath my fingertips. I continued my exploration down to his perfectly sculpted glutes, cupping them and pulling him deeper with each stroke.

A sheen of sweat broke across my skin, my breathing ragged and panting. My hips kept pace with Gabe as he moved faster and faster.

"Gabe." I moaned his name. A silent plea to give me what I needed.

He was watching me, his dark eyes, as always, capturing every detail. "You're so beautiful, Alex."

His words washed over me, nearly drawing tears to my eyes.

So, this was what it felt like to have a man make love with

reverence. Gabe and I were connected. Each of us asking and answering with our bodies in a way that didn't require words.

The pressure built. And when I thought I couldn't stand anymore, I cried out, a wave of ecstasy crashing over me. I shattered into a thousand pieces as wave after wave of sweet pleasure erupted through me. I was still lost in my own release when Gabe went rigid, his muscles straining beneath his skin, his mouth pressed into a firm line. He gently rocked into me as we rode the echoing waves together.

We lay there for several minutes, a tangle of limbs, before Gabe rose from the bed. Pulling the covers back, he lifted me into his arms and slid me beneath the sheets. Once I was tucked in, he disappeared into the bathroom and was back a moment later, climbing into bed next to me. He wrapped his arms around me and pulled me against him, kissing my temple before settling his head on the pillow beside mine.

The weight of his arm across my abdomen was oddly comforting. It made me think back on my life with Robby. I had never liked snuggling in bed with him. I preferred my space when I slept. But with Gabe, I was surprised to realize I didn't want him to take his arm away.

Completely satiated and feeling the heavy pull of sleep on my eyelids, I took a deep breath, and as I released it, I noticed the knot in my chest was gone.

"You doing okay?" Gabe asked as he nuzzled my hair.

"Mmm" was all I could manage in response.

I tucked myself in a little closer to him, and as his arm tightened around me, I drifted into the deepest sleep I'd ever known.

CHAPTER 27

Alex

THE SOUND of someone hollering woke me from the sleep of the dead. Confused, I lifted my head and looked around the room, rubbing my eyes in an attempt to bring things into focus. Gabe, pressed against my back, his arm still over my waist, was beginning to stir as well.

"Gabe! Alex!"

The sound of Trevor's voice drifted down the hall. Gabe, suddenly alert, bolted out of bed in search of his jeans. "Be right there," he called back.

The door to my room was still partially open, so he closed it before diving for his shirt. Throwing back the covers, I made a beeline for my dresser, grabbing a matching pair of green panties and a bra before disappearing into my walk-in closet to dress.

A moment later, Gabe and I made our way down the hall to the foyer where Trevor was waiting, hands on his hips, head down. When we approached, he moved only his eyes, lifting them to gaze at us through his lashes.

The look on his face turned my blood to ice. Instinctively, I reached out and gripped Gabe's hand. He gave me a squeeze and said to Trevor, "What? What's wrong?"

Trevor wiped a hand across his mouth like he didn't know

how to begin. "I've been trying to get you on your cell for the past hour."

Gabe patted his pocket. "Shit. I must have left it in the truck."

Trevor nodded, his face sober. "Yeah, well, you can expect a lot of pissed-off voice mails from the chief. He's been trying to reach you too."

"Why? What the hell is going on?" Gabe's voice held an edge. He clearly wanted Trevor to get to the point.

Trevor glanced at me and then down to where my hand was joined with Gabe's. "There was another leak this morning." Trevor locked his eyes back on Gabe.

What could have possibly been leaked now? I couldn't think of anything else that would be as damaging as the divorce papers and the truth of Robby's and my relationship.

Gabe gripped my hand a little tighter. "For fuck's sake, Trevor. Spit it out."

"A video was released to several media sites and fan pages early this morning. Well"—Trevor tipped a hand—"two videos, actually. The first was of Alex in her office. It was the day she found out about the divorce papers having been leaked."

"Why would anyone care about that?" I asked, my brow furrowing as I looked between Gabe and Trevor.

Trevor shifted his gaze to me. "Because you were on the phone with your publicist. You were pretty angry, and the video clearly captures you saying that you don't give a damn about your publisher or your fans."

I pressed my palm to my head as the floor swayed beneath my feet. Gabe's head snapped around to me. Removing his hand from mine, he slipped his arm around my waist and steadied me.

Tears rose in my eyes until everything blurred. "I-I didn't mean it!" I focused on Trevor, silently pleading with him to believe me.

He lifted a hand, palm to me. "I know, Alex." His tone was soft. "It was taken out of context, but that was the point. This video was clearly intended to destroy your career."

Losing the battle with my emotions, tears began to stream down my face. I was helpless to stop them.

Gabe rubbed my back in slow, firm circles. He looked back to Trevor. "You said there were two videos."

Trevor pressed his lips together and glanced at me again. Sensing he had saved the worst for last, nausea rolled through my stomach.

He dipped his chin, avoiding eye contact, and scratched the back of his head. "Yeah. The, uh . . . the second was, uh . . ." Trevor exhaled sharply and squared up with Gabe. "It was a video of the two of you having sex."

If I'd thought I was in danger of fainting before, this time I was certain I was going down.

When I started to sway again, Gabe scooped me into his arms and carried me into the living room with Trevor right behind. Once I was settled on the couch, Gabe sat on the coffee table opposite me and placed one hand on my knee and the other on my cheek.

"Alex? Talk to me."

I couldn't look at him. I was too ashamed. Tears ran down my cheeks in torrents. Embarrassed by them, I propped my elbows on my legs and dropped my face into my hands, trying to stifle the sobs.

"Did you see the video footage?" Gabe asked.

Trevor cleared his throat from somewhere over my left shoulder. "Yeah, I saw enough."

My entire body flushed. It was bad enough realizing millions of strangers were witnessing one of the most intimate moments of my life, but it was mortifying thinking about all of the people who would see it that I *knew* and would have to face again. A fresh wave of sobs racked my body, and Gabe's hands moved to my arms, sliding up and down in an effort to comfort me.

Despite my meltdown, he was still focused on the information Trevor could provide. "Were you able to determine how the footage was obtained?"

Trevor's voice was farther away now. The sound of a glass being pulled from the cabinet and the tap turning on preceded his answer. "In both instances, the camera was inside the house and had a top-down view, so I'm guessing the perp either drilled down from the attic or placed a wireless lens on a light fixture or something to camouflage it."

Trevor's voice came near again. "Here, Alex. Drink this."

I lifted my face from my hands and saw a glass of water suspended in front of me. Unable to meet his eyes, I quietly thanked him and accepted the water.

Gabe stood and paced between the kitchen and the fireplace, his hand resting on the back of his head. "We need to get the team out here to sweep for surveillance equipment." He stopped and looked at Trevor. "Have they been mobilized?"

Trevor shook his head. "Nope. Not yet. We have a more pressing matter we're trying to rein in at the moment."

Gabe shot Trevor a glare. "What the hell is more pressing than *this*?"

"Well"—he drew the word out—"as I said, the chief's been trying to get a hold of you all morning. The media descended on Eden Falls like a plague of locusts before daybreak. They're demanding answers, and it's only a matter of time before they find out where Alex lives." Trevor crossed his arms over his chest and lifted his eyebrows. "The chief hasn't stopped swearing since the inquiries started flooding our dispatch center early this morning."

Gabe blew out a slow, heavy breath, his head dropping to his chest. The guilt I carried over Robby came back in full force, but now it grew even stronger as it bled into the guilt eating me alive as I watched the effect this was having on Gabe.

If I hadn't been so selfish and desperate to escape the sins of my past, this never would have happened. I never would have allowed Gabe to comfort me. I never would have sought escape in his arms. Now, he was reliving a nightmare where everyone he knew and loved would once again gossip about his personal life and what bad taste he had in women. *He's going to hate me.*

Trevor turned his body toward me. "Alex, I almost forgot to tell you . . ." The look of pain on his face had my stomach plummeting again. "Your publicist has been calling the station all morning. She tried repeatedly to reach you, and when she couldn't, she started calling us, demanding that someone get over here to get you on the phone with her."

Panicked, I pushed off the couch and ran down the hall to my office, where I'd left my phone last night. When I snatched it from the desk, it lit up, displaying an endless string of missed calls and texts. Without checking any of them, I dialed Cass.

The phone didn't even make it through one full ring before she picked up. "Alex? What. The. Fuck?" Cass's California girl accent was prominent. "Where the hell have you been?"

I walked my free hand along the desk for balance as I made my way to my office chair and dropped into the soft leather.

"I'm sorry, Cass. I was—"

"It doesn't even matter now." The irritation in Cass's voice was palpable. I crumpled, realizing this was yet another relationship I had just destroyed.

I remained silent, giving her room to say her piece.

She sighed. "There's no easy way to break this to you, so I'm just going to say it. Your publisher has dropped you. They're demanding the advance back immediately, or they'll pursue legal action."

My hands began to shake as I fought for the strength to keep the phone pressed to my ear.

"Your fans have had it, Alex. A lot of them could have gotten past the Robby thing once they made peace with the fact that their image of you wasn't completely accurate, but this . . ."

I heard the beep of Cass's car alarm being disarmed. The sound of a door opening and slamming a moment later came before her engine turned over. "I've done everything I can to help you through this,

Alex, but it's time to accept that your career is over. No publisher is going to touch you after all of this, and your fans are never going to be able to forgive hearing from your own lips that you don't give a damn about them. At this point, you're unrecognizable to them."

The black shadow of despair began to encroach. Like a snake slowly uncoiling itself from a slumber, it unfurled within me, seeking every crevice of warmth, every bit of hope that had begun to bud during my night with Gabe. As the shadow took over, I grieved for what might have been.

* * *

GABE

I STOOD in the middle of Alex's foyer, silently watching my team canvass her house for surveillance equipment while enduring furtive glances and hushed whispers as penance for my idiocy and unprofessionalism. I sensed movement behind me and recognized my partner's footfalls.

"Did Chief rip you a new one?" Trevor asked.

I scoffed. "Twice."

"Did he tell you to take a few days on the beach?"

"Nope. Worse." I glanced over my shoulder at Trevor. "He said he was disappointed in me."

My partner remained silent. He knew the chief was like a second father to me and that his disappointment was about the worst punishment he could have doled out.

"After swearing at me for about twenty minutes, he asked how the one officer he's never worried about doing something stupid managed to fuck up so royally by sleeping with the victim in a high-profile case while he was on duty." I gripped the back of my neck and let my head fall back, my voice growing quiet. "He said since it was a first offense and he couldn't afford to lose any manpower right now, he's going to pretend it didn't happen."

I let my head fall forward again, my arms crossing my chest, wishing the chief had done more to punish me. Forced leave without pay, maybe. Or feeding me to the media rather than taking the blows *for* me.

Trevor came up alongside me and smirked. "That's one of the perks of working for such a small department. The chief can exercise a lot more discretion without having to answer to anyone, and he knows his people well enough to know when one of us simply fucks up or when there's a larger issue to deal with."

I didn't respond. I was too ashamed. Ashamed that I had given Alex's stalker the opportunity to humiliate her. Ashamed that I had brought this media shitstorm down on the department and put the chief in a position to have to defend me. And ashamed that I had embarrassed my family and neglected my responsibility while on duty.

I scrubbed a hand down my face, my eyes vacantly watching uniformed officers moving from one room to the next.

Three times. That's exactly how many times I'd had sex between the time Olivia had left town and when Alex had arrived, and I not only chose *this* situation to break my months-long celibacy, but I do it while on duty? What the fuck was wrong with me?

I thought back to the night before. To Alex's confession, recalling the pain on her face and the guilt binding her body. The way she looked at me with those big green eyes and how they shone bright with vulnerability and a silent plea not to see her as the hateful bitch the rest of the world was determined to make her out to be.

And as I'd fallen deeper into those eyes, I had felt the walls of ice I'd so carefully constructed around me break. They had tumbled down until all reason went out the window and instinct took over. I had needed to hold her. To feel her soft skin under my fingertips. To give her strength and to show her that someone cares for her. The urge to take her away from her pain, even if only temporarily, had been all-consuming.

As if he could read my thoughts like a ticker tape flashing

across my face, Trevor clapped a hand on my shoulder and squeezed. "It's all going to work out, man. No one is going to kick your ass for this more than you will. We're all behind you. And Alex. This shitstorm will blow over, folks will have something new to talk about by the time the weekend comes to a close, and we *will* nail this asshole's balls to the wall."

Taking a deep breath, I managed a slim smile. I was so damn lucky to have a friend like Trevor. Someone who always had my back, no matter what. Someone who wouldn't sugarcoat the truth but also always reminded me that we'd figure things out together, as we always had.

Giving myself a mental shake, I nodded once, signaling to Trevor that I had my head on straight again. I'd spent enough time feeling sorry for myself. What was done was done, and the best way to help Alex through this was to find the son of a bitch who was trying to destroy her life.

"What kind of surveillance have the guys found so far?" I asked.

"Three cameras." Trevor pointed to each of the locations where they'd been found. "One in the living room, which also captured the kitchen. One in the office, and one in the bedroom. They also found bugs attached under Alex's desk, on the fireplace mantel, and along the back of her bedside table."

I chewed the inside of my cheek, trying to see the full image amongst the missing puzzle pieces. "Does something feel off about this?"

Trevor laughed. "The whole fucking thing is off. That's to be expected when you're dealing with psychos."

I shook my head. "No. I mean, these last few incidents haven't felt like the work of someone who thinks they're in love with Alex. It's more like someone who hates her. Someone who wants to take everything from her." I turned to face Trevor head-on. "It feels personal."

Trevor nodded slowly, mulling it over. "Yeah, but when did you and Alex start getting close?"

"What do you mean?"

"Seems to me that if this guy is in love with Alex and he sees you moving in, and she's receptive to it, crazy love can turn to crazy hate in a flash."

I nodded. "You're right. And if that's the case, we just kicked one hell of a hornet's nest."

Various scenarios and possibilities zoomed across my mental landscape, the situation unfolding in my mind like a giant chessboard consisting of moves and countermoves.

"We need to find someone who's good with computers," I said. "See if they can track down where those videos and the divorce papers were leaked from. Do you have any idea where to look for someone with those kinds of skills?"

Trevor grinned like the Cheshire Cat. "No. But I'm sure my girl does, and she's no doubt suffering withdrawals from me by now." He pulled his phone out of the chest pocket of his uniform. "I'll give her a call."

I shook my head, unable to stop the grin spreading across my face. "She's seriously going to give you nothing but paper as soon as this case is over if you don't stop giving her shit."

Trevor's blue eyes took on a devilish gleam. "It'd be worth it."

"Just don't piss her off to the point where she refuses to do all this extra legwork for us. This guy's been ten steps ahead the whole time. Trying to track him through his online dealings is a good place to start, but it's not enough."

"What are you thinking?" Trevor asked, scrunching his brow.

I ran my hand along my jawline, barely noticing the stubble. "We've been chasing our own tails trying to catch him. Maybe it's time we bring him to us."

"You want to set a trap?"

"Yeah, I do."

"Such as?"

I gazed into the living room and through the patio doors, my eyes drawn to the tree line that bordered Alex's backyard as I considered the question.

"I'm not sure yet. Let me think on it." With my thumb, I pointed over my shoulder. "I'm going to go check on Alex. She's still in pretty rough shape. You talk to Quinn and see what you can do to get a cyber freak on the tracking."

Trevor nodded once and was already putting the phone to his ear. Before I could turn to head down the hall, he beamed and said, "Quinny-baby!"

I couldn't hear Quinn's reply, but judging by how far and fast he pulled his phone away from his ear, I didn't have to guess how wrong he'd been about Quinn having withdrawals.

I chuckled, already feeling a little lighter. It was hard not to laugh whenever Trevor and Quinn came into contact. Quinn, known for her ability to always remain poised and in control, lost that superpower faster than a ball gown on prom night whenever Trevor was around. And Trevor had made trying to beat his time to detonation a hobby.

Leaving Trevor to try to soothe Quinn's ruffled feathers, I headed down the hall on my own mission, praying I would have more luck with my woman than Trevor was having with his.

CHAPTER 28

Alex

THE GLOW from my laptop screen cast a ghostly pallor on my skin as I stared down at the never-ending comments plastered across my social media and fan sites. I'd been sitting cross-legged on my bed with the laptop balanced on my knees for so long my feet had gone numb, but I couldn't bother to care. With the blackout curtains drawn across my windows, I was surrounded by darkness other than the screen chronicling the end of my career.

A heavy weight had settled in my chest, my breathing so shallow I could hardly perceive the rise and fall of my chest.

Everything I had feared about myself was there on the screen in front of me, confirmed by thousands of spectators. Comment after comment, I read what people now knew to be true about me.

She made all of her fans feel sorry for her, thinking she was in mourning while she was really just shacking up with some other guy.

If I was her husband, I would have gotten drunk and killed myself just to get away from her too.

She's such a fraud.

Does she even feel guilty for causing her husband's death?

I'll never read this author again on principle alone. I'm sorry I ever supported her career.

On and on it went, each comment a wave sending me deeper and deeper into the suffocating depths of guilt and self-loathing. Even worse—I had taken Gabe with me.

I squeezed my eyes shut, trying to pretend that none of this was real. This was punishment for seeking a respite from the self-recrimination and isolation. For allowing myself to escape into pleasure, even for a moment. I didn't deserve happiness, and I certainly didn't deserve love and understanding. I knew that. And yet, I had sought those very things in Gabe's arms, selfishly wanting to feel something good again.

I knew I was a terrible person. I knew that my own selfish desires had led to the events of Robby's death. Despite everything that had happened between us, I had never stopped loving him as a friend, and I had sent him to his grave thinking I didn't care.

A single tear leaked from the corner of my eye. I didn't wipe it away. I would bear my tears and wear them as the scarlet letter I had earned.

The aroma of Gabe's aftershave still surrounded me, captured in the fibers of my sheets. The woodsy scent, *his* scent, was the only thing anchoring me to reality. I wasn't sure if that was a good thing. A big part of me just wanted to give in to the darkness. It would be so much easier to just stop fighting.

In my mind, I saw the shadowy figure that had emerged from my nightmares to haunt my waking hours. I couldn't escape him. He was too smart. Too determined. Somehow I knew that he would not stop until he had decimated every piece of me.

His job was almost done. There wasn't much left to destroy.

My fingers fumbled with the trackpad on my laptop, and I clicked over to my email, where I had a message from my now-former publisher sitting open. The correspondence detailed the exact amount of the advance owed to them and the date they expected its return. My stomach clenched as my eyes focused on the number.

The only piece of my life that remained private was the fact that I was not the wealthy heiress everyone thought me to be.

When I had disentangled myself from my toxic parents, they'd disowned me, no doubt believing the desire for my inheritance would draw me back into their controlling grip. It hadn't.

Robby and I had done fairly well for ourselves, but without my parents' old money behind me, the lavish lifestyle we had maintained to keep up appearances had quickly buried us in a mountain of debt. For years, I had begged Robby to leave Los Angeles along with the social circle we had been born into. I wanted a simple life, a *real* life, and I had hoped that if we could just get away from all of our superficial relationships, we might rediscover the genuine friendship we had started with, and perhaps it would blossom into something more.

I sighed and felt a sharp ache in my chest. I didn't just grieve for the way things had turned out between Robby and me. I grieved for the innocent and hopeful children we had been.

Doing my best to shove those images back into the locked room in my mind where I kept all of the things I couldn't bear to examine, I clicked out of the email, unable to stare at that impossible number any longer.

I had no idea how I was going to pay back that money. There was absolutely no way I would return to my parents on bended knee, begging them for it in exchange for my freedom. I had used that advance along with the payout from Robby's life insurance policy to pay off our debt. And with the remaining funds, I had picked up what was left of my life and purchased the house in Eden Falls. Even if I sold the house, I didn't have any equity in it yet.

A burn started in the back of my throat, and I slammed my laptop shut. I clung to the anger that simmered beneath everything else, trying to stave off the tears.

A gentle knock at the door made my breath catch. The officers had already searched this room. I didn't want to have to face anyone else for the rest of the day. Before I could send whoever it was away, the door opened slowly, and Gabe poked his head inside. With my laptop closed, the room was completely dark with the exception of the small stream of light coming in from the hallway.

Voices floated into the room from behind Gabe, their murmurs too low to discern. Gabe stepped through the door and closed it behind him. I listened as he moved through the room, and a moment later, the light in the bathroom switched on. Gabe pulled the door so it sat only half-open, allowing a gentle glow to slice through the obsidian prison.

"Hey," he said, moving toward me as though I were a wild animal he didn't want to spook. When he reached the bed, he eased onto it, pulling one leg up so it sat bent between us. "How are you feeling?"

I stared at him for a moment, wondering why he was being so gentle with me. I was the reason he was reliving the worst experience of his life. Except this time, it was on a global scale.

Gabe reached up and ran a lock of my hair through his fingers, watching it as it slipped through his grasp and fell back to my shoulder. His eyes returned to me, his irises nearly as dark as the room.

I cleared my throat, hoping my voice would sound fairly normal. "Fine. You?"

Gabe offered a small smile. "Alex, you're sitting in a dark room, curled into a ball on your bed, in the middle of the day. If you don't want to talk, I understand, but don't tell me you're fine when clearly you aren't."

I shrugged. "What do you want me to say, Gabe?" I watched him as his image began to shimmer behind the tears trying once again to take hold. "I'm humiliated. I'm sad. I've yet again been splashed all over the internet when all I wanted when I came here was to disappear and be left alone." My voice rose, pent-up emotion taking control of me. "And to top it all off, I've lost the *one* thing I managed to build on my own. The *one* thing that made me feel alive when I felt dead in every other regard." I quickly swiped at the tears and looked away.

Gabe was quiet for several agonizing moments, and my anger

was slowly replaced by a new wave of guilt for taking my pain out on the one person who had remained firmly in my corner. Gabe was dealing with his own fallout over this situation and here I was acting like I was the only one suffering.

I raised my eyes to his, expecting to see disgust reflected back at me. Instead, I saw only sympathy. I blew out a resigned breath. "I'm sorry." Shaking my head, I placed a hand on his knee. "I'm so sorry, Gabe. You didn't deserve that."

He laid a rough hand on top of mine. "Don't apologize, Alex." His thumb drew soft circles on my hand. "You have to stop apologizing for being honest with people just because they might not like what they hear. I asked you for the truth, and you gave it to me."

I think I would have felt better if he had yelled at me. This care and understanding was killing me. It was more than I deserved.

Gabe scooted a little closer, keeping his voice gentle. "I want to get you out of here, Alex. I want to take you someplace where you can feel safe. Where you haven't been violated and the media will have a harder time finding you."

I sniffled. "Where is that?"

"My place."

My eyes rounded, but Gabe's were resolved. Finally, I shook my head. "Gabe, you don't want to invite this mess into your home. Trust me. It's not just the stalker. In a town this small, it's only a matter of time before the media find out who you are and where you live. Once they do, if they find me there, you will lose every bit of privacy you have. It's better if you just distance yourself from me."

Gabe lifted a hand and combed his fingers through the hair at my temple, the simple gesture soothing my rough edges. "First of all," he said, leaning in closer, "I'm not going anywhere without you. Second, as gossipy as the people of this town are, they only gossip to each other, and at the end of the day, we all protect one another. I trust that no one is speaking to the media. And if by chance I'm wrong . . ." He lifted a shoulder as if to say no big deal.

A war was raging inside of me. Part of me wanted to run away and never look back. The other part of me wanted to run right into Gabe's arms and never let go.

"Besides," Gabe said, "maybe the change in scenery will help you get some writing done."

I leaned back a bit. "Gabe, my career is over. No one in publishing is going to want to take a chance on me after this, even if I write under a pen name. I've made too much of a mess of things."

Gabe smiled with his eyes. "I didn't say anything about your career. I said you could write."

I studied him, not understanding where he was going with this. If my career was over, what was the point of continuing to struggle over the story that wouldn't come?

"Alex, why did you become a writer?"

Were we really sitting here in the middle of an inferno with a crazed stalker watching from the shadows of my life discussing my career choice?

I cleared my throat, my eyes searching the bedspread between us for answers. "Well—" I sighed deeply, thinking back to when I was a little girl sitting at my desk with one of those clunky old typewriters. My parents had furnished my room with the latest and greatest computer for me to complete school assignments on, but in my spare time, I loved sitting at that old typewriter, feeling the keys give way to the pressure of my fingertips, the melodic clicking of each stroke pulling me deeper into the trance of my story world.

Without my realizing it, a smile spread across my face, and I drew my eyes to Gabe's. "I loved disappearing into worlds that only existed in my imagination. I loved knowing that I could live a thousand different lives and experience endless adventures."

Warmth began to spread in my chest, chasing away some of the cold dread that had settled there. I held on to that feeling, the one I had had when I first discovered the stories that lived in my head. "I loved the way words would pour out of me without conscious thought, breathing life into something that came into existence right before my eyes." I smiled wider. "And I *loved* that it was something special, meant only for me. Something that my parents couldn't take away or use against me. Later, it became the thing that had given me my freedom."

Gabe's smile matched my own. He brought his hand to my cheek, his thumb caressing my skin. "And that's why you should keep writing, Alex. You think the person terrorizing you has taken everything from you. But he can never take what you just described to me. That lives inside of *you*. No one can touch that. No one can steal the joy that it brings you. So write."

I brought my hand up to cover Gabe's as he continued to stroke my cheek. "I don't know if I can," I admitted. "I'm worried I've lost it."

Gabe shook his head slowly, holding my gaze. "You can't lose it, Alex. It's too much a part of you. Maybe all of this is actually a good thing."

I scrunched my forehead.

Seeing my confusion, he elaborated. "Maybe without a publisher, and a publicist, and fans breathing down your neck for the next best seller, you can get back to just focusing on the joy. Maybe when you stop chasing everyone else's approval, your muse will see fit to return."

I felt the tension slip from my face and shoulders and took the first deep breath I'd been able to manage all morning. Something in Gabe's argument rang true. A part of me was nervous that I would sit down to write and the story still wouldn't come. But a bigger part of me was excited to try.

I smiled at Gabe and gave him a little nod.

His eyebrows lifted. "Yeah?"

I nodded again.

He smiled and brought his other hand up to my face so that his palms warmed my cheeks. He leaned down and covered my mouth with his. Though the kiss was gentle, he still managed to leave my lips tingling.

Gabe rose from the bed. "Pack an overnight bag with enough things to last you for a few days. I can always come back and get more if you need it." He walked to the door and turned back. "I'm going to go clear all of this with the chief and then we'll get out of here."

I nodded and quickly climbed from the bed, suddenly anxious to escape my house. Knowing my stalker could somehow manage to enter anytime he wanted, and worried that the police might have missed another camera or listening device, I knew Gabe was right. I needed to go someplace where I hadn't been repeatedly violated. Somewhere I could feel at least a small slice of safety.

My only fear was that my presence would cause Gabe's home to become my stalker's new playground.

Alex

GABE OPENED the front door of his house and stepped back so I could enter first. My breath caught, and I came to a sudden stop the moment I walked inside. His modern ranch-style home could have graced the cover of a magazine. He had chosen a navy-gray paint with dark wood accents for the outside, and he carried those same wood elements and masculine colors inside. His living room opened right off the foyer, and the dark-stained wood beams that ran along its vaulted ceiling created the perfect contrast against the white walls and black steel-framed windows.

The rich wood floors beneath my feet continued to my right, down a long hallway, while the flooring that ran to my left eventually met tile where the kitchen began. I could just make out a few stainless-steel appliances and a dark gray backsplash behind the black marble countertops. The overall aesthetic was cozy yet sophisticated. The perfect blend of simple and elevated—just like Gabe.

Feeling the cold air of an approaching winter at my back, I realized I was blocking Gabe from being able to come inside and shut the door.

"I was going to put your things in my room," he said, setting my large suitcase on the floor while keeping my overnight bag slung over his shoulder. "But if you'd rather, I can put them in the guest room."

I pulled my lower lip between my teeth and worried it as I glanced down the hall to where I assumed the bedrooms were situated. After a moment, I looked back at Gabe, who was watching me with a stoic expression that gave nothing of his thoughts away.

"I don't want to get you in any more trouble," I said finally.

He gave the smallest shake of his head. "You won't. I'm not on duty tonight, so it's no one's business where either of us sleeps."

I glanced down the hall again. I wanted to say yes, but I felt a little brazen doing so. "How 'bout I put them in my room for now and you can think on it," Gabe said, sensing my discomfort. "It's easy enough to move them."

I smiled and looked at the floor before meeting his eyes again. "Yes, that sounds good."

Gabe's answering grin made those butterflies start up in my stomach again. He was gorgeous as it was, but when he grinned like a schoolboy who had just heard the final bell before summer break, the effect was staggering.

After Gabe got my bags settled in his room, he gave me a quick tour of the house and set out towels for me in the bathroom. He then took me by the hand and led me to his home office across from the guest bedroom.

The room was a decent size and furnished with an executive black-walnut desk that would be the envy of any writer, a plush executive chair, and a tall oak bookcase. What really caught my attention, though, was the large window running seamlessly from one side of the far wall to the other. Since it was one sheet of glass, the view was unobstructed. And what a view it was.

Gabe's house was situated on the same piece of property as his parents' and Liz's houses, but it sat higher than either of those homes. The office was located on the back side of his house, so there was nothing but nature outside those windows. A gentle slope started about fifty yards from the patio area. It was covered in magnificent evergreens with a few boulders scattered amongst the foliage. I could easily imagine how it would look in winter with a thick blanket of glittering snow on the ground and the deep-green boughs dusted in powdered sugar. It was so spectacular, it felt as though it shouldn't exist outside of my dreams.

"Make yourself at home," Gabe said, cutting into the wintery wonderland of my imagination.

I twisted to glance at him over my shoulder.

"There are pens in the drawer," he said, waving his hand toward the desk. "The Wi-Fi password is taped to the side of the printer, and that's a wireless printer, so you shouldn't have any problems connecting." He ran a hand up and down the back of his head. "Is there anything else I can get to make you more comfortable?"

I smiled and shook my head. "No, this is . . ." My eyes traveled around the office, taking in all of the exquisite detail. "This is perfect," I said, bringing my gaze back to him. "Your home is beautiful, Gabe. I don't know how you ever manage to leave it."

Gabe laughed and scratched the thick stubble on his jaw. "Thanks. It was a fun project."

My eyes widened, and my mouth flopped open and shut without producing sound. "Are you saying you built this?"

I had never seen Gabe shy, but the bit of blush that rose in his cheeks along with his bashful grin was much too endearing.

"Yeah. Liz and I always knew we wanted to build homes on this property." He walked to the window wall and looked out, scanning the land of his childhood. "We each designed our dream homes back in high school, and I promised Liz I would build them someday."

Gabe was thoughtful for a moment as he continued to take in the scenery. Then he turned back to me, stuck his hands in his pockets and shrugged. "I like to work with my hands, and so does my brother."

"You have a brother?" I asked.

He nodded. "Mason. He's in the Army. Special ops, so he doesn't make it home very often. He helped as much as he was able with the construction, though."

The more I learned about Gabe's family, the deeper the ache in my chest grew. Despite the fact my parents were still living, I didn't truly have anyone that gave me a sense of love and belonging. Even with the small amount of time I had spent with his family, though, I was happy to know that such good people had been blessed with something that special.

Gabe clapped his hands together and started toward the door. "I'm going to get out of your hair. If you need anything, I'll just be down the hall keeping Aderes company."

A smile stretched across my face at the thought of Gabe and Aderes hanging out while I worked. There was something so domestic and entertaining about the idea.

As soon as the door closed behind Gabe, I went to the desk and pulled my laptop and notes from my bag. Sinking down into the plush chair, I took one more look out the window, drew a deep breath, and opened my computer.

The hours ticked by like minutes, my fingers never ceasing their flight across the keyboard. My notes lay forgotten beside me, and my words constructed the walls of a new world as Gabe's office faded away.

By the time I looked up from my work, darkness had fallen, and only the dim light of my laptop illuminated the office. I scrolled back up through my words, page after page slipping down the screen. I knew I had been writing a while, but I could hardly conceive of how many pages I had actually managed to fill. The story that had poured out of me without conscious thought was different than anything I had written in my adult life. But as I relived the images that I had transcribed, I realized it was very much in line with the kind of stories I had written as a child. Just a more grown-up version.

I smiled with unmitigated joy at the burgeoning novel and stood as I closed my laptop. After lifting my arms over my head and eliciting a pop from my back, I left the office in search of Gabe and Aderes. As soon as I rounded the corner to the living room, a chuckle bubbled up in my chest and turned into a hysterical laugh when Gabe and Aderes noticed me. Gabe was sitting on the couch watching ESPN highlights, Aderes beside him, on her back with all four legs in the air as her new friend scratched her belly. When she turned to look at me, her tongue lopped out of the side of her mouth, which was hanging open in a goofy grin.

"What?" Gabe asked, the corner of his mouth lifting.

I wiped my eyes and tried to get my giggles under control as I moved to sit on the arm of the couch next to him. "I just didn't expect to see a big, scary guy like you snuggled up to my pup, scratching her belly while watching sports."

Gabe snaked his arm around my waist and gave it a squeeze. "Don't worry. I'll rub your belly later, too, if you're a good girl."

Fire rose in my cheeks and grew so hot I thought I might go up in flames when our eyes connected, and I read the intentions behind his smile.

And there go the butterflies again.

Noticing my blush, he chuckled and squeezed me one more time before standing. He faced me, placing his hands on his hips. "Are you hungry? I've got dinner warming in the oven."

My eyebrows shot up. "You cooked?"

"I'm surprised a California girl would be so shocked by a man cooking," he teased.

Grabbing my hand, he pulled me behind him into the kitchen. When he bent and removed a homemade lasagna from the oven, the aroma of cheese, red sauce, and garlic permeated the space. It smelled so incredible I almost grabbed a fork to dive in before he'd even set it on the stove.

"So, how did you do with the writing?" Gabe asked as he pulled a couple of salads from the fridge.

My smile was so big that my cheeks nearly forced my eyes shut. "Good. You were right. With all of the external pressure gone, it just came rushing back. It was so exhilarating getting to write the story that was in me rather than having to write what was expected."

Gabe pulled a couple of plates from a cupboard. "I'm glad to hear that, although I had no doubt. You're too talented a writer for your well to dry up for good." He walked to the fridge and pulled out an amber bottle and showed it to me. "What would you like to drink? I've got beer, red wine, milk, and OJ."

I surveyed the label on the beer bottle and nodded. "I'll take a beer, please."

His eyebrows shot up, a ghost of a smile on his lips, but he said nothing and pulled a second bottle from the fridge.

I studied him for a moment. "How do you know I'm a talented writer?"

He glanced at me quickly before returning his focus to the table that sat in a small alcove adjacent to the kitchen where he was arranging the last of the dinner items and shrugged. I continued to wait for an answer. He sighed, finally realizing I wasn't going to let the topic go. "I read a couple of your books."

It was my turn to look surprised. Refusing to meet my eyes, Gabe pulled a chair out for me and waited. I moseyed over, never taking my gaze off him, and sat, waiting for him to join me.

We each dug into dinner as though neither of us had eaten in a week. The lasagna was the best I had ever had, and it had me contemplating how many more pleasant surprises I might have during my stay with this incredibly thoughtful, complex, sexy cop.

Once I had taken the edge off my hunger, I stopped inhaling my food and took the time to savor it, using the opportunity to return to the subject I was sure Gabe was hoping I'd dropped.

"You're not exactly my target audience," I said, giving him a teasing smile.

His neck turned a little red, and he leaned back in his chair, mischief in his eyes as he chewed the bite he'd just taken. Swallowing, he said, "I thought you'd let that go too easily."

I merely smiled and continued to pin him with my stare.

After a brief standoff, he growled and leaned forward, placing his forearms on the table. "I was curious about you, so I downloaded one of your books. It was good, so I downloaded another." His eyes crinkled and his smile spread.

"You really liked it? I never would have thought you'd get into romance."

He shrugged again. "Normally, I don't, but you balanced it with a good mystery, and you have a way with words that makes a person want to keep reading." He reloaded his fork. "That, and . . ."

I waited for him to finish his sentence, but instead, he took another bite, leaving me hanging on the edge of my seat. "And what?" I leaned forward, waving my hand for him to get on with it.

He considered me with that same look of mischief and took his sweet time chewing, clearly enjoying that I was now the one teetering on *his* cliffhanger.

I exhaled sharply and flopped back in my chair.

Laughing, he finally gave in. "Well, I figured your sex scenes are probably a reflection of your own fantasies, so I made sure to commit them to memory."

It was suddenly way too hot for my sweater. A trickle of sweat ran down my back as the blush ran up my chest and neck. I straightened and ducked my chin, taking a rapt interest in my lasagna. Out of my periphery, I could see Gabe's shoulders shaking in silent laughter—the ass.

We spent the rest of dinner discussing neutral topics and the lack of progress on the case. Gabe's frustration with the latter was evident. I wasn't at all surprised to hear that Maxwell Hargrove was proving rather elusive. Though he was completely delusional, he was also highly intelligent. A particularly scary combination. The thought of him walking around, free to do as he pleased, sent a tremor down my spine. I had no doubt that had the police not captured him when they had the last time, I would have met a fate worse than death at his hands. I didn't mention any of that to

Gabe, though. He and his team were doing their best, and he didn't need more to think about.

After we finished dinner, I helped him put away leftovers and wash dishes. Then he went outside to check in with the officer standing watch while I disappeared into his en suite to get ready for bed.

Ten minutes later, I exited the bathroom rubbing the remnants of the lotion I'd applied all over into my hands, surprised to see that Gabe hadn't returned yet. A moment later, I heard the front door close and expected Gabe to come strolling down the hall any second. I tightened the belt on the short silk robe I wore, listening for approaching footsteps. The house was silent. I listened for another minute, and when he still didn't appear, I decided to go check on him.

Just as I reached the door, Gabe emerged from the dark. We collided, our bodies flush from chest to knee. Gabe's hands darted out, gripping my upper arms to keep the impact of running into his wall of muscle from sending me flying across his bedroom floor.

His eyes captured mine, their smolder forcing my lips to part. Gabe's gaze dropped to my mouth and lingered. He continued to hold me against his body, his calloused thumbs stroking my arms through the silk of my robe, the erotic sensation drawing goose bumps to my skin. A small smile lifted the corner of his mouth as he slowly guided me back into the room. My breathing quickened along with the pounding of my heart.

Gabe removed his hands and, without breaking eye contact, pulled his white T-shirt over his head. My eyes traveled down his torso, admiring his broad shoulders and sculpted abs. My body pulsed for him, its silent thrashing begging him to consume every part of me.

Instead, he kissed me softly on the tip of my nose and then swaggered into the bathroom in nothing but his jeans, the denim riding low on his hips.

I stood frozen, caught off guard by a crashing wave of

emotion at this achingly beautiful scene of domesticity. The whole evening had been the exact picture of what I had longed for for so many years. Sharing space with a man who delighted and surprised me. Talking about our day over dinner while Aderes rested in her bed by the fire. The small, intimate touches in passing that sent chills through my body and raised goose bumps on my arms. Those deep, meaningful glances while doing something as mundane as cleaning up after dinner.

In the short time we had known each other, Gabe had given me more support and understanding and encouragement than I had received from any one person in my entire life, and my growing feelings for him left me deeply conflicted.

I went to my suitcase and began repacking the items I had removed to locate the emerald camisole and matching shorts I wore under my robe, all the while lost in thought as the sound of Gabe's electric toothbrush faded into the background.

Having tasted the temporary serenity that being in this place, surrounded by Gabe and all of his things, had given me, I craved more of it. His presence had become a drug that I couldn't get enough of. It went deeper than my physical attraction to him. It was as though something inside of Gabe called out to and connected with something deep inside of me. Like our souls recognized each other. Were *part* of each other.

And while I wanted more days like this one, that same connection urged me to pull back. My life had become a bomb that had exploded, taking as casualties all those who were near. I cared too much for Gabe, and for his family, to bring that destruction to their doorstep any more than I already had. Maybe all the damage that he could suffer from being close to me had already been done. But maybe it hadn't.

The truth was, as long as I remained in the public eye, anyone closely associated with me would always be at risk of getting caught in the blast. I had chosen this path, knowing the potential cost. Gabe had never consciously made that choice.

Then again, if my career really was over, maybe I could finally disappear the way I had wanted to. Maybe once we caught my stalker, I could actually settle into a quiet, simple life here. Or . . . maybe I was hoping for things I had no right to hope for.

Gabe emerged from the bathroom, drawing me from my thoughts. He smiled as he came into the room, stopping at the foot of the bed to unlace and remove his boots. I reached up to free my hair from the claw clip holding it in place, the action causing my robe to open as long, soft curls fell gently around my face. Gabe straightened and went perfectly still, his eyes dilating and sliding to the ample cleavage peeking out from my low-cut camisole.

My stomach seized, and my breathing faltered at the sight of his rigid frame and the hunger in his eyes, anticipation making my knees weak as I waited and prayed for him to make a move.

CHAPTER 30

Gabe

Hot damn.

This woman should come with a warning label. Caution: may cause public humiliation by instant and irreversible hard-on. Consume in private.

My brain was short-circuiting by trying—and failing—to decide what to focus on. Her gorgeous green eyes were emphasized by the matching color of her robe and that sexy little number beneath it. And the way her eyelids lowered in response to her arousal made her gaze even more hypnotic in the low light of my bedroom.

But, *damn*, that cleavage was calling to my primal side. I was itching to put her back to my chest, cup those perfect breasts, and bite her neck as she moaned for more.

Then there were those long, creamy legs. They begged for my attention, too, their slight sheen saying *you know you want to lick every square inch of this.*

My mouth went dry as I pictured kissing my way up those thighs, her squirming beneath me as I inched closer and closer to what we both wanted.

The slightest blush rose in her porcelain skin, but the shyness she'd shown earlier was otherwise gone. She was ready and waiting for me to make a move.

I went to the light switch near the door and flicked it off, never taking my eyes from her. The moon was bright tonight. Its pale beams streaked through the windows, providing ample light in which to enjoy the breathtaking woman before me.

I went to her, my movements unhurried so I wouldn't spook her. I got the sense she was still grappling with the idea of moving on after her husband's death. Understandable. Especially since she blamed herself for his accident. I could only imagine the complicated and confusing emotions she battled on a daily basis.

I stopped with only inches between us. She tilted her head back to meet my gaze, her eyes wide and filled with vulnerability. I could almost hear the whisper from her heart, pleading with me not to cause her more pain.

I brought my hand to her cheek and felt my walls crack a little more when she closed her eyes and leaned into my touch. Wrapping my other arm around her waist, I pulled her to me until we were pressed so close a whisper couldn't pass between us.

I bent to take her lips, and she opened for me immediately. Sliding my tongue against hers, I kept my strokes slow, drawing that moan I'd spent so much time fantasizing about. I smiled against her lips and plunged deeper, my hips grinding into her with each penetration of my tongue.

Alex's arms wound around my waist, her hands sliding down until each palm cupped my ass. With every thrust of my hips, she pulled me tighter against her.

The woman was driving me mad. Her soft whimpers, begging for more. The way her fingers gripped me like she couldn't get close enough. *And her tongue*—that angelic face had one wicked tongue. I was dying to get my hands on her bare skin. To feel her beneath me, her hips rising and falling enthusiastically in time with my own thrusts.

My fingers found the neckline of her robe, and I made short work of relieving her of the material. Pulling back from her just enough to enjoy the view, I lifted her arms over her head, then gripped the bottom of her top and pulled it off. Her hair caught in the fabric, and as I pulled the silk away, that dazzling mane fell free, cascading over her shoulders and across her back.

I canvassed her face, drinking in all the little details that, when put together, made her uniquely Alex. The woman I was falling head over heels for.

My eyes journeyed from her eyes to her nose. Down to her pouty lips and the hollow of her neck. And finally, they came to rest on the two most beautiful breasts to ever grace this earth. Winding my arms around her waist, I bent her back and drew her nipple into my mouth. Her hands gripped my shoulders as her eyes fluttered shut. Slowly, I drew small circles with my tongue around her erect nipple. A shudder rippled through her, and the caveman in me roared in triumph.

Still holding her with one arm, I used my free hand to roll her other nipple between my fingers, all the while sucking and biting at the one in my mouth.

She tasted so sweet. My senses were in overdrive. I'd never been this consumed by a woman before. My head was yelling at me to stop acting like a lovesick puppy. She was Hollywood. Glitz and glamour. Big city, high heels, and designer clothes. I was asking for trouble letting myself get this wrapped up in her. But I couldn't help it. She had captured me before I'd even realized I'd walked willingly into the lion's den.

Still, I'd seen a different side of her lately. And something about the Alex I had come to know in private seemed so much more real than the woman who had blazed into town, stirring up a ruckus with her presence.

Alex squirmed against me as my hand traveled down her belly and dipped inside the waistband of her shorts. I brought my lips to her neck and smiled as I rested my fingers just above her clit, causing her to whimper and lift her hips higher.

I had always trusted my instincts. They'd gotten me through a lot of crazy shit in combat when I'd listened to them, and I'd fallen to my lowest with Olivia when I'd chosen to ignore them. Ever since the night Alex had joined my family for dinner, my instincts had slowly gotten louder and louder, telling me she wasn't who I'd first thought her to be. She felt right. When we were together, everything just fit. I was already lost to her, so I figured I might as well trust my instincts and go all in. No guts, no glory.

Alex, growing frustrated with my teasing, gripped my wrist and tried to push my hand lower. Chuckling, I finally gave her what she wanted. I ran my fingers up and down her slick folds and then settled over her clit, making small circles and varying the pressure. I brought my mouth to her other nipple and sucked hard, winning another shiver.

I stroked her sex and nibbled her neck until she was right at the edge of release. Then I pulled my hand away and walked her backward to the bed, kissing her gently, my fingers tangling in her hair.

I laid her back, her creamy skin illuminated in moonlight and standing in contrast to the dark-gray bedspread. She drew her knees up and lifted her hips as I worked her shorts down, leaving her bare to me.

Stepping back, I unbuttoned my jeans as my eyes raked over her, taking in her pink nipples, the hourglass shape of her torso, and the blue polish on her toenails.

Her eyes watched as I peeled off my jeans and boxer briefs, stroking myself as I reached into the nightstand and pulled out a condom. Once I had it in place, I gently pressed her knees apart and settled in between her legs, reaching down to stroke her to make sure she was really ready for me.

She bucked beneath me, crying out in pleasure when I entered her with a finger.

"You feel so good, Alex." I spoke into her neck, my teeth nipping at her delicate skin.

"Gabe, please," she whimpered, gripping my shoulders so hard I could feel her nails biting through my skin.

I grabbed her hips and positioned myself at her entrance.

When she lifted her hips again, I plunged inside in one smooth stroke, nearly coming at the sound of her breath catching and the feel of her body wrapping around me.

I withdrew until only the tip of my shaft was still inside of her and then thrust deep again before settling into a gentle rhythm, losing myself in all the tiny sounds she made. It felt like our bodies were made for each other. She fit around me like a glove, her movements matching my own in perfect symphony.

I drove into her, increasing my pace as she tightened around me, her fingers digging even deeper into my skin. My body wanted to let go. Wanted to give in to the ecstasy beckoning from the other side. I ground my teeth together, unwilling to come until she did. Just when I was nearing my breaking point, Alex's muscles spasmed around me, her orgasm setting off my own. A burst of stars filled my vision, the roar of blood in my ears shutting out all other sound.

Alex shuddered once more beneath me, and then I felt her body go limp, a look of complete bliss on her face. A possessive instinct settled over me as I held her close, wanting never to let go. I bent down to kiss her and let my lips linger on hers. Her eyes were closed, but her mouth smiled against mine.

Rising from the bed, I tucked her beneath the covers and then disappeared into the bathroom to discard the condom. When I returned, she was lying on her side with her arms wrapped around one of my pillows, holding it to her chest, the covers draped loosely over her waist. She looked so adorable lost in the early clutches of sleep that I just stood there for several moments, painting a memory, ensuring that I had every detail memorized well enough that I could conjure the image whenever I wanted.

When I crawled into bed behind her, I tucked my arm over her waist, and she wiggled backward until she was pressed against me. Thoroughly depleted by both the hellish morning and our passionate lovemaking, it didn't take long for me to give into sleep as well. And as I drifted, I pictured a life in which I could live this moment on repeat.

CHAPTER 31

Gabe

SUNLIGHT STREAMED through the bedroom window, pulling me from sleep. I rubbed my eyes, trying to banish the exhaustion that had become my constant companion these past couple of weeks. Turning my head, I found Alex still peacefully lost within her dreams, her mahogany hair fanned out across the white pillowcase, her long eyelashes fluttering against her cheeks.

Waking up to a beautiful sight was a daily occurrence on our ranch. Each morning the sun ascended from behind eminent mountains, painting the sky in bold strokes of pink, orange, and yellow, its golden rays slowly spreading across the land, catching the millions of dewdrops that clung to the grass and made our entire valley sparkle like a city of glass. The deer would emerge from the surrounding woods to get their fill of the rich grass that lay in thick blankets around the few homes dotting the open landscape. Still, the majesty of each morning failed to compare to the beauty of the woman lying next to me.

I eased out of bed, carefully tucking the covers around Alex, before pulling on a pair of jeans and slipping into the hallway. Aderes was sitting outside the bedroom door, patiently waiting for someone to play with, but at the first sight of me, she scrambled to her feet and came to my side, her tail stirring up a strong wind, blue eyes filled with expectation.

A wide grin broke across my face as I knelt down next to her and used both hands to scratch along her collar. I knew I'd found the exact right spot when one of her hind legs started bobbing up and down. With a final ruffle of her ears, I made my way to the kitchen, Aderes trotting beside me.

Taking the empty coffeepot to the sink to fill, I gazed out the window, drinking in the sight of the morning light painting itself across the steep face of the mountain range that ran along the back of our property. The combination of the captivating view and the sound of the water as it left the faucet and collected in the carafe lulled me into a trance, allowing the thoughts I'd pushed aside to deal with at a later time to surface.

I was getting in deeper and deeper with Alex, and reason told me I should pull away, put more space between us. At least until the case was closed. When we finally caught the asshole who'd made it his mission to terrorize her, I didn't want there to be *anything* that could compromise our case against him. I was going to make it my personal mission to see to it that this guy got the maximum sentence. That meant ensuring no slick attorney would be able to argue that my personal relationship with Alex had biased the evidence against his client.

Even knowing all of this, I couldn't bring myself to leave her side. To keep it strictly professional. I could tell myself it was because she was, for all intents and purposes, alone in this world, and I wasn't going to be one more asshole who left her to fight her battles alone. That was partly true. But even if she had all the support in the world, selfishly, I wanted to drink in every bit of her like a man whose thirst couldn't be quenched. When it came to Alex, I had a feeling I'd never be able to get my fill.

With the coffeepot set and the grounds loaded, I punched the button to start the brew, then went about making breakfast. The tile floor was cold against my bare feet, but the sensation was soon lost to me as my movements became automatic and my mind returned to the situation at hand.

A small part of my brain had been whispering to me, warning that this would end badly, since the first time I'd admitted to myself I wanted Alex. She had spent her life with all of the luxuries and opportunities this world had to offer. And until recently, she'd lived the big-city life where there was nothing that wasn't at her fingertips, never a night where there wasn't something exciting and novel to do.

She was accustomed to being in the spotlight, one way or another, and though she talked as though that wasn't what she wanted anymore, I knew damn well that that sort of thing became an addiction for most people. Could I really hope that I'd ever be able to offer her enough to keep her happy? Could I really expect that she wouldn't outgrow this town sooner rather than later? If not, then where would I be? The chump, once again, whose woman ran out on him because she found something better.

With the eggs and sausage spitting and sizzling in the pan, I distracted myself from the direction of my thoughts and the growing anger over the memory of past events by pouring some dry dog food into Aderes's bowl and mixing it with the wet stuff she liked. My hand barely escaped the bowl before she dove in, scarfing down her breakfast like a wild beast.

The grunts and snorts coming from Aderes competed with my brain as it continued to do its best to build a case that Alex and Olivia had more in common than not, but I wasn't willing to go there. I wasn't sure where Alex and I were headed. I had no idea what she wanted, but what I did know was that I wanted more nights like last night. So, I shoved my doubts back into the corner of my mind where I tucked away all the things I didn't like to bring into the light of day, and after checking on breakfast once more, I filled a travel mug with the freshly brewed coffee and delivered it, along with a microwavable breakfast sandwich, to the officer who'd been on watch all night.

By the time I returned to the kitchen, breakfast was done, and

I could hear water running through the pipes, signaling that Alex was awake. I grabbed my phone from the counter and called Trevor as I went to work plating the food and pouring the coffee. He picked up on the second ring.

"Good morning, gorgeous." As usual, Trevor sounded upbeat and poised for trouble.

"Morning, dipshit. You on your way yet?"

Trevor sighed loudly as though my question had put him out. "Yes, Mother, I'm walking out the door now." I heard the jingle of Trevor's keys moments before his engine growled to life.

"Does Alex want to hang at your place, or should I take her home?" he asked.

I was about to tell Trevor she was going to stay at my place but pulled up short, realizing that was what *I* wanted, but I had no idea if Alex would want to stay. "I haven't talked to her about it yet."

With the table set, I leaned against the counter, positioning myself across from the open doorway leading from the kitchen, giving myself full view of the hall on the opposite side of the house. "Alex is still getting ready. I want to talk to you about something before she gets out here."

"Uh-oh. Trouble in paradise?"

I rolled my eyes but bit back the sarcastic remark attempting to spring off the diving board of my tongue. "I want you to take sole lead on Alex's case." I crossed my ankles, leaning more of my weight against the counter.

Trevor was silent a moment and sounded as though he was choosing his words carefully when he finally spoke up. "Sure, I've got no problem with that as long as the chief signs off on it. You wanna tell me why you want off the case?"

I shook my head. "I don't want off the case. I just want off lead." I scratched the back of my head, searching for the right words to explain why I was requesting the change. Realizing there was no way to say it without making myself sound like a lovestruck schmuck, I finally just decided to give it to Trevor straight.

He was my oldest friend, and while he liked giving me shit, he always had my best interests at heart, and deep down, I knew he'd understand where I was coming from on this.

"When we finally catch this guy, I don't want my relationship with Alex to give him a get-out-of-jail-free card. I could end things with her, put space between us, but if there's going to be any fallout from the fact people know we're involved, that die has already been cast." I paused, stalling to make the admission that was coming. Trevor seemed to sense there was more that needed to be said and remained uncharacteristically quiet.

I blew out a deep breath and let him have it. "Look, the truth is, I'm not going to walk away from Alex. I don't know how she feels about whatever this thing is between us, but I . . ." I pressed my lips together, frustrated that this was so hard to say out loud.

"You want to see where it can go," Trevor finished for me.

I nodded, my gaze locked on my feet. "Yeah, I do." Those three quiet words hung between us in the long silence that followed. Clearing my throat, I straightened and glanced down the hall once more, my voice restored to its usual volume. "Anyway, I figure if you take over as the sole lead, it at least creates a buffer and helps to protect the integrity of the investigation."

"Yeah. Makes sense." There was no judgment in Trevor's voice. No speculation about what this request might mean. Only acceptance.

Trevor's turn signal clicked steadily like a metronome keeping time and marked his progress toward my place. He lived in town, so it was only about a ten-minute trip.

Shifting gears, I switched back into cop mode. "When you get here, I want to discuss how we can draw this guy out of the woodpile."

"You come up with any ideas?"

"Yeah, but I haven't mentioned any of this to Alex yet. I'm not sure how she's going to feel about it."

The sound of a door opening drew my attention to the hallway again. Alex stepped out of the bedroom, her bare feet falling quietly on the hardwood floor as she walked toward me. My eyes traveled up her long legs, clad in dark-blue jeans fitted at the ankle. She wore a simple white T-shirt that she had tucked into the front of her jeans while the rest of the shirt moved freely around her hips. I could see the faint outline of her white bra beneath the shirt and a thin gold chain glittered around her neck. But all of that paled in comparison to the fresh innocence of her face.

She had foregone makeup, allowing her natural flush and the dewiness of her skin to steal the show. Her dark hair was piled on top of her head in a messy bun with a few fallen tendrils tucked behind her ears. And her bright-green eyes, the color of Irish hills in spring, were calling to me like a siren at sea. When her gaze found mine, a smile, so full of joy and free of worry, spread across her face, reaching her eyes and drawing one of my own.

Suddenly remembering that I still had Trevor on the phone, I walked toward Alex as I wrapped up the conversation. "We can go over the details when you get here. I'll see you in a few."

As soon as we disconnected, I wrapped my arms around Alex and pulled her close. She settled her cheek against my chest, her forehead pressed against the side of my neck as her arms banded around my waist. I bent and kissed the top of her head before resting my cheek where my lips had just been.

"Did you sleep all right?" I asked.

"Mmm," she murmured into my chest. "I can't remember the last time I've slept that hard. Well—except for the night before last."

We both chuckled, and I gave her a final squeeze before stepping back and taking hold of her hand to lead her to the table, where I had breakfast waiting. Her sharp inhale when she saw the spread thrilled me way more than I would ever admit to another living soul.

"Oh, Gabe, this looks wonderful!"

The childlike gleam in her eye as she slid onto one of the

kitchen chairs, surveying all of the morsels, was one of the cutest things I'd ever seen.

"Well, dig in and get your fill, because Trevor's on the way, and he'll wolf down whatever is left when he gets here."

She laughed and plunged into her food with the same enthusiasm as she had the lasagna the night before. I tried not to stare, but I couldn't tear my eyes away from her. She was one of the most beautiful women I'd ever seen regardless of what she wore or how she styled herself, but the look she sported today—this was my favorite. She looked like a small-town country girl. A girl who got excited about things like a hearty breakfast and town baseball games.

As she lifted her coffee mug to her mouth, the steam rising and swirling until it tickled her nose, I found myself once again wondering which Alex was the real Alex. The one who had blown into town driving a Range Rover and sporting designer clothes, with an impeccably painted face ready for the bright bulbs of the red carpet? Or the one sitting beside me like the perfect fit for my simple life?

I didn't get a chance to contemplate the question further. Trevor came sailing through the front door, allowing it to slam behind him.

"What up, mis amigos?" He strolled into the kitchen like this was the best day ever and pulled out a chair across from me, joining us at the table. Glancing down at the food, his eyes went wide the moment he spotted the bacon. "Score!" His hand darted out and snatched three pieces, devouring them just as fast.

"I guess I should be glad you're so fast on the draw." My dry tone drew a sheepish grin as he licked his fingers.

"I'm a growing boy. I need to feed this machine!" Trevor waggled his eyebrows at Alex. She ducked her head and brought a hand to her mouth, trying to hide her amusement.

I fought my own smile. I liked that Alex could have fun with my friends. Olivia had never been impressed by any of the people in my inner circle. And because she never wanted to hang out with them, I gradually spent less and less time with the people I loved most in an attempt to keep harmony in my relationship. I'd been such an idiot.

"So," Trevor said, drawing out the word and darting his eyes back and forth between Alex and me.

I cleared my throat and sat a little straighter, leaning my forearms on the table. I guessed now was as good a time as any to broach my proposed plan with Alex. She seemed to pick up on the fact that there might be a difficult conversation heading her way. Her eyes locked on me, a small crease between her eyebrows. She had one knee drawn to her chest, her coffee cup perched on top of it as she nursed it with both hands, silently waiting for me to explain.

I glanced at Trevor, and with a single nod from him, I started to lay out the plan. "Alex, I have an idea for how we might be able to bring this stalker situation to an end."

Her eyebrows lifted as she shifted in her seat. "How?"

"Well . . . what we've been doing obviously hasn't been working. This guy is smart, and somehow, he always seems to be at least two steps ahead. So far, we've been on the defensive. He acts, and we react. We've made attempts to get out in front of him, but as I said, he's good at covering his tracks and anticipating our moves."

Alex nodded, her gaze one of concentration. I knew pretty well how her mind worked by now. She was trying to follow my argument to its endpoint to determine where I was headed with this.

I gripped the seat of my chair between my legs, turning it toward her and scooting a little closer. "What I'm getting at is that we need to go on the offensive. We need to be the ones acting, forcing *him* to respond."

Alex scrunched her forehead. "How do you propose we do that? It's not as if we can call him up and invite him for brunch."

Trevor snorted from across the table. When I cast a scowl in his direction, he coughed and looked out the window.

I ignored the interruption and continued. "We need to tempt him with something he wants. Something he can't resist."

The confusion cleared from Alex's face. Her eyes rounded as her mouth fell open in silent protest. When she recovered enough to find her words, they came out in a rush and about ten decibels above her normal volume. "Are you saying you want to use me as bait?"

I shook my head quickly, trying to calm her down before I lost control of the situation. "Only in a manner of speaking."

I glanced at Trevor for help, but the dolt just sat there, chair tipped back, arms crossed, and a shit-eating grin on his face.

I sighed, expressing more exasperation than I intended, mostly aimed at Trevor, but Alex interpreted that it was meant for her, and her shock quickly morphed into indignation. This runaway train was gaining speed fast. If I didn't regain control of it, there was a massive train wreck in my immediate future.

I softened both my expression and my voice. "I understand why this idea seems crazy and how scary this all is for you. I would never put you in direct danger."

Alex's shoulders relaxed a little, her face taking on a more neutral expression.

"What I meant," I continued, "was that we make him *think* he's getting you. You, however, will be nowhere in sight and under tight guard."

Alex looked between Trevor and me for a moment as though trying to discern if we were insane or might actually be onto something. After a moment, she asked, "As you said, he's smart. How are you going to get him to believe you're just handing me to him on a silver platter?"

I directed my attention to both Alex and Trevor now to explain the plan I'd come up with last night while Alex was writing. "We hold a press conference. The chief goes on air telling everyone we've caught the guy who's been stalking you and that the protection detail has subsequently been lifted."

I waited for the idea to sink in. Trevor spoke first. "So the stalker thinks Alex is wide open, but really, Alex will be some-where else, and we'll be waiting for him at her house."

I nodded.

"So you want him to think you have the wrong guy in custody?" Alex asked.

"Yes."

"Do you really think he'll fall for that?"

I nodded again. "I do. See, I'm not only banking on how badly he wants you. He has one other Achilles' heel that we know of. Arrogance." I stood and walked into the kitchen to grab the coffeepot and pulled down another cup from the cupboard before returning. "This guy thinks the cops are incompetent and that there's no way we could ever outwit him. His own arrogance, along with his excitement at having a clear path to you, is going to be too much for him to resist. He's going to be chomping at the bit, which means he's not going to be as methodical as when he's calling the shots and doing everything in his own time."

I placed the empty coffee mug in front of Trevor and filled his cup before refilling Alex's and mine as well. All the while, Trevor and Alex silently contemplated the plan.

Trevor took a sip of his coffee and winced when the hot liquid hit his palette. "I think it's a solid plan, man. And Lord knows we need to bring this thing to a close." His eyes pinned me, his subtext clear when he added, "If anything big were to go down in our town, our resources are stretched too thin to handle it appro-priately."

I nodded, thinking of the pending ambush the Serpents were planning. Jace could reach out any day to inform us that the MC was moving on their target. We had to be ready, and that meant having our force at its strongest.

Even if the MC wasn't an issue at this point, Alex needed her fucking life back. She needed to be able to feel safe in her home. To have her privacy restored. She needed to be able to run long and hard without a babysitter or fearing that someone was going to murder her along the way or assault her upon her return. And *I* needed to know my woman was safe when I wasn't able to be with her.

I raked my eyes over Alex, trying to figure out what she was thinking. She stared out the window across from her, chewing on her lower lip, something she did when she felt anxious.

I reached out and placed my hand over hers, which was resting on the table. "Alex, if this plan makes you too uncomfortable, we'll think of something else."

While technically I could force this plan on her, I wanted *her* to make the decision to take her life back. To go from being the prey to being the hunter. Only she could decide how far this guy was going to make her fall.

Her eyes found mine, the anxiety in her features replaced by determination in a flash. "No, it's a good plan. And you're right. We need to try a different tactic if we want a different result."

I squeezed her hand as Trevor reached over to clap her on the back. "Attagirl," he said before tipping back in his chair once more, his thumbs hooked through the loops on the waist of his jeans. "We've got the perfect opportunity with all of the media in town too. There'll be widespread coverage of the press conference, so regardless of whatever hole this guy has slithered into, it'd be pretty hard for him not to catch wind of it."

Alex set her coffee cup down on the table with a loud thunk, snapping our attention to her. "There's one change you need to make."

My eyebrows drew together. "What's that?"

"Use me as live bait."

CHAPTER 32

Gabe

"Come again?" I leaned forward, cocking my ear toward Alex, convinced I'd missed her meaning.

Her gaze was steel as she repeated herself. "I said, you need to use me as live bait. I need to be there. At the house, as you draw him in."

I shook my head. "No. It's too dangerous."

Trevor jumped in next. "Though I'm violating one of my basic principles here, I have to agree with Gabe, Alex. Besides, it's not necessary for you to actually be on scene. He just has to *think* you're there."

Alex stabbed her pointer finger into the table. "Whoever is behind the mask, it's clear that he has a very specific plan for me. He has systematically dismantled everything in my life that means something to me, is trying to alienate me from anyone who might offer support, and has been psychologically tormenting me, watching me suffer and *enjoying* it. The only thing that's left is the grand finish."

Seeing my hesitation, Alex leaned forward, her eyes boring into me. "As you said, I am his great temptation. He needs to *see* me. He will be so focused on me and the culmination of his master plan—on *winning*—that he'll be far less likely to notice the officers lying in wait. He'll make his fatal error."

I stared at her for a long moment trying to think of a counter-argument that was stronger than the case she'd just made. But I came up empty. I looked to Trevor, hoping he had something in his arsenal that would prove we didn't need Alex on scene to make this work. But when he shrugged and shook his head, I knew he also couldn't argue with her reasoning.

Trying for a Hail Mary before consenting to this crazy plan that had turned on me like a rabid dog, I asked Trevor, "Did you talk to Quinn about the trace?"

Trevor lowered the front legs of his chair to the ground and leaned his arms on the table. "Yeah. She has a contact at Las Vegas PD. Apparently, they have a guy who works as a free agent and contracts with various law enforcement agencies when they need someone who's . . . *gifted* with technology."

"A hacker," I said.

"Yup. Anyway, the contact is going to work on putting Quinn in touch with this guy, but it's likely to take a few days before we know anything."

Fuck. It was something, at least, but knowing that this thing with the Serpents was likely to blow up any day now, and the fact that Alex's stalker was picking up speed and becoming more venomous with each attack, my gut was telling me we just didn't have that kind of time.

I assessed Alex once more. She looked as determined as ever to get in on this fight. I took a deep breath and released it slowly. Well, I *had* wanted her to dig deep and find her courage. Guess I'd gotten what I'd asked for. "All right, Alex. We'll have you at the house and ensure he's able to get a good look at you. But you are not, under *any* circumstance, to leave the house or the immediate presence of the officers guarding you. Are we clear?"

Her eyes sparked with a fire I hadn't seen since our fight in her foyer when I'd thrown her over my shoulder.

"Crystal."

* * *

GABE

TWO DAYS LATER, we were set and ready to roll. Trevor and I had just finished briefing our team on their respective roles. We were now essentially in a holding pattern, waiting for the next piece to drop into place. I stood in Alex's living room, surveying the scene. More than half our force was decked out in black tactical gear and milling around the living room and kitchen as Alex flitted between them, refilling coffee cups and setting out snacks. To anyone else she would have appeared calm, focused only on keeping her guests comfortable. I knew better.

Her bottom lip kept finding itself ensnared between her teeth. When her hands were empty, she laced her fingers together, the tips turning white. And though she'd already given my guys so much coffee I was about to cut them off for fear their shooting accuracy would go to shit, she made another round each time she found herself with nothing to do but wait. I knew her well enough to recognize that she was distracting herself from the nervous energy threatening to tear her apart.

A beefy hand clapped my back as Trevor settled in next to me, his eyes alert, taking in every nuance around us. "The chief is about to go live."

I nodded, trying to ignore the anxiety fighting to take root in my stomach. If this had been any other operation, I would have been stone cold. Focused on the facts and what needed to be done without any emotional attachment. But this was the first time I'd ever had something on the line that I was terrified to lose.

My eyes returned to Alex. She was laughing at something one of the officers had just said, and, like him, I couldn't tear my attention from the woman who shone with the dazzling brilliance of sunlight on a fresh blanket of snow. I never should have agreed to her being present for this operation. It just wasn't worth the risk of something happening to her.

Trevor nudged me with his shoulder. When I swung my gaze to him, his expression was filled with compassion and understanding.

"We're going to keep her safe, brother. This will all be over soon."

I nodded again, apparently having lost the ability to speak. In an attempt to distract myself, for the hundredth time, I went down my mental checklist of all the elements that needed to be in place for this thing to work.

It had been a long day. We'd started early in the morning to ensure we were set up before the chief's news conference, which was scheduled for the afternoon. After we had conducted another full search to confirm no new surveillance equipment had been installed during our absence from Alex's house, we went to work sweeping the perimeter, identifying the most advantageous positions for our officers who would be stationed outside.

Then Rob, our K9 officer, and I had taken a little stroll over to Mr. Kensington's place. He was one of Alex's closest neighbors and, as luck would have it, a retired law enforcement officer, so I knew I could rely on him for both his cooperation and discretion. When we'd explained to Mr. Kensington that we needed a place to conceal Rob and his K9 partner, Ace, and that his house put us in the best tactical position, the old man had been thrilled to be of assistance and hadn't even tried to get the dirty details. He'd simply removed his car from his garage, parking it in the driveway, so Rob could park his patrol SUV out of sight.

Now that everyone was briefed on their assignments and we'd gone over the plan and all possible contingencies multiple times, all that was left was to wait for the chief to deliver the bait.

Trevor checked his watch and then located the TV remote. A moment later, everyone was gathered around the flat-screen, looking at an empty podium and a *breaking news* banner running across the bottom of the picture. I stood in front of the television with my feet planted wide, arms crossed over my chest, trying to keep myself anchored as the seconds ticked by, both too fast and achingly slow.

I twisted to look over my shoulder, searching for Alex, and found her standing at the back of the group, peering around the stocky frame of one of my guys. When our eyes met, I could see the full depth of her unease in the slight strain around her mouth and the way her eyes were just a little wider than usual.

I wanted to go to her, to wrap my arms around her and tell her that I was going to banish this nightmare for good. But I had to keep a professional distance. I couldn't afford to undermine my leadership or distract from the job at hand. It was essential that everyone remain alert and focused.

The sound of the chief's voice drew my attention back to the television. He squinted against the bright afternoon sun, his electric-blue eyes and bald head both holding a gleam from the harsh rays. The faint sound of cameras clicking and dying chatter faded into the background as the chief's commanding presence and sonorous voice filled the stage.

"There has been much interest," he began, "in the recent circumstances involving Ms. Alexandra Reilly and the threats and crimes against her. While it has been the department's position to limit the information released to the public out of concern of compromising the ongoing investigation, I am pleased to announce that we have brought Ms. Reilly's case to a successful conclusion."

A chorus of questions and waving hands erupted, each trying to rise above the rest. Chief Kelly lifted his hands, palms toward the crowd, calling for silence. "As I stated at the beginning of this press conference, I will not be accepting questions at this time. While there are still many details that we are not yet prepared to release, here is what I can tell you. The perpetrator who has been stalking Ms. Reilly, invading her privacy with the intent to sabotage her career and place her in constant fear for her safety, has been apprehended. We are not releasing the identity of the suspect at this time. Ms. Reilly has been safely returned to her home, which she had temporarily vacated due to the threat against her. The police protection assigned to her has been removed, and she is asking that her privacy and need for some peace and quiet be respected. A representative of Ms. Reilly's will make a statement at a later time. That's all for now."

The chief exited the stage, ignoring the litany of shouts and questions calling for his attention. Trevor and I exchanged glances, acknowledging that there was no turning back now. The bait had been delivered. Now all we could do was wait.

My cell phone vibrated in the pocket of my black cargo pants. The Velcro keeping the flap to my pocket closed protested as I yanked on it and retrieved the device. Expecting to see the chief's number displayed on my screen, I frowned when I saw an unknown number instead.

I answered. "McNeil."

"It's Jace."

Jace's tone was hushed, his words hurried. I stepped away from the crowd, finding a quiet space down the hall.

"Jace? Are you in trouble?"

"No, but I don't have long. I'm calling from the office line at the coffee shop."

The hair on the back of my neck stood up. Something big must be going down for him to sound so bugged out.

I kept my voice low. "What's going on?"

"The Serpents are moving on the Reapers tonight. Sometime around midnight. They're going to wait near the rest stop just outside of town and then follow at a distance until the truck carrying the weapons gets near the turnoff to the logging roads."

Shit. I closed my eyes and tilted my head back. What a clusterfuck.

I took a deep breath, trying to recenter my focus. "You're certain?"

"Yeah. I just came from there. Dawson had me doing cleanup from one of their ragers last night. He brought everyone in for church, and I listened at the door."

My chin dipped to my chest, and my shoulders dropped. This was getting worse by the second. I didn't want to chastise Jace. He never should have put himself in such a dangerous position as eavesdropping on a Serpent meeting, but I admired the hell out of the kid for how badly he wanted to help end the Serpents and right his wrongs.

I released the breath I'd been holding. "You did good, Jace. Now I want you to lie low. Go about your normal business. Leave the rest up to us. Got it?"

"Yeah. Stay safe, Gabe."

Jace disconnected and I stared at my phone a moment. It was strange to think how this kid had gone from being a town terror and a royal pain in the department's ass to being the most competent and useful informant we could have hoped for and someone I genuinely cared about.

I pocketed my phone and walked back to the entrance of the living room. After catching Trevor's eye, I hooked my head toward the hallway and waited for him to join me.

"We've got a situation," I said once he was in earshot. "Jace just called. The ambush is happening tonight."

Trevor rolled his eyes and ran a hand down his face, dragging his features with it. "You've got to be shitting me."

I quickly briefed him on the details. When I was finished, he said, "Well, I've got one more wrench to throw on the pile."

Of course he did. I raised my eyebrows, waiting for the next sucker punch.

"Rob's been tracking the weather," he said. "That little drizzle we were supposed to get tonight? It's now been reclassified to an Adios, Motherfucker."

My fists balled at my sides. I needed to hit something, to get some of this rage and anxiety out of my system before I exploded on everyone. This shit was circling the drain fast.

"What do you want to do?" Trevor asked.

I threw my hands out to the side. "What choice do we have? The chief already made the announcement that Alex's protection detail has been removed. It's not like we can call another press conference and say *just kidding—we got the wrong guy, so we're guarding her again.* We can only pull this rope-a-dope once."

He nodded. "And we might not get another opportunity this good to annihilate Dawson and his snakes."

The storm would definitely add an extra layer of danger to both operations, reducing visibility and potentially making it more difficult for the dog to track if that became necessary.

"We've got one more problem," I said. "We don't have enough manpower to run both ops at the same time."

"I'll take care of it," Trevor said. "You keep the team we've already briefed for this op. I'll talk to the chief about taking patrol down to a minimum tonight and calling in some off duty to handle the Serpents."

I shook my head vehemently, bringing my hands to my waist. "That's nowhere near enough bodies. Not to mention, we've got most of our seasoned officers here. You can't run an op like that with a bunch of greenhorns."

Trevor smiled like he was about to stir some shit up. "No time like the present to rub the bloom off."

Seeing that I wasn't amused, he chuckled and grasped my shoulder, giving it a hard squeeze. "Don't worry, bro. I'm going to call County for an assist. This could easily spill into their backyard, and I'm sure the sheriff's office will be itching to get in on the action."

I worked my jaw, mulling the idea over. It was a viable plan. The sheriff's department had had plenty of run-ins with the Serpents and other biker gangs who'd traveled into the territory over some beef with Dawson and his crew.

Still, the idea of not having Trevor's back or being there to see the case we'd been building for over a year through to the end left me feeling like I'd swallowed acid. The only alternative was to leave Alex under someone else's protection while I went after the Serpents. But really, that wasn't an option at all. There was no way in hell I was leaving her side. Especially after we'd just dropped her blood in the water and called the shark to dinner.

Reluctantly, I nodded, signaling to Trevor the plan was a go.

He stuck out his hand, waiting for me to shake it. When our palms met, I tightened my fingers around his grasp and pulled him into a bro hug. When we broke apart, he turned for the door and left without another word, and I prayed it wouldn't be the last time I saw my best friend.

CHAPTER 33

Alex

I GLANCED AT GABE, who was circling my walk-in closet like a caged predator. Dressed in black with face paint to match, he looked like murder walking. Especially when you took into account his intimidating frame and the scowl he'd been wearing since this afternoon.

I'd tried asking if he was all right, but the most I had gotten out of him was a grunt and a view of his back as he walked away.

Now, folding clothes on my bed, I kept my mouth shut and only glanced at him every so often as he made another lap inside the closet, remaining out of view to avoid casting shadows that might show through the blinds.

"Alex."

I turned, surprised that he was addressing me.

"You should head out to the main part of the house. Odds are, he's going to approach from the woods. It's better if you stay in the kitchen and living room where he can see you."

Gabe's tone was flat. Matter of fact. It held none of the warmth and intimacy to which I had grown accustomed over these past few days. I tried to tell myself that he was just remaining professional, ensuring that our relationship was kept separate from the job he needed to do. But deep down, I feared that this had all become too much for him. That somewhere between me sleeping in his arms and that national news conference about the mess that had become my life, he had decided that the drama was more trouble than it was worth. More trouble than *I* was worth.

There were so many things I wanted to say to him, to apologize for, and to plead with him to talk to me about what was going on in his head. Instead, I simply nodded and started for the door.

"Alex, wait."

I turned, hoping for an explanation that would make me feel better.

"Remember," he said, "this guy is smart. He's not going to blindly trust what he heard at the press conference. He'll sneak in. Waiting and watching for anything that seems out of place. You have to do your best to go about your business as normal. Try to look like a woman who's relieved that the threat is over."

I took a deep breath, feeling my shoulders rise and then fall as I released it slowly. I had to get my head on straight. I had to do my part to make this mission a success. I couldn't do that if I was preoccupied by whatever was going on between Gabe and me.

I nodded and forced a reassuring smile before leaving the room.

The sound of rain beating its fists against the house grew louder as I made my way toward the kitchen. Sheets of water cascaded down the windows, making it impossible to see anything beyond. Not that I could have seen much anyway. It was nearing midnight, and what little moonlight we would have had was fully obscured behind a thick and unyielding blanket of clouds.

As I reached the kitchen, another peel of thunder was unleashed across the heavens. It joined with the howling winds to rattle the windows and add to the deafening rage of the elements.

I went to the stove to collect the teakettle and glanced into the living room, where Aderes laid on the couch with her head propped on the arm, gazing at the patio doors. A fire roared in the hearth across from her, the warm glow of the jumping flames casting shadows that danced around the room.

Staring out the kitchen window as the teakettle filled, my eyes tracked the flashes of lightning that bounced across the sky. I thought of all the officers standing watch in the mud and these horrible conditions and hated knowing they were enduring this misery because of me.

When the teakettle was finally full, I set it to heat on the stove and then went about cleaning the kitchen and tidying the living room. If all I could do to help this situation along was play a worm on a hook, I'd ensure I was the most tempting worm that had ever dangled on the line. Then maybe we'd all be able to put this behind us, and Gabe and his people could return to life as usual.

Another half hour passed without incident, and I was just finishing emptying the dishwasher when Aderes's head shot up from the arm of the couch. Her body remained very still, her eyes trained on the patio doors, a low growl emanating from her chest. I froze, my eyes fixed on her rigid body. Goose bumps erupted on my arms as her steady growl intensified, taking on a savage tone.

With my next heartbeat, Gabe tore through the house, swearing on a snarl, his gun drawn.

"Stay put!" he barked before wrenching the patio doors open and disappearing into the night.

* * *

GABE

I SPRINTED into the woods at a hazardous pace, rain pelting my face and blurring my vision.

I keyed my mic and bellowed into the mouthpiece, trying to ensure I could be heard over the squalling storm. "Adam Nine, what was his direction of travel?"

The radio squawked with static, the storm making our already shitty reception even worse. "East. Parallel to the main road."

"Copy," I replied. "All units, I'm going to proceed directly east from the residence. Units on the north side of the property, spread out and head east along the road. Units to the south, reposition a hundred yards southeast of the residence, then canvass to the east and south. K9, you copy?"

"K9 here."

"Take your partner and start a track south from your location."

"Ten-four."

With my units in position, I resumed my pursuit. Holding my Glock in one hand and my flashlight in the other, I moved deeper into the woods, keeping the light off for the time being. The last thing I wanted was to reveal my location before I had a better idea of where our perp was.

After a few minutes of navigating over some fallen trees and ripping through low foliage that tangled around my boots, I watched an arc of lightning slice across the sky, and for a moment, the woods were cast in an ominous glow. The light was fleeting, but it was enough for me to catch a glimpse of movement straight ahead with about a fifty-yard lead.

I tucked my flashlight under my arm and keyed my mic again. "Adam Two to all units, the suspect is directly ahead of me, still proceeding due east, twenty-five yards south of the main road. Dressed in all black."

With one rookie already having fucked up this operation, I prayed that another didn't get an itchy trigger finger and mistake one of our own for the perp, considering we were all dressed similarly and the visibility was shit.

"K9, what's your status?" I asked. The sound of a thousand boulders careening down a mountain erupted around me as another burst of thunder joined the madness.

The radio traffic was breaking badly, but I could make out

enough of K9's transmission to know that if I didn't catch up to our suspect, there was a good chance he was getting away.

"Ace is having trouble following a line!" Rob shouted into his mic. "The heavy winds and high rainfall are scattering the scent."

I clicked my flashlight on and directed the beam along the forest floor ten yards ahead of me. The guy had a large enough lead and knew there were several officers in pursuit, so I doubted he'd try to lie low and take aim somewhere. With the addition of the light, I made quick work of eating up the distance between us, the lightning flashes coming rapidly enough now that I was able to keep fairly good tabs on where he was.

The wind roared in my ears and joined with the sound of my wildly beating heart and ragged breaths, the noise removing one of the senses I relied on heavily in situations like this.

After several minutes of giving chase, I was deep in the woods, towering evergreens standing over me like obsidian giants. I knew I was being stupid. If this were any other case, I would have called off the pursuit long ago. Visibility was practically zero. The radio interference from the storm made it nearly impossible to keep track of my team. The dog couldn't follow the perp's trail, and we were virtually begging for someone to get shot, either by a desperate suspect or by friendly fire.

Knowing all of this, I still couldn't bring myself to terminate the pursuit. I couldn't return to Alex and tell her that I had failed her again.

But I could at least protect my guys. "All units, pull back and wait for my command."

As soon as the words were out of my mouth, another bolt of lightning rippled through the dark clouds. This time, I couldn't see movement ahead of me. I slowed my pace in case this guy *was* reckless enough to try ambushing an officer with a dozen others nearby and hot on his trail.

I turned the beam of my flashlight in a slow arc, looking for any signs of movement, but with the torrential rainfall and high winds, *everything* was moving. The only thing that would help now was catching another glimpse of my target.

Seconds later, my stomach dropped, my ears picking up a sound that was most definitely not the storm.

CHAPTER 34

Alex

I TRIED to see Gabe through the blurry window, but the darkness had swallowed him instantly. Movement in my peripheral snapped my head around. I jumped, my hand flying to my chest, when I saw a dark figure standing just inside the doors Gabe had left open. The storm was so loud, I hadn't heard anyone approach.

Aderes jumped to her feet, her front paws positioned on the arm of the couch as she barked viciously at the intruder. Though his face was painted black, I recognized the youthful features and the red hair peeking out from under his black beanie. The young officer put his hands up in front of him, not daring to move with Aderes inches from his throat, her lips peeled back and drool streaming from her canines. I went to her, placing my hand on her head, stroking her soft fur.

"It's all right, sweet girl," I cooed as I soothed her with my touch. "It's all right." Aderes cast a furtive glance in my direction as if to ask if I was sure I didn't want her to tear this guy's throat out.

"Yes, it's all right, Aderes. We're okay."

She stopped growling and relaxed ever so slightly, but her muscles were bunched, ready to pounce if necessary.

The officer let his arms fall and slowly turned to close the patio doors behind him. He was soaking wet, a large puddle of water surrounding his feet.

"Officer McNeil sent me in to watch over you," he said.

The poor kid held nothing of the bright smile and twinkling eyes I had seen earlier in the day as he'd bantered with his colleagues. Now, his head hung low, and it was all I could do to get him to make eye contact with me.

"What happened?" I asked.

He grimaced and looked down at his feet. "I fucked up." His head snapped up, eyes wide. "Ex-excuse me, ma'am. I didn't mean any disrespect." He removed the beanie from his head, wringing it in his hands, sending a stream of water to collect with the puddle at his feet. "What I meant was that I made a huge mistake. The suspect was nearby, and I alerted him to our presence."

My heart beat painfully against my chest as adrenaline shot through me like a live wire. "Where did he go?"

The officer ran his hand through his hair, causing the strands to stand up in various directions, giving him an even more youthful appearance. "He took off through the woods. Officer McNeil and the others are in pursuit."

My blood turned to ice in my veins. If Hargrove really was the one behind all of this, he wouldn't think twice about shooting anyone who got in his way. And in these conditions, Gabe and his team had the disadvantage.

* * *

Gabe

I RUSHED FORWARD, my arms extended, shoving branches aside as I pushed through the dense trees.

No, damn it! No!

All thoughts of personal safety gone, I didn't even take the time to advise my partners of what was happening. Seconds mattered, and I couldn't waste even one.

Almost. You're almost there.

The sound had died nearly as quickly as I'd heard it. Branches scraped against my face and hands. My clothing snagged and pulled away from my body. Cold air burned my skin where my shirt had torn. I was hardly aware of any of it.

I leapt over a large tangle of weeds, my boots sliding in the mud when I landed on the other side.

Another crack of thunder.

As the night sky became a sea of white once more, I looked ahead and saw that the trees thinned considerably.

Still no sight of my prey.

With one more burst of energy, my boots tore up the sodden earth, and the trees suddenly fell away. I came to a halt, my head swiveling in all directions as I realized I was standing in a clearing and completely exposed. Stepping back to the tree line to get some cover, I turned my flashlight on and surveyed the area, realizing I had stumbled upon a narrow dirt road.

It only took a moment for my eyes to find the source of the sound I'd heard. Directly in front of me, a fresh set of tire marks were scored deeply into the muddy terrain, the tracks rapidly filling with water.

I swept my flashlight along the road, noting that the tire marks died where I was standing. I was certain they belonged to our suspect. He'd driven in, parked his car here, and then left the same way. We were close enough to the main road that he was long gone by now.

I took a moment to exhaust my full arsenal of expletives before calling my second-in-command to advise the suspect had escaped and I was on my way back to Alex's. By the time I walked through her front door, everyone except my K9 officer had congregated in the living room. One look at Alex's wet, muddy floor and I decided I'd start making up for my failure by calling in a professional cleaning crew.

The look of relief on Alex's face when she spotted me was the only thing that had ever come close to breaking me. Before I could go to her, Rob walked through the open patio doors, Ace on a tight lead at his side.

With a room full of people between us, all of them busy reliving the excitement of the past twenty minutes, I caught his eye and jerked my chin up.

He pressed his lips into a firm line and slowly shook his head. My last hope had rested on my K9 unit finding something, *anything*, that could lead us to this guy.

I was about to debrief everyone so they could get the hell out of here and shuck their wet clothing when my phone buzzed. One glance at the screen and my adrenaline spiked again.

"Is it over?" I asked.

I pressed my phone hard against my ear, trying to make out Trevor's muffled words.

"We're code four," he yelled into the line. "But the sting was a bust."

"What the hell happened?" The lid I'd been trying to keep on my anger all evening had finally disintegrated along with my ability to speak in anything other than a shout. All eyes turned on me, and Anderson, still undoubtedly drowning in his own shame for botching the operation, shrank even farther into the corner he was occupying by himself.

"We got the Reapers, and they were running guns, just like you-know-who said. But there wasn't a Serpent in sight."

"Are you sure you guys weren't spotted before you moved in?"

"Positive. We even had units hang behind to monitor the rest stop once we realized something was up. The Serpents were never there. We tracked the cargo several miles beyond where the hit was supposed to go down. We finally just had to make the call to move on the bust before the target got into someone else's jurisdiction."

Fuck. How had everything gotten so royally screwed up?

"It's still a hell of a bust," Trevor said, trying to make the best of the situation, as usual. "After this, the Reapers are pretty much dead in the water. All of their biggest fish are going away for a *very* long time."

He was right. It was still a win, just not the one we were hoping for.

"How is everything going there?" Trevor asked. "Has our guest arrived yet?"

My blood boiled again at the reminder. "You could say that." Icicles could have hung from the statement.

"Yikes. Dare I ask?"

My eyes locked onto Anderson. "We almost got him, but *someone*"—I spoke the word loudly to get everyone's attention—"forgot to put his cell phone on silent, and the asshole got away by inches."

Anderson caved in on himself further, looking as though he wanted to locate the smallest, darkest hole he could find, crawl in, and die.

Alex stood near him, the look of pain and sympathy in her eyes conveying that she thought I was being a dick and way too harsh.

I couldn't share in her sympathy, though. Having spent over a decade in the company of both soldiers and cops, I knew the only way he was going to have this lesson seared into his memory was to make him feel the full weight of his shame and what his mistake could have cost someone.

I'd take him aside later and help him to understand that it was a mistake, and we all make them. The important thing is ensuring you never make the same mistake twice.

Trevor whistled through his teeth. "Someone's gonna be on paper duty for the foreseeable future."

I took a deep breath and reminded myself that Anderson was the rookie, and I was the seasoned vet and the lead on this op. It was my responsibility to ensure my officers were prepared for what we faced. Many of them had never seen the kind of action we'd encountered tonight. I should have reminded everyone to put their phones on vibrate.

"Nah," I said more quietly. "He's just green. I didn't lead him well enough. I'll talk to him about it later."

Trevor was quiet a moment, only the shouts from those working the scene around him coming through the phone. When he finally spoke, his tone was somber. "Gabe, Jace had everything else right. You know what that means."

I released a breath, my shoulders falling as I felt the full weight of the night's events. "Yeah. I know." I wiped my hand down my face, removing the water running down from my hair.

Either the Serpents knew they had an informant in their midst and they were trying to smoke him out, or someone had found out about the sting and given them a heads-up. Either way, there was a very strong possibility that Jace's cover was blown. If that was the case, Jace would be skinned and disemboweled before the week's end.

CHAPTER 35

Gabe

I SMOTHERED a yawn as I steered my truck through town. The late-afternoon sun beat through my windshield, its warmth making it even more difficult to remain conscious. I glanced at my reflection in the rearview mirror and immediately regretted it. I looked like a fucking hobo. My eyes were bloodshot. I had several days' worth of dark stubble on my jaw. And because I hadn't even had time to buzz my hair lately, it had grown enough that after last night's playdate in the rain, it was plastered to my head in some places and sticking straight up in others.

Just thinking about last night had me grinding my molars again. What a fucking shitshow. Trevor and I had been so sure we were going to bring both cases to a successful conclusion before morning broke. But instead of savoring victory, we'd spent the rest of last night and all of today in the war room with the chief trying to figure out how we'd gotten our asses kicked so badly and what we were going to do to clean this clusterfuck up.

Another yawn broke free. My fingers automatically went to the buttons on the side panel of my door, and I rolled my windows down in hopes the blast of cool autumn air would help to keep my eyes open.

I came to a stop at the last traffic signal between me and the familiar country road that would take me home. Out of habit, my eyes raked over my surroundings, taking in all the details while my brain sorted the information. School had gotten out a short while ago, so the sidewalks and the park were full of kids. A part of me envied their rosy, smiling faces. Little legs carried them across the grass as they reached for a friend they were trying to tag or had them skipping from the ice cream parlor with dairy in varying colors dripping down their faces. Their foreheads were smooth, devoid of the creases that came with worry and heartbreak.

A smile tugged at my lips. A couple decades ago, I had been one of those kids. Despite having acres upon acres on which to run and play, Liz, Mason, and I had always joined our friends in the park after school to run off some of the energy that long hours spent at a desk had forced us to contain. Growing up in this town had been one of my greatest joys. Everyone here was family. Mom and Dad never had to worry about where we were or what we were doing, because there was always someone with eyes on us.

It truly was one of the last great places on earth. And that was why I had wanted so badly to raise kids here. I wanted them to experience the same joy and magic that I had been given. I wanted them to know what it was like to grow up in a community where people genuinely cared about each other.

Even as an adult, after I'd joined the Marines, whenever I came home on leave, it wasn't just Mom and Dad waiting to welcome me home. The whole town showed up to hug me or shake my hand, bringing with them food and stories from the past.

Shouts and shrieks of laughter brought my attention back to the park, and my eyes settled on one little girl sitting beneath a massive Sycamore tree. She had dark-red hair, and she sat with her back to the trunk of the tree, her legs tucked under her, a book in her hands. I imagined that that was what Alex had looked like as a young girl. A loner, preferring the characters of her books to the company of other children. Intelligence shining from her eyes and the red tones of her hair glowing like a torch under the sunlight streaming through the leaves of the tree that sheltered her as she dreamt of endless adventures.

Realizing the traffic beside me was moving, I flicked my eyes to the light and saw that it had turned green. I waved an apology to the car behind me and hit the gas to head out of town. As houses and buildings fell away and were replaced by endless rows of trees, a backdrop of lush mountains all around, my mind returned to the situation at hand.

Trevor and I had gone round and round about whether we should bring Jace in. If his cover was blown, we didn't have much time to get him to a secure location. The problem, though, was that there was still a possibility that his cover was intact. If Trevor and I made a move to extract him, we would essentially be signing his death warrant and labeling him a rat. Whatever decision we ended up making, if we chose wrong, Jace would be tortured and killed. I would never be able to scrub that mark from my soul.

And then there was the issue of Alex. I feared that all we had accomplished last night was pissing off a very deranged, very capable psychopath. There was no way he'd fall for another con, so we were back to the game of cat and mouse with him striking out of the blue and us watching for any misstep that would reveal him to us.

But my biggest concern about last night's fiasco was what he would do to retaliate against Alex. And there was no doubt in my mind he would.

As the miles disappeared behind me, and the sun sank lower in the sky until it hovered just above the mountain range in my rearview mirror, I continued to turn each situation over in my head, convinced that there was a solution I simply wasn't seeing.

By the time I parked in front of Liz's house ten minutes later, I was still short on ideas, and my mood had darkened even further. Before heading inside, I took a moment to run my hands through my hair and get my head on a little straighter. I hadn't spent much time with my family these past couple of weeks, and I didn't want the few moments I could spare to be tainted by work.

Once I felt I had a solid lid on my emotions, I hopped out of the truck and went inside. Lily was playing on the living room floor, and the sound of pots and pans banging trickled out from the kitchen.

Lily looked up at the sound of the door, her blue eyes growing as big as her smile when she saw me.

"Uncle Gabe!" She squealed and jumped up from the floor, clutching her toy under her arm as she ran toward me.

I bent and scooped her up, laughing as she threw her arms around my neck, choking off my air supply. Her bouncy blond curls tickled my nose, and as I held her tight against my chest, all of the anger and frustration melted away.

"Hey, Lily-pad. How was school?"

Lily kept her chubby arms around my neck but pulled back and placed her forehead against mine. "Good. Where have you been, mister?"

I laughed again, enjoying how cute she looked with her bottom lip sticking out in a pout. "I know, I know. I haven't been around much. But hopefully that's going to change soon."

I kissed her cheek and shifted her weight so she was perched on my hip. One arm remained snaked around my neck while the other held her toy. Not recognizing it, I took it from her to get a closer look.

"Did you get a new toy?"

"Mm-hmm."

It was a stuffed pig. An interesting choice since Lily was obsessed with princesses. Anytime we got her something new, it was always somehow tied to a girl in a pretty dress and crown.

I turned the stuffed animal over, looking for something that would indicate why Lily would be interested in this toy, and noticed a black mark on one of its sides.

When I brought the toy in for a closer look, my heart jumped to my throat.

"Lily, where did you get this?"

"From my friend."

"Which friend?"

"The one with the loud bike."

Lily wiggled down my body, and as soon as her feet hit the floor, she ran down the hall toward her bedroom.

The loud bike. No fucking way.

I looked at the black mark on the pig again. There was a small X drawn in permanent marker where the animal's heart would be. Obviously a threat meant for me.

Just as I was about to follow Lily to get more information, I heard the clatter of her small feet running toward the living room. She rounded the corner a moment later, holding a big white envelope in her hands.

Brushing a curl away from her cheek, she stood in front of me. When I squatted down so that I was eye level with her, she handed me the envelope.

"The man said if I gave this to my Uncle Gabe, I could keep my present." Her sweet, lilting voice gripped my heart, acid rising in my stomach as I thought about how vulnerable she'd been.

"Lily, what did this man look like?"

Her eyes swept up to the right, her pink mouth puckering as she tried to remember. "He was a giant!"

"Okay. What else?"

"Hmm." She tapped her lips. "He had brown hair. But not like yours. It was long, like mine."

"That's good. What else? Do you remember what he was wearing?"

She nodded enthusiastically, her curls dancing and catching the light filtering in through the large front window. "A black shirt, but it didn't have arms. It had a scary picture on the back."

A cut. "What was the picture, Lily?"

"A scary red man with lots of snakes crawling all over him." She stuck out her tongue and faked a shiver.

A sensation of cold washed over me as though I'd just fallen through a frozen lake. I looked down at the envelope in my hand, the sound of Liz's movements in the kitchen turning into muted background noise as all of my senses heightened and focused on it.

I flipped it over and ripped open the flap, pushing the sides of the envelope open so I could see inside before sticking my hand in it. A glossy image of Lily playing in the yard stared back at me.

I gripped the stack of photos by their corners and pulled them free. Careful not to get fingerprints on any of them, I flipped through the stack. One after the other revealed my family, each taken at a distance as they went about their normal routines. A picture of my mom watering her garden. One of Connor at soccer practice. And Liz, carrying Lily on her hip as Lily pointed to something ahead of them.

I returned the photos to the envelope and propped my elbow on my knee, allowing my head to drop into my hand. Tiny fingers patted my shoulder.

"It's okay, Uncle Gabe. Don't be sad."

I met Lily's concerned gaze and reached out, pulling her into a hug.

How had I let this happen? How had I led one of the most violent gangs in the country right to my family's fucking doorstep?

I was failing everyone who trusted me to keep them safe.

The sound of high heels on hardwood grew louder as Liz exited the kitchen and joined us in the living room.

I released Lily and stood. Liz had her hands on her hips and an apron around her waist. The sparkle in her violet eyes faded the moment she saw me.

"Gabe?" Her forehead creased, waiting for me to tell her what was going on.

I shook my head. "I'll talk to you about it later. I need to make a call."

She hesitated and looked as though she was about to protest. Finally, she nodded and told Lily to help her in the kitchen.

I pulled my phone from my pocket and stepped out onto the front porch, walking to the corner closest to the road.

"Hey, man. What's up?" Trevor's voice was groggy. He'd undoubtedly fallen asleep the second he'd arrived home.

"We've got a situation." My voice was a low growl, ice in every word.

The rustle of covers told me I had Trevor's attention. His voice was alert when he spoke again. "What's going on?"

I glanced at the envelope still clutched in my hand. "A snake paid my family a visit."

I filled Trevor in on my conversation with Lily. With each new detail, the menace in his deep voice grew to match my own.

I released a frustrated breath and stared at the blue and gray shades of twilight just beginning to rise in the distance. "This needs to end," I said quietly. "One way or another, I'm bringing this whole fucking shitstorm down."

CHAPTER 36

Alex

THE RAPID CLICKING of my keyboard marked the minutes and seconds ticking by as I tried to lose myself in the story that clamored for life. Dying rays of amber light filtered through my office window, mixing with the soft glow of lamplight that fell in sheets around the room. Despite the words forming in front of my eyes, I had little awareness of what was actually unfurling on the page.

My movements halted, my fingers hovered over the keyboard. I stared at my screen and the blinking cursor, but the only image I saw was one I held in my memory. I huffed, releasing all of the air from my lungs, and flung myself against the backrest of my chair. Squeezing my eyes shut, I tried to banish the storm of emotions that kept surfacing, threatening to spill over, despite my attempts at distraction.

I took a deep breath and slowly released it, telling myself that I'd walked through hell before, and I could do it again. After a few more breaths and a few more recitations of my mantra, the storm within began to settle. With my head still leaning against the back of my chair, I rolled it to the side and let my eyes trace the few leaves that remained on the tree outside my window as the images of last night were projected onto the movie screen in my mind.

I'd been beside myself with worry when all of the officers had trudged through my patio door, one after the other, sopping wet, heads hanging low and no sign of Gabe. They had assured me they still had radio contact with him, but the thought of Gabe chasing a madman through the woods in the dark of night, alone, was almost more than my nerves had been able to handle.

I'd paced, stopping every few seconds to scan the woods from my open patio doors, each time growing more anxious when I saw only shadows. Finally, the front door had slammed shut. We'd all turned to see Gabe standing in the archway between the foyer and living room. He had water cascading down his body like the rest of them, but the look of murder shining in those dark eyes belonged to him alone.

I had wanted to go to him. To put my arms around him and reassure myself that he was whole and sound. But one look at the hard planes of his features and the balled fists held against his rigid body had me stepping back.

He'd seemed off all day, but that was the first time I'd truly felt I couldn't approach him. The mood in the room was as dark as the night, and my heart had broken for the young officer who had been shamed in front of his colleagues.

I knew Gabe, Chief Kelly, and all of the officers on my case were ready to put this situation behind them. So was I. And I couldn't help but wonder if that was the reason for Gabe's sudden change in mood. Maybe he blamed me for how much trouble this case had caused his department. Maybe he was tired of babysitting me and wanted to get back to real police work. *Or maybe . . .*

The thought forming had visited on many occasions, and each time, I tried to pretend it wasn't there, but with the way Gabe had been acting the past couple of days, it was getting harder and harder to ignore.

Maybe I remind him of Olivia.

Mentally, I began to tick off all of the ways in which I was similar to the woman who had betrayed and humiliated the proud man for whom I'd been falling.

I had intended to leave the man I'd promised my life to. I was the reason Gabe's personal affairs had been blasted all over town, not to mention the internet and national news. He had given me so much and remained by my side when most people would have left me standing in my mess alone. But what had I given him in return? Nothing.

The anguish, the guilt, and the shame surfaced again and would not be tempered. That was okay, though, because this time, I would force myself to feel them. To bear every agonizing ounce of what I deserved.

I stood and walked to the window, leaning my shoulder against it. Given the cold temperatures and damp conditions, the ground was still saturated from last night's storm. I unlatched the lock and lifted the window a few inches, allowing the scent of damp earth and decaying leaves to permeate my sanctuary.

An image of Gabe, smiling, his eyes crinkling at the corners as his body hovered over me beneath the warm covers of his bed, sprang forth, bringing with it a lump in my throat and burning in my eyes.

I had been so careful, so determined, to keep people at a distance. When I'd come to Eden Falls, it had been with the intention of living a solitary life. A life where I could neither hurt anyone nor allow them to hurt me. But somehow, that damn Marine had broken down my carefully constructed walls and waltzed right into the deepest caverns of my heart. Feeling him pull away was a fresh kind of pain, one I had never felt before and so much more excruciating than I could have imagined.

Water welled in my eyes. I tried to blink it away, but the tears refused to be denied. One by one, they fell to my cheeks and carved a path down my throat and onto my chest.

A *ding* came from my computer. I swiped at the trail of tears on my face and moved back to my desk, praying it wasn't another piece of hate mail. I wasn't even sure why I was still checking my correspondence at this point. Perhaps a part of me hoped that someone out there was willing to publish a tarnished brand so that I wouldn't have to admit my life's work was over.

I opened my email and found the most recent message. In the *From* field, it simply showed *A Fan*.

My forehead furrowed as I clicked on the message and began to read.

Dearest Alexandra,

I would have thought by now that you would have realized I cannot be bested. Last night's child's play accomplished nothing other than trying my patience and convincing me that more is required to teach you the lesson you seem so unwilling to learn.

Since you seem unable to understand that this is my *game, and I am the only one who can win it, I will make your next move excruciatingly clear. You will get rid of the cop you've been fucking. If you fail to do so in a timely manner, I will ensure he suffers dearly before I dismember and dispose of him. Do not test me, Alexandra. You know well by now what I am capable of. Nobody takes what is mine. Get rid of him.*

My hand flew to my mouth, my fingers trembling against the soft skin of my lips as my eyes stared disbelieving at the sadistic message. Images of Gabe, beaten and bleeding, rushed forward, quickly replaced by the sight of his lifeless body lying carelessly in some forgotten wood.

I stood so fast my chair slammed against the wall behind me. I took two steps toward the door, about to call out to the officer on duty, when my feet halted. I glanced back at my laptop.

I couldn't tell anyone about this. If last night had proven anything, it was the fact that my stalker was always, *always*, one step ahead. He hadn't shown an ounce of hesitation or remorse in any of the sadistic acts he'd carried out. There was zero doubt in my mind his threat against Gabe wasn't idle.

If I told Gabe or any of his officers about the email, there was no way they would back off this case. And despite whatever Gabe did or didn't feel for me at this point, I knew his sense of duty and honor would only fuel his determination to stay near.

My shoulders fell. With slow, heavy footsteps, I returned to my chair, rereading the email, hoping a solution that would resolve this whole situation would magically appear.

Instead, as the minutes ticked by and the light was swallowed by the dark, another fissure in my battered heart was the only thing I gained.

* * *

THE DOORBELL RANG. I set an unopened tea bag down on the kitchen counter and started toward the front door, clueless as to who would be paying a visit this time of night. The officer on duty intercepted me in the foyer, holding up a hand to signal that he wanted me to stay put. I nodded and took a few steps back as he approached the door, opening it only after peeking through the side windows.

The officer's tall frame and broad shoulders made it impossible for me to see who was outside. He spoke quietly to someone, his head bent at such an angle it appeared that whomever he was speaking to was much shorter. Finally, the officer stepped back and permitted my guest to enter.

My mouth parted when Bree stepped inside, carrying a plate covered with a dish towel. She smiled brightly when she saw me.

"Hey, Alex. I'm sorry to stop by without calling first, but I didn't have your number. I hope you don't mind."

Recovering from my surprise, I smiled in return and shook my head. "No, not at all. I was just about to fix some tea. Would you like to join me?"

"Ooh, that sounds fantastic. It'll pair perfectly with these."

She moved closer, pulling the towel that matched her vivid red top from the plate to reveal crescent-shaped shortbread cookies dusted in powdered sugar. My mouth began to water as the decadent scent of sugar and butter hit my nose.

"They're lovely!" I said.

Her smile deepened as she tried to tuck a stray lock of hair back up into her messy bun while balancing the plate. "I know you've been under a lot of strain lately, and I just wanted to do something to remind you that you've got friends in your corner."

I felt the familiar sting of tears trying to work their way to the surface and swallowed hard in an attempt to keep them from springing free. The last thing I wanted was to give the appearance that I was falling apart. True as that might have felt.

"Thank you, Bree." I held her gaze, hoping she could feel the sincerity and heartfelt gratitude behind my words.

She simply nodded and said, "Lead the way."

I took her into the kitchen and set out two mugs on the long counter that doubled as a breakfast bar. She placed the cookies in between and grabbed a couple of napkins from the stack I kept near the sink. With our backs to the living room, we settled on the barstools, steaming liquid in hand.

"How have things been at the coffee shop?" I asked, angling my body toward her.

"It's pretty much been business as usual," she said. "A bit more volume with all the visitors in town." She gave a wry smile over the brim of her cup before taking a cautious sip.

Visitors. That was a thoughtful way of referring to the swarms of media trying to dig up every dirty detail of my life. I appreciated that she was sidestepping the elephant in the room, giving me the freedom to choose whether or not I wanted to discuss it.

I smiled, but try as I might, I couldn't force it to reach my eyes. "At least with the local businesses getting a bump in revenue, something good is coming out of all this."

My hands were wrapped around my mug, trying to draw every ounce of warmth from it. Bree reached over and placed her hand on my wrist and waited for me to meet her eyes.

"Alex, I know we haven't known each other long, but I want you to know I'm here for you if you need anything. I haven't really followed the details. I don't like getting into people's business, but working in the coffee shop, I hear enough to get the gist of what's going on in town. With what I've been hearing, and the fact I haven't seen you around the coffee shop lately, I figured you've been taking quite a beating."

For a moment, I resisted the urge to let my cheerful facade fall, but I finally gave in, releasing my breath and allowing my shoulders to crumple. "The truth is, I feel like I'm trapped in a nightmare and can't wake up."

I don't know why I made the admission. Bree was right. We hadn't known each other long, and I had made it a practice years ago to keep my cards close to my chest after having learned there are far too many people in this world who are good at pretending they care only long enough to gain information that serves them. Maybe I was just too used up at this point to keep such a tight hold on those reins.

Bree ran her thumb back and forth across my skin before withdrawing. She turned her body so she could face me more directly. "What can I do to help, Alex?"

A shaky smile formed on my lips. The sincerity in that question was threatening to break the dam holding my emotions back. I shrugged. "Honestly, you're already doing it. These cookies," I said, gesturing toward the plate. "Your concern. They mean a great deal."

Her gaze fell as though she were trying to work out a difficult problem. Then she suddenly looked up, a mischievous smile forming. "Well, since everyone is getting their gossip jollies by talking about you, how 'bout I share some of the goings-on with the rest of the townsfolk?"

She waggled her eyebrows, drawing a giggle from me, and spent the next half hour regaling me with all of the funny and outrageous things that our community had been up to. Everything from old Mr. Finnigan watering his lawn in nothing but a pair of lace-up boots to Mrs. Cagney siccing her cockapoo on one of those nosy reporters.

By the time Bree was through, I felt a little lighter, the tears not nearly so close to the surface. The respite was short-lived, however.

The officer standing guard had remained close during our visit, pacing slowly between the living room and the front of the house. His phone rang, and when he greeted Gabe and stepped away to keep his conversation private, my heart fell at the reminder of the man I loved but couldn't have and the horrible decision I needed to make.

"Hey," Bree said softly, placing her hand on my shoulder, her slate-blue eyes filled with concern. "What just happened?"

I shook my head, trying to put my mask back in place. "It's nothing."

"Alex, something is clearly weighing on you. I know you to be a pretty private person, and given your lifestyle and work, I can understand why. But if there's something going on that's bigger than you know how to deal with, it isn't good to try to keep it locked inside." Bree shifted in her seat and crossed her arms in front of her on the counter. "If you don't feel comfortable talking to me about it, I understand. But you need to find *someone* to talk to."

I meditated on her words for a moment. She was right. This threat against Gabe—I didn't know how to handle it. I just didn't know who to talk to. Liz was out. She was way too close to Gabe. She'd tell him, and then it would have been no different than me telling him or his officers myself. Cass and I still had radio silence. And my parents—that would only make the situation ten times worse. They would care nothing of the threat against Gabe and would merely proceed to tell me how I had brought all of this on myself.

I glanced down the hall where the officer was still talking to Gabe. Convinced I wouldn't be overheard, I turned back to Bree and lowered my voice.

"Bree, if I talk to you about this, you absolutely cannot tell another soul." I dipped my chin and held her gaze, my expression conveying that I was dead serious.

She eyed me warily but finally nodded. "You have my word."

I took a deep breath and checked one more time to ensure we still had privacy.

"I received an email earlier today," I began. "It was from the person who has been stalking me. He threatened someone close to me—"

"Gabe," she cut in matter-of-factly.

My eyebrows shot up. "How did you know?"

The corner of her mouth curled. "It's not hard to put together. This guy is obsessed with you, and everyone knows you and Gabe are an item. It makes sense he would threaten the competition."

I looked down at my mug again, which was nearly empty now.

"Go on, Alex."

I bit my lip, praying this wasn't going to come back to haunt me. But trying to solve this on my own had left me with more doubts and confusion than when I'd started. "He threatened to kill Gabe if I didn't end things with him."

Now it was Bree's eyebrows that shot up. "Did you tell Gabe?"

I shook my head.

"Why not?"

"Because I'm not sure that's the best course of action." Now that I had admitted the worst of it, my words were falling out of my mouth faster than my brain could track. I knew we wouldn't be alone much longer, and I wanted to get Bree's input before my guard returned.

"If I tell Gabe, or any of his partners, he's not going to walk away. If anything, he'll stay closer." I stabbed my pointer finger into the counter to drive my point home. "Whoever is behind all of this is dangerous, Bree. And he's very smart. I have no doubt that he will make good on his promise to dispose of Gabe if I don't get him to stay away."

Bree nodded slowly, her eyes drifting off into the kitchen as she digested what I'd just told her. "Well," she finally said, "it sounds like you feel the best thing to do is to end things with Gabe and not tell him about the threat, so why did you say you're not sure what the best course of action is?"

"Because there's a chance my stalker would go after Gabe either way, even if I do what he says. If that's the case, Gabe is more likely to be caught off guard if I don't tell him about the death threat."

Understanding replaced confusion on Bree's face. "So, what are you going to do?" she asked.

"I don't know," I whispered.

Bree studied me with a look I couldn't quite discern. Then she opened her mouth to speak but promptly shut it again and took another sip of tea.

I leaned closer, putting my hand on her arm. "What were you going to say?"

She shook her head. That errant strand of dark-blond hair she'd tucked away earlier fell again, and she promptly brushed it behind her ear.

"Bree, please. I'd appreciate your thoughts. I don't have anyone else I can talk to about this. I don't want something to happen to Gabe because I made the wrong decision."

Bree set her mug down, the ceramic making a dull thunk as it met the tiled surface. She hesitated long enough I expected her to refuse.

"You're right about Gabe," she finally said. "He doesn't walk away. If he knows about the threat, he'll only push harder. The same is true of his relationships."

I was with her until that last sentence. "His relationships?"

She nodded. "He won't walk away because things are less than rosy. I mean"—she flicked her wrist, waving her hand in a small circle—"look how long he stayed with Olivia despite her treating him like garbage and everyone around him telling him to get rid of her."

I nodded slowly, my eyes cast to the floor.

Bree continued. "If he's going to stick with someone like that, it's going to take a *lot* to get him to walk away from someone like you."

My eyebrows drew together. "Such as?" I asked, unsure if I really wanted to hear the answer.

Bree's eyes ticked back and forth between mine, her lips pressed together. She sighed. "Well, I hate to say it, but . . . Olivia is Gabe's kryptonite. Maybe if you trigger some of those old wounds, he'll back away?"

I studied Bree. Her features were relaxed, her eyes patient and waiting. Sitting this close, I realized from the plumpness of her soft skin and the natural flush in her cheeks that she really was as young as I had first thought, though she spoke and conducted herself with the poise and self-possession of someone with another decade's worth of life experience.

I chewed my lip, realizing I was distracting myself from facing the decision I didn't want to make.

Bree was right. Gabe wouldn't walk away easily. And while I hated myself for even considering bringing up those old wounds with Olivia, I would rather Gabe hate me and go on living than love me and end up in an early grave. I could *not* cause the death of another man in my life.

My shoulders fell, and my eyes squeezed shut. "You're right," I said, barely loud enough to hear.

Bree's hand went to my shoulder. "I know it's hard, Alex. But if you truly believe his life is in danger by being near you, it's the only way to keep him safe."

I nodded, swallowing against the tears that hammered against my eyelids. Had I known I would face this fork in the road, I would have savored those last moments of intimacy with Gabe. My lips would have lingered on his just a bit longer. My arms would have held him just a bit tighter. And I would have taken those extra few seconds to study every nuance of his face, etching into my mind an indelible picture of the man I had loved and then let go.

Gabe

I PULLED up in front of Alex's just in time to see one of my officers walking out the front door. When he caught sight of me, he waved, meeting me at the hood of my truck.

"How's it going, Gabe?"

I adjusted the holster on the waistband of my jeans. "Good. You?"

He nodded, his gray eyes taking in our surroundings. "Got no complaints. Shift is nearly over, and the wife is making her potpie tonight."

I laughed. "Doesn't take much to keep you happy."

"Nope." He hooked his thumb toward the rear of the property. "I was just headed out to do another perimeter sweep before I lose the last of the sun."

The days were getting much shorter. Toward the east, the indigo sky ushered in twilight. In the west, the sun gave a silent nod to the night amid a wash of fuchsia and vermilion.

"I'll let you get to it," I said. "Just stopped by to check on Alex and update her on the case."

With a casual salute, he set off on his rounds and I made quick work of the steps leading to Alex's door. It felt like days since I'd seen her. I was anxious to feel her warmth pressed against me, to smell the intoxicating scent of her coconut shampoo and lavender body lotion.

I entered the house as Alex emerged from the hallway, headed toward the kitchen. She halted when she saw me, storm clouds filling her eyes and then disappearing just as quickly.

"Hey," I said, wanting to go to her but registering something in my gut that told me to approach with caution.

She slid her hands slowly into the pockets of her skintight designer jeans. "Hi." Her voice was demure. Stoic.

My eyes raked over her, taking in the expensive high heels and the soft pink cashmere sweater with a plunging neckline.

She remained silent, apparently waiting for me to say something. I studied her for a moment, sensing that something was off but unsure of how to approach the subject without having a better idea of what kind of hornet's nest I might be stepping into.

Thinking that maybe she was stressing about the case, I figured I'd start there and gauge her reaction.

"Thought I'd stop by and give you the latest development in the case."

She continued to stand perfectly still, her expression one of stony indifference, all emotion masked even further by the heavy makeup, painted to perfection to match the twist her hair was styled into. Every strand exactly where it should be.

I moved a few steps closer and shoved my hands into my pockets, mirroring her stance. "You know that hacker that Trevor mentioned one of our dispatchers was trying to get into contact with?"

Alex gave a curt nod.

"We wanted to see if he could trace the videos and documents that were leaked online back to the person responsible."

Alex showed the first sign of life I'd seen since walking through the door. Her eyebrows lifted ever so slightly, her eyes sparkling with hope. "Was he successful?"

My stomach turned sour seeing how badly she wanted me to say yes. I should have never brought this up. I should have kept my mouth shut until I had a major triumph to lay at her feet. I pressed my lips into a tight line and quietly shook my head. Her eyes closed, her chin dropped to her chest.

I wanted to reach out and pull her against me. I wanted to hold her so tight that the pain she was feeling would drain out of her and pour into me. But something about the way she held her body so rigid, the invisible wall she had erected between us, kept my feet planted where they were—three feet away in distance but an ocean's breadth of what wasn't being said.

Alex recovered quickly. She lifted her chin and met my eyes, her stoic mask back in place, shoulders squared.

"Quinn's guy is going to stay on this, Alex." My eyes pleaded with her to believe that this was all going to work out. "He's watching. Waiting. All he needs is for this asshole to make one little mistake."

Alex resumed her trek to the kitchen. "It doesn't matter."

Confused by her reaction, I watched her retreat. When she disappeared around the corner, I followed. Before I could reach her, she was already coming out of the laundry room that opened off the kitchen, adjacent to the garage. She carried a stack of folded clothes, her sky-high heels clicking on the kitchen tile as she brushed past me.

What the fuck? I spun on my heel and followed her down the hall to her bedroom. "What the hell is that supposed to mean?"

Alex walked to her bed, where she had a huge duffel open, and began carefully placing her stack of clothes inside.

"What are you doing?" I started to cross the room, and that was when I saw the other suitcases sitting inside her walk-in closet. Dread landed like a weight in my stomach.

"Alex, what the fuck is going on?"

She didn't even bother looking up from her work. "I'm packing."

"I can see that. But *why*?"

Alex turned from the bed and went into the bathroom, where

she started pulling things out of drawers, setting them on the bathroom sink.

"Alex!"

She turned to face me, throwing her hands up before settling against the bathroom counter, legs crossed at the ankles, arms crossed over her chest. Waiting.

"For fuck's sake. Talk to me." I stood before her, a man stripped bare, not even trying to hide the agony her cold facade was causing me. It was just yesterday morning when I'd last seen her. She had been quiet, but she'd been every bit the warm, beautiful, vivacious woman I had fallen for. I didn't even recognize the person standing in front of me now. The Alex I'd left yesterday was Eden Falls down to her bones. This woman screamed Hollywood.

Alex sighed, glancing at her shoes as though she was irritated she was having to take time out of her busy schedule to have this conversation. "I'm leaving. I'm going back to Los Angeles."

My eyes searched hers. This wasn't making sense. What the hell could have happened to have flipped this switch?

"I have a friend there," she continued. "He's going to arrange for private security. I'll be staying with him for the foreseeable future."

She turned her back on me again, pulling makeup from one of the vanity drawers and dropping it piece by piece into a small bag.

I tried to swallow the bile rising in my throat, but my mouth had gone dry. She wasn't leaving. She wasn't taking off to go live with some other guy. She couldn't be.

"Alex." I kept my voice low, approaching as if she were a feral cat. "I know this whole situation has been scary for you, and I'm sorry that it's taking longer to bring it to a close than we first thought—"

She scoffed and spun around. "Please, Gabe. You guys are no closer to catching this guy than you were when you all attempted to throw me out of the police department and label me crazy."

I stared at her, my mouth hanging open, speechless for the first time in my life. I didn't even know how to begin fixing things between us, because I still had no fucking idea where I'd gone wrong.

"I'll be better off in Los Angeles, where the police have a lot more experience and a higher success rate." She turned her back on me once more and continued packing her makeup.

I looked to the ceiling and ran my hand up and down the short hair at the back of my head, then returned to the bedroom trying to regain control. The sound of Alex opening and closing drawers faded into the background as I studied the floor, trying to figure out what I could say to bring her back to me.

She returned to the bedroom a moment later, adding her toiletries to her duffel.

I started toward her. "Alex—"

"Gabe—" She turned to face me and held up her hand. "Just stop. I'm tired of this boring little town. I came here to get some peace and quiet so I could write. Since that plan clearly isn't working out, there's no point in me staying here and suffering any longer."

She didn't even give me a chance to respond. Just gave me her back and dismissed me. A white-hot burning filled my throat. Memories of Olivia smirking as she threw her bags in the trunk of that asshole's Audi swam amongst images of Alex living it up in some swanky Los Angeles high-rise with a guy who lived in Armani suits.

My fists clenched at my sides, pain and anger battling like a blaze gaining strength in a windstorm.

I took one more look at the woman who had managed to fool the biggest fool of all, then turned on my heel and walked out her front door for the last time.

CHAPTER 38

Gabe

I AIMED my truck for the station, punching the gas and relishing the sound of my engine roaring as it ate up the road. The sun was nearly hidden behind the mountains now. In another hour, night would consume my world, turning everything as black as my mood.

With my breath tight in my chest, I fought the temptation to hold the gas pedal to the floor. The trees were already screaming past my windows. My body thrummed with the blood pounding through my veins, my fury like a live wire threatening to set fire to anything it could touch. The gym at the station had served as my salvation on many occasions. Tonight would be no different.

Trevor and I had volunteered to cover patrol tonight for a couple of guys who had really stepped up and put in the overtime so we could focus on the Serpents and Alex. I had little more than an hour to expel these demons and get my head on straight before hitting the streets. I needed to focus on something else. Something that would keep me from living those last minutes with Alex on repeat.

Eyeing the phone in my cupholder, I snatched it up and punched Trevor's number. After several rings, his groggy voice came on the line. "Unless you're a blonde with big tits, long legs, and more into action than talk, I'm hanging up."

I didn't waste time with banter. "Meet me at the station in ten."

A loud yawn filled my ear. "Jeez. Don't have to worry about *you* winning Miss Congeniality."

"We've only got an hour before shift change, and we need to talk about what we're going to do with Jace."

Trevor groaned. "Remind me why we agreed to patrol tonight?"

"Because we're a couple of pitiful motherfuckers who go home to empty houses, and Nash and Rogers both have good women who love them and haven't gotten to see their husbands in weeks thanks to us."

"Yeah, well, she might not be a permanent staple in your house yet, but at least you have Alex to warm your bed on the regular."

Silence.

"Bro?" Trevor's tone indicated my partner's intuition was as sharp as ever.

I expelled the air from my lungs. "She won't be warming my bed anymore." Try as I might, I failed in keeping the disappointment and defeat out of my voice.

There was a long pause before Trevor spoke again. "What happened?"

I shook my head, unable to find the right words. *I* still wasn't even sure what happened. "I don't know, man. She's not the woman I thought she was."

Trevor didn't respond. I knew my friend. He was searching for the right thing to say to keep from making me feel even shittier than I already did and was coming up short.

I shifted in my seat, a deep growl emanating from my chest. "Look, it doesn't matter. Just get your ass to the gym so we can figure out what we're going to do about Jace before we have to hit the street."

Trevor yawned again, but I could hear covers rustling. "All right, all right. I'm up."

I hung up and threw my phone back in the cupholder. With Alex leaving town, Trevor and I could get back to focusing on the MC, which was what we should have been doing all along. Jace's ass had been hanging in the wind far too long with our attention divided.

It's a good thing she's leaving. It was bound to happen sooner or later. Better that it's sooner.

My grip on the steering wheel tightened as I narrowed my eyes at the road ahead, the lights of Eden Falls just beginning to come into view. All I needed was one good sweat session and some distance from the woman who had reminded me why I don't get emotionally involved. Holding on to that thought, I accelerated toward town, anxious to throw myself into anything that didn't involve Alex Reilly.

* * *

BY THE TIME Trevor walked through the doors of the gym a half hour later, I had already gone several rounds with the punching bag. He had one hand wrapped and was finishing with the second as he moseyed over. When he reached me, he pulled the heavy bag to his chest and held it still while I hammered into it.

My gray T-shirt was soaked through, and if my black basketball shorts had been a lighter shade, the sweat would have darkened them too. The mats beneath my feet silenced the shuffle of my steps but revealed the exorcism of my emotions in the dark spots accumulating with each drop of water that fell from my body.

Trevor's muscles flexed as he gripped the bag tighter, fighting to keep it in place as my punches grew stronger. "You want to talk about it?"

"No."

Trevor shifted so the bag was now pressed against the other

side of his chest, his voice vibrating each time he absorbed another hit. "Come on, Gabe. Don't shove this shit down again."

"What the hell are you talking about?" I was breathing so hard, the words came out two at a time. My pace never slowed.

"You know what I'm talking about. When Olivia picked up and walked out, making sure the whole town knew she'd been fucking some rich asshole who was going to give her more than anyone here could ever dream of, you didn't say one word about it."

I threw a couple of knees into the bag, ignoring him.

"You just let everyone in town get their jollies gossiping about your love life, and you *changed*."

"I didn't change."

"You changed, man. It used to be that nothing could wipe the smile off your face. Hell, it got to the point where sometimes even *I* wanted to kick the shit out of you for being such a damn Pollyanna all the time. But after Olivia . . ."

I stopped hitting the bag, my chest heaving, a stitch forming in my side. I squared off with Trevor. "What?"

He didn't say anything, just held my gaze.

"After Olivia, what?" I demanded.

Trevor sighed and released the bag. "After Olivia you didn't smile as much. You became cynical. Expected the worst of people and kept everyone except me and your family at arm's length. Until Alex."

I turned away and walked a small circle, bringing my heart rate and breathing down. I didn't want to hear this.

Trevor came closer, his hands resting easily on his hips, his voice low. "These past couple of weeks, the old Gabe showed up again. You laughed more and snapped less. You were excited to go home because you had someone to go home *to*. Hell, you even started cracking your lame jokes again." Trevor smiled, but the humor didn't chase the concern from his eyes.

I stopped moving away from him—from the truth he was forcing on me—and turned to face him.

I held my arms out to my sides, showing I had nothing more to give. "It doesn't matter now, Trev. She's going back to LA and made it clear that we're just some hick town. That there's nothing for her here. She used me to get what she wanted, and when that didn't pan out, she showed her true colors and tossed me aside like yesterday's news."

Creases formed in Trevor's brow. "Used you how?"

I laced my fingers together behind my head and looked up at the ceiling. "I don't know. I guess by sleeping with me, making me think we actually had something, she thought it would get us to focus harder on her case, bring it to a close faster."

Trevor cast his eyes to the floor, his lips pressed together. Slowly, he shook his head. "I don't know, man. I saw you two together. It looked as real for her as it was for you."

I scoffed and went back to the bag, throwing half-hearted jabs.

"You brought out the best in each other." Trevor moved to stand at my side. "She got you to believe again in the future you once wanted, and you helped her to find her fight."

I stopped hitting the bag and lifted the hem of my shirt to wipe the sweat from my face. Trevor was nothing if not persuasive. The fact that Alex had managed to pull the wool over *both* our eyes said a lot about her acting skills. When it came to Olivia, Trevor had seen that train wreck coming even before the train was on the track. But I didn't want to talk about this anymore. I didn't want to think about what I had thought I'd found and then lost. I didn't want to see her face in my mind anymore. Didn't want to picture the way the morning sun set the red in her hair on fire or the way her green eyes sparkled like diamonds when she laughed. I didn't want to think about how many times these past few weeks I'd gotten in my truck and blazed a trail straight to her, anxious as a teenager to get his hands on the girl who tortured his mind. And I *definitely* didn't want to think about all the things I'd seen in our future that would never come to pass.

"Look," I said, "it's strictly business with Alex now. She's packing up and will head back to LA soon. We'll keep the guard on her as long as she's in our jurisdiction. Once she's gone, things can go back to normal."

I circled the bag and pulled it against my body, giving it a couple pats to invite Trevor to have a go. He hesitated, smashing his lips together like he was fighting the temptation to say more on the matter, but finally yielded.

We fell silent as Trevor warmed up with some easy punches. As much as I was trying to act like Alex wasn't my concern any longer, the thought of her being out on the road alone left my stomach in knots. Even with the private security her mystery man was arranging, I still believed deep down she'd be a sitting duck. No one would protect her as fiercely as I had, as though their very existence depended on her survival. And this stalker was way too obsessed with Alex to ever give up.

Trevor's punches halted, pulling me from my thoughts.

"I've been thinking about the situation with Jace," he said. "We obviously don't have anywhere safe we can stash him in Eden Falls."

Grateful for the subject change and the chance to think of something other than Alex, I jumped all over his line of thought. "You're thinking we should pull him out."

Trevor threw a couple of hooks into the bag. "Yeah, I do. I know it's been quiet, but my gut is telling me it's time to get him the hell out of Dodge."

I nodded. "I've been thinking the same."

Trevor put his hands on his waist. His tanned arms held a subtle sheen, and his green tank top was already developing dark spots around the armholes and neckline.

"I know we had planned on shipping him off to Billings and putting him under watch with your contact at the PD there, but I think we might have a better option."

I raised my eyebrows. "What's that?"

"You remember that fed I talked to about Charles Bailey?"

"The dead CI?"

"Yeah. I was thinking of reaching out to him again. Asking if he would arrange for Jace to go into WITSEC."

I leaned against the punching bag, mulling it over. "It's not a bad idea. The feds have a hell of a lot more resources than we do and can get him far away from here."

Trevor nodded. "And since we now know the feds are gunning for the Serpents, they have a reason to say yes."

Part of me hated sending Jace away with federal agents. That kid's life had already been fucked in too many ways to count. But I'd been working closely with him this past year, showing him that someone actually gave a damn about what happened to him. He had ambition now. He wanted to join the Marines, like I had. I was helping him to get his life in order to make that happen. I had no way of knowing how placing him in WITSEC might affect that outcome. But, at the end of the day, Jace *having* a life was more important than figuring out what he was going to do with it right now.

Trevor was watching me, waiting for my answer. With one nod, I gave him all the go-ahead he needed.

CHAPTER 39

Alex

THE BATHROOM WAS FILLED with steam by the time I stepped out. Even after a long, hot shower, I still felt cold and empty inside. It had taken nearly an hour for me to pull myself up off the floor and dry my tear-stained face after Gabe had turned around and walked out of my life. For a split second, I had considered running after him and explaining everything. But then his words had echoed in my head. *Quinn's guy is going to stay on this, Alex. All he needs is for this asshole to make one little mistake.*

Only, my stalker didn't make mistakes. He was the puppet master, and we were controlled by the strings he pulled. He had proven time and again that he could crawl through the window of my little world whenever and however he wanted. I wasn't going to let Gabe or any of his people get hurt because of me.

I plugged my hair dryer in and flipped the switch, falling deeper and deeper into my thoughts as my hair flew around my head, the red undertones catching the dull yellow light in the bathroom. My reflection in the mirror soon faded, replaced by Gabe's face, betrayal in his eyes and pain etched into his features. As long as I lived, that memory would haunt me. I would never forgive myself for causing him that kind of pain. Would he ever be able to trust and love again after this? Had I robbed him of any chance at future happiness?

My stomach turned over at the thought of Gabe with another woman. His hands on her naked body, sending waves of pleasure crashing over her as she cried out for him.

I squeezed my eyes shut and tried to shove the image away. If I kept thinking like this, I'd go running back to him and ruin everything. It was good that he hated me. It would be easier for him to forget me that way. My throat grew thick with emotion, and I gave myself a mental slap. *Get it together, Alex. You did what you had to do. Let him go.*

I turned my hair dryer off and shook myself free from the anguish and what-ifs snaking their bony fingers around my throat and turned my attention to what lay ahead. Dressing in my favorite green camisole set, trying not to think about the last time I'd worn it, I ran through the game plan Cass and I had conjured when I'd called her late last night, after Bree had left, to make amends.

I'd only fibbed to Gabe a little. I was going to be staying with Cass, not some man who I thought could protect and provide for me better than Gabe. But I figured the lie was necessary to give Gabe enough of an incentive to *want* to stay away from me. As for the private security, Cass had generously agreed to help me cover those costs for a reasonable period of time until I could get my finances straightened out.

Once I was back in Los Angeles, I'd ensure my case was on the LAPD's radar. From there, the only other item on my agenda thus far was to reach out to my former publisher and do everything in my power to secure an in-person meeting so that I could face them as I made my apologies and explained the situation. Perhaps they would grant me one more chance. Perhaps not. But I had to try. It was time that I started fighting for my life.

I pulled my short silk robe from the hook on the back of the bathroom door and belted it tightly around my waist. I stepped into the bedroom, the steam from the bathroom swirling around me, happy to escape its confines.

Aderes, who had been asleep on my bed ever since Gabe had left, no doubt sensing I shouldn't be alone, lifted her head sharply, the tags on her collar jingling with the sudden movement. Her icy blue eyes transfixed on the dark hallway beyond the bedroom door.

Following the direction of her gaze, I moved slowly toward the door, my bare feet silent on the wood floor. Perhaps the officer on duty had returned from his walk around the property. But Aderes knew all of the officers by scent at this point. She never batted an eye when they were around anymore.

I inched closer to the hallway, the light from the bathroom reaching just beyond the bedroom door before fading into black. I made it to the entrance of the hall just as Aderes released an earsplitting bark. I jumped, looking back at her to see her hackles rising. When I swung my gaze to the hall again, my breath caught. A tall shadow, darker than those around it, had materialized at the other end.

Tingles ran down my arms and legs. The hair on the back of my neck began to rise. Was I seeing things?

I crept forward, my eyes transfixed on the silhouette. It wasn't moving. Just standing there like a statue.

My fingers shook as they slid along the smooth surface of the wall beyond my bedroom, searching for the light switch. Before I could reach it, the shadow lunged forward, booted feet thundering toward me.

I screamed and jumped back, the beat of my heart as loud as the footsteps barreling toward me. My fingers fumbled for the door. Managing to get hold of it, I tried to slam it shut, but a large, calloused hand snaked around the edge, blocking my attempts. I shoved at the door with my shoulder, but the shadow was too strong. With one thrust, he sent me flying backward onto the floor, the door slamming into the wall behind it.

Aderes was on her feet on the bed, barking and snarling, her teeth fully bared. I tried to scramble away, but the moment my eyes landed on the face towering over me, my limbs went limp. Before I could recover, Aderes launched herself over me, latching her teeth around my assailant's arm. She shook her head savagely, trying to rip through flesh until she hit bone.

With an angry growl, the man lifted his beefy arm with Aderes still attached and slammed her into the wall beside the door. Aderes lost hold of him on impact, her silver body sliding to the floor. I could see that she was dazed, but my sweet girl thought nothing of herself. She was too focused on protecting me. She launched for the man again, blood glistening on her canines. Before she could make contact, her target turned and planted a foot into her side, sending her sailing through the open door into the hallway.

Aderes whimpered, but she got up and scrambled toward the bedroom once more, unable to reach me before the door was slammed and locked in her face. The sound of whining and claws scratching mercilessly at the door couldn't dampen the cold chills that raked my body at the sound of a voice I had prayed I'd never hear again.

"Hello, beautiful."

I was still seated on the floor, my hands braced behind me as I stared into yellow-green eyes.

Maxwell Hargrove planted his feet on either side of my legs and gazed down at me as though he had all the time in the world. He smiled wide, showing two rows of crooked teeth. "Did you miss me, Alexandra?"

I didn't so much as breathe.

"I've missed *you*." He bent down and pulled a lock of my hair through his fingers. "Not an hour has passed when I haven't thought of those creamy thighs wrapped around my waist. You moaning beneath me, begging me to fuck you harder."

A shiver arced down my back. I pressed my knees together, my movements painfully slow for fear of triggering his next move.

"Tonight . . ." He paused, his eyes running down my breasts, my torso, my hips. He licked his lips and brought his gaze back to mine. "You're going to know what it's like to have me inside you."

Aderes's clawing was growing louder. I could hear her snout puffing air in the crack below the door. Hargrove reached out to grab my throat, and as he did, I kicked hard against his shins. He lost his balance just enough that I was able to scramble backward and get to my feet. I turned to run for the bathroom and cried out as a hand tangled in my hair and yanked backward, dragging me toward the bed.

When the back of my thighs hit the mattress, Hargrove let go of my hair and shoved me backward so hard my body bounced on the soft surface. I knew if he got his weight on top of me, my chances of surviving this night were practically zero, so I clawed against the covers, trying to fling myself over the opposite edge of the bed.

My lungs burned from the ragged breaths that tore from my chest. I could feel the adrenaline thundering through my body, but I was also desperately aware of how heavy my limbs were beginning to feel. I had only managed to make it halfway across the bed before Hargrove laughed and clamped his hands around my bare thighs with bruising force.

With one yank, he pulled my body flush with his, holding my legs on either side of his hips as he ground his pelvis against mine. He released one of my thighs and ripped at my robe, tearing it open. His eyes went straight for my breasts, a look of feral hunger enveloping his poison-colored irises.

A tear leaked from my eye and ran down my temple, disappearing into my tangled hair. I tried kicking against the incarnation of my nightmares, but he was so strong. My thrashing didn't faze him at all.

Another tear slipped from my eyes, its path drawing my fear and sadness over the contours of my skin. Amidst the anguish and disbelief, one thought rose to the surface, reverberating against the inner chambers of my soul.

This can't be how it ends.

CHAPTER 40

Gabe

I CRUISED down the desolate streets of town in my black-and-white. The silhouettes of the broad-leafed trees that lined the street and stood between quaint buildings waved gently in the night breeze. Their dance was the only movement aside from the slow crawl of my headlights painting the blacktop ahead of me. Though Eden Falls wasn't the type of place to have a lot of activity after the sun went down, something about *this* night felt eerily still. As if the place itself was waiting with bated breath.

I yawned loudly over the sound of static and the quiet chatter of radio traffic. I had the radio in my unit turned low, preferring to copy the traffic through my earpiece. I glanced at the clock, groaning when I realized it was just after twenty-one hundred. This was going to be the longest fucking shift I'd had in a long time. And that was saying something.

I blinked a few times, trying to banish the sensation of sandpaper from my blurry eyes, but my effort proved just as futile as my attempts to banish Alex from my mind. Coming to an intersection, I flipped my blinker on with more force than necessary. With the roads clear, the steady click, click, click of my turn signal was a respite from the silence for only a moment.

Guiding my cruiser down the alleys behind the businesses on

Main, I shone my spotlight anywhere the shadows collected, ensuring that all was as it should be. Despite my efforts to keep my mind occupied on business, it fought me at every turn, insisting that I let it dwell on the jade-eyed beauty who had bewitched me.

I couldn't, for the life of me, fathom how I had been so far off base where she was concerned. Even with Olivia, I could look back and see the writing on the wall clear as day. Hell, even while I'd been in the middle of that mess, deep down I'd known what was up. I just hadn't wanted to admit it. I was too stubborn to admit to everyone, myself included, that I had ever been stupid enough to get ensnared by a woman like that.

But Alex? Even now, as I played the past few weeks over and over in my head, I couldn't spot even one moment that revealed she was anyone other than who I'd thought.

I came to a stop at the end of the long alley and allowed my cruiser to idle. In my rearview mirror, my brake lights turned the brick buildings and the alley between them a fire truck shade of red, exhaust billowing and curling like some portal to hell.

Crrrsh. Static crackled through my earpiece, followed immediately by Quinn's sultry voice. "Attention all units, Adam Seventy-eight is failing to respond to status check."

Adam Seventy-eight. That was the call sign for Alex's guard duty. Anderson was assigned to that detail tonight.

I picked up the handheld on the radio next to my hip and keyed up with my call sign.

"Twenty-Five Adam Two, when was the last time Dispatch had contact with Adam Seventy-eight?"

Quinn responded immediately. "Fifteen minutes ago. Adam Seventy-eight advised he was initiating a perimeter check."

I rolled my eyes. Anderson was on my last fucking nerve these days. Given that Alex was leaving because she found us incompetent, I was more pissed than ever that his asinine mistake had cost us our best opportunity to take her stalker out. On top of that, he was notorious for not hearing his call sign whenever Dispatch tried to raise him.

I keyed my mic again. "Ten-four. I'm ten minutes out and en route to check his status."

Trevor's voice came over the radio as soon as I'd clicked off. "Twenty-Five Adam Four, I'll back Adam Two."

I was back on Main and headed west less than sixty seconds later, the low rumble of my cruiser's engine growing louder as my speed climbed steadily.

My plan had been to avoid Alex from here on out. Let her slip out of town without another face-to-face encounter. Now, thanks to Anderson, it appeared I was going to have to look into those hypnotic eyes once more and pretend I didn't feel a thing.

A buzzing came from my chest pocket. I reached inside and extracted my phone, glancing at Trevor's name on the screen. He was already talking when I put the phone to my ear.

"So, what do we think it is this time? Head up ass, or he forgot to check the charge on his radio?"

I slowed to a stop at the last traffic signal before the city limit sign. "Who knows. Either way, he's off this detail. Two fuckups is more than we can afford."

"Agreed. I'll try calling his cell."

"Copy that." I disconnected and scanned the dark streets as I waited for the light to change. My thumb drummed the steering wheel, a small tingle starting at the base of my skull. I had no reason, really, to believe that anything was wrong. This kind of thing happened all the time—officers not hearing their radio. Trev would call back any minute to advise that Anderson was code four and up shit creek.

Still, the tingle grew stronger, and I questioned why, if I really believed everything was fine, did I have the urge to blow this red light and put the accelerator through the floor?

CHAPTER 41

Alex

THINK, Alex. Slow down and think.

Hargrove's hot breath washed over my face as he bent over me, one hand holding my wrists over my head as the other hand tangled in my shorts.

My thoughts were erratic. In one moment, I was consumed with regret, hating how I had left things with Gabe and the fact that he would never know the truth of my feelings. In the next, I accepted my defeat. Accepted that there was no way out of this, and no one was coming to save me. And finally, determination to fight. An unwillingness to accept that Hargrove's plans would be my fate.

Think, Alex.

I fought to slow my breathing, to tell my body and my brain that this wasn't over. Not yet.

Think.

And then there it was. Hope. Glimmering like a solitary firefly in an endless night. Small and fragile. But it was there.

I lifted my head just enough to gaze through the open door of my bathroom and found what I was looking for.

My phone.

My phone was on the counter. I just needed one small opening, one moment of weakness in Hargrove, to have a chance.

He was bigger and much stronger. He knew that. He was relishing it. And that sense of security was my greatest weapon.

My shorts were tied at the waist, and Hargrove was growing impatient as he struggled to remove them with one hand. When he let go of my wrists to work the knot, I had my opening. He pulled back just enough to see what he was doing, which happened to be all the space I needed.

With the heel of my hand, I struck his nose with every ounce of strength I possessed. His eyes watered immediately as his hands flew to his face, cupping his nose. He stumbled backward, giving me more space to work. Just as quickly as I'd struck him in the face, I drew back my leg and slammed my heel into his crotch. It might not have incapacitated him as much as a direct blow to his testicles, but it was enough.

I launched off the bed, running straight past Hargrove and into the bathroom, slamming the door behind me. Once I had it locked, I spun around to the bathroom counter and snatched my phone up. I fought with the lock screen, cursing the damn thing, then remembered there was a way to call emergency services without entering my code.

A loud bang came from the door, causing me to jump and drop my phone in the sink. I grabbed it once again, and this time, I managed to put the call through.

Hargrove's deep, raging voice on the other side of that pitiful piece of wood that served as my only barrier set my body to trembling so violently, I was forced to hold the phone with both hands.

A female voice came on the line. "9-1-1, what is th—"

"This is Alex Reilly! There's a man in my house attacking me . . . I don't know what happened to the officer who was here!"

Bang!

I screamed into the phone.

Hargrove threw his weight against the door again, each time

causing the wood to rattle and creak. There was no way it would hold much longer. I was regretting more than ever having a bathroom without a window.

"Ma'am!" the dispatcher shouted, trying to get my attention.

"I-I'm here."

"We've got officers on the way. Does the man have a weapon?"

Bang!

Shit. My hand flew to my forehead, my fingertips pressing into my skin. I tried to focus. "I—didn't see one . . . but he had one last time." My voice trembled as badly as my hands.

"What do you mean last time?"

Hargrove threw himself into the door again, and this time, it was accompanied by the sound of wood splitting.

"Last time . . . when he . . . he—it doesn't matter! I need help now! Please!"

Just then, a loud thud accompanied the cracking and splintering of the doorframe. Hargrove shoved his way into the bathroom, a maniacal look in his rage-filled eyes that told me I was going to die tonight.

His fingers wrapped around my throat, the sound of my own gasps for air drowning in the blood rushing to my ears.

Hargrove slammed me against the bathroom counter, causing the phone to fall from my grip and slide across the floor. Pain radiated from my hips and up my back. Keeping a hold of my throat, he wrenched me toward the bedroom and let go, sending me sliding across the wood floor on my side, my thigh burning as my bare skin dragged across the tacky surface.

Hargrove pounced, landing on top of me before I had even managed to get my bearings. Placing one knee on either side of my hips, he gripped my head in both hands, lifted, and then drove it hard into the floor. The room spun, colors and objects blurring into one swirling mass.

I felt my head lift from the floor again, and then another burst of pain and white lights. I could feel myself slipping away, my body growing heavy. I fought to stay awake. If I let go, if I succumbed to the sweet pull of unconsciousness, my life was over. So I opened my eyes and stared at the face of evil, focusing on those yellow eyes, refusing to let them be the last thing I would ever see.

* * *

GABE

I WAS five minutes out from Alex's when my phone rang again. I answered without looking, knowing it was Trevor.

"Anderson isn't answering his phone." Trevor's tone was sharp.

Before I could respond, my radio crackled to life. "Adam Two and Adam Four, we've just received an emergency call from the location of your response. A female caller advised there is a man in her house attacking her. The line is open with ongoing sounds of a struggle."

Fuck! My foot slammed the gas pedal to the floor. A cold sweat broke on my brow. I raised my mic. "Ten-four, we're en route code three."

My lights and sirens roared to life and blazed a trail through the starless night. Trevor's voice, coming through the phone I'd thrown in the passenger seat, was lost to me.

Why didn't I listen to my fucking instincts?

I should have raced over there the second Dispatch had advised Anderson wasn't answering his radio.

What the hell happened to Anderson?

I thought of Alex, alone and scared. If anything happened to her, I'd never forgive myself. I should have fucking been there.

The lines on the road turned to solid yellow, and still my car wouldn't go fast enough. One thought kept pounding against my brain with every beat of my frantic heart.

What if I don't get there in time?

Alex

NAUSEA ROILED in my stomach and sat thick in my throat. I shoved and clawed at Hargrove's chest, but my weakened muscles had little effect. Still straddling my hips, he let go of my head, the weight of his body growing even heavier as he straightened, reaching behind his back.

My eyelids fluttered as I fought to keep them open, but they were heavy. So heavy.

My head lolled toward the sound of Aderes's whimpers drifting under the door. She could smell that I was near, her agitation growing in her inability to get to me. I focused on her. If I was leaving this world, my last thoughts would not be of the ugliness of this enduring night. It would be with the love of Aderes on my heart and in my mind.

A flash of steel drew my eyes back to Hargrove, a large, serrated hunting knife gripped in his hand. His smile was one of triumph, a goal long sought and finally attained. My fingers curled around his wrist as he placed the blade against my throat, the sting of violated flesh communicating his intention.

A trickle of blood traveled down my neck as he pushed deeper. I closed my eyes and focused on the memory of when I'd first brought Aderes home. She was a little white-and-silver ball of fur, her piercing blue eyes so full of joy and expectation. She had claimed me at once, paying little attention to Robby and refusing to leave my side. An explosion of images presented themselves, one after the other, of Aderes growing, our relationship evolving into one of the most important I'd ever had.

And then I saw Gabe.

I saw him on the couch, snuggled with Aderes, watching TV. I saw him leaning over me, a cup of coffee in his hand as he kissed my forehead to rouse me from sleep. I saw him with Lily, her chubby little arms around his neck as he held her close and hung on every word she said.

My heart squeezed at the exquisite memories, the love that had surrounded me these past few weeks, often without me even recognizing it. And as my last memory of Gabe surfaced, the hostility on his face, the betrayal in his eyes, the pain of the knife cutting into the tender flesh of my neck was nothing compared to the pain in my chest for hurting the only person who had ever loved me so completely.

I kept my eyes closed, waiting for this to be over, praying that Gabe wouldn't be the one to find my mutilated body. That wasn't an image I wanted haunting him for the rest of his days.

I could almost hear his voice, hear him shouting. It was muted, like the remnants of a dream disturbed, but it gave me comfort.

A loud noise erupted nearby, loud enough to pull me from the blackened fringes of defeat. My eyes flew open, and my head turned automatically toward the source of the noise. Confused, I blinked slowly, my heavy lids protesting, as I tried to make sense of the open space where the door should have been.

Boots. I saw boots.

My eyes traveled up the legs attached to the boots and kept climbing. A loud ringing in my ears added to my disorientation.

Light. I felt lighter.

My eyes abandoned their course to look down at my body. It was then that I realized Hargrove was gone. With his weight no longer pressing down on me, I had the sense that I could finally move. Finally breathe. I started to roll to my side, away from the door, and it was then that I saw Hargrove lying facedown on the floor beside me.

"Alex."

Was someone calling me?

"Alex!" My head whipped around to find the voice. "Alex, look at me!"

My eyes returned to the form in the doorway and finished their ascent. Gabe's large frame blocked out everything beyond the door, his black uniform and shiny silver badge drawing me in like the strobe on a lighthouse. His gun was extended in front of him, aimed at Hargrove, vengeance in his eyes.

"Are you all right?" he asked.

I heard the words, but my brain still wasn't cooperating.

He removed one of his hands from his gun and keyed the mic on his shoulder.

"Twenty-Five Adam Two, what's the ETA on medics?"

A woman's voice squawked through the radio at his hip, but amid the static and my confusion, I couldn't begin to decipher her response.

Gabe's eyes dropped to my neck, his lip curling before he returned his attention to the man beside me.

A moment later, Trevor's face appeared beside Gabe's, his expression unrecognizable. Where he normally wore a smile, his mouth was pressed into a hard line, accentuating the squareness of his jaw. His sky-blue eyes, usually so calm and friendly, swept my body and filled with fury as they landed on Hargrove.

Gabe and Trevor moved farther into the room, Gabe keeping his gun trained on his target while Trevor pulled handcuffs from the pouch at his back. He stepped over my legs, careful not to clip me, and then kneeled down next to Hargrove and drove a knee into his back, right between his shoulder blades.

Hargrove grunted but otherwise remained silent, staring at me, his eyes crinkling at the corners as his grin stretched wide.

The moment Trevor had the cuffs secured around Hargrove's wrists, he hauled the man in my nightmares to his feet and shoved him out the door.

Gabe holstered his gun and moved to my side, dropping to a knee so he was closer to eye level. His fingers gently grazed my cheek, then pushed my hair behind my shoulder so he could get a better look at my injuries. His dark eyes held nothing of the anger he'd shown earlier.

He opened his mouth to speak, but before he was able to say anything, Bryan—the firefighter I'd met at the town baseball game—appeared in the doorway wearing an Eden Falls Fire Department T-shirt, a medic bag in his hand.

Whatever Gabe had intended to say, I likely would never know. After exchanging a few quiet words with Bryan, he turned and walked back down the hall, moving like a shadow in his dark uniform, the sound of the last piece of my heart breaking, the only exchange between us.

* * *

Gabe

AFTER LEAVING ALEX WITH BRYAN, I walked out to where the cruisers and medic units were parked just in time to see Trevor slamming the door of his black-and-white in Hargrove's smug face. Standing with my hands on my hips, eyes taking in the flashing blue and red lights and the various uniforms scurrying around like a colony of ants, I resisted the urge to turn around and glue myself to Alex's side.

I had argued with Bryan at first when he'd asked me to step out and give him a moment alone with Alex, but he had made the right call. He wanted her to be able to speak openly about what she had endured tonight, knowing there might be injuries for which she needed to be treated and wasn't ready for anyone to know about. Bile rose in my throat at the thought, and I clenched my molars to force it back down.

No. It didn't get that far. She still had her clothes on.

I told Bryan I'd give them a moment, but I never said I wouldn't return. As soon as I was confident the scene was under control, I was going back inside to stay with Alex, and heaven help Bryan or anyone else who tried to stop me.

Trevor climbed the steps and came to a stop beside me, the emergency lights bouncing off his skin.

"How's she doing?" he asked.

I lifted a shoulder. "I don't know. Bryan kicked me out." Trevor didn't miss the edge in my voice.

"And you listened?"

My eyes locked on the rear window of Trevor's cruiser. Between the moonless night and the tinted glass, I couldn't see Hargrove sitting inside, but I could feel him watching me.

"He thought she might have an easier time letting him examine her if I wasn't there . . . just in case there was anything she wouldn't want me to hear." My voice cracked on the last word.

Trevor repositioned himself to stand between me and Hargrove. His hand was heavy on my shoulder, and he dipped his chin, compelling me to meet his eyes. "Gabe, I know you well enough to know what you're thinking."

My eyes flicked back and forth between his, my jaw flexing.

"This was *not* your fault."

His hand still on my shoulder, he shook me hard when I shifted my gaze to look past him.

"You can beat yourself up all you want," he said, "but that's not going to help Alex right now. Regardless of what went down between you two, you love that woman, and right now, what she needs more than anything is to feel loved and protected."

My eyes swung back to his, and he raised his eyebrows as if asking what the hell I was going to do about it.

He was right. I needed to be with Alex. She might not want

me. She might send me away again. But she was at least going to have the option.

"I've got things under control here, man." Trevor twisted to survey the scene at his back, then hooked his thumb toward his patrol car. "I'll take this asshole back to the station and place him in interrogation."

I gave a single nod. "Don't question him without me. I want to hear every detail from his own lips and watch him squirm when he sees his future in my eyes."

I spun away without waiting for an answer and headed straight for Alex's bedroom, slowing as I reached the door. My chest squeezed at what I found.

Alex was seated on the edge of her bed, Aderes pressed firmly against her side, head between her paws, while Bryan knelt in front of them both. Bryan was grinning in that way that had always made women fawn all over him, and Alex was looking down at him, a brilliant smile on her face that lit up the room and belied the terror she'd just lived through.

The lilting sound of her laugh drifted through the open doorway as Bryan took each of her hands in his and helped her to her feet. Once she was steady, he bent to pick up his medic bag, then wrapped an arm around her slender waist and absorbed her weight as she leaned into him. I swallowed hard against the lump in my throat, unable to stop my brain from comparing how cold Alex had become toward me and how smitten she appeared with Bryan.

As the two started toward the door, I quietly retreated down the hall, stepping into the dark space of the guest bedroom, feeling the last embers of hope fade as they went by.

Deciding it was best to keep my distance, I sent an officer out to get a status update on Alex and Officer Anderson while I touched base with our crime scene techs. A weight lifted from my chest when the officer returned a few minutes later, reporting that both Alex and Anderson were going to make full recoveries. Alex was being treated for a concussion and abrasions, and Anderson had a nasty goose egg on his head where Hargrove had knocked him unconscious.

By the time I emerged from the house, the medic rigs were pulling out of the drive, leaving only my officers and a small swarm of media on scene. Aderes's frantic whining drew my gaze to where an officer held the squirming dog, trying to keep her from chasing after the rig carrying Alex.

I went to Aderes, kneeling in front of her, stroking the soft fur at her chest and behind her ears. She stared into my eyes, a plea to help her get to Alex.

"Easy, girl." My voice was low and smooth. The same tone I used with victims who were traumatized by their ordeal. She whined again and leaned into me.

I looked up at the officer and nodded, signaling I'd take care of her. Looping my fingers under Aderes's collar, I walked her to my patrol car and loaded her in the passenger seat before heading inside to leave a note for Alex.

I returned moments later with Aderes watching my every move, but she seemed to trust that I was going to make sure everything turned out okay, because her whining had ceased, and she sat alert, monitoring the activity around her and no longer agitated.

I wished the same could be said of me. Though my adrenaline had settled from a pounding force to a dull hum, I still buzzed with a rage that could only be quelled by exacting a pound of flesh from the man who had terrorized the woman I couldn't seem to uproot from my soul.

My eyes narrowed as I stalked to the driver's side of my patrol car.

A pound of flesh was exactly what I required.

CHAPTER 43

Alex

I UNLOCKED my front door and stepped inside before turning to wave to the officer who had brought me home. It was too dark to see if he waved back, but his unit slowly backed out of the driveway, leaving me alone for the first time in several weeks. I breathed deeply, expecting a sense of peace to wash over me in the stillness of my private space. But it didn't come.

It was too quiet. I didn't know *how* to be alone anymore.

I rubbed my forehead, trying to ease the nagging headache that continued to dull my senses. When I'd left the hospital a short while ago and only an hour after arriving, it had been against medical advisement. The ER doctor and nurses had put up one heck of a fuss, but I wanted to be in my own space, finally free from the myriad pairs of eyes that had been watching me during this whole ordeal.

Something fluttered near my head. I drew back, trying to get my eyes to focus, and found a piece of paper taped to the wall just inside the door. Flipping the foyer light on, I closed the door on the growing wind and pulled the paper from the wall, immediately recognizing Gabe's handwriting.

Alex,

I'm taking Aderes to the station, where she'll have more atten-

tion than she knows what to do with. Let me know when you're ready for me to bring her home.

Gabe

A sad smile formed on my lips as my thumb brushed over the hastily scrawled words. A deep ache pressed against my chest as gratitude for Gabe's affection toward my dog mingled with regret of what might have been. Tearing my eyes from the paper, I squared my shoulders, reminding myself I had packing to get on with.

Although . . . My eyes traveled to the note again. *Now that the threat is over and Hargrove is behind bars, maybe I don't have to leave.*

A sliver of hope bloomed in my chest before disintegrating like a fallen leaf in a bonfire. My shoulders fell, my fingers working the paper into a tight ball in my hand.

I couldn't stay. Not after what I'd done to Gabe. Using his past with Olivia against him, convincing him that he had yet again failed to be enough—it was unforgivable. And I couldn't bear the thought of remaining in this small town, running into him at every corner, knowing that he would never again be mine. The day would come when he was ready to move on, to try to love again. And when that day came, I didn't want to be here to see him give his heart to another. To know that every touch, every kiss, every glance kindled with desire had been mine to lose.

I spun from the door, marching to the kitchen, not even bothering to turn on any lights as I went. When I reached the counter that separated the main living space from the kitchen, I threw my oversized purse down and dug out my phone. Opening the string of texts I shared with Gabe, I tried to ignore the last message that had been sent, but the words *Miss you already, beautiful* drew my eyes like a moth to a flame.

I drove my gaze back to the flashing cursor and began to formulate a text, telling Gabe I was home, and he could bring Aderes back whenever it was convenient. I was only halfway through the message when a noise caught my attention.

I paused, my fingers hovering over my phone, nothing but the light from the foyer and the blue glow from my screen to give context to the shadows.

I strained my ears, waiting to see if I heard it again. I couldn't be sure, it was so faint, but it had sounded like the creak of stiff leather. After several moments of absolute silence, I was convinced it was my imagination playing tricks on me.

Returning to my text, I reread what I'd written so far. Before I could finish, my hands began to tremble, and tingles erupted across my skin.

My eyes slid to the left, my body still, breath caught in my chest.

A whisper of movement behind me.

* * *

GABE

I stood in the corner of the interrogation room, my arms crossed, back to the wall. Trevor was seated across from Hargrove, doing all the talking at the moment and serving as the only barrier between me and the old-school justice I sought to serve.

The white fluorescent lights bounced off the pale-gray walls, the only color in the room the cheap wooden table that had more dings than all the souls brought before it to answer for their sins. My eyes bore into Hargrove, studying his every twitch, looking for confirmation that this was finally the end.

I took in the hard planes of his body, the way he sat like a powder keg of pure power waiting to blow. The man was a beast. It was a miracle Alex had managed to fight him off as long as she had. At six four and two hundred eighty pounds of muscle and bone, he would have been intimidating to most *men*.

He had tested his boundaries when he'd first been brought in, throwing his weight around, laughing as Trev and the officer assisting him had wrestled Hargrove into his seat. But now . . . he sat so still he mimicked a marble statue. Except for those eyes. Snakelike and cunning, they drilled into Trevor, a smirk his only sign of emotion.

It took every ounce of concentration to keep my face a blank mask, to give Hargrove nothing he could use against me. But inside, the fires of hell were raging.

"Why did you break into Alex Reilly's home this evening?" Trevor asked.

Hargrove remained silent.

"What was it you intended to do to her?" Trevor held Hargrove's gaze, the intensity in his own eyes every bit as potent. My partner, for all of his carefree, playboy ways, was no pussy. If Hargrove's goal was to intimidate Trevor into backing off, he was going to have to get used to disappointment.

Trevor's tone shifted, taking on an easy, conversational style. "I admire that you aim higher than you deserve. A guy like you" —he paused, allowing his eyes to travel down Hargrove's frame and back up again—"could never hope to turn the head of a woman like Alex Reilly."

I waited, watching Hargrove to see if the tactic would work. Trevor was smart, attempting to trigger this man's greatest weakness—his ego.

For a second, it looked like Hargrove was going to give something up. His smug grin twisted into a sneer. But just as quickly as his features had morphed, he schooled them back into a placid mask.

Hiding my disappointment, I focused on taking my emotions out of the situation. Something about this whole thing wasn't sitting right with me. My gut had been nagging me since I'd left Alex's. The whole drive back to the station, my mind turned all the evidence over and over, trying to confirm that the pieces fit together. To everyone else, they did fit. So much so that the chief had removed Alex's protection detail, telling the officers who had gone with her to the hospital to go home and get some much-needed rest.

As for this interrogation, Trevor was merely working to make a strong case even stronger. But still, my gut nagged.

Shifting my focus from Hargrove for a moment, I went inside myself, banishing my emotions and calling on the part of me that was ice-cold and fully tactical. A soldier focused on one mission. I couldn't approach this as Alex's lover if I was going to spot what my gut was trying to tell me.

Stilling my mind and sharpening my senses, I brought my attention back to Hargrove. I looked past the exterior, past what he wanted us to see, and peered into the soul behind those yellow eyes.

What does he want? The question echoed across my psyche until it became a quiet chant.

Tick, tick, tick. The cheap bold-faced clock on the wall marked the seconds, a hazy truth beginning to form.

Tick, tick . . . And then there it was. Part of the missing piece.

Hargrove wanted Alex more than anything. She had said that in his letters, he'd talked about wanting to possess her, and a man like him doesn't just take the hint and move on. It also meant that he had motive to try to remove anyone who held her affection.

So, if that was the case, and Hargrove wanted me out of the picture, or at the very least, had every reason to despise me, why hadn't he looked at me even once during this entire interrogation? It definitely wasn't because he was intimidated by me. This guy made it a point to show how little he cared about what anyone else might try to do to him. Instead of acting like I was a threat to something he wanted, he acted like I was just another uniform he didn't give a shit about. As though he wasn't even aware of my relationship with Alex.

The zing through my veins told me I was on to something. I needed to test the theory. Knowing that Trev would pick up my lead without missing a beat, I shoved off from the wall and swaggered to the table. Trevor sat at my right, never taking his eyes off Hargrove, but for the first time, Hargrove's eyes shifted to me. Slowly, I leaned forward, bracing my palms on the rough wood of the table. I let Hargrove get a good look in my eyes, showing him exactly what he was up against. His smug facade blinked for just a second, before he regained control.

Good. Right where I want you.

The right side of my mouth curled into a smile. "See, the reason he knows a guy like you could never tempt a woman like Alex is because it took a *man* like me to make that flower bloom." My tone was silk. I let the challenge hang between us. It took only a second for that smooth mask to fall as pure, unadulterated hate flashed in his eyes.

Hargrove's body began to tremble, his eyes wide and locked on me.

Now this *is the reaction I expected from the start. He didn't know.*

Without showing that I had gotten exactly what I was after, I straightened slowly, the smug look on my face conveying to him that my statement was nothing more than a cock-swinging contest rather than the bait he'd just swallowed whole.

I swaggered to the door, taking my time. Once my hand hit the knob, I caught Trevor's eye and jerked my head, telling him to meet me outside. As soon as I was clear of Hargrove, I entered the room connected to interrogation and watched through the one-way mirror as Trevor collected the file in front of him and stood to leave.

My mind was racing, trying to figure out what we were still missing. When Trevor joined me a minute later, he held his hands out to his side. "What the hell was that? I thought we agreed you weren't going to talk to him."

I kept my eyes trained on Hargrove. He was still vibrating with barely contained rage. "I know, but I got a hunch and ran with it."

"Okay," he drawled. When I didn't respond right away, he said, "Are you going to share with the rest of the class?"

I turned to face him. "This isn't adding up, Trev."

His brow creased. "What isn't adding up?"

"Did you see how he responded when I told him about me and Alex? He acted like he didn't know."

Trevor put his hands on his hips and turned his head to look at Hargrove.

"Whoever has been stalking Alex made me a target the moment we slept together. This guy acted like I was about as significant as a bug until I told him I had taken what was his."

Trevor scrunched his face, a slow shake of his head telling me he wasn't nearly as convinced as I was. "I don't know, man. This guy knows the game. He could be putting on a good show to make it look like he was only responsible for the part where we caught him in the act."

I blew out an irritated breath and scratched the back of my head. "What about his MO?"

"What about it?"

"When he stalked Alex before, he didn't hide. He *wanted* Alex to see him and know he was there. That wasn't the case this time." I punched my pointer finger into the palm of my other hand. "Whoever was behind the stalking this time was careful to remain hidden. And he was cold. Calculating. Every move carefully weighed and measured. That's nothing like Hargrove. His attack on Alex tonight was just like it had been before. Passionate. Emotional. Obsessive."

Trevor stared at Hargrove while he chewed the inside of his cheek. I remained quiet, allowing him to filter through his thoughts.

Finally, he said, "I get where you're coming from, man, but it's been almost two years since the first stalking. Hargrove was locked up for a long time with nothing to do but focus on Alex and plan how he could make sure he was successful the next time. I mean, fuck—" Trevor walked to the glass and threw his knuckles against the wall beside it, hard enough to make his point, but not enough to alert Hargrove to the fact we were watching him. "He went on the lam for six weeks completely undetected. Not so much as a blip on our laser-focused radar."

It was my turn to think. He was right. Criminals often became better at their craft during incarceration. Hargrove clearly had a lot of self-control, as demonstrated by his carefully maintained facade during arrest and *most* of interrogation. He had gone to Alex's prepared, knowing there would be an officer on duty and when and where that officer would be vulnerable during a perimeter check. That definitely took planning. He had even parked in the same location on the obscure dirt road where I had chased our target the night we'd laid the trap.

Trevor could see that I still wasn't convinced. "What about all the evidence we found in his truck?" He ticked off the items, one by one, on his fingers. "The photos of Alex in private moments that could have only been taken by someone in these past few weeks. The laptop that has the videos that were leaked online as well as the divorce documents. Add to that his past stalking of her, and, well . . ." He shrugged as if to say *I rest my case*.

It did add up.

But was it adding up too nicely?

After thinking it over for another minute, I jerked my head toward Hargrove. "Let's let him fester for a bit. I want to take a closer look at that evidence."

To his credit, Trevor didn't roll his eyes or do anything to suggest he was irritated that I wouldn't let this go. We trusted each other, and we had a silent pact that we both had to feel good about a case when we put our final stamp on it and sent it off to the prosecutor.

As we made our way to the evidence room, the leather of our boots creaking with each step and lulling me deeper into the puzzle in my head that was slowly taking shape, a prickle at the back of my neck set my teeth on edge. Though I didn't have anything other than my gut as proof, I sensed that secrets and lies would soon be revealed. My only fear was, would we see them in time?

CHAPTER 44

Alex

I SCREAMED and turned to run, but I didn't make it two steps before a meaty hand clamped over my mouth and a strong arm snaked around my waist, hauling me back against a wall of flesh. I thrashed, kicking my legs and twisting my body, but I only succeeded in weakening myself further. My head throbbed, and the dizziness returned.

A mouth brushed against my ear, filling it with a raspy chuckle as hot breath skated across my cheek. Confusion washed over me as I squinted against the pain in my head, trying to make sense of the fact that I was being held in place at the same time a dark form was walking toward me.

I stopped kicking and allowed my frame to go limp, my chest heaving as I panted for air. If I had any chance of getting out of this, I had to be smart about how I used my dwindling energy.

I watched the figure in front of me move closer, my eyes tracking every movement as it bent to pick up the phone that had fallen to the floor, the screen still glowing with my unsent text.

Then it straightened and brought my phone closer to its face, revealing a man with pockmarked skin and a heavy dark beard.

He scoffed as he scrolled through the text messages between Gabe and me. "Guess Golden Boy's got it bad." His voice, tarnished by years of smoking, matched the crooked yellow teeth that were displayed as he grinned at me like some prize.

From the mouth beside me, a tongue snaked out, its rough, wet texture meeting the soft shell of my ear. "Too bad he's not going to want you after we're done with you." The arm around my waist tightened, pulling me snug against my captor until the bulge in his pants pressed into my lower back.

My mind grappled with the situation, struggling to comprehend how this could really be happening twice in one night. What did these guys want? Hargrove's attack at least made sense, but these men were strangers to me.

My eyes snapped back to the man holding my phone, searching his features as his words echoed in my head. He called Gabe Golden Boy.

They know him. Maybe this wasn't about me at all. Maybe it was about Gabe. Maybe I was part of some kind of vendetta.

The man with the marred face put my phone in his back pocket. "Get her to the van. No telling how soon McNeil will catch on to the fact that something's wrong."

A knee pressed into the back of my thigh, causing my leg to buckle. As I worked to catch myself, the man behind me shoved me toward the foyer while the other man made a move for the patio doors. I eyed the scissors standing in the penholder I kept next to the pad of paper on my counter. As soon as I drew even with them, I lunged, hoping my sudden movement would catch the man at my back off guard.

I managed to break free only long enough to land on top of my purse, still situated at the edge of the counter. A bone-crushing weight came down on top of me, pinning me to the cold tile surface.

"Try that again, and I'll take you right here and leave the cum stains for your boyfriend to find." The malice in his voice cut like a razor.

His hand pressed between my shoulder blades, keeping me pinned to the counter. A moment later, hard plastic slipped around my wrists. *Zip ties.* With my wrists bound, he hauled me off the counter, catching part of my purse in the process. The bag fell to the floor, the contents scattering everywhere. He paid them no mind as he crushed the mess beneath his boots and continued to shove me toward the door, and for the second time that night, I was grateful that Gabe had taken Aderes from this place.

As I stepped onto my front porch, my breath caught at the sight of a black van idling in the driveway, exhaust billowing toward the navy sky. *How many of these guys are there?*

A man exited the driver's side and dipped out of sight, reappearing at the back of the van as he swung the doors open. The moon was hidden tonight, but the taillights gave off enough light that I was able to catch sight of a black vest with white writing on it. As we moved closer to the van, I made out the words: *Satan's Serpents.*

My blood chilled. I dug my feet into the earth, subconsciously resisting getting any closer to the van. I had no idea who Satan's Serpents were, but it didn't take a genius to figure out this situation was not going to end well for me.

Alone and outnumbered with no way of knowing how long it would take for someone to figure out something had happened to me, I was caught in fear's grip once more, paralyzed from being able to do anything but imagine the worst.

The man behind me threw a knee into my leg again and shoved me forward until I was at the opening of the van. I pressed backward, doing everything in my power to keep my feet on the ground, but when my eyes landed on a form huddled in the back of the van, my surprise gave my abductors the opening they needed, and they wasted no time thrusting me inside. My shins scraped against the high bumper, my shoulders screaming in pain as my bound arms absorbed the shock of the fall. With a slam of the doors, I was engulfed by darkness.

* * *

GABE

TREVOR CLICKED through the laptop recovered from Hargrove's truck while I leafed through the stack of photos, all of which contained Alex as their only subject. I tried not to get distracted by image after image showcasing her exquisite beauty, but the woman was hard to ignore. Each time my eyes locked on her, they sought to memorize every detail, and I had to force my brain back into an analytical state. The point of examining these pictures was to identify anything that could either prove or disprove Hargrove was the person we'd been after all these weeks.

"I don't know, man," Trevor said, shaking his head but never taking his eyes off the screen in front of him. "It's all here. Hundreds of hours of video footage taken from the surveillance cameras in Alex's house, the divorce documents, her restraining order and copies of court proceedings from the original stalking case, and his browser history is full of articles about Alex. This whole laptop is like a shrine dedicated to her."

My eyes narrowed at the laptop. Sitting across from Trevor, I was unable to see the screen, but I didn't need to. I had never doubted what we would find when we opened it up. I was more interested in digging to see if there was anything *beneath* the obvious.

"It's a little too convenient, don't you think?"

Trevor looked up from the screen. "What do you mean?"

I extended my hand toward the computer. "Everything we need to convict this guy and put him behind bars for the next decade was sitting right there in his truck for us to find?"

Trevor shrugged. "You saw that prick. He's so arrogant, he never thought there was a snowball's chance in hell he was going to get caught. He planned on being long gone and back under the radar before anyone knew that something was up."

"All right," I said, drawing out the word. "I can get on board with that theory, but what about the passcode?"

"What about it?" Trevor went back to clicking and scrolling.

"This guy is computer savvy enough to escape detection by Quinn's contact—*a contracted hacker*—but our in-house IT guys were able to crack through his security on this laptop?" My eyebrows nearly met my hairline as I waited for him to explain that one. Instead of responding, Trevor leaned closer to the screen, his features scrunched in concentration.

"What?" I asked.

"Did Alex ever mention anything about a death threat?"

I scoffed. "This whole fucking thing has been a thinly veiled death threat."

Trevor shook his head. "No. I mean this." He turned the screen around so I could see it. It was an email sent to Alex. As my eyes skated along the text, my heart began to beat faster.

"Judging by the look on your face, I'm guessing the answer is no." Trevor laced his fingers together behind his head and leaned back in his chair, watching me.

My eyes scanned the screen, looking for a date and time. As soon as I found what I was looking for, my galloping heart came to a dead stop.

"This was sent the night before Alex told me she was leaving."

Trevor nodded slowly.

Realization struck, sharp as a tack. "That's why she was acting so off. She was trying to get me to walk away."

A slow shit-eating grin spread across Trevor's face. "I told you she loved you."

Heat crawled up my neck, my brows drawing together. "She should have told me."

Trevor brought his chair back to center and placed his forearms on the table. "If you knew about this"—he motioned to the laptop—"you would have handcuffed yourself to her and refused to leave her side. She knew that, so she did what she thought she had to to keep you safe."

My heart felt like it was too big for my chest as hope swelled, and the vision of the future I'd seen for us barreled to the foreground of my mind. *Maybe we can still have that.*

Then the prickle at the back of my neck returned, more persistent than ever. If that future was going to exist, I first had to make sure the threat was truly over.

I slid the laptop back to Trevor. He snapped it shut, watching and waiting for me to accept this case was a wrap. I pictured Hargrove, seated at the table in the interrogation room, recalling his body language and the way he had or hadn't reacted to certain questions. The longer I focused on his image, the stronger the nagging in my gut grew. What was it? What was I missing?

Almost as soon as I'd asked the question, it clicked. I snatched a box from the end of the table and slid it toward me. It was one of our earlier evidence boxes where we had collected the letters Alex had supplied when she'd first brought this case to our attention.

I flipped the brown cardboard lid off and rummaged through the contents until I found what I was looking for. Extracting a file, I slapped it on the table and leafed through the documents and images, pulling one photo from the stack and sliding it across the table to Trevor.

He picked it up, and after only a few seconds, the creases in his forehead disappeared.

"Hargrove couldn't have made those prints," I said.

The photo was of the footprints I'd found outside of one of Alex's windows the first day of the protection detail. The image showed a measuring apparatus next to the print, which was clearly much smaller than Hargrove's massive hooves. And someone his size would have left a much deeper impression in the soft soil.

Trevor's eyes lifted to mine, concession in his features. "All right, I'm convinced. That puts us back at square one. If it's not Hargrove, who is it, and why did Hargrove have all of this stuff in his possession?"

My brain went back to fitting different pieces together. "Whoever this guy is, he's not just smart, he's analytical. He thinks three steps ahead, pushing here, pulling there, playing everyone like pawns." I rubbed the scruff on my jaw that was quickly becoming a full beard. "He could have easily discovered Alex's history with Hargrove. It was in all the papers, not to mention public court documents. Seeing an opportunity, all he had to do was check the inmate system where Hargrove was doing time to discover that he was no longer behind bars, and boom!" I slapped my hand on the table. "Instant scapegoat."

Trevor nodded slowly, keeping pace. "So this guy makes contact with Hargrove, dangles the object of his obsession right in front of him, and gets Hargrove to take the bait."

I nodded. "And while Hargrove is making his move on Alex, the real stalker plants this evidence in Hargrove's truck, escaping before anyone is the wiser." I leaned back, staring at the table. "The question is, why? If the real stalker wanted Alex for himself, why let Hargrove get his hands on her?"

"Maybe he thought the officer on watch would stop Hargrove before it got that far. Then Alex remains untouched, and our guy gets to disappear free and clear."

"Maybe." I scratched the back of my head. We were close. I could feel it. But something still wasn't lining up. "I can't imagine this guy just walking away without his prize, though. Can you?" Before Trevor could answer, the last piece of the puzzle slid into place.

My skin flushed, adrenaline racing along every nerve.

Trevor straightened at the change in my body language.

I shot up from my chair, my palms slamming on the table. "This is exactly what he wanted." My lips peeled back from my teeth. How could I have been so stupid not to see it sooner? "We removed the protection detail. We're all here focused on this guy while Alex is wide open."

Trevor put his hands up, palms facing me. "It's okay. She's at the hospital surrounded by dozens of staff." He pulled his phone from his chest pocket. "I'll call the hospital and put security on alert. They can stand watch until we get there."

I shoved my hand through my hair, feeling like I was about to come out of my skin.

Trevor's right. She's fine. No one would try anything with all of those witnesses.

It sounded like Trevor was making contact with the ER first, telling them not to allow any visitors access to Alex. It was the sudden spike in his volume a moment later that sent my stomach through the floor.

"What? When?" Trevor's eyes were wide, his fingertips growing white as he gripped his phone. When he ended the call abruptly, I knew my night was about to get a whole lot worse.

Trevor shot to his feet. "Alex isn't at the hospital. She left AMA a half hour ago."

I was running for the door before he could finish. "Get every fucking unit going code three to her place!" I shouted over my shoulder.

The thought of Alex alone and vulnerable was like having a hot poker shoved down my throat. As soon as I was in my patrol car and blazing a trail to her house, I pulled my phone out and called her cell. She had no idea she was in this psycho's crosshairs. When the phone went straight to voice mail, I broke into a cold sweat.

Please, God, don't let me be too late.

CHAPTER 45

Alex

Hard plastic bit into my wrists as I twisted my hands, trying to create a weakness in the bonds, but it was no use. They were holding fast. The van bumped along, my already battered body protesting the constant assault of the cold, hard floor. I lifted my eyes to my fellow hostage and found him watching me, something akin to pity etched in his features.

I recognized him immediately, but his name was lost to me. Despite ardent efforts to conjure the memory of his name tag, my traumatized brain just wouldn't cooperate. But he'd made an impression. Every time I went to the coffee shop and saw him working behind the counter, I couldn't help but wonder about him—a young man who looked more like he belonged under the hood of a car than in a barista's apron.

The van hit another bump, causing the kid's shaggy brown hair to fall across his right eye, but he continued to hold my gaze. Though the light filtering in from the windshield was minimal, I could see that his eyes kept jumping to his boot. With his legs stretched out in front of him, his feet rested mere inches from my crisscrossed legs. My eyes narrowed, ensnared by his as they climbed to meet me once more. Though I wasn't gagged like he was, I didn't dare speak with our kidnappers only a few feet away.

He continued to stare at me with a burning intensity. I could practically feel him willing me to read his mind. My eyebrows drew together as I tried to push the foggy feeling in my brain aside. The concussion was taking its toll, no doubt helped along by the heavy shaking the baboon sitting in the passenger seat had delivered.

When the boy's eyes flicked to his right boot again, so did mine. Did he have something in his boot that could get us out of this mess?

I glanced to the front of the van. The two men charged with our transport were absorbed in a conversation about boxing, paying us no mind, convinced our bonds were all the security they needed.

The van continued its bumpy pursuit toward our destination, and I used each bounce to my advantage, scooting myself closer to my companion. Once my arms, still bound behind my back, were even with his feet, I angled my body away from his, so my fingers could search him.

The rough denim of his pants scratched against my fingertips. I didn't feel anything but bone beneath the fabric at his ankle. So, I reached a little deeper, diving into the top of one of his boots. It took a moment, but I finally came up against something smooth and hard. My fingers fought for purchase, the awkward angle of my hands making it difficult to grasp the object. I pressed my lips together, willing my body to contort like some kind of circus performer so I could get a hold of what felt like the metal handle of a knife.

After several minutes of bouncing and repositioning, not to mention the sharp sting from the zip ties cutting into my skin, I finally felt the handle wiggle free a bit. It had moved only an inch higher, if that, but it was progress. My heart beat wildly in my chest, the fear of getting caught mingling with the desperation of escaping whatever these men had in mind. And as I wiggled that handle, knowing full well both the boy's life and mine depended on me getting it free, I froze when I realized the chatter up front had died.

* * *

GABE

GRAVEL SPRAYED beneath my tires as I turned into Alex's driveway and gunned my engine. My cruiser shot forward, sprinting toward her front walk. I didn't hit the brakes until I was practically on the cement. The car barely had a chance to recover from the sudden stop before I ripped my seat belt free and sprang out. I raced for the house, my blood running cold when I saw the gaping black hole of the open doorway.

"Alex!" My voice was savage, her name a promise of agony to anyone who dared touch her.

I drew my gun, slowing just enough to scan the exterior of the house for signs of a trap. "Alex!"

Answer me, baby. A cold sweat broke on my forehead, mingling with the pelting rain.

When I reached the door, I pulled my flashlight free, swinging the beam in an arc, my eyes moving methodically from one side of the vast opening to the other. It wasn't until I swung the light toward the kitchen that I could see several small items scattered across the floor.

The sound of tires crunching behind me, a siren dying on a wail, informed me of Trevor's presence. He was at my back before I'd even had time to blink and placed a hand on my shoulder, signaling he was ready to enter. My mind told me to hurry, urging me to burst inside without regard for my own safety. But my instincts and training fought my desperation, beating it back until I once again became the merciless soldier.

If something happened to Trevor and me, it would only slow down any progress on finding Alex. And no one would ever look for her as hard as I would.

Staring down the sights of my gun, I eased inside, taking the left while Trevor took the right. Aside from the rain beating against the house, the place was silent and still. I tried not to allow myself to be distracted by the items beneath my feet as I stepped into the kitchen, but my mind started racing with images of how that purse and its contents had ended up all over the floor.

Trevor and I moved quickly, clearing one room after another and coming up empty, a mix of relief and fear battling in my chest. As grateful as I was that we hadn't found Alex's mangled body or any signs of blood, I was equally worried by the thought of what she could be enduring at this very moment.

I returned to the kitchen and flipped on the light, squatting down to inspect the items on the floor more closely. I recognized Alex's makeup bag and the small notebook she always carried with her. Her keys had slid halfway under the fridge, and her wallet was peeking out of the fallen purse. Picking up her wallet, I opened it, noting all of the cash and credit cards were still inside. I checked the interior of her purse next. With the exception of a few pens and a pack of gum, it was empty.

My head swiveled as my eyes scanned the full length of the floor. Then I placed my hands on the ground to look underneath the fridge and the base of the cabinets.

Trevor came from the back of the house, the wet soles of his boots squeaking on the hardwood floors. "It doesn't look like she was here very long. The bedroom looks exactly like it did when she was taken to the hospital."

I straightened, my forehead creasing.

"What are you doing?" Trevor asked.

I brushed off my hands and climbed to my feet, pulling my cell out. As I dialed Dispatch, I said, "Alex's phone isn't here."

Quinn's voice promptly came on the line. "Dispatch, this is Quinn."

"Quinn, it's Gabe. Alex is missing. I need you to start a trace on her phone."

"Sure thing. Do you know the number?"

I rattled it off and heard her passing the information to one of her partners to get started.

"Gabe . . ." Quinn's voice was tight. "I know you've already got your hands full, but . . ."

It was so unlike Quinn to hesitate, even for a second, that a new sense of dread settled over the cold knot that was already sitting heavy in my stomach. "What is it, Quinn?"

"Emmy Dixon is here at the station. She's frantic."

The creases in my brow deepened. "Frantic about what?"

I signaled to Trevor that I wanted to do a perimeter search. He nodded and we headed outside. The rain was falling in solid sheets, our uniforms soaked through and clinging to our bodies. We walked slowly, our flashlights guiding our feet, the elements adding an additional challenge. Alex's kidnapper would have had to leave a pretty big fucking clue if we were going to find it in the dark with the rain washing the soil away.

I pressed the phone harder against my ear, trying to hear Quinn over the roar of the storm.

"She was supposed to meet up with Jace Maloy at Grind. He was closing tonight, so he told her to come in through the back door in the alley. When she got there, the place was empty, and Jace's phone was lying next to the dumpster, smashed."

My hand tightened on my cell. This was *not* happening. The two people I was responsible for protecting had not both gone missing on the same night.

My brain immediately began to sort through the details of each situation, working to adjust our strategy as the pawns on the board and the rules of the game kept shifting.

Prioritize and clear.

I returned my attention to Quinn. "Have you dispatched units to the coffee shop?"

"Yes. Nash and Garrett are just getting there now." The clicking of Quinn's keyboard never slowed as she got me up to speed, pausing only to respond to the radio. "The only reason I'm telling you any of this right now is because Emmy is still here, beside herself, stating that Jace had once told her if anything happened to him, he wanted her to go straight to you."

Trevor and I had worked our way to the rear of Alex's house. I bumped him on the shoulder, and when he turned to look at me, I nodded toward the woods, telling him that's where I wanted to check next. We continued sweeping our flashlights across the ground in front of us, the dense tree line drawing nearer and nearer.

"All right, Quinn. Let me know as soon as you get that trace on Alex's phone, tell Emmy to go home and wait for me to contact her, and advise Nash to call me as soon as he's checked the surveillance footage at the coffee shop."

"Copy that." Quinn's tone was as calm and smooth as ever despite the fact the dispatchers were surely getting their asses handed to them right now.

As soon as we disconnected, I filled Trevor in on the phone call.

"What the ever-living *fuck* is going on?" he shouted above the rain and wind.

I squinted against the water dripping into my eyes. We were approaching the edge of the grass that marked the boundary of Alex's yard. The towering black trees of the woods I had practically memorized at this point stood like sentinels.

"I don't know," I said. "But if this is a coincidence, I'll run down Main Street wearing nothing but a fucking tutu."

My mind reeled as I willed my eyes to find something, *anything*, that would guide me to Alex.

Minutes later, the beam from Trevor's flashlight sliced across a reflective surface. I knew right away what we were going to find. It was Alex's phone, and it was smashed. Just like Jace's had been. My heart squeezed as my light landed on large boot prints in the mud, visible only where the canopy of trees was thick enough that the rain hadn't yet washed them away.

I squatted to examine the tracks more closely. There were two sets of prints headed out of the woods toward Alex's but only one set returning. And no sign of Alex having come this way.

She could have been carried out, but considering the prints leaving weren't any deeper than the ones coming, it didn't appear that whoever left this way was carrying extra weight.

Given the fact one of her abductors clearly hadn't come back through here, and Alex's car was still in the garage, I was willing to bet she'd been loaded into another vehicle. One that had arrived only after she had. Which meant there had been at least three abductors.

My teeth ground together as my brain filled in the question of what had gone down here not even an hour before I'd arrived.

My phone vibrated in my pocket. It was Nash. I didn't waste any time demanding the information I wanted. "What did the surveillance show?"

His voice was grim. "Nothing."

"So, what? Jace just walked out and never came back?"

"No. I mean it didn't show *anything*. The system was turned off."

"Fuck!"

Trevor's head snapped toward me.

"The fucking cameras were off at the coffee shop!" I told him, kicking a clump of mud. Pulling the phone from my ear, I put it on speaker so I wouldn't have to waste time filling Trevor in.

"I *do* know that he was taken by two members of the Serpents, though," Nash said.

My gut already knew that, but it didn't stop my stomach from plummeting.

"How the hell do you know that, and why didn't you start with that information?" Trevor growled at the phone.

Nash ignored Trevor's irritation. "I recalled that Barney at the hardware store two doors down installed cameras in the alley about two months ago when he was having some vandalism issues. I called him and asked him to forward the footage from the last two hours to me."

"And?" I asked.

"A large black van pulled up out back. Two Serpents got out. You can see their cuts clear as day. They entered the rear of the coffee shop and emerged less than a minute later dragging Jace. It looks like his hands were bound behind his back, and he was limp."

"What was the time stamp when they hauled him out?" I asked.

"Twenty-two fifteen."

Fire ripped through my veins, realization dawning. Every Eden Falls police unit had been at Alex's house while Jace was being abducted. Could the Serpents really have orchestrated such a convoluted plan?

"Nash, how many units do you have there?"

"Three. Why?"

"Send two of them to the Serpents' clubhouse. I want the place torn apart and every one of those assholes questioned on the whereabouts of Jace Maloy and Alex Reilly."

"Alex Reilly?"

"Just get them over there now!"

The sound of a siren grew louder as Trevor's and my backup drew near. It was only then that I realized the units who had initially been responding to Alex's must have been diverted to the coffee shop.

I glared into Trevor's eyes. "They took her because of me. This is them making good on that warning they left with Lily."

He slowly shook his head. "You had no way of knowing they would come after Alex."

I spun away from the woods and stalked toward the house. I wasn't going to let Trevor give me an excuse not to feel guilty. This was on *me*. All of it.

Jace had *trusted* me. Alex had *needed* me. I knew the risks, and I had failed them both.

"Get whoever's headed this way to divert to my place." My tone was sharp enough to cut glass, my thumb nearly breaking the screen on my phone as I pulled up Liz's number. "I want a guard on my family until we know how far Dawson and the Serpents intend to take this tonight."

CHAPTER 46

Alex

AIR ESCAPED my lungs in a whoosh when the chatter from the front of the van resumed. I cast a glance at the kid, watching the tension ease ever so slightly from his features. With a single nod, he urged me to keep trying for the knife. I was grateful for the rain beating down like war drums on the metal hull of the van, as it would mask the sound of my movements. At the same time, with my back turned toward our captors, my ears were the only thing I could rely on to alert me to any change in their behavior. I feared that at any moment they were going to glance back, and I wouldn't realize it until it was too late.

I glanced over my shoulder at the boy again. He kept his eyes trained on the men up front. When his foot frantically tapped my hand a moment later, I let my arms fall and sat perfectly still, hoping that the fact I was now sitting in the middle of the van rather than at its edge would be dismissed as a result of the bumpy ride.

When the kid tapped my hand again, I slowly turned my head and met his eyes. With his nod, my fingers flew back to his leg, grasping the handle of the knife that now sat several inches higher than the top of his boot. I was nearly there.

With my arms tied behind my back, my range of motion was

limited. Realizing there was a better way to do this, I gripped the knife as hard as I could between my thumb and first two fingers. Then I caught the kid's eye again and jerked my head toward the opposite side of the van. He squinted his eyes, then almost immediately, the confusion cleared. He glanced toward the men once more, and finding them still deep in conversation, he thrust his body forward, effectively dislodging the knife as I held it in place.

I took a deep breath, trying to ease the shaking in my hands. If I dropped the knife, the sound of it hitting the metal floor would, without doubt, travel above the din of the rain. Feeling along the edges of the handle, I tried to figure out how to expose the blade. It was taking too long. We had already been driving for what seemed like hours. Without the ability to see any road signs or mile markers, I couldn't be sure of how far we'd gone, but the winding road and the change in elevation causing my ears to plug suggested we were traveling deeper into the mountains.

My frustration growing, I ground my teeth as my fingers searched for a break in the smooth metal. I felt a nudge at my shoulder and realized the kid had managed to turn himself so he sat facing the front of the van with his shoulder next to mine. He hooked his head as if to say *give it to me* and waved one of his hands up and down. Pivoting away from him, I leaned over and dropped the knife the moment I felt his warm flesh come into contact with mine.

I heard a snap and looked down, realizing it was a switchblade. The kid fumbled with it for a moment until he had the blade pointed straight up. Turning my back to him fully, I leaned forward to raise my arms and then carefully brought them down until the switchblade was between me and the zip ties at my wrists. I sawed up and down, leaning forward to apply more pressure from the blade into the hard plastic. My shoulders screamed in protest, the ache going bone-deep, but I shoved the pain aside, knowing there was worse to come if this kid and I didn't get free of these bonds before we arrived at our destination.

Several agonizing minutes later, I felt the first tie break, followed almost immediately by the second. Relief flooded my shoulders and neck as my arms fell forward, but I didn't allow myself time to enjoy the release. Spinning on my butt, I snatched the knife and went to work freeing my ally. The moment the plastic fell away from his wrists, he pulled the gag from his mouth and leaned in close, clutching my upper arm to pull me in tighter.

His breath was hot against my ear, his whisper barely audible above the raging storm and the sound of the van's engine revving as it catapulted us up a particularly steep incline.

"Ms. Reilly, it's me, Jace, from the coffee shop."

Jace, that's it.

He rushed on without waiting for me to acknowledge him. "These guys are taking us somewhere isolated to kill us."

Fear plunged its icy fingers down my throat, choking off my words. I still wasn't even sure why I was here. A part of me had been reasoning that this was some big mistake. These guys clearly knew Gabe, but that didn't necessarily mean that that had anything to do with why they had broken into my home and kidnapped me. Perhaps they were after money. I doubted they knew of my success because they were fans of my books, but with all of the news coverage I'd been getting lately, the whole world knew me as the heiress-turned-best-selling romance author.

I turned my mouth to Jace's ear. "I'll offer them money. Whatever they want. That's got to be what they're after—"

"They're after our blood." Jace's tone was absolute, as though he knew with certainty why we were here. "I'm here because they know I ratted on them. And you're here because they want to hurt Gabe. Teach him a lesson."

An arctic wave washed over me, sending my body into a fit of shivers. *This can't be happening.* After all of these weeks of being terrorized by Hargrove, who was once again locked behind bars, and I still end up with my life dangling off a precipice because of someone else's enemies?

Jace didn't allow me time to process his words. He spoke quickly, glancing toward the front of the van every few seconds.

"They have a place where they take people to dispose of them. We *cannot* let them take us inside. Our only chance to escape is to catch them off guard and run the second we clear this van."

He pulled back, his eyes boring into mine, waiting for acknowledgment. I swallowed hard and nodded reluctantly.

His mouth was at my ear once more. "You're going to scoot back to the other side of the van. Keep your arms behind your back. Make it look like you're still tied up. When they open the door and go to pull us out, act like you're struggling to move around. Make them think there's no way you could put up a fight."

I fought to pay attention, but my mind kept resisting, insisting over and over that this was just a ploy for money. That I would be able to figure out a way to buy our freedom.

Jace nudged me with his shoulder, his eyes capturing mine before he leaned in again. "Alex—"

The switch to my first name, and the steel beneath it, had the intended effect. I turned my head to look at him.

"I need you to trust me and do as I say. I *know* these men. I know what they're capable of. And I know what they intend to do to us. Even if we die trying to escape, it's a faster and better death than we'll have if we let them get us inside that cabin."

I scanned his face. The truth of his words was written plainly in the crease between his eyes and the frown at his lips. Nausea burned the back of my throat as my anxiety climbed, causing my body to tremble even harder. I dropped my chin, fighting the tears that emerged on the dying gasp of my hope.

Jace scooted closer, pressing his shoulder against mine, his voice deep and reassuring. "Alex, I'm going to do everything in my power to get you out of this. But I need you to help me."

How could this boy, who was so young, be so fierce? I should be helping *him* to keep it together right now, not the other way around. But as I gazed into his sable eyes, I saw the undeniable spirit of a warrior. He showed no fear. Only a desire to fight and a willingness to die trying.

I inhaled deeply, forcing the fear into a dark corner in my mind, deciding to place my trust in Jace. He must have sensed the shift. His lips turned up ever so slightly before he continued laying out the plan. "As soon as we're both out of the van, run. Don't look back and don't worry about me. Just *run*. Understand?"

I nodded, and he jerked his chin, signaling that he wanted me to get back on the other side of the van. As I scooted, he reclaimed his original position and pulled his gag back into place. With my hands clasped behind my back, alarm flooded my system as the van slowed and turned off the main road. Gravel crunched beneath the tires, the van jostling even more violently than before.

Though I tried to control my breathing, my heart was thrashing against my chest, causing the panic to rise until I was panting. I closed my eyes, and for the first time in far too many years, I prayed. Prayed that I could have one more chance to right my wrongs. That I could have one more chance to show that I had learned how much I had to be grateful for. And one more chance to open my heart and let down my walls. To love and live without guilt or condition. Just one more chance . . .

CHAPTER 47

Gabe

THE MINUTES WERE TICKING BY, and every one of them propelled Alex and Jace closer to death while Trevor and I were still wading waist-deep in shit and without a clue as to where to search next. The units we'd sent to the Serpents' clubhouse had already reported back that there were no signs of Alex or Jace on the premises. I wasn't surprised. Drake Dawson wasn't stupid enough to do his dirty work that close to town and in a place where law enforcement would check first. Still, we had to ensure we covered our bases.

Though every person in that clubhouse was currently being questioned, I didn't hold out much hope. None of the senior members had been present during the raid, which meant no one there had the kind of sensitive information I was looking for. So, Trevor and I went to work figuring out our next move. Now that I knew my family was armed and guarded by officers, I could give my full attention to Alex and the kid again.

Trevor and I sat in my patrol car, staring into the black night through the sheets of water pouring down my windshield. I ground my molars, the tension in my shoulders pulling tighter as seconds vanished.

Trevor exhaled sharply. "I should have just put unauthorized trackers on Dawson and his inner circle." He punched the dashboard. "How many times did I say I was going to do that in case Jace went missing?"

We couldn't even try running a trace on any of the members' cell phones. They were too careful about using burner phones and leaving their personal cells away from club business.

"It's not going to help worrying about what we *should* have done," I said. "We've got to focus on finding wherever the hell it is they do the worst of their deeds."

If only dead men could talk. Then Charles Bailey could tell us where he'd been when they'd slit him from groin to sternum.

Before I'd even finished the thought, my mind was jumping to our next-best source. My head snapped around to Trevor. "Trev. Did you ever get in touch with that fed again to ask about witness protection for Jace?"

Trevor's eyes widened. "Yeah. He was practically drooling at the thought of getting his hands on someone with that kind of insider information. He was going to notify me when the pieces were in place."

Already knowing where I was headed with my question, Trevor pulled out his cell phone and scrolled through his contacts, placing the call that I prayed would put us back on the trail. Trevor put the call on speaker and held his phone between us so I could hear over the rain pelting the car like BBs off a tin can.

"Moss." It sounded like we'd roused the agent from a dead sleep.

"Moss, this is Trevor Ryan, Eden Falls PD. I need your help."

Moss cleared his throat, accompanied by the sound of a bed squeaking. "What's going on?"

"I'm here with my partner, Gabe McNeil. That kid I told you about? He and a woman have been taken by the Serpents. We need to know if you have a way of tracking the senior members or any idea where they might have taken the hostages."

When Moss spoke next, his voice was crisp and alert. "What woman?"

"Alex Reilly."

"The author?"

"Yes."

"What the hell would they want with her?"

Trevor glanced at me before answering. "We're not sure, but we think it was to send a message to my partner."

"What kind of message?"

"He's involved with her. The Serpents delivered a warning to him a few days ago, threatening the people closest to him."

Moss groaned. "Fuck. It's not their MO to mess with someone that high-profile. They dispose of people no one will miss, not prominent heiresses who make regular appearances in the media." He paused, the sound of papers flipping in the background. "How do you know the Serpents are responsible for both the kid and the woman?"

Trevor detailed the events of the evening, trying to be as brief as possible. Every once in a while, he'd glance over at me again like he was afraid I was about to detonate.

He was right to worry.

I knew Moss was just doing his job. Covering his bases. Making sure he wasn't going into something blind and likely to end up in hot water with a whole lot of explaining to do. But we didn't have time for this. The Serpents never kept their targets alive for long, and Dawson knew me well enough to know I would sprint into the pits of hell to get my people back. He wouldn't risk keeping them in his possession any longer than he had to.

As soon as Trevor finished relaying everything Moss needed to know, including Emmy's account of what she'd found and the video footage of the Serpents carrying Jace to their van, Moss spoke again. "I don't have any way to track them yet. I'm working on it, but the warrant hasn't come through."

My stomach twisted. If this guy couldn't give us something, *anything*, to at least point us in a direction, our chances of getting to Alex and Jace in time were slim to none.

Unable to stay silent any longer, I snatched Trevor's phone, growling into the mouthpiece. "Look, I get that you feds don't have a habit of playing nice with local law enforcement, but if you have *any* information that could be of any fucking use to us, you'd better hand it over unless you want my boot so far up your ass, you'll be spitting leather for a year."

Heat emanated off my body, my rage coiled so tightly in my gut, my body vibrated with it.

There was a long pause. Then Trevor took the phone. "Look, Moss. I get that you've been working on this investigation for a long time, and you don't want us barreling in there, ruining the case you've been building against these guys." Trevor's voice was surprisingly calm, his hand rubbing the back of his neck the only indication of the emotion he was suppressing. "But we're talking about an innocent woman and a kid who put his ass on the line to help us end these guys. Are you really going to let them suffer what Drake has in store for them?"

Silence filled the air for more than a few heartbeats. Then, finally, Moss spoke, his words resigned and delivered on a sigh. "There's a cabin in the mountains, about an hour outside of Eden Falls. We suspect it's where they do their really dirty work. It's far enough removed that there's no chance of anyone hearing the screams or witnessing the cleanup."

My blood ran cold. Images of the Serpents' filthy hands on Alex, of Jace being sliced open, a scream dying on his lips, became the only thing I could see.

I turned toward the phone Trevor still held in front of him and stared daggers that I hoped Moss could sense on the other end of the line. "If you know about this cabin and what they do there, why haven't you raided it yet?"

"Because we're not certain." Moss sighed again, sounding as though he was growing weary. "Look, we're only going to get one shot at catching these guys off guard. If we're going to get a conviction that sends them away for life, we have to ensure that we strike when we can do maximum damage. The truth is, they're very good at cleaning up after their messes, and our intelligence has always come *after* the fact. We need to catch them in the act if we want to nail their asses to the wall and make it stick."

Instinctively, I brought my emotions back under control. The red-hot rage tearing through me became a blue flame that settled in the pit of my gut. I reached for the key in the ignition, revving the engine as it roared to life. "This might just be your lucky night." My voice was ice, the promise of violence dripping from every word. "Where is the fucking cabin?"

Alex

THE VAN CAREENED over the rough gravel road, each spin of the tires taking us closer to the moment that would deliver us to either victory or death. I had no way of knowing how long it had been since we'd turned off the main road. My sense of time had long since been warped by the fear clawing at every piece of me.

I swung my gaze to Jace. Now that we were traveling deeper into the woods, the heavy boughs of the trees lining the gravel road blocked out what little ambient light had previously been afforded, making it difficult to pick out details. But from the subtle light emanating from the electrical elements on the dash, the hard lines of Jace's face, the stillness of his body, indicated that fear had made no purchase where he was concerned.

The moment the van began to slow, the brakes shrieking like nails on a chalkboard, my heart leapt into my throat, and my mouth went dry. Movement from Jace got my attention. When I glanced at him again, he nodded once. His eyes narrowed and mouth set with a silent promise that we *would* get out of this alive.

I closed my eyes and inhaled deeply, drawing strength from Jace. Something told me that this kid had tangled with the devil before and lived to tell the tale. When I opened my eyes, he was still locked on me. I squared my shoulders, sitting a little straighter, and inclined my head. That seemed to be all the reassurance he needed, because he returned his attention to the men up front.

The van lurched as it came to a stop, the driver killing the engine. I leaned forward to look through the windshield, expecting to find some kind of structure where they intended to hold us. Instead, the only thing I could see in the yellow beams of the headlights was the gravel road stretching toward eternity.

My heart beat savagely against my rib cage, my breaths coming in ragged pants as the blood rushed to my ears and drowned out the sound of the rain. I looked down at my white sweater, silently cursing my wardrobe choice. Had I known I'd be running for my life through the woods in the dead of night, I would have chosen something a little less easy to track.

The two men exited the van, slamming the doors behind them. The gravel crunched beneath their boots and grew louder as they approached the rear doors. I drew one more deep breath through my nose, forcing my mind away from the grisly images I feared would come to pass and instead focused on what needed to be done. My life was not the only one hanging in the balance. Jace had given me a chance at escape and a promise to fight for my survival. I would give him no less in return.

The rear doors swung open, framing two dark figures. The big bald man who had forced me from my home reached in and grasped me around the arm, dragging me toward him. Just like Jace had instructed, I kept my arms banded behind my back, scooting toward the exit with great effort.

Jace scooted with me, but the barrel-chested man who had been driving the van threw his hand up. "Not you, rat. Just the woman."

I paused, whipping my head around to look at Jace. His brows drew together, giving him a sinister look, but he jerked his chin toward the doors, telling me to keep going.

When I reached the edge of the van, the barrel-chested man spoke again. "Don't even think about it, kid."

I glanced over my shoulder at Jace, seeing that he had positioned himself on his knees, hands still behind his back, breathing hard against the gag. His eyes were locked on the man giving him orders.

A tug on my arm reminded me I had my own adversary to deal with. Why were they pulling me from the van but leaving Jace behind?

A knot formed in my stomach, my intuition telling me that the surprises of this night were far from over. With no clue about what I was supposed to do given this hiccup in the plan, I swung my legs over the edge of the van and allowed the man holding my arm to pull me to my feet. The moment he did, his eyes widened, and his partner let out a gasp.

I shrieked when something went flying past my shoulder, knocking the shorter guy off his feet. Jace landed on the man and tussled with him for only a moment, throwing a bone-crunching punch into his nose. Jace then jumped to his feet; without a second's hesitation, he lowered his head and charged toward the giant still holding my arm, driving his shoulder into the guy and forcing his grip to loosen.

As soon as I was free, Jace shoved me toward the woods. "Run, Alex! Go!"

We had only made it a few feet when the gravel rolled beneath my Keds, throwing me off-balance for just an instant. But it was enough to sabotage my getaway. Strong fingers tangled in my hair and yanked back, pulling me into familiar arms. I wiggled and kicked my heels into the bald man's shins, but his grip only tightened.

Ahead of me, Jace's steps faltered as he looked to his left and realized I wasn't there. He spun around, eyes widening when he saw me. Without missing a beat, Jace sprinted to where I stood captive and launched himself at us. The momentum of his weight sent us all flying into the back of the van, landing in a tangle. The man lying beneath me grunted as Jace slammed his fist into the guy's face. After two more punches, he finally released me so he could use his arms to block Jace's assault, allowing me to roll away from the pair.

"Run, Alex!" Jace grunted, dodging a wild punch.

Out of my peripheral, the man Jace had sent flying through the air was climbing to his feet, his eyes taking in the melee in the back of the van. My head swiveled wildly, searching for something I could use to help Jace.

Where was the knife I'd pulled from his boot? Had he put it back? Was it in his pocket? Or was it lying outside on the ground somewhere?

The van shook violently with the force of the struggle between Jace and his opponent. The man beneath him bucked like a rodeo horse, attempting to unseat Jace from his chest. Jace threw a knee into the man's side and then craned his neck around to find me.

"Run, Alex! Now! Run!"

I bit my lip, the thought of leaving him in the hands of these monsters shredding my insides. But as the man outside the van staggered to his feet, I knew that if I didn't leave now, we were both as good as dead. Our survival depended on my escape so I could return with help.

I catapulted from the van, narrowly avoiding the outstretched fingers of the barrel-chested man, and I ran. My legs stretched out before me, the way they had a thousand times before. The wind and the rain whipped across my face; the rough branches of trees and shrubs clawed at my skin and clothes. And still I ran.

The baritone shouts of my captors and the man who'd sacrificed himself to save me died in the wail of the storm. My legs hurdled fallen trees, and my feet moved so fast that not even the slick mud could slow me down.

Deep into the heart of night, swallowed by a raging storm, I ran.

CHAPTER 49
Alex

TERROR GRIPPED my body as I stumbled over unfamiliar terrain. My breath was ragged, threatening to burst my lungs, the darkness so consuming, I navigated by shades of black. It wasn't the fact that I was in the woods in the dead of night. It was that these weren't *my* woods, and I had no idea if I was running toward help or right into the devil's outstretched arms.

The pine needles beneath my feet, squishy with rain, muted the sound of my footfalls. Unfortunately, that meant my pursuer had the same advantage.

A twig snapping to my right whipped my head around. Was it the storm shearing smaller branches from the trees? Or was my lead shorter than I thought?

I clenched my jaw, willing my feet to keep going, to push through the heaviness that had settled in my legs, making every step harder than the last.

He's counting on you. You have to get out.

The rain fell in blinding sheets, even through the thick canopy of overlapping pine branches, and the wind howled as it ripped through the trees, twisting the drenched fabric of my sweater around me. The sting of the water and cold on my face taunted me with the reality that this was not a nightmare from which I would wake.

Passing the thick black silhouette of a tree standing sentinel, I threw my back against the rough bark and consciously fought to slow my breathing, the ragged bursts of air making it difficult to hear and threatening to reveal my location.

I closed my eyes and strained my ears.

Nothing.

Nothing but the sound of rain falling and small creatures scurrying amongst the fallen foliage that blanketed the woods.

I swiveled my head, scanning my surroundings, but it was pointless. The darkness was too profound. Getting out of these woods alive would be a damn miracle. I was tempted to crawl under some brush and hide until morning. But I couldn't do that. I wasn't the only one running out of time.

He's probably dead by now.

I gritted my teeth and forced the thought aside, refusing to entertain that possibility. Sending up a silent prayer that I was headed in the right direction, I stepped away from the tree and started forward again, quickly glancing over my shoulder. When I turned back, my stomach lurched, and my steps faltered. A shadow unfurled from the dark mass of trees dead ahead and stalked toward me.

How could they have possibly gotten ahead of me? Though I wasn't exactly sure how close I had made it to the road, I was confident I was still headed away from the van.

A low laugh rode the currents of the wind, its pitch so unexpected my confusion held me in place. The figure moved closer. Slowly. Methodically. As if time didn't exist and this place was just a dream that it controlled.

A beam of light erupted from the darkness. I threw my arm up as a shield when it landed on my eyes. Blinded, I had no way of knowing if the figure was still coming toward me or how close it was getting. Instinctively, I took several steps backward, my movements cautious. Then the light dropped to my chest, and a pale hand extended beyond the darkness into the ethereal glow, the black barrel of the gun it held causing my steps to falter.

But it was the red polish and slender fingers that commandeered my attention.

"You just couldn't walk away, could you?" The voice calling to me over the storm tickled a memory, as though I'd heard it before, but my sluggish brain couldn't place it.

"The heiress turned America's sweetheart and world-renowned author just has to take it all."

I shivered, but it had nothing to do with the icy water gushing from the heavens. The malevolence dripping from that disembodied voice foretold gruesome intentions. My eyes drilled into the sheet of black that obscured the identity of the person standing before me, but with the way the light was affecting my eyes, the effort was futile.

"I gave you a chance to leave. I warned you that things would get bad if you didn't." The voice shifted without warning from chillingly calm to vicious. "But you're a selfish whore!"

I jumped and took a step back. As I did, the figure moved into the light, swinging the flashlight up as a child telling ghost stories would do. My breath caught when the light fell across a face I had seen dozens of times.

"Bree?" I breathed her name, too stunned to do more.

The menacing smile that spread over her face reached across the distance between us and seized my heart. Like her voice, though her features were the same, nothing about them was familiar. Where her eyes had once been soft and understanding, they were now filled with a maniacal gleam. Her hair, usually tossed casually into a messy bun, now clung to her face and neck like tentacles.

"I don't understand," I stuttered against the cold and fear.

Her answering laugh was caustic. "Of course you don't, Alex. That would require you to actually think about someone other than yourself."

I glanced at the gun again, sickened by the fact it didn't quiver in the slightest. She had no fear, no hesitation over what she was doing.

She had turned the flashlight so it was once again pointed at me but held it low and stood close enough that we were both engulfed in the light. I raised my eyes to hers. "What do you want with me, Bree? I thought we were friends."

She sneered. "You thought what I wanted you to think. It was the only way I could get close enough to you to gain the access I needed to destroy your life."

My eyebrows drew together. None of this was making any sense. "Why would you want to do that?"

"Because you tried to take what isn't yours!" She jabbed the gun toward me.

I threw my hands up, hoping my show of submission would calm her rising agitation. "Bree, I want to make this right." I searched her eyes, the irises nearly completely eclipsed by her pupils. "I just need you to tell me how I can do that."

The calmness of my voice belied the terror arcing through my body. I had seen crazy like this before. Had already stared it down once tonight. I knew trying to reason with her wasn't going to do any good. But I had to do something to stall until I could see an opportunity to get the upper hand.

Bree stepped toward me, closing the distance between us until the barrel of the gun brushed my sternum, her lips peeling back from her teeth. "It's too late for that." Her words were so quiet they were nearly lost in the storm. She reached out with the hand that held the flashlight and shoved me away from the road and deeper into the woods, forcing me to feel my way over the rocks and shrubs that rose from the mud to sabotage my steps.

If I could distract her, maybe throw her off by triggering another emotional outburst, it might create enough of an opening for me to escape. I was fast. Even in the dark and unfamiliar terrain, I was confident in my ability to put distance between us. I just had to get her to lower that gun for a few seconds.

I straightened my shoulders and slowed my steps a bit, giving her a hint of resistance. "So, what's the plan, then?" I forced boredom into my tone. "Shoot me and leave me here for some hunter to find?"

She shoved at my back and snickered, the hard edge of the flashlight causing a twinge as it met my shoulder blade. "Shoot you, yes. Here, no. We're much too close to the road." She shoved at my back again and sent me stumbling forward a few steps before I caught myself.

"No," she continued, "your final resting place will be where the wildlife will find you long before a hunter even has the chance. Your bones will be picked clean. Every remnant of Alex Reilly consumed and defecated until you're erased from existence." She sighed dramatically. "But, since those idiots couldn't manage to hold on to you, we're just going to have to walk a little farther than I intended."

The complete lack of emotion as she uttered those words was more terrifying than anything she said. Maybe it was the writer in me. The fact that my brain detested loose ends. But I *had* to know why this was happening. Jace had said those guys had taken me to get back at Gabe. If that was the case, how the hell was Bree involved, and why did it seem like this was very much about *me*?

I continued the conversation as if we were chatting like two friends. The way we had the night before. "Is that how you found me out here? Are you working with them?"

She scoffed. "*They* are working for *me*."

I infused my voice with skepticism. "They didn't strike me as the type to work for anybody, let alone a skinny twentysomething-year-old woman."

She brought the flashlight down hard across my back, drawing a grunt from me. "They're too stupid to realize when someone is using them. You have that in common."

Deeper into the woods we marched, the road slipping farther and farther from my reach. If I was the only one I had to think about, I would just bide my time, waiting for the right opportunity to escape and then hide for as long as it took to find my way out of this mess. But every step in the wrong direction was a step closer to Jace's death. If he was even still alive.

I chided myself for the thought. Jace deserved better than to have me giving up on him already. I *would* find a way out of this. For both of us.

"All right," I said, continuing my search for answers as fervently as my eyes swept for escape. "If that's the case, then what could you possibly want with Jace?"

She snorted. "I don't give a rat's ass about Jace. He simply provided an opportunity that was too good to pass up."

"How so?"

Something pressed into my back. Given the fact the flashlight was still swinging wildly around us, I suspected it was the gun. "Talk less and walk more!"

I steeled my spine and took a deep breath, about to take a risk that I prayed with every fiber of my being would pay off. Spinning around, I threw my arms out to the side. "Look, you've won, Bree. I'm out in the middle of the woods. No one knows where I am, and you've got a gun pointed at me. The least you could do is slake my curiosity and fill in a few blanks before you kill me."

I waited, my breath caught in my chest. Either I would have succeeded in keeping us from getting any farther from that damn road, or she was going to shoot me here and drag my body the rest of the way.

Her eyes narrowed, lips pursed to the side. I could practically hear the cogs turning in her head. Finally, she relaxed her frame ever so slightly but kept the gun aimed at my heart, the flashlight hanging limp at her side. "Fine. I'm a charitable woman. And truth be told, I like drawing out the kill."

My stomach plummeted. *What the hell? Has she done this before?*

CHAPTER 50

Gabe

THE RED TAILLIGHTS from the government-issued SUV ahead of me glowed like demon eyes as we wound our way up the mountain. Towering evergreens pushed in all around us, crowding the road and waving their arms as if warning us to turn back. My hand choked the steering wheel, the sound of the plastic protesting beneath my grip the only outward sign of the tension I was feeling.

Trevor glanced at me out of the corner of his eye. "We're not that far behind them, brother. We'll make it in time."

I pressed my lips into a firm line. "If we're even heading to the right place."

We fell into strained silence again, both of us knowing that was a big *if*.

It didn't take long after threatening Moss with the anal insertion of my boot for him to agree to some cooperation on the condition that this became a DEA bust on the Serpents, with hostage rescue a happy side effect. I didn't care what we called it or who got the credit as long as Moss disclosed the location of the damn cabin.

The convoy of black SUVs snaked its way through the fog that had descended like a veil across the road. Trevor and I were the only ones in a black-and-white, relegated to the rear of our procession to minimize the chances our squad car would be spotted before we were ready to reveal ourselves.

I shifted in my seat and glanced at the rearview mirror. The prickle at the back of my neck was growing more persistent with each mile that fell behind us. We were still missing something. I could *feel* it. And that knowledge was like bugs crawling beneath my skin.

I shook my head and expelled an aggravated breath. "Trev, this isn't right."

His head swung around, eyes narrowed. "What do you mean?"

"This feels like a puzzle where we're just jamming pieces together that don't fit." My eyes raked back and forth across the road, my body directing the car on autopilot while I thought through the sequence of events from the past few weeks for the thousandth time. "The Serpents taking Jace, that makes sense. I still can't figure out how they made him as a rat, though. We were so careful."

I slammed my hand against the steering wheel. "And Hargrove attacking Alex. That makes sense too. He had motive. Opportunity. A history of the same behavior. But Drake Dawson and his band of Merry Men pulling off a double kidnapping as sophisticated as this?" I pressed my lips together and shook my head, allowing the insinuation to hang between us.

Trevor sighed, propping his elbow on the windowsill. "Yeah, that *is* a little tough to swallow."

"Either we're grossly underestimating the Serpents, and they really did arrange for Hargrove to attack Alex as a decoy, or we're on the wrong track, and the MC doesn't have Alex."

My stomach tightened, sensing that the latter was true. Still, the MC *had* to be involved somehow. It was just too coincidental that Jace had gone missing on the same night, not to mention the multiple sets of booted footprints we found on Alex's property and the fact her phone had been left smashed at the scene, just as Jace's had been.

"The MC couldn't have been involved the whole time," Trevor said, his words slow like he was working out a difficult problem. "The letters Alex received. The picture of her that was nailed to that tree. It all happened before you two were anything to each other." I could feel his eyes more than see them in the dark as he turned to look at me. "The MC wouldn't have had a reason to zero in on her. It's like Moss said, they don't go after high-profile figures people will miss."

I opened my mouth to respond when the headlights from one of the SUVs ahead of us glanced off something on the side of the road. As we drew nearer, I slowed, squinting to try and make out what it was. A second later, I spotted it. A black car parked off the road and partially hidden by the tree line.

The tingle at the back of my neck grew, cascading down my arms and torso. On a hunch, I pulled over, allowing the feds to disappear around the next curve.

Trevor leaned forward, his face scrunched as he tried to get a better look at the vehicle through the rain and the windshield wipers sweeping wildly across the glass.

Ripping my seat belt free, I sprang out of the car, pulling my flashlight from my duty belt. I swept the light through the trees, looking for a body to accompany the vehicle. I found none, but as I walked around the car, one set of footprints led from the driver's door into the woods. But that didn't trouble me half as much as the black apron tossed casually in the back seat, the words *Rise &* *Grind* printed in white script on the front. There was only one person who worked at Grind that drove a car like this.

Bree.

After conducting his own sweep of the car, Trevor came to a stop at my shoulder. I turned to meet his eyes and yelled over the raging wind. "Why the hell would Bree be all the way up here in the dead of night, taking a stroll through the woods?"

Trevor didn't reply, but the look he gave me said plenty.

What motive could Bree possibly have for being involved in all of this? Was she in bed with a member of the MC?

Then Jace's words came back to me. *Dawson is paying spies . . . it could be anyone.*

Was that it? Was she on Drake Dawson's payroll? Acid rose in my throat. I had delivered Jace right into Bree's hands. The trees and sky began to swirl around me when, in the next breath, a new realization took root.

"Trev, we were in the back of the coffee shop when Jace told me about the ambush the Serpents were planning on the Reapers." My mouth went dry, my throat trying and failing to swallow.

Trevor closed his eyes for the briefest of moments. When he opened them again, they held an edge that matched his rigid form.

I jerked my chin toward the pocket where Trevor kept his phone. "Call Moss. Tell him we're headed into the woods from here while they continue to the cabin."

Whatever Bree's role in this whole situation, it didn't matter. I knew, without a shred of doubt, that she was intimately involved. I could figure out her motivation once we had Alex and Jace back and every single asshole involved in their abduction was wearing metal bracelets.

While Trevor placed the call to Moss, I placed a call to my other right hand.

"Dispatch, this is Quinn."

Just hearing Quinn's soothing voice helped to downshift my own emotions.

"Quinn. I need you to run another trace, and I need it yesterday."

By the time I got off the phone, Trevor was ending his own call. It would take a few minutes to hear back on the trace, and I would spend that entire time praying that Bree's cell phone was turned on and with her.

I pulled my gun from my holster and looked at Trevor. He palmed his own weapon and gave a quick nod.

With my partner at my back and my woman somewhere in those woods, I stepped into the tangled labyrinth of trees. Under the dark canopy of pines, the rest of the world disappeared, an eerie sense of isolation descending as the enemy's playground unfolded before us.

CHAPTER 51

Alex

I COULDN'T GET over the change in Bree. There was nothing of the woman with whom I'd had countless conversations—the woman who'd brought me cookies and given me a shoulder to cry on. The memory of that last encounter came rushing forward, and like the final digit that opens the safe, something clicked.

"Gabe." I spoke in a whisper, but the grotesque twist of her face told me she caught his name on my lips.

"Not so stupid after all," she said.

"You want Gabe." I said the words slowly, speaking aloud the montage of memories streaking across my mind as the haziness gave way to clarity. "You sent the email telling me to break things off with him." My eyes darted back and forth between hers, searching for confirmation. "That's why you came over last night. To get me to confide in you so that you could convince me to go through with it."

One corner of her mouth lifted. "And like a lamb to the slaughter, you blindly followed."

My brows knitted together. "If I did what you wanted, why are we here? Why do you still want to kill me?"

She considered me for a moment before answering. "It was obvious you had your hooks in Gabe too deep. Even after you did as I suggested and betrayed him, pulverizing every bit of faith he'd put in you, he still looked at you like a lovesick puppy."

I shook my head. "He doesn't—"

"I was there," Bree cut in. "I saw him when that moron Hargrove almost ruined everything."

"Hargrove?" I was having trouble keeping pace with her thoughts. "How is that possible?"

Her eyes lit up. "Well, I arranged your little reunion, of course." She waved her hand in the air, a goofy look on her face meant to patronize. "He was never supposed to get close enough to do any real damage. I'd only provided him with enough information to get himself caught and fingered as your stalker. I guess even the brain-dead get lucky sometimes." She rolled her eyes. "I thought I was going to have to interfere there for a minute when Anderson got himself knocked out. I mean, there was no way I was letting Hargrove claim my kill. But then sweet Gabe, even after *everything* you'd done to him, came racing to your rescue." Her eyes trailed off into the woods behind me as she escaped somewhere beyond what I could see.

A wistful yearning ghosted across her face for the briefest of moments, then morphed into a glare when she remembered I was there. "I was still hiding in the tree line after they hauled Hargrove away. Even after Gabe knew you were safe, he kept returning to check on you. You were too busy acting the poor, helpless victim to notice how his eyes kept searching for you." She shrugged. "I'd already decided to let the rest of my plan play out, though. Everything was progressing exactly as I'd arranged, each domino falling into the next. And you deserved to die for stealing the love of my life right out from under me." Bree's voice began to shake, the tips of her fingers blanching as her grip on the gun tightened. "But when I saw the look in his eyes as he watched the ambulance take you away, I knew the only way I was going to get him was to get rid of the harlot who had seduced him."

My brain screamed at me to run. To take my chances of catching a bullet in the back rather than remain where I stood, facing certain execution. But I forced my feet to stay put and shoved my fear down as best I could. Bree had every advantage at the moment. I needed to tip that scale, even just a bit. I held her eyes, my foot reaching out and testing the area around me, praying she didn't swing that flashlight low again. I needed to keep her talking—to anger her enough that she would launch into another bitter tirade but not so much as to prompt her finger to pull that trigger.

"If all you wanted was me dead, there were much simpler ways to take care of that." I kept my tone even, inquisitive. "Why the elaborate scheme? Why toy with me for weeks?"

My foot paused its inspection of the ground as she brought her face closer to mine. "Your death wasn't enough. You needed to learn what it feels like to have what you love most taken from you." Her mouth twisted, her words dropping to a hiss. "And *he* needed to pay as well."

Confusion momentarily stunted my search for escape. "Who needed to pay?"

She didn't answer, so I took a wild stab. "Gabe?"

Rain streamed down Bree's face and dripped off the end of her nose, but she made no attempt to remove it. She was too focused on what she'd come here to do to care about anything else.

"He betrayed me the moment he climbed into your bed!" She took an aggressive step forward, forcing me back a few feet. "He had to pay for his weakness. For turning away from me and running straight into your arms after all I'd done to be the woman he needed."

Her features softened once more, along with the tone of her voice. The frequent and instantaneous shifts of her affect sent panic prickling through my nerves.

Keenly aware of precious seconds escaping like sand through an hourglass, I arced my foot out once again, testing the ground, searching for a clear path and anything I could use to my advantage. When I moved my foot behind me, careful to keep my body rigid so that it wouldn't betray my intentions, my toe knocked against something firm. A few probing taps indicated a rock roughly the size of a softball with sharp protrusions.

"After I leaked your little sex tape," Bree continued, "I figured he'd dump your ass for turning his private life into a spectacle, just like Olivia had. But what did he do instead? He moved you into his *fucking* house," she roared, the veins in her neck popping, eyes bulging. "That was it. The final straw." With the hand holding the gun, Bree groped at her hair, causing it to tangle on top of her head, giving her an even more disheveled appearance. "So I played my ace and reached out to my new friends. The ones whose loyalty I'd earned by giving them some very valuable information about a certain employee who was snitching to the cops."

Her statement captured my full attention. *Jace? She's the reason he got caught?*

He had warned me we'd never get out alive if we didn't find a way to escape those men, but this revelation brought a fresh wave of nausea to the surface. Short of a miracle, there was no way Jace would live to see morning. He had known that when he'd sacrificed himself so I could get away.

I pressed my lips together, anger surging above the fear and the cold. Whatever happened tonight, I would *not* allow Jace's gift to be in vain. My toe returned to the rock, tapping against its edges and angles, collecting additional information about its girth and weight as Bree continued to regale me with the evidence of her genius.

"I made sure those boys knew how badly Gabe was pushing to burn the club to the ground and cart all of their members off to prison. Then I conveniently suggested that by helping me, they'd be helping themselves." Bree's lips spread wide, fully displaying her teeth. "So, I arranged to have Jace close the café alone and ensured all of the surveillance was turned off. We, of course, knew at this point that all of the cops in town would be busy at your place for quite a while. And once I assured them that Gabe's woman would meet a fate worse than any Drake and his baboons could cook up, they were only too happy to deliver you to me on their way to deal with their little rat problem." Bree snickered and ran her eyes down my torso before returning them to my face. "It's a good thing you decided not to stay at the hospital, where it was nice and safe. Your unexpected field trip almost ruined an otherwise perfect plan."

She rolled her eyes and sighed dramatically. "Of course, you just had to go and put yet another hiccup in everything when you decided to run. Fortunately, I'm a lot brighter than you, so it wasn't hard to track you down." With the barrel of the gun, she gently traced a line down the curve of my neck, her voice dropping to a caress. "You failed to notice I was parked nearby, so when I saw you take off, all I had to do was head down the road a ways and wait. I knew you'd do the predictable thing and try to find the road they'd brought you in on. And sure enough, my little trophy didn't keep me waiting long." Her eyes dropped to my sweater, a smile curling her lips. "Thanks for the great wardrobe choice, by the way."

My head swam with the intricacy of her plan. She really had been playing us all like marionettes. The only one who hadn't responded the way she'd anticipated was Gabe. But one thing still wasn't adding up.

"So you think I stole Gabe from you, and you're getting even with me for our relationship." I shook my head. "But I started getting those letters and threats before Gabe and I were even an item."

Her face turned to stone. "Maybe officially, but like every pathetic man out there, his head turned the moment you wiggled your ass in front of him."

I started shaking my head again, but she cut me off before I could protest.

"He was *finally* getting over that lying, cheating bitch Olivia! I had been patient. I'd been there for him every step of the way. Laughing at his jokes. Giving him his coffee on the house. Always there to greet him with a smile and ask him about *his* day, while everyone else only wanted to tell him how he could improve theirs. He *relied* on me. That's why he asked me to hire that little juvenile delinquent in the first place. Said he was grateful that he could always count on me to come through in a pinch."

She jabbed the flashlight into her chest, her pale skin glowing white under its beam. "*I'm* the one who deserves his love. And he was just beginning to realize how perfect we are for each other when *you* showed up. Ever since the first time you breezed into that coffee shop and every head turned, including *his*, he hasn't been able to look away." Bree advanced again, but this time, I didn't budge. I needed that rock to stay right where it was.

"You think I didn't notice how he started coming in every day during the same two hours you always came in to write?" Her eyes went wide, and the pitch of her voice turned shrill. "You'd sit there and act like you didn't know he was dangling on your hook. I gave you plenty of warnings to walk away and leave this place. And what did you do? You *threw* yourself at him!"

My face pinched, my hands fisted at my sides. "What are you talking about? I'd never even met Gabe until the day he spilled his coffee on me!"

"Yeah," she spat, jerking her chin up. "And the very next day you show up to Rustlers, leaning your ass over the counter, drawing him into your little web. And like a dog, he ran over with his tongue wagging." Bree pushed the barrel of the gun between my breasts, pushing so hard I knew I'd have a perfectly cylindrical bruise there.

"That's when I decided you didn't deserve to walk away," she said. "I *craved* the chance to take everything from you, and once everyone hated you and realized how stupid they'd all been to worship the ground you walk on, I would take your life." Bree brought her nose to mine, her eyes holding nothing but disdain and a thirst for vengeance.

I softened my gaze, trying to get her to connect to the friendly moments we had once shared. "Bree—"

"Shut. The. Fuck. Up." Bree punched the gun into my sternum, causing me to bow to the blow. "Enough story time. Walk."

This time, I didn't protest. Straightening, I turned, and as I took my first step, I allowed my toe to catch under the rock and fell to the soggy ground, crying out to feign surprise.

Bree's voice sounded like rusty nails on a tin can. "Oh, for fuck's sake. Get your spoiled, pampered ass up! Let's go!" She shoved at my back with her hand fisted around the flashlight.

My fingers curled around the cold, jagged surface of the rock. I used the direction of her voice and the pressure of her hand at my back to visualize her precise location, knowing I had only one chance to make this count.

Gripping the rock, I kept it close to my body, allowing it to skim up my leg as I stood. My clothes were heavy with rain, my jeans and sweater clinging to me like a second skin. Overhead, the thunder roared with Mother Nature's battle cry.

Bree shoved at my back once more, and when she did, I twisted, causing her hand to fall away. With a feral scream, I swung my makeshift war hammer around in a sweeping arc, the jagged edges of the rock splitting the side of Bree's head open with a sickening crunch. I didn't pause to decipher how much damage I'd done.

The mud shifted and squished beneath my shoes as I sprinted away from Bree and past the same trees I had navigated before. On my heels, a banshee's scream ripped through the night, seconds before the gunshot rang out.

CHAPTER 52

Gabe

I WAS SLOWLY PICKING my way over dense foliage and broken tree limbs, listening for anything out of place, when my phone vibrated against my chest. When I answered, Quinn didn't waste any time rattling off the coordinates I'd been waiting for.

After entering the lat and long into my phone, I glanced up at Trevor. "Bree's phone is pinging about a mile from here, dead ahead."

He nodded, and we resumed our trek, picking up the pace while remaining alert for hidden threats. Unable to use our flashlights without turning ourselves into easy targets, we navigated the slick footing that, combined with the downward slope of the hillside, made for treacherous conditions. But all that was forgotten the moment a scream and a gunshot pierced my soul. I broke into a dead run, not giving a second thought to how easy it would be to fall and break my neck.

My heart beat viciously against my rib cage, its cadence matching the pounding of my boots on the soft soil as I raced toward a location I was both desperate to reach and terrified to find. Behind me, Trevor shouted and tried to keep pace.

"Gabe! No!"

I paid him no mind. A fallen tree blocked my path. Placing a palm on its rough bark, I catapulted over it without missing a beat.

Trevor cursed and grunted from somewhere near my shoulder. "Gabe! Damn it! We have no idea what we're running into. You're going to get both our asses pumped full of holes!"

Some distant part of my brain told me he was right. I knew the element of surprise was our best asset in this situation, but none of that logic, none of the years of combat and training, could break through what now possessed me.

I could focus on only one thing. And if I was too late . . . there was more than innocent blood that would be spilled in these woods tonight.

* * *

ALEX

I PUMPED MY ARMS HARD, propelling myself forward as I tuned in to the sensations of my body, scanning for a new source of pain. Finding none, I figured I had literally dodged a bullet.

White puffs of air escaped my lungs in spurts, my breathing making it impossible to hear anything else. I was once again running blind, with no idea of how close danger lurked. But this time, I wasn't the only prey.

Not daring to glance behind for fear of taking a fatal step, I scanned the dense forest, looking for a spot where I could make a sudden disappearance. Not a minute later, a thick black mass of towering trees, grouped together in tight formation, sprang out of the darkness just ahead on my left.

I reached it in seconds, throwing my body to the side, pressing my back into the moss-covered bark. Squatting down, I patted the wet ground, my hands searching for a sturdy branch. I knew Bree would expect me to run as far and as fast as I could. Just like she'd anticipated me trying to find my way back to the road when I'd escaped the men in the van. But I wasn't going to

369

play into her hand. This time, I'd be the shadow that emerged from the dark.

Coming up empty, I leaned a little farther to my left, trying to keep my white sweater hidden behind the tangled tree trunks. At this point, I'd probably be better off going topless. I swallowed hard, trying to slow my breathing so I could better hear Bree's approach. Assuming I hadn't lost her altogether. Should I hope for that? Maybe. But I didn't. I wanted this to end. Now.

I was done living in fear. I was done feeling helpless. I was done living in the dark while she watched my life unfold under the floodlights. One way or another, this ended tonight.

I withdrew my hand, growling at its emptiness. Pressing my palms to the tree at my back, I began to slide up, stopping only a few inches later when my skin scraped against the jagged edges of splintered wood. My hand groped the precarious bits until it found a branch, two inches in diameter, clinging to the tree by only a few layers of soggy bark.

I cocked my ear toward the heart of the forest, holding my breath as I listened for the sound of snapping twigs and ragged breath. When nothing but rain and the occasional peel of thunder met my ears, I turned to face the tree, drew my knee up and slammed my foot into the branch. Under dry conditions, it would have snapped free in an instant, but the soggy wood was proving more stubborn. After three more kicks, it finally tore free. I bent to claim my prize, holding it like Excalibur as I pressed my back to the tree again. And not a moment too soon.

Over my left shoulder, I peered through a small gap in the trees that sheltered me. A beam of light bounced erratically through the woods, its forward movement stalling now and then to swing in a smooth, wide arc. Bree was headed straight for me.

I leaned my head against the tree, closing my eyes and inhaling deeply. *She is not the sweet, kind person who welcomed you to town and brought you treats. She is a crazy, psychotic bitch who's trying to kill you and handed a boy off to brutal criminals who are likely torturing him at this very moment.*

Committed to what I knew had to be done, I choked up on the branch, twisting my palms around the shaft as though I was trying to grind it to dust. Bree's footfalls drew near, her ragged breathing helping me to gauge the distance she closed between us.

Her small frame jogged past my hiding spot and stopped. I hesitated, fearing that something had given me away. She held the light out in front of her, turning slowly from left to right, her feet shifting in small degrees as she worked her way through a full turn. Any moment, that light was going to fall on me, and a bullet from the gun held beside it wouldn't be far behind.

I held my breath, waiting. Deciding to attack and then second-guessing my timing, knowing she would see me the instant I made my move. I had to get this right. A mere heartbeat later, Bree turned toward me. I was out of time.

I twisted from my torso, drawing the branch over my left shoulder. Stepping into the swing, I unwound my body, the momentum turning my weapon into a blur as it sailed toward its target. Bree's eyes found me a split second before the branch made contact with the back of her skull.

Grunting, she dropped to her knees. My branch fell with her as I stared with wide eyes at the blood dripping down her face and now matted in her hair from each of my assaults. Between the rock and the branch, I had really done a number on her. Face-to-face with the trauma I'd inflicted on another human being, I clutched my stomach as bile and vomit fought for the surface.

Bree shrieked, the violent sound crashing into my ears and drawing me from the shock just in time to register my fate suspended in the black hole of the barrel of her gun. I dove to the ground in the same moment a red-and-orange flash burst in my peripheral, the acrid scent of gunpowder filling my nose before the rest was lost in the wind. My ears rang from the blast. I cupped my hands over them, trying to orient myself following the loss of one sense after another, the whole world seeming to teeter on its axis.

Fire erupted in my right bicep when I lifted my arm. The

vague realization I'd been shot skipped across my consciousness and was gone just as quickly when I noticed Bree rotating toward me. Struggling to my knees, I picked up the branch carrying her blood and cracked it across her back. She fell facedown, a small groan muffled by the fallen leaves and dirt. I jumped to my feet. Finding the gun still gripped in her fingers, I smashed my heel into the back of her hand, grinding it into the ground like a cigarette. She screamed again, sounding more feral each time. When her crippled fingers finally loosened from the grip of the gun, I snatched it up and aimed it at her head, relishing the chance to give her a taste of what she'd been dishing.

"Don't move." My voice was firm despite the trembling of my body.

Bree didn't even attempt to roll over. She just lay there, writhing now and then from the pain.

I released the breath I felt like I'd been holding for weeks, allowing the cold rain to wash down my face.

But the respite was short-lived. The sound of twigs snapping and bodies pushing through the brush came from somewhere behind me.

Alarm zipped through every cell of my body. I was certain the men who abducted me had caught up to us, and my brain scrambled for my next move. There was no way I could hold them *and* Bree off at the same time.

Just as I was about to take off running again, my name, shouted into the dark, held me in place. My head whipped around, eyes searching over my shoulder, trying to determine if I was imagining things.

"Alex!"

Gabe.

He was here.

I took a step toward his voice. "Ga—"

Arms snaked around my knees. One hundred twenty pounds of dripping-wet psycho barreled into the backs of my legs, carrying me to the cold earth. Bree was pressed into my back, her slender fingers reaching overhead to where I held the gun, her nails digging into my skin as she tried to pry it loose.

I managed to roll onto my side, but Bree was fast, moving like smoke in a strong breeze. She scurried off my back before I could pin her and wrapped her legs around my waist, pulling herself over me until I was on my back with her straddling me.

We continued to wrestle for the gun, Bree's face a mask of evil, her eyes boring into mine with pure venom. In a surprise move, she released her hands from mine and gripped my head instead, slamming it into the ground. Dazed, I felt my grip slacken just enough that the gun fell free. Bree dove for it. On instinct, my palm struck up, smashing into her windpipe. She sat back, both hands going to her throat as she gasped for air. Drawing my knee up, I wedged it between us, and with a guttural roar, I drove it into her and sent her flying backwards.

"Alex!"

Gabe's voice was so close. My gaze searched feverishly for his face, the need to see him, to have him by my side, so strong I could think of nothing else in that moment.

"Gabe! I'm here!" I shouted, clamoring to my feet. A flashlight clicked on, its swath of white light finding me in the dark.

"Alex." He breathed my name, his boots pounding the earth as he ran toward me. Relief flooded my limbs so that I struggled to stay erect.

With less than twenty feet between us, he stopped suddenly. The beam of his flashlight no longer bobbing, his boots falling silent. I took a step toward him and froze when another blast filled the air.

CHAPTER 53

Gabe

ALEX WAS PARALYZED, her eyes wide with shock, her body rigid. I kept her in my peripheral as I walked slowly toward the crumpled body behind her, my light just as focused on the form as my gun. A part of me was grappling with the fact I'd just shot Bree, someone who I had considered a friend. But then the flashback of her rising to her knees and pointing that gun at Alex's back came flooding into focus, and my remorse was nothing more than a memory.

Trevor skidded to a stop beside me. "*Fuck me,*" he breathed.

"You got her?" I asked.

"Yeah." He kept his gun trained on Bree. "You just take care of your girl."

I holstered my weapon and spun toward Alex, my hand cupping her cheek. "Baby?"

I ran my light over her, looking for injuries, noting the blood staining the sleeve of her sweater. When I raised the light just enough to check her pupils, I wasn't surprised to find that her eyes were no longer green but black. I moved in closer, not wanting to startle her, and wrapped my arm around her waist, pulling her tight to my chest, while my other hand gently brought her head to my shoulder.

Trevor didn't take his eyes off Bree when he spoke. "She okay?"

I kissed her head and rocked her slowly. "Yeah, I think so."

I breathed deep, drawing her sweet scent into my nose and closed my eyes, overwhelmed by gratitude to have found her in one piece. I just prayed I'd be able to say the same about Jace.

My muscles tightened around my girl, a fear of ever having to let her go settling deep in my gut. I would worry about that fear another day. Right now, I'd savor this taste of heaven.

* * *

WE PULLED UP TO THE SERPENTS' cabin an hour later, Trevor driving my cruiser while Alex was tucked under my arm in the back. She clutched the blanket I'd placed around her shoulders tightly, her fingertips having long since turned white. Though she was still pale, her pupils were slowly returning to normal, that gorgeous shade of green once again rimming the black. I watched as she ducked her head to look through the windshield, taking in the flurry of activity.

At least a dozen federal vehicles sat parked at odd angles in front of the cabin, their red and blue lights illuminating the night. Several men and women wearing black jackets with three letters across the back jogged in and out of the house and around the compound. I heaved a deep sigh, bracing myself for what we would find.

Once Trevor and I had confirmed that my shot to center mass had claimed Bree's life, we'd called Chief Kelly and Agent Moss to inform them of the situation. The chief had several of our units, along with our crime scene techs, on location within the hour. As soon as they'd arrived, I turned Bree's body and evidence collection over to them, anxious to get to Moss's location and to get Alex out of the cold. Fortunately, the rain had finally ceased, but our soaked clothing still felt like a bitch every time the wind blew.

I squeezed Alex's shoulder. "You want to wait here?"

She shook her head, never taking her eyes off the cabin.

Sliding from the back seat, I held my hand out to her. Trevor stood at the hood of the car, waiting for us. A silent declaration that we would face this together.

With Alex wedged between us, we made our way to the cabin and climbed the stairs to the porch. The structure was smaller than I had imagined. Maybe twelve hundred square feet, but according to Moss, it appeared they really only used it for the basement, where they were set up with bleach, a power hose, and a drain that carried away their sins.

As we stepped across the threshold, Moss met us at the door, holding up his hand. The grave lines etched into his face made my stomach clench.

"Like I said, he's in bad shape." Moss's eyes flicked between Trevor's and mine. "We're rendering what medical aid we're able, and we've got paramedics on the way, but . . ." He shook his head solemnly and stepped back, holding out his hand to direct us into the next room.

We passed through the claustrophobic entryway, skirting the agents clustered in groups, each holding a small notepad and pen, and entered a large living room. A broken-down box TV sat to my left against the wall, and directly across from us, a green couch, stained and torn, was the only other piece of furniture.

My breath caught at the sight of Jace's badly bruised and bloody body sinking into that filthy couch. An agent wearing white latex gloves leaned over him, speaking too quietly for me to hear. We waited to approach, my eyes taking the opportunity to assess the damage.

Several white squares of gauze dotted Jace's torso, each one steadily turning bright red. His arm was in a makeshift sling that he kept clutched firmly to his chest, and his left eye was black and purple and completely swollen shut. The bruises and swelling across his face, along with a puffy split lip, made him almost unrecognizable. And it was obvious from the way his chest rose and fell erratically that he was having trouble breathing.

A sniffle from my left drew my attention to Alex, the tears streaming down her cheeks as she gazed upon Jace the first sign of emotion since I'd found her.

My arm tightened around her waist as I gave her space to deal with everything she'd been through tonight.

"He saved me," she said, her voice small and fragile. Her big, beautiful eyes swept up to mine, imploring me to understand the magnitude of what she was saying. "He sacrificed himself so *I* could get away."

I nodded grimly, pressing my lips together to bite back the fury stirring in my middle. I wanted to rip into Drake and the assholes who did his dirty work. I wanted to tear them into the tiny bits to which they had reduced so many men. But Moss had scooped them up and shuttled them out before anyone else could get their hands on them.

So, for now, I would focus all of my energy on getting Alex and Jace on the other side of all this.

When the agent moved away from Jace, I pressed gently against the small of Alex's back and nodded to Trevor. Together, we approached the unspoken hero that an entire town had written off. Jace must have sensed our presence, because he opened the one eye that wasn't swollen shut and turned toward us. When he saw Alex, a ghost of a smile tugged at his lips.

Alex knelt on the floor beside him, placing her hand on his head, caressing his hair as a mother would.

Trevor took up a spot near Jace's feet so Jace could see him without having to crane his neck. "I hate to break it to ya, kid, but you're not so pretty anymore." The sad smile on my partner's face showed a vulnerability he rarely exposed.

Jace spoke quietly, as though every word required a huge effort. "That's okay," he said. "I hear chicks dig scars." He tried to take a deep breath, but the rattle in his chest kept him from succeeding.

I placed a hand on his shoulder. "Hang in there, Jace. Medics will be here any minute, and you'll be back on your hog, terror-izing the town in no time."

He closed his eyes, small lines turning up at their corners.

Alex put her mouth next to his ear. "Thank you, Jace. Thank you for saving my life."

Jace's hand lifted from the couch, and Alex placed her palm in his.

"You did good, Jace." My voice threatened to crack. Some-thing that had *never* happened prior to these past three weeks. "I'll make sure that Emmy knows you're safe. She flipped the entire police department on its head to get everyone out looking for you."

Jace didn't respond. I watched his chest, noticing how his breaths were growing more shallow.

We fell into silence, allowing Jace peace as twenty of the longest minutes of my life passed by. Each of us kept contact with him, Alex with her hand in his. Me with my hand on his shoulder. And Trevor gripping his shin.

It was in those moments, where Jace's life hung in the balance and my chest loosened just a little bit having Alex safe by my side, that I realized how much love I had turned my back on, so deter-mined never to be someone's fool again. But somehow, that didn't seem to matter anymore. I would make a fool of myself every day for the rest of my life to ensure the people I loved never had to question their place in my heart.

CHAPTER 54

Gabe

Hours later, with Alex snuggled safely under the covers of my bed and Liz keeping watch over her, I met up with Trevor at Bree's house, where Moss's team had joined forces with the Eden Falls Police Department to conduct a search. By the time I arrived, the place had been pretty well turned upside down and inside out.

The small house had an open floor plan, with the living room to the left of the front door and a breakfast nook to the right. Beyond the breakfast nook sat the kitchen, the bright whites and gleaming steel of the decor belying the dark soul that had possessed the space.

I scanned my surroundings, only half aware of the visual information my brain collected. I still, for the life of me, could *not* figure out how I'd managed to miss the sociopath living beneath Bree's cheerful exterior.

Trevor's voice drifted from the back of the house. I followed it past the living room and kitchen and into the hallway that sat opposite the front door, finding him almost immediately in the first room on the left. Placing my hands on the doorjamb, I leaned my body inside, taking in the blackout curtains over the windows and a surveillance and computer setup that would have had the CIA drooling. Trevor sat on a stool next to an agent who looked all of about sixteen with sandy-blond hair and a pair of round black-rimmed glasses that pegged him as a Harry Potter fan.

A computer monitor sat in front of them, their bodies leaning forward, engrossed in whatever was on the screen.

"What's going on?" I asked.

Trevor's head snapped around and he jumped to his feet. He pointed his thumb over his shoulder toward the agent. "This is Agent Gallagher. He's the tech guy. He, uh—" Trevor twisted at the waist to glance back at Gallagher before turning back to me. "He's found some interesting stuff."

I walked into the room, my forehead lifting. "Oh yeah? Like what?"

Trevor nudged Gallagher with the back of his hand. "Show him, Doogie Howser."

Gallagher pursed his lips at the nickname but didn't respond. Instead, he swiveled in his seat, holding out his hand to shake mine. "Call me Luke."

"Gabe," I said, squeezing his hand.

I took up a position behind Gallagher, Trevor standing beside me. We watched over his shoulder as the computer whiz clicked through file after file, explaining what he'd found so far, my stomach tightening with each revelation.

Bree had been *very* thorough in both her research and reconnaissance. There were endless pictures, articles, and video clips of Alex, some that were in the public domain and many that were taken in private moments. Gallagher clicked into another folder, this one containing all of the police reports and court documents from Alex's case against Hargrove. With it, there were also encrypted communications in which Bree had reached out to Hargrove, enticing him to go after Alex and providing everything he would need to track her down and finish what he'd started.

When Gallagher switched over to another cluster of files, my jaw clenched. An audio recording popped up, Jace's voice clear as a bell as he detailed the ambush the Serpents were plotting against the Reapers.

I turned my head to Trevor. "She bugged the coffee shop?"

Trevor nodded. "We found a sort of diary vlog she was keeping. It took a while for Doogie here to break into it, but she was meticulous and didn't seem to miss much. Always on the lookout for opportunities." Trevor scratched the back of his head and adjusted the sunglasses that sat on top. "She got curious about why we had taken such an interest in Jace. Once she learned he'd turned on the Serpents, she saw the perfect opening to get them to help her with her dirty work, and to teach you a lesson in the process."

I scrunched my face. "Me?"

Trevor pulled his lips in and nodded. "Pull up the video diary," he said to Gallagher.

A moment later, Bree's face filled the screen. But it wasn't the Bree I thought I knew. This woman looked crazed. Where Bree normally had a sweet smile, this woman's lips were pulled back, revealing clenched teeth. Her eyes were wide, pupils dilated—she looked possessed.

Gallagher hit Play, and Bree's voice reverberated off the walls of the small room. Over the next half hour, I heard from the lips of the woman I'd shot and killed how much she loved me. How we were soulmates. And how much she hated Alex for ruining everything between us. My heart twisted just a little each time she mentioned some small, innocuous thing I'd done that had proven my love for her in return. A part of me felt guilty because none of those actions had been special. They were simply the kind of things I did for everyone. But somehow, in her mind, I'd led her on.

My ears perked up, something Bree had just said pulling me from contemplation. "Wait, can you pause it right there?"

Gallagher complied, waiting for further instructions.

Bree had just said that when she met me, she realized Gary wasn't the one.

"Who is she talking about?"

Trevor nudged Gallagher's shoulder again. Apparently, the

two had spent enough time together this morning to have developed their own code.

Gallagher opened another file. A scan of a black-and-white newspaper photo popped up in front of all the other open windows. A man who looked to be in his midforties, wearing a collared shirt and tie, smiled at the camera. Beside him, a woman with light-colored hair worn in the elegant waves of a 1950s starlet was tucked into his side, a string of pearls decorating her throat.

The caption beneath the photo read: *Professor of political science at local university and wife found beaten and stabbed to death inside their Grand Estates home Sunday afternoon.*

My blood turned to ice.

"That's Professor Gary VanButen and his wife, Genine," Trevor said. "Gallagher found a bunch of files on the couple, just like with you and Alex. I called over to Seattle PD this morning when we found this." Trevor extended his hand toward the monitor. "According to what the lead detective on the VanButen case told me, along with the news articles Bree has on her computer, it appears Professor VanButen was having an affair with one of his students. His wife found out and threatened to leave. Guess who the student was?"

My eyebrows shot to my hairline. "Bree?"

Trevor nodded and crossed his arms over his chest. "Except she wasn't Bree then. Her real name is Jessica Marx. The cops could never *prove* she was the one who killed the couple, but they had enough evidence to bring her in for questioning. She took off before they got the chance, went underground, and resurfaced in Eden Falls as Bree Sherman."

My mouth went dry as my mind grappled to reconcile the Bree I knew with the one who had beaten and eviscerated the couple on the screen.

Trevor continued. "According to sources close to the couple, VanButen chose his wife over Bree, ending the affair and promising to do whatever he had to to keep Genine from leaving him. You can imagine, that didn't go over too well with Bree."

I swallowed hard, realizing just how close Alex had come to being the next life Bree claimed. I blew out a deep breath as my hand went to my mouth and dragged down to my chin. It was disorienting seeing everything from this angle. The death threat against me that was sent to Alex. I'd assumed that was Hargrove trying to get me out of the picture. But really, it was Bree trying to get *Alex* out of the picture. The threat from the MC, hand-delivered to Lily, was a direct result of Bree trying to teach me a lesson for being *unfaithful* to her.

And to think, had Charles Bailey not ended up on a slab in *our* coroner's office, we never would have been able to find Alex and Jace last night. Bree had played one card too many by bringing the MC into her nefarious plot.

"Oh. . ." Trevor raised a finger as though to signal he'd just remembered something. He walked to the far corner of the room and stopped in front of what I assumed was a closet door. "I solved the mystery of those footprint impressions we took outside of Alex's windows."

Trevor opened the door to reveal a dark space no bigger than a coat closet. Inside, a pair of men's boots sat on the floor, covered in dried mud. On the rod above them, a single item swayed on a set of wire hangers. I went to the closet and gripped the garment, turning it to get a better look. *So that's how she did it.*

"She wore a weighted bodysuit and men's boots to make us think Alex's stalker was a man," I said, turning to Trevor.

He nodded, glancing back at the garment with an air of appreciation. "You gotta hand it to her, taking the time to sew all these weight packs into this getup. She was good at thinking outside the box, I'll give her that."

I bit the inside of my cheek and let the bodysuit slip from my fingers, watching as it swung in the empty space. Maybe in time I'd be able to admire the genius and dedication she'd demonstrated throughout this whole ordeal, but right now, I was just ready to wrap up this investigation and forget Bree Sherman had ever existed.

* * *

A FEW HOURS LATER, the last of the evidence was collected and added to the brimming trunks that loaded down a number of patrol cars. I stepped out of the house, the weight of the oppressive atmosphere slipping away as the sunshine soaked into my skin.

I took a deep breath and closed my eyes, turning my face to the cerulean sky. A hand slapped down on my shoulder and squeezed. I didn't need to look to know it was Trevor.

"Why don't you head home? I think you and Alex are due some makeup sex."

I couldn't help the grin that spread across my face, my cheeks pulling tight. I squinted one eye open and turned to look at him. "I'd be happy just watching her sleep."

"Ugh." Trevor rolled his eyes. "Don't tell me that now that you're in love, you're going to turn into one of those castrated sissies who forgets he's got a pair."

I laughed and raised my eyebrows. "Have you *seen* my woman? We'll be seventy and still going at it like a couple of teenagers."

Trevor barked out a laugh and clapped me on the shoulder again before heading to his squad car. I wasn't far behind when I climbed into my truck and headed back through town, anxious to get home before my green-eyed beauty awoke. As the buildings and houses I'd seen all my life faded in my rearview mirror, images of Alex walking those streets with her hand in mine and a couple of kids on our hips brought a sweet ache to my chest. Somehow, I knew deep in my bones that Alex Reilly had changed my life for good.

Epilogue

EIGHT MONTHS LATER . . .

I sat on a bench, my back warmed by the sun and my laptop balanced on my knees. Aderes was propped up against my leg, enjoying the cool cement beneath her paws and the breeze caressing her face. I smiled and reached down to stroke her soft fur, the diamond on my finger sparkling like Caribbean waters. Aderes's eyes began to drift close, the warmth of the day combining with my rhythmic strokes to induce a trancelike state. A moment later, she flopped to the ground, her breathing deep, a goofy smile playing at her lips.

I laughed and shook my head, returning my fingers to the keyboard. It was hard to believe how *much* my life had changed in the short time since I'd come to Eden Falls. Had I known what awaited me here, I would have left my old life long ago.

I was putting the finishing touches on the third book I'd written and published as an independent author. A venture that I was pleased to report was doing incredibly well. Though I had been able to smooth things over with my former publisher once I'd had an opportunity to explain, *in person*, the events that had unfolded, complete with extensive police documentation, in the end, I'd still chosen to walk away from the contract.

Now that I was finally free to write the stories that were brimming inside of me, my writing block was a thing of the past, and after profuse and heartfelt apologies, my fans proved more forgiving than I could have ever imagined.

Fortunately, the settlement I'd won from suing the various media outlets who'd posted the video footage and documents obtained by Bree's illegal surveillance and hacking allowed me to pay back my advance to the publisher and left enough to start a nonprofit aimed at protecting and supporting victims of stalking. Liz, my soon-to-be sister-in-law, being the incredible organizer that she was, had proved instrumental in getting that pet project off the ground and running.

My phone dinged beside me on the bench. I picked it up, glancing at the name on the screen, and smiled. "Speak of the devil."

It was a text from Liz. *We still on for this afternoon?*

Liz and Lily were taking me wedding dress shopping. Considering that just six months ago, I'd wanted to lock myself away and have nothing to do with the world, it was a wonder to feel the giddiness bubbling up inside of me at the thought of a girls' day with two of my favorite people to pick out a dress that would mark the rest of my life with Gabe.

I typed out a quick reply. *Definitely. Can't wait!*

As soon as I'd hit Send, a shadow fell across my lap, drawing my eyes skyward.

Soft chocolate eyes looked down at me as Gabe's hand moved to my hair, stroking the tresses that fell loosely down my back. "Hey, beautiful. You waiting on anyone special?"

My smile was so big my cheeks nearly forced my eyes shut. "Not really. Just the love of my life."

Gabe gave me a wolfish grin and bent down, planting his luscious lips on mine. The kiss was sweet at first, tender and slow, but quickly became filled with an aching hunger. My arms lifted to loop around his neck. His hands tangled in my hair, drawing me closer to him. As our tongues dueled against each other, our breaths intertwining and becoming one, we were lost to the world. So much so that we didn't realize we were no longer alone.

Aderes jumped to her feet between us, planting her paws on the bench and forcing us apart just as the sound of someone clearing their throat reached my ears. My head snapped around, heat flooding my cheeks when I saw Jace standing a few feet away, his hands in his pockets and rocking on his heels awkwardly as he waited for us to notice him.

Gabe, not one to embarrass easily, didn't miss a beat. He shot Jace a brilliant smile as he walked over to him and shook his hand. "Well, this is it," he said.

Jace smiled and ducked his head, adjusting the large duffel draped over his shoulder. "Yeah."

I tucked my laptop into the bag at my feet and rose from the bench, joining the boys. Standing on my tiptoes, I wrapped my arms around Jace and pulled him close. He kept one hand on the strap of his duffel, the other sliding around my back.

"We're going to miss you around here," I said.

He squeezed me a little harder but remained quiet.

We broke apart a moment later when a cop car came around the corner, sirens blaring and a voice through the PA system reverberating off the brick buildings lining Main Street.

"Jace Maloy," Trevor's voice boomed through the speaker. "Local hero and resident shit-starter—"

Gabe groaned and palmed his face, every head in the vicinity turning to gawk at the commotion.

"Today is the day you become a man," Trevor continued. "Today is the day you become all that you can be."

Jace burst into laughter, my eyes growing wide as my head whipped toward him. Rarely had I even seen this kid smile. The sound of his heartfelt joy shattered my heart in the best way, and my eyes flooded with the realization that he was going to be okay. Trevor was right. Today was the day Jace left behind the troubles of his past and started a new adventure. One that I hoped would someday allow him to see the incredible man the rest of us already had the pleasure of knowing.

Trevor pulled the cruiser into the curb, and the car rocked back at the sudden impact. He sprang from behind the wheel and jogged over to the bus bench where we were gathered.

He stuck out his palm to Jace, pulling him into a bro hug as they shook hands. "This is it, kid. Just remember, those Marines are mean sons of bitches. Don't do anything to piss them off." Trevor flashed a cocky grin at Gabe, who was glaring in return.

I pressed my lips together, trying and failing not to laugh at the way Trevor was so easily able to get under Gabe's skin.

Before Gabe could retaliate, squeaky brakes filled the air and drew our attention as the bus that would carry Jace out of town rounded the corner.

Shielding my eyes, I glanced around, my brow furrowing when I couldn't find what I was looking for.

"Wasn't Emmy planning on seeing you off?" I asked Jace.

The smile dropped from his face, his eyes finding his shoes. "No." He shook his head subtly. "She, uh, she had some things she needed to do."

Considering it was obvious to everyone but Jace that the sun rose and set with him as far as Emmy was concerned, I found that explanation incredibly odd. But Jace didn't seem to want to dwell on it, and we were here to support him, so I let it go.

The screech of the brakes assaulted my eardrums as the bus pulled to a stop in front of us. Jace cast one more look around at each of us, a lump rising in my throat as I went to him and pulled him in for one more hug. Unable to speak through the tears threatening to burst free, I stepped back and allowed Trevor and Gabe to say their goodbyes.

Trevor gripped Jace on the shoulder and leaned in, whispering something in his ear. Jace nodded, a shy smile forming as he shook Trevor's hand one more time.

Gabe stepped forward next. He placed a hand on either of

Jace's shoulders and dipped his head to meet his eyes. Jace locked onto him as though Gabe was the only thing keeping him anchored to the ground.

"Just remember, Jace," Gabe began. "You have people in your corner who will never abandon you. We're right here. Always."

Jace's jaw flexed, his gaze never wavering from Gabe.

"Where you start in life does not mean that's where you have to end up." Gabe's eyes bored into Jace as he waited for him to acknowledge that he understood.

With the subtlest of nods, Jace stepped into Gabe and wrapped his arms around him, hands fisting behind Gabe's back. Gabe returned the embrace just as fiercely, something passing between the two that only they could fully understand.

And with that final farewell, Jace boarded the bus, looking back only once as though he was trying to sear this moment in his memory. And then he was gone, the taillights of the bus fading as it disappeared from Eden Falls.

We shared a moment of silence. Then Trevor cleared his throat. "Well, I guess it's back to business as usual."

Gabe nodded, his arm snaking around my waist and pulling me into his side. Trevor walked back to his patrol car and climbed inside but left the door open.

"You heading out soon to go shopping?" Gabe asked, looking down at me.

I nodded. "The distraction will be good."

He lowered his head to drop a kiss on my lips, then jerked back suddenly. His fingers pressed into the earpiece connected to his radio. My forehead creased as I leaned back to look at him.

"What's wrong?" I asked.

Trevor jumped out of the patrol car, his arm hanging over the door. "Did you catch that?" he shouted to Gabe.

Gabe nodded and turned back to me, his eyes narrowed and his mouth set. "Baby, I gotta go." He gave me a quick peck and spun away, jogging to the passenger side of the cruiser. Over his shoulder he yelled, "Have fun and let me know when you guys make it back!"

Before I could respond, he disappeared into the patrol car. Trevor threw the vehicle into reverse, the tires squealing when he changed directions and hit the gas. They sped off, their lights and sirens blazing a trail through town.

Accustomed to Gabe having to leave suddenly, I collected my things and called Aderes as I loaded up the car to head out and meet Liz. Whatever had sent the boys running, something whispered at the back of my mind that our sleepy town was about to be turned upside down. Again.

What's Next?

Want more Gabe and Alex? Visit RileySkov.com to sign up for the newsletter and receive three **exclusive When Shadows Fall bonus scenes** and updates on future releases.

* * *

Continue the fun, passion, and thrills with Trevor and Quinn's story!

WHEN MIDNIGHT STRIKES

*A calculated killer. A pile of bodies. A Casanova with a badge. And **me**, the woman at the center of it all.*

Praised for her intellect and ability to stay calm when the world is burning down around her, Quinn Martin is a star in the Eden Falls police dispatch center, and she has never met a challenge she couldn't defeat—until one call changes everything.

When the brutalized bodies of local women darken the borders of Eden Falls, and the man responsible chooses Quinn as his confessional, she is determined to prove she can help bring the killer to justice. But Quinn soon realizes she may have met her intellectual match. When the killer threatens to reveal a past she is desperate to keep hidden, Quinn must decide how far she will go to catch a killer, even if it means getting caught in his trap.

Trevor Ryan, Eden Falls police officer and proverbial ladies' man, has spent the past five years hiding the fact that he's in love with the sassy and wickedly smart Quinn Martin. He's done a good job of it, too, considering she hates his guts. But when a sadistic woman-killer comes to town and insists on making Quinn part of his game, Trevor finds himself doing double-time to protect his town and the woman who will never be his.

With the body count rising, and the clock ticking down, can Trevor and Quinn outwit the killer before he claims a soul too close to home?

Love This Book?

Thank you for reading *When Shadows Fall*! Creating stories has been a lifelong passion of mine, and people like you are a part of making the dream a reality.

If you enjoyed this book, please consider leaving a quick review. Reviews help other readers to find the book and take a chance on it, and they are one of the best ways you can support an author.

You can jump to the review page by scanning the QR code below.

With gratitude, Riley.

About the Author

With a passion for justice and a heart for people, Riley is a former emergency dispatcher living out her dream to write stories that exemplify the healing power of love and the eternal battle between good and evil.

Riley holds a bachelor's degree in criminal justice and master's degrees in counseling and forensic psychology. Her education, professional experience, and slightly macabre mentality set the stage for her novels and fuel an imagination that sends tingles tripping down her readers' spines.

Living in Montana with the man who stole her heart, and the two rescue pups who took a piece as well, Riley is hard at work bringing love, passion, thrills, and chills to all who dive into the pages of her books.

Subscribe to Riley's newsletter by scanning the QR code and receive *exclusive* bonus content, updates on book news, and behind-the-scenes shenanigans!

Also by Riley Skov

EDEN FALLS MONTANA SERIES

When Shadows Fall

When Midnight Strikes

When Secrets Kill